Lynne Graham was b has been a keen roman She is very happily ma husband who has learn started to write! Her five children keep her on her toes. She has a very large dog, which knocks everything over, a very small terrier, which barks a lot, and two cats. When time allows, Lynne is a keen gardener.

When **Kali Anthony** read her first romance novel at fourteen she realised two truths: that there can never be too many happy endings, and that one day she would write them herself. After marrying her own tall, dark and handsome hero, in a perfect friends-to-lovers romance, Kali took the plunge and penned her first story. Writing has been a love affair ever since. If she isn't battling her cat for access to the keyboard, you can find Kali playing dress-up in vintage clothes, gardening, or bushwalking with her husband and three children in the rainforests of South-East Queensland.

THE MAID'S PREGNANCY BOMBSHELL

LYNNE GRAHAM

CROWNED FOR THE KING'S SECRET

KALI ANTHONY

MILLS & BOON

First published in Great Britain 2023
by Mills & Boon, an imprint of HarperCollins*Publishers* Ltd,
1 London Bridge Street, London, SE1 9GF

www.harpercollins.co.uk

HarperCollins*Publishers*, Macken House, 39/40 Mayor Street Upper, Dublin 1, D01 C9W8, Ireland

The Maid's Pregnancy Bombshell © 2023 Lynne Graham

Crowned for the King's Secret © 2023 Kali Anthony

ISBN: 978-0-263-30700-9

11/23

THE MAID'S PREGNANCY BOMBSHELL

LYNNE GRAHAM

MILLS & BOON

CHAPTER ONE

THE GREEK TYCOON Ares Sarris was a billionaire loner. He had shed his team of bodyguards for the occasion of the Durante wedding because they kept everyone at arm's length and he did not like to lend truth to the rumour that he was antisocial...even if he *was*. His unusual silver-blond hair glittered below the lights, his dark eyes very serious, his lean, strong face taut.

He had had a long hard road to the remarkable triumphs that were now his. Born in the back streets of Athens, he was the child of a drug-addicted mother and a rich man, averse to taking responsibility for his blunders. Furthermore, his earliest memory was of his mother calling him a mistake and abandoning him. He didn't look back to those days very often because his childhood had been a nightmare.

Yes, he acknowledged with the grudging aspect of an intellectual man who refused to dwell on the past, his life was very much better now. People didn't tell him what to do any more. They didn't denigrate him or hit him. They didn't act as though his genius level IQ were either some hellish annoying fault or a blessing he didn't deserve. Why? He was much too rich now to be that vulnerable and that made him smile because he had only first set out to make money at the age of eighteen to feel *safe*.

His immense wealth, nonetheless, had failed to protect Ares from being coerced by an old, bitter, snobbish woman he had never met into doing what he didn't want to do. To inherit the Sarris ancestral home as the bastard that he was, he had to be married. *Married!* As desirable a prospect to a male as private and reserved as Ares as sticking his hand into an open fire and the vindictive old witch had known it too! Why else had his grandmother imposed that clause in her will? By law, prevented from leaving the property to anyone other than the last living Sarris, she had contrived to slip in, 'Ares and his wife'.

Katarina Sarris had been well aware that Ares, foolishly frank in the only press interview he had ever given at the age of nineteen, on the acquisition of his first billion, had sworn *never* to marry. Although he had never met the woman who had been his late father's mother, and only a disastrous plane crash killing both his father and his half-brothers in adolescence had finally allowed him to be publicly recognised as a Sarris, Ares longed to possess that firm family foundation of history that had eluded him all his life.

His birth father's denial of his existence when he was a child had broken something in him while also warning him that his bone-deep need for validation was a dangerous weakness. Through DNA tests done at the time, the family lawyers, however, had acknowledged that Ares was a Sarris and had ensured that his educational needs were met. His grandmother, appalled by his background and antecedents as only a very snobbish woman could be, had refused to meet him even after the rest of her family had died. That the sudden death of his father and legitimate half-brothers had immediately given Ares recognition as a Sarris had been a tragic truth. But sadly, no warm welcome had awaited Ares in the bosom of his long-lost family when he'd finally arrived.

Ares had long told himself that he did not need that welcome now that he was an adult. But that house, the home of his paternal ancestry, could not, *should* not be denied to him by some petty clause in a will. Of course, he could have gone to court and easily overturned his grandmother's will but Ares refused to allow his sordid background to be exposed in an open court. As a child and teenager, he had undergone deep humiliation on that score. He would never subject himself to that anguish and embarrassment again. No, marrying a stranger simply to meet the exact terms of the will was, by far, the wiser option and a quick, clean solution to a thorny problem.

And that recollection brought Ares straight back to this evening's idiocy. He groaned, pacing restlessly in the well-lit boarded seating area by the side of the hotel's ornamental lake. His future bride, Verena Coleman, very much a paid role-player in his determination to inherit that property, had demanded this private meeting with him. That the woman should *demand* anything set Ares's even white teeth on edge. Until that evening, he had never actually met the lady in the flesh although she would become his wife at the end of the month. His lawyers had dealt with her. She had signed the watertight complex contract and for a very handsome price she would show up at the altar and start acting as his fake wife.

For a split second, Ares thought that he saw an odd shimmer of movement in the darkness below the trees and he spoke in Greek to ask if anyone was there, and then in Italian. After all, he *was* in Italy. Silence rewarded him and he shrugged a shoulder, reckoning that nobody but him was chilling down by the lake unless they were a smoker and, for very good reasons, he would never belong to that tribe.

At last, he heard the sound of feminine heels tap-tapping down the path to the beach and he frowned. Verena had pushed her way into his presence during the wedding reception and thoroughly exasperated him. She was provocatively dressed in a style he viewed as vulgar and everything he disliked in a woman but, for all that, she would still be his wife come the end of the month. She swam into view, all smiles and heaving cleavage on display. She was a curvy brunette from a minor English aristocratic family but if there was a hint of refined blue blood in her it definitely didn't show on the surface. His lawyers had not done well in choosing her.

'Ares!' she carolled, hurrying towards him as if they were friends when they were not even acquaintances.

It had been an unpleasant surprise to meet her at the wedding, which he guessed she had only gained entrance to by accompanying the glitzy wedding planner.

'You were directed to address any enquiries to my lawyers,' he reminded her. 'Why would you need to speak to me in person?'

'This is something that only *you* can deal with,' she announced importantly. 'I'm in a bit of a pickle, I'm afraid. I'm pregnant.'

'Pregnant?' Ares exclaimed in disbelief, and as quickly added, 'That means you've broken our marriage contract—'

'But why should it matter?' Verena demanded angrily. 'It's not as though sex is included in our arrangement. It's not as if you're even planning to share the same house.'

'If I marry you when you're pregnant, the child will be assumed to be mine and that is a legal maze of complication which I have no intention of touching in these circumstances. I do not want your child approaching me in the future believing that I may be his parent. I do not want the squalid rumours that would engulf us all over time either.'

'So, you're asking me to terminate my pregnancy?' Verena assumed.

Ares lifted his proud fair head high. 'I would not dream of making such a request of any woman, nor would I wish such a sacrifice to be made and laid at my door. No, it is much simpler than that: you've broken the contract. Our arrangement is now at an end.'

'You can't do this to me! I was depending on that money!' Verena flashed back at him furiously.

Ares said nothing because he truly had nothing more to say. Verena had after all already received a substantial payment for merely signing the contract.

'But you *need* a wife by the end of the month!' Verena reminded him.

'You are not the only woman who would be willing to enter a marriage of convenience for a price,' Ares retorted with precision.

Verena slung a handful of filthy curse words at him and stalked off. Ares was appalled and he swung away to look out over the moonlit lake. It had been an error not to request a personal meeting with her *before* he signed that contract. His legal reps had certainly not done him proud with her selection, he reflected grimly. She was too ignorant. She might only have been a fake bride-to-be, but naturally he did not want a boorish woman carrying his name or potentially figuring in the media as *his* wife. The binding NDA she had signed would keep her quiet though. He dug out his phone and texted his chief lawyer to warn him that the search was back on for a bride.

As he spun back round, intending to leave, he was taken aback to find a blonde in a long green dress that shimmered standing barefoot in the sand only a few feet away, her shoes clutched in one hand. It was, to his astonishment, the bridesmaid who had caught his attention earlier that day. Why? She was downright stunning from her sheet of natural blonde hair to those bright aqua-green eyes framed in her heart-shaped face with skin so flawless her complexion glowed. He had watched the men queuing up to take her onto the dance floor, all of them desperate to impress her, and he had noticed her seeming indifference to their efforts with detached amusement. Had he thought of approaching her on his own behalf? No…she was far too young for him, barely out of her teens, in his estimation.

'Can I help you with something?' he asked politely in English because he was aware that the sole brides-maid was the bride's sister.

Nervousness made her twitch, and her extraordinary clear eyes evaded his. 'I was rather h-hoping I could help you,' she stammered in a rush. 'If you need a fake wife in a hurry for a price, *I'd* like to put myself forward as a candidate.'

And Ares, who was very rarely surprised by any development in life, was totally astounded by that proposition. It was a dazzlingly inappropriate offer as well and he rather thought that her new distinctly rich brother-in-law, Lorenzo Durante, would be shocked to the core by a member of his family approaching any wealthy stranger with such an offer.

An hour earlier

Alana had never had as much attention in her life as she received from the men at her sister, Skye's wedding. But once the novelty wore off, she had no interest. She didn't have room for a man in her life when she was too busy working and the reasons *why* she had to work so hard and so endlessly boiled up afresh in her on the dance floor, making her eyes sting with sudden tears.

She was in debt to her eyeballs but that had to remain a giant secret. Yes, her new brother-in-law, Enzo, could have rescued her from her problems in five minutes. After all, Enzo was very generous. He had bought her a car as a bridesmaid's present, even offered to help her return to her art and design course at university. But to request Enzo's help, she would have to lie to her sister and she couldn't imagine Enzo lying to his bride if she told him the truth. Enzo and Skye had a thing about not keeping secrets from each other and Alana was hiding a *huge* secret that she was determined not to share with the big sister she adored.

Skye had idolised their stepfather, Steve Davison. Absolutely idolised the man who had adopted them and whom they both had called Dad. But the older man had been rather more flawed than Skye could ever have suspected. Unbeknownst to their mother and his eldest daughter, Steve had been a gambler and when he had got into trouble with money he had approached Alana for help, knowing that she was the least judgemental person in his family.

Alana had been far too fond of him to refuse to borrow money on his behalf with the loan shark he had taken her to meet. Every week out of his earnings as a taxi driver, Steve had faithfully brought her his payment towards the loan and there hadn't been a single problem. Well, the problem had really only begun when her mother and stepfather were killed in a train derailment the year before and Alana was left struggling to keep paying that loan out of what little she earned as a hotel maid.

But even worse, the debt kept on growing at a fantastic rate. She was paying a phenomenal interest rate and she knew it was illegal but there was nothing anybody could do about that aspect when the loan was in her name and her stepfather had picked a moneylender who was more of a criminal than an upstanding loan officer. Steve Davison had wanted that debt off the books, under the counter, *hidden* and she had made the biggest mistake of her life when she had agreed to the debt being placed in her name.

And when it had occurred to Alana that the best thing she could do with that lovely new car Enzo had bought her would be to sell it for the cash, she had cringed in shame and guilt and had left the wedding reception to seek the darkness down by the lake to lick her wounds. Of course, she couldn't *sell* that gift, but she genuinely didn't have the money to run a car in any case. She got around on a bike for good reasons. Not because she was obsessed with keeping fit, as her sister had teased…oh, if only Skye knew the truth!

But as Alana sank down on a rock in the shadows of the thick belt of trees girding the beach, she knew she wasn't ever going to tell Skye the truth about their stepfather's gambling debts. They had two younger siblings, Brodie and Shona, aged two and one, and Skye had taken full charge of them. She and Enzo were currently in the process of adopting Alana's little brother and sister. Skye had done enough. She had already made more than enough sacrifices on their family's behalf and she *deserved* to retain her illusions about the late father she had adored.

Now it was Alana's turn to do *her* bit and continue to handle the unfortunate financial repercussions of their parents' premature demise. Making heavy weather of her difficulties wasn't going to change anything, she scolded herself impatiently.

As footsteps sounded on the board path above the beach she glanced up, momentarily drawn from her unhappy reverie. A very tall, broad-shouldered male stepped into view below the fairy lights strung round the seating area. Instantaneous recognition leapt through Alana: it was Ares Sarris. That platinum fair hair was unmistakeable, although it had got a little longer since she had first seen him at the Blackthorn Hotel where she worked. He was probably a guest at her sister's wedding, although she hadn't noticed him at the reception because there were hundreds of guests.

The one and only time she had seen Ares Sarris before had been in the Presidential Suite at the Blackthorn Hotel. A US president had stayed there once to play golf and there was a plaque on the wall commemorating his visit. Ares had taken Alana's breath away at first glance. Give him a pair of feathered wings and a sword and he would resemble a warrior archangel. Her cheeks burned in the darkness. What a silly comparison! But, seriously, the guy *was* heartbreakingly beautiful from the crown of his silvery blond head to the soles of his doubtless handmade shoes. He had stopped her in her tracks, made her fumble her words and stare and she still winced thinking about that moment and of how she had later watched him leaping into his helicopter to leave again. She was a grown woman, not an adolescent fangirling over a popstar.

As a female came tripping down the same path, Alana looked on curiously while also beginning to rise to her feet to leave and then the woman announced quite loudly that she was pregnant and Alana dropped back down on her rock perch in shock because she definitely didn't want to walk out into the middle of *that* kind of scene and the only way off the beach would be past the couple. Their voices carried very clearly even though she was trying hard not to listen. The conversation was too confidential to interrupt, she told herself, all the while as her brows rose so high they vanished into her hairline because the idea that Ares Sarris, in all his gorgeous bronzed-angel glory, could have to *pay* a woman to marry him shook her rigid.

By the time, the foul-mouthed lady had departed in a snit, however, Alana's brain was engaged in an entirely different direction. The baby wasn't his? He *needed* a fake wife? He was willing to pay for the service? No sex was involved? In the midst of her frantic ruminations, it struck her that here was a vacancy she could fill, a job with better prospects than the one she had because she knew that Ares Sarris was even richer than her brother-in-law. According to repute, the Greek technology mogul was one of the richest men in the world.

Was she a gold-digger to even think of approaching him?

It was disgusting, wasn't it? To be so desperate for money that she would consider such an option? But that same desperation moved Alana stiffly and uncertainly out of the shadows. What drove her forward was remembering the days she'd lain sleepless, fretting about how she would scrape enough cash together to make the next payment to Maddox, the moneylender. He was a nasty, revolting little man, who had told her more than once that there were *other* options if she was struggling to find the money. She strongly suspected that Maddox was a pimp.

Focusing on a point somewhere to the left of Ares Sarris, after he had asked her whether he could help her with something, she heard herself stammer in a mortifyingly little voice, 'I was rather h-hoping I could help you. If you need a fake wife in a hurry for a price, *I'd* like to put myself forward as a candidate. I'm in debt and I need the money,' she added, like an afterthought.

Ares loosed an unexpected laugh because she was so embarrassed and so gauche and so young that she couldn't even look him in the eye. 'Does Enzo know about this?'

Alana's cheeks flamed and she looked up at him, disconcertingly aware of his great height in comparison to her below average five feet three inches, to say, 'Of course, he doesn't. There are very good reasons why I can't go to Enzo for help.'

Credit-card debt, Ares ruminated, extravagance,

drugs? 'If it's drugs, I should be sharing this conversation with him. I'm not a snitch but you are his family now and, in his position, I would want to know such a thing.'

Alana blanched. 'It's not drugs!' she gasped in horror. 'What do you think I am?'

Ares chuckled, amused yet again by her sheer incredulity at such a suggestion. 'I know nothing whatsoever about you. How do I know whether or not you're a party girl?'

'Well, I'm *not*!'

'But you are an eavesdropper,' he pointed out drily.

'I heard the woman say she was pregnant and then I thought I couldn't interrupt because it was too private and I didn't want to embarrass anyone,' she protested vehemently. 'I didn't intend to hear the rest of it. I just felt trapped there in hiding. I'm very sorry that I heard what I shouldn't have.'

'How can you possibly apologise when you're trying to *use* what you heard?' Ares demanded unanswerably.

'If I wasn't pretty desperate, I wouldn't have dreamt of coming up to you like this!' she muttered shakily.

He gazed down at her. The jewelled eyes glistened with tears. A rare shard of compassion infiltrated Ares Sarris, by repute a male with a heart of stone. Yes, he would be asking her to sign an NDA on his behalf in the near future, but she couldn't hide a single emotion that crossed her lovely face. Honesty, innocence and regret shone out of her like a luminous light and he found that weirdly attractive because he was infinitely more accustomed to women who concealed every genuine feeling.

'How old are you?' he enquired.

'Twenty-one,' she told him with a hint of defiance.

She was a little older than he had guessed but not by much. Listening to her, he felt about a century more mature because he didn't believe that he had ever enjoyed such innocence. 'Sit down,' he urged.

'Why?' she asked even as she obediently sat down.

In silence he detached her shoes from her loose grip and crouched athletically low to attach them to her sandy feet. 'I'm assuming you don't want to walk them into the water first?'

Swallowing hard, she shook her head in agreement, seemingly dumbstruck by his assistance with her shoes. He brushed sand away with a light sweep of his hand across the top of her foot and Alana shivered, extraordinarily conscious of the firm fingers at her ankle holding it steady. Unwarily, she looked up at him for the first time and sank into dark eyes that under the lights above were tortoiseshell perfection set in his lean bronzed face. Every shade of amber and gold swirled in those eyes. And those cheekbones, she enumerated, that sculpted shadowed jaw line, that unexpectedly full sensual mouth and the faint breeze playing with the silvery fair strands across his sleek dark brows. She wanted to *touch* him. In all her life she had never wanted so badly to reach out to touch anyone and she pushed her hands below her thighs to ensure that she kept them to herself.

'You're not even considering me for the job, are you?' Alana condemned. 'You think I'm—'

Ares looked levelly back at her. 'Too young, too naïve and probably unreliable into the bargain.'

'You're only twenty-nine. I read that somewhere!' she added with the speed of embarrassment lest he suspect that she had searched out information about him, which she had many weeks earlier after his stay at the hotel. And in terms of an online search the known facts about Ares Sarris were very few and far between beyond his meteoric success as a tech mogul. Ares certainly didn't live a playboy lifestyle in the public eye as her brother-in-law had done before he'd met her sister. He had been described as reclusive and mysterious because nobody seemed to know how or, indeed, even quite *when* he had appeared in the Sarris family.

'And I'm not unreliable, not the least bit unreliable!' she snapped in fiery addition.

Ares vaulted upright again, amusement his guiding principle in her presence and a rare experience for him. But for all that, he was very much aware that she was a true beauty in that unadorned classic way that so many women sought but missed out on. She sported nothing greater than a hint of shadow on her lids and lip gloss. And as he straightened and caught an accidental glimpse of her full creamy breasts below the neckline of her dress, he went momentarily rigid, fighting off an erection, because, in truth, it was quite some time since he had been with a woman. The reminder that he was a fully adult male with hormonal impulses was unwelcome to Ares. He had always put work first and foremost, scheduling occasional sex into his timetable while simultaneously reminding himself that sex was an indulgence he could do without.

He extended his hand. 'Let me walk you back to the hotel,' he suggested smoothly.

'I would be really good as a pretend wife,' Alana told him earnestly, much as if she were trying to sell herself in an interview.

His handsome mouth quirked. 'Why do you think that?'

'I'd do everything I was asked to do and think myself lucky to get the opportunity,' she continued winningly. 'I'd also hopefully be a bargain in terms of price!'

Above her down-bent head, Ares could not resist a wicked grin. 'Let's hope nobody else overhears *this* particular conversation.'

'I only want enough to settle my one debt,' she continued doggedly.

'And how much is this debt?' Ares could not resist asking, ridiculously diverted by her and not bored the way he usually was with her sex.

'It's a *lot*,' she warned him in an undertone and then she practically whispered, *'Thirty thousand pounds...'*

Ares was trying hard not to laugh out loud. 'Yes, you would be a very inexpensive acquisition for that amount—'

'Are you considering me yet?' she prompted hopefully, pausing on the path as the lights of the big hotel loomed into view ahead of them.

Ares gazed down at her with eyes that were now black as the night sky. 'I'm afraid not. What's your name? I don't even know your name.'

'Alana… Alana Davison. You're not giving me a chance,' she complained.

'Why would I?' Ares asked drily.

'Because it would be perfect for both of us. Obviously, you don't want a proper wife and I certainly don't want a husband!' she pointed out cheerfully. 'And I'm very trustworthy. I promised my dad before he died that I would never tell my sister, Skye, about what he had done and I never have because if I did tell her, it would *hurt* her too much. I also have no family other than Skye and Enzo to be suspicious and, let's face it, like most newly marrieds they'll be very much wrapped up in their own little bubble. I'm a very hard worker—'

'I wouldn't be hiring you to do actual work,' Ares inserted into that animated flood.

'I'm sure I could do something. I'm very willing and adaptable. I like kids and pets…' Alana looked up at him hopefully.

'I have neither to offer for your care,' he divulged ruefully, finding himself strangely reluctant to hurt her feelings when she was trying so hard to impress. 'Is the hard sell over? Could we now return to the hotel?'

Her expressive face reddened as she moved on down the path. 'At least promise to think about it…about me as a possibility,' she pressed.

Ares released his breath on a slow hiss, drew out his phone and opened it. 'Give me your number but, in all likelihood, you *won't* be hearing from me,' he warned her wryly. 'But my lawyers will be asking you to sign a non-disclosure agreement very soon.'

'Of course I'll sign it,' she muttered hurriedly, keen to reassure him.

'I could pay you for doing that—'

'No, no, no!' she exclaimed in dismay. 'You can't pay me for having done something I *shouldn't* have done—surely you see that?'

And that immediate refusal of cash when she was desperate for it was the most eye-opening experience that Ares had had in years. She had a sense of honour and that was rare indeed, he conceded as he strode away. She had connected with him on some level he didn't understand but that didn't mean that he appreciated her appeal. Ares didn't like impulsive promptings or anything out of the norm for him. In fact, it made him immediately suspicious and ill at ease, although, he recalled, he had not felt uncomfortable while in her company. For curiosity value alone, he would have a background check done on Alana Davison and his lawyers would have the NDA signed. There would be no further personal contact. Why the hell would there be?

CHAPTER TWO

Where are you?

THAT WAS THE text from Ares four days after Alana had left Italy.

Alana rolled her eyes as she emptied rubbish from a bin and wheeled her trolley back down the corridor. It was seven in the evening. Alana worked a permanent nightshift and the very wealthy clientele she served on the upper floors of the exclusive hotel often arrived and departed at unconventional times. The Blackthorn Hotel offered twenty-four-seven service to their guests.

UK. Working. Busy.

She texted the triple-word response with pleasure, thinking it served him right when he had blown her off in Italy. Doubtless he wanted that NDA signed, she reflected ruefully, her punishment for having listened to a private conversation when she should have revealed her presence.

That brief text response made Ares grind his teeth

together. She was a hotel maid, not a neurosurgeon. She could have spared him a little more information. Of course, if that was how she wanted to play it, he would respond in exactly the same way. He signalled a PA to get Enzo Durante on the line because he wanted a favour. He would buy the Blackthorn. Game on, he thought without really thinking about what he was doing, a reaction weird enough to Ares's precision-orientated brain to have usually inspired deeper reflection. Only it didn't on this occasion because Ares was in full attack mode like a guided missile taking aim at a target.

Forty-eight hours later, as she began her shift at six in the evening, Alana was cornered by the night manager, Martin. 'Why does the new owner of the hotel want to see you?' he demanded.

'The hotel's been sold?' Alana was ridiculously surprised by that news and, as quickly, she scoffed at her reaction. Had she really thought that Enzo would retain ownership purely because she worked in a lowly capacity there? Naturally, that wouldn't strike her brother-in-law as an important fact. Besides, in response to his offer of financing her return to university, she *had* mentioned searching out a better job as her current ambition. That had been her handy excuse when she was not in a position to admit that she could not afford to stop earning while she had a debt to service.

Her brow furrowed as she mulled over the rest of what the night manager had said. 'Why would he want to see *me*?' she asked.

'Maybe because your rich brother-in-law asked him to check on you or something,' Martin replied cuttingly.

Alana reddened. 'I doubt that.'

She was paying the price for the time off she had been granted for her sister's wedding. Initially it had been refused because the hotel was fully occupied and then an order had come down from the owner of the chain to say that she was to receive *any* leave that she requested and her family connection to Enzo had been exposed. And ever since her return she had been treated with suspicion at work, being viewed either as a potential spy or some little rich girl playing at a low-paid job she didn't really need. Nobody seemed to accept that Enzo's wealth had nothing whatsoever to do with her.

'He's in the Presidential Suite so you had better get up there,' Martin said thinly just as a slender brunette came walking down the corridor with a winning smile aimed at him, and Alana lost his attention altogether.

A couple of months earlier, Alana had applied for the assistant night manager position when it came up. Enzo hadn't known about it because Skye hadn't wanted to ask her fiancé for a favour for her sister. And Alana hadn't got the job she was qualified to do because married Martin was illicitly involved with the equally married colleague of hers who *had* got the job.

Wondering if the new owner was one of the men she had met at Skye's wedding and very much hoping he wasn't, Alana ducked into the staff cloakroom to check that she was tidy and wash her hands. Her simple brown overall and maid's frilly mob cap were brown and uninspiring, her hair braided up beneath, her face bare of cosmetics. Maybe it was just a case of the new owner being a friend of Enzo's and wishing to be polite and acknowledge her, she thought wryly.

She knocked on the door of the Presidential Suite and it was swiftly opened by a guy in a suit wearing one of those earpieces that signified that he was in protection work. Her face tense, Alana moved deeper into the very large reception area with its opulent seating and a fireplace blazing with the logs provided.

A very tall figure clad in a black pinstriped suit of impossibly well-tailored cut rose from behind the desk in the corner, lean bronzed features so instantly recognisable, she gasped. 'Alana—'

'*You're* the new owner?' The accusation flew from Alana's lips in angry disbelief, instant wariness and suspicion flooding her. 'Why on earth would you buy the hotel where I work? Is that supposed to be some nasty, aggressive threatening move? *Why?* I agreed to sign an NDA, didn't I?'

Utterly taken aback by that verbal assault, Ares strode round the desk and right over to her. 'Nasty? Aggressive? *Threatening?* Of course not, not in *any* way,' he assured her with taut emphasis, his startlingly handsome face reflecting distaste at the very suggestion.

'Well, it looks like a dodgy move after the conversation we had on the beach last weekend,' Alana told him roundly, noting how very tall he was again. 'It's intimidating.'

'My apologies. That was not my intention,' Ares lied, and he *knew* he was lying but he still didn't understand why he had bought the wretched hotel in the first place and now had nothing more to say on the subject. It was a good investment, that was all, he reasoned inwardly.

'So, where's the document for me to sign?' Alana prompted. 'I need to get back to work.'

Unaccustomed to such a summary dismissal, Ares breathed in deep, wondering how their meeting could have travelled in such a disconcerting direction. Like a grenade thrown into a room, she had exploded his every expectation because he had vaguely pictured her greeting him with smiles and warmth. 'I wish to discuss the debt you told me about—'

Alana tilted her chin, green eyes like emerald fire throwing defiance. 'That's nothing to do with you—'

'You have no debts to your name. I had a background check done on you,' Ares revealed with calm assurance.

Her delicate brows shot high, her slender frame growing even more rigid. 'And why would you do something nosy like that?' Alana demanded. 'My background is none of your business!'

'When you asked me to marry you, you neglected to mention how belligerent you could be,' Ares breathed with icy restraint.

'Well, now you can be grateful that you're not suffering a bad case of buyer's remorse!' Alana shot back at him quick as a flash.

'Miss Davison?' another voice unexpectedly inter-posed into the seething silence that had fallen after that response. 'Why don't you come this way and we'll get the document signed without further ado?'

In shock that there was another human being pres-ent, because she had assumed that she was alone with Ares, Alana glanced across the room to see an older man standing in the open archway that led through to the dining area and she turned the colour of an over-ripe tomato in embarrassment. She had contrived to have an argument with Ares Sarris, and she honestly didn't know how that had happened. His unforewarned appearance as the new owner of her place of employ-ment had set off every alarm bell she possessed and only now did it occur to her that she might have over-reacted, and she regretted the hot, quick temper that her sister had once told her she should always control.

Her newly guilty mood at having humiliated herself was not improved by walking through that archway to find another two men already seated at the polished table. Both of them studied her as though an alien crea-ture had joined them without warning. Doubtless they had heard every accusing word she had flung at Ares.

Ares disconcerted her even more by stepping past her to politely tug out a chair for her and she sank into it like a stone dropped from a height. 'We'll have some supper after this,' he murmured smoothly as if the pre-vious five minutes hadn't happened.

Her ears almost shot out in incredulity at that an-nouncement. *Supper?* She thought of the excuse of working again and shelved it because he *was* the boss and how had she forgotten that for even five minutes? Was she totally stupid around Ares Sarris? The NDA agreement was explained to her at great and very boring length. Ares sat across the table from her, probably afraid of her accusing him of intimidation again if he even sat beside her, she reflected with an inner wince of shame.

In any case, Ares was still showcased in her mind by the first glimpse she had caught of him as she'd walked through the door: her warrior angel, lean, strong face gorgeous but cool and composed as ice, not even a twitch of a smile anywhere near his wide mobile mouth. She hadn't seen the tiniest hint of welcome or friendliness in that image and maybe she had reacted accordingly because wasn't she entitled to expect him to have been a little less frozen after their frank discussion in Italy? Or was it simply the truth that that reckless and spontaneous dialogue by the lake had merely increased his frozen aspect by a factor of ten?

Afterwards, she had barely been able to believe the foolish things she had said to him. What an idiot she had been to corner so sophisticated and wealthy a man with her stupid irresponsible idea! Of course, he had said no! She had probably struck him as being not just a little off the wall but a touch unhinged.

Alana scanned through the document as fast as she could without her reading spectacles while one of the lawyers present offered to take her into the other room to discuss anything she didn't understand. 'That's unnecessary,' she parried, thinking that it took an awful lot of words to warn her that she was never to talk about Ares, write about him or his business or make use of any photographs of him.

As Alana rose upright, Ares stood up as well. 'Let's relax now…'

Alana shot him a look of visible wonderment at that suggestion and Ares almost physically etched a one-up symbol in the air between them. He was relieved, in fact, that she had shown him that she was not fault free. A quick temper and a habit of expecting the worst from people were bearable flaws, although it was not as though he would be spending much time with her, he reminded himself, frowning at the random weird thoughts that infiltrated his very orderly brain in her vicinity.

'Take a seat,' he invited as the legal team filtered out of the suite.

Alana settled down into the sort of sofa that almost swallowed her alive because it was soft and comfortable. The lights dimmed a little and the fire crackled in the grate. 'Isn't this cosy?' she muttered uncomfortably.

'Is that sarcasm?'

'No. I was just thinking that this is much better than vacuuming. But I don't blame you for being wary,' Alana acknowledged, finally looking up to focus on him where he sat opposite. 'I kind of lost the plot earlier. I wasn't expecting to see you ever again. I thought you'd send the NDA in the post…or something.'

'You've seen me at this hotel before, haven't you?' Ares prompted.

Alana nodded. 'I delivered your coffee one night when you were working late. I'm not expecting you to remember me. Guests don't really look at staff in uniform or remember faces.'

Ares said nothing. He didn't remember her. But he imagined a certain type of male would notice her even with her hair hidden. Her shapely legs, her slender yet curvy figure, the vivacity of her green eyes, the flawless skin. The sleazy ones would notice her, he reckoned. 'It's rather an old-fashioned uniform,' he remarked.

'Suits the antique style of the hotel and at least they didn't model it on a French maid's outfit.' She laughed as a knock sounded on the door.

Without any prompting, Alana jumped up and went to answer it. Tom, one of the young waiters, wheeled in a trolley and grinned at her.

'Sit down, Alana,' Ares instructed.

Talk about the habit of command, Alana thought ruefully, wondering why he would insist on having supper with her. Just to be friendly because of the Enzo connection? Or was there something else? It occurred to her that Ares was as naturally friendly as barbed wire.

'I would still prefer to settle that debt for you,' Ares informed her loftily. 'You have signed the NDA. You could have made a lot of money selling the story of my intended fake marriage to some tabloid newspaper and I am very grateful that you didn't.'

'Because I'm poor and in debt, I can't be expected to behave decently?' Alana quipped. 'I still have standards, Ares.'

'You've had time to think now. Will you…?'

Alana jumped upright with a bright and determined smile. 'Coffee or tea?' she asked, stationed by the trolley.

'Coffee…but—'

'I don't want you offering me money again when I didn't do anything for you. I did what I *should* have done,' she pointed out. 'Don't embarrass me.'

Unfamiliar with interruption and anyone guessing his intentions before he even expressed them, Ares released his breath in a hiss. 'You frustrate me. You are very stubborn. At least tell me what this mysterious debt is.'

Alana breathed in deep and reckoned that there was no harm in clarifying the situation on that score. 'My stepfather was a gambler. Backroom illegal card games, as far as I was able to work out. When he got into trouble with money, he came to me for help,' Alana explained. 'He was deeply ashamed of the gambling, and he couldn't bring himself to confess to my mother or my older sister. I think he was terrified that Mum would leave him over it…he loved her *that* much—'

'But not as much as he loved gambling,' Ares interposed cynically. 'If he'd loved her as much as you think he did, he would have got professional help with his addiction and come clean.'

'In an ideal world,' Alana agreed. 'But he was a

weak man, Ares. I'm strong, and my mother was and my sister is, but he *wasn't*. It's a shame because our stepfather was a kind and loving man. In every other field, he was pretty perfect as a dad.'

While she talked, Alana acted like a maid serving him, offering him snacks from the containers on the trolley, furnishing him with a napkin and a plate, pouring his coffee exactly as he liked. And it thoroughly irritated Ares. He didn't like her waiting on him in that demeaning way. He didn't like seeing her in a maid's uniform either. He supposed it was because he felt sorry for her, an unbusinesslike, impractical sensation that was incredibly new to him, but then nobody had ever told him that he should have no feelings whatsoever. Even though he usually did not have.

'How did you get involved with your stepfather's gambling debts?'

'He asked me to take out the loan in my name with the moneylender so that it couldn't come back to him and expose his secret,' Alana explained.

Ares was so outraged by that casual explanation that he clenched his teeth together, sooner than risk saying something offensive, but he couldn't hold it back. 'He was your adoptive father. It was his duty to *protect you*. Instead he took you to a moneylender and bulldozed you into signing up. Is it an illegal loan?'

'I assume it is. But I don't want you thinking badly of Dad. He brought me the money to pay that loan every week for over a year before he died,' she countered. 'He would never have left me to cope with it alone.'

Ares studied her with hungry intensity. Even in a maid's uniform, he found her appealing. Did that mean that *he* was a sleaze? In haste, he averted his attention from her but the vision of her face and curvy little body went with him. What was wrong with him? The heaviness at his groin told him that he was getting hard *again*. It was the originality of her, he told himself. She was like no woman he had ever met before and naturally novelty was a draw. For once, he wasn't bored. He couldn't second-guess her responses. She didn't fish for compliments or talk endlessly about herself and her accomplishments in an effort to impress. But why was he even thinking in such a manner about her?

He had come in person to the Blackthorn because he had wanted to see her again. *Needed* to see her again, no matter how odd that key instinct still seemed to him. For the first time in his life he couldn't fathom what was happening inside his own head and it was driving him crazy. It had to be sex, *lust*, he assumed, compressing his lips on the shocking suspicion that such a base prompting could control him to such an extent. Characteristically, he was appalled by the idea.

'I understand,' he remarked on her defence of her father.

'And I hope you also understand now that you don't owe me anything whatsoever for signing that NDA,' Alana pressed, her green eyes welded to his bronzed features while she tried feverishly hard to fight off her fascination. But he was *so*…together, she selected distractedly. Controlled, contained, impregnable, she sensed, the core of him locked behind high walls. She was all on the surface, nothing concealed or, certainly, very little and he was her total opposite, not a shred of emotion displayed on that lean, darkly handsome face of his.

'I get that that is what you want me to feel but I don't agree with your outlook,' Ares admitted tautly.

'I don't suppose you do, because you're used to putting a price on everything and I suppose people expect to enrich themselves at your expense.'

'That's an odd remark to make when you're the woman who offered to marry me for a price.'

'I'm in a bind, Ares. While I have to service that debt I can't get on with my life or do anything that I want to do.'

'And what do you want to do? Assuming you had a choice.'

Ares watched her emerald-bright eyes cloud in contemplation. 'Return to your university studies?'

'I didn't like my course much. I signed up for it because I wanted a marketable job when I finished because of the loans I took out to finance it,' she admitted. 'I'd probably most enjoy something arty, possibly painting, although I'm not particularly talented as an artist.'

Ares was impressed that she could admit that. He pictured her painting in one of his houses. He himself did not have an artistic bone in his body but he collected art that he enjoyed for more than its investment value. He liked her utterly unashamed honesty, her unexpected standards, her confidence even though she was sitting in front of him in a maid's uniform. He knew Edwin Graves, his suave chief lawyer, would turn white overnight at what he was about to do but, for once, he didn't care about the formalities. He would take a risk on Alana Davison and, although he had only briefly discussed the idea with his lawyers, who had expressed reservations, he knew that *he* had already made up his mind and for that reason he had instructed his lawyer to bring the marriage contract with him for him to look over.

'I'm offering you that job you said you wanted,' Ares intoned. 'That's why I had the background check done.'

Her green eyes widened, and her soft pink lips parted in surprise. 'Oh, well…er…what does it entail?'

'We go through a legal ceremony, because I need a wife for legal reasons,' Ares advanced. 'It will last from a few months to, at most, a year. The signing of a contract will be required. If you break the terms included it will be punitive, I warn you. For the period of time that you are pretending to be my wife, you will conduct yourself as though you truly *are* my wife and will engage in nothing that could cause me embarrassment. You will dress well and behave well and that is pretty much it.'

'And I don't even have to live with you?' Alana checked anxiously.

'No. I like my privacy but, for the sake of appearances, I will occasionally visit whichever property you are using.'

'OK. I'm signed up,' Alana told him with a huge inhalation of sheer relief at the very idea of finally being free of the debt that haunted her every waking hour.

Ares frowned, black brows pleating. 'Are you always this impulsive?'

'Don't say it like it's a fault.'

'I see it as such.'

'Do you ever let loose and relax? Because after meeting you twice, I have to wonder.'

'We will have a businesslike arrangement,' Ares countered levelly. 'We will not have conversations like this. Indeed, you will hardly see me for the duration of the contract.'

Alana lowered her hopelessly disappointed gaze and swallowed hard.

'Being attracted to me is unlikely to be a plus in this scenario,' Ares warned her quietly.

Alana's head came up again in a rush. 'I'm not attracted to you!' she snapped.

Ares was almost pleased to discover that some things she would lie about, if cornered. But he was attracted to her too, although he would not have admitted it either, he conceded absently. 'I spoke merely because I don't want any misapprehensions arising between us. There will be no intimacy of any kind.'

'Not a problem,' Alana replied with insouciance.

Ares experienced an extraordinary desire to simply lift her into his arms and show her how much of a problem that hunger could be, but he was too disciplined to succumb to such an urge. 'The contract is on the desk.

When you've read and digested it, I'll recall my legal team to act as witnesses.'

'I don't need to read it—'

Dark eyes as sharp as ice picks landed on her. 'You *will* read it from start to finish.'

Alana watched him vault upright with that smooth easy grace that she found so noticeable in his every movement, as if his limbs and his muscles were composed of stretchy silk. He swept a document off the desk and strode back to her extending it and she reckoned that she would not miss his bossy presence in whichever property of his she ended up living in. The fat document was at least a hundred pages long and she looked at him in wonder as she glanced through it.

'You shouldn't punish me just because the last candidate was stupid.' She sighed, beginning very slowly to leaf through, peering at the small print. 'I can't read this without my specs.'

'You read the NDA,' he reminded her.

'As well as I needed to,' she qualified.

'Go and get your spectacles,' Ares instructed impatiently.

Alana got up, which took effort when the squashy cushioning of the sofa wanted to hold her back. 'Gosh, is this what happens when you get rich...you want everything signed, sealed, and delivered like...yesterday?' she commented.

'It is,' Ares responded without apology.

Alana heaved a long-suffering sigh but inside she was crowing in heady delight. She was about to get rid of her stepfather's debt, she was going to get her life and her freedom back! She could hardly believe the sheer joy of release that was flooding through her veins.

Ares watched her bounce out of the room and he smiled. She was pleased. She was happy. Strangely that knowledge satisfied something in him. He assumed it was relief from being at the end of the bride hunt again.

His chief lawyer had intimated some doubts on the score of Alana being the right choice. He had produced exactly the same objections that Ares himself had cherished on first meeting Alana. But some stubborn trait inside Ares had refused to give ground to those sensible doubts. He *liked* Alana and he trusted her. It really was that simple. Her silence in recent days, when she could have spilled what she had overheard to the press and made herself a fortune, had been the conclusive proof he needed that Alana was the absolute right choice.

Alana raced back to the Presidential Suite, her glasses firmly anchored on her nose. She used her key to gain entry, saw no sign of Ares and walked into the dining area to sit down at the table and immediately read the contract. She could have done with a dictionary to interpret some of the words but glossed over those phrases regardless.

'Any questions?' Ares enquired from behind her.

'Yes, what does that word mean?' she asked, pointing a finger.

Ares leant down close to her to look over her shoulder and explained, silvery hair brushing her cheek. He smelled *divine*. Some sort of cologne mixed with warm, clean, male earthiness. Her nostrils flared on the scent of him, her body warming without her volition, her nipples tightening into hard little buds, her legs quivering and pressing close together. Only chemistry, she told herself squarely, nothing to feel bad about. Or at least, she conceded, she wouldn't have felt bad had a guy ever affected her that way before, only no one had until now. Ares Sarris was like a hidden patch of black ice on a road. She needed to learn avoidance techniques. Or did she? Hadn't he said that they would barely see each other?

'My lawyers are joining us to witness the signing,' Ares informed her. 'You'll leave this job in the hotel today.'

'I can't just—'

'If you want this contract, you will. How many people would credit that I've married a maid?' he sliced back at her. 'And I want the details of the debt so that it can be dealt with.'

'Maddox operates out of the back room of the pool hall in town. That's all you need to know. Give me the money and *I* will settle it—'

'No,' Ares said succinctly. 'You will not return to the moneylender in person. It could be dangerous. That is not negotiable.'

'There isn't very much negotiable with you,' Alana dared to say. 'But then you're paying for this, so I suppose that's how it should be, but I can't see what you're getting out of it.'

Ares's innate reserve prevented him from telling her. He would gain immediate ownership of the house he had never once entered as a boy or young man. He would see the portraits of the Sarris family as their last descendant and the name would die out after him because he wasn't planning on providing the next generation. He would pass on single, childless and without fanfare and leave the medieval ancestral estate to the state to use as a tourist attraction.

'All the same, I enjoy a mystery,' she said lightly, turning another page. 'Where will I be living?'

'I haven't decided yet.'

'Well, if you could make your mind up now I could tell Enzo and Skye that you've hired me as a housekeeper for it.'

'A lie of that nature won't work, not when you'll have staff of your own looking after you and calling you Mrs Sarris. Tell your family that we fell in love at first sight and when it doesn't last very long, nobody will be too surprised,' Ares disconcerted her by suggesting with a cynical twist of his lips as though the very idea of love at first sight was preposterous.

'But then they'll expect a proper wedding and I assume you're not planning on that.'

'I'm planning a quick civil ceremony—'

'So how do I explain that when I'm a fairy-tale-bride kind of girl?'

'You tell them that Ares doesn't do parties or celebrations.'

'But that makes you sound really dull, serious and selfish—'

'I am,' Ares slotted in without hesitation.

Alana tilted her head back and looked up at him awkwardly. 'You don't look or act dull.'

Ares shrugged a broad shoulder, unconcerned by her opinion. Certainly, he wasn't a fun guy, a prankster or a party animal or even a womaniser. He was a workaholic. His only other interest was working out in the gym and that was only sensible to maintain good health.

'You'll need to be ready to leave in the morning,' he informed her. 'So, pack tonight.'

'Tonight?' She gasped. 'Where am I going?'

'London to facilitate the rest of the arrangements. I have accommodation ready there for your arrival.'

Alana winced. 'I didn't realise everything would be happening so soon. Saying we fell in love at first sight is not likely to work when I only met you first at the wedding—'

'You say you met me several times here while you were working.'

'Guests don't *meet* chambermaids.'

'You *did*. Let your sister think what she wants of that. It scarcely matters in the scheme of things. We won't be married for very long,' he pointed out carelessly.

Alana compressed her lips and said nothing. She

had to adapt to the truth that, for the next few months at least, her life would no longer be her own to direct. 'Can't I tell Enzo and Skye the truth?'

'I thought you read that contract. You tell a single living soul and you're in breach of contract,' Ares reminded her.

CHAPTER THREE

'YOU CAN'T JUMP into marriage with some guy you hardly know!' Skye fired at her younger sister in incredulous disbelief later that same evening.

'I've clarified everything as best I can but I'm an adult,' Alana forced herself to proclaim even while she had every sympathy for her sister's feelings on having to listen to such unlikely fabrications as Alana had been forced to tell. 'Nobody can stop me marrying Ares and I'm leaving with him in the morning. I won't risk losing him.'

Her sister's husband, Enzo, studied her anxious face with penetrating force. 'He made you sign something to keep you quiet. That's why you can't explain, isn't it?'

Stunned by that accurate reading of the situation, Alana paled and then, overwhelmed by relief by his grasp of the situation, she nodded confirmation in haste.

'What on earth are you talking about?' Skye demanded.

'We're getting fairy stories because she *can't* talk,' Enzo guessed. 'Ares Sarris is notorious for having legal eagles who fire off more non-disclosure agreements than a celebrity's lawyers do. He's a very private individual. I would surmise that Alana is entering a marriage with him because he requires a wife for some business purpose?'

Wearily, Alana nodded again and then just dropped her head, not knowing whether to be pleased or aghast at the impressive level of Enzo's shrewdness. But at that mention of the lawyers' use of NDAs on Ares's behalf, she was suddenly worried that she might have leapt from the frying pan into the fire. Had she been too impulsive? After all, in much the same fashion she had signed that loan agreement in haste and nothing good had come of that decision.

'Does this have anything to do with his sudden desire to buy the hotel from me?' Enzo queried.

'It could do. I'm not really sure,' Alana admitted.

Skye heaved in an audible breath and perceptibly relaxed. 'But what I don't understand is *why* Alana would agree to such a thing when she could come to you for any financial help she might need. Do you know what you're doing right now?'

'Yes, as far as I can establish stuff,' Alana reasoned carefully.

'Is he a trustworthy guy?' she asked her sister, with a nudge of her shoulder to make her younger sibling look directly at her again.

'Very much so,' Alana declared, perspiration marking her short upper lip now that the worst was over and the act of sharing that marital announcement was achieved.

'And obviously you're attracted to him—'

'Obviously.'

'With Ares, you're talking about the ultimate serious, steady male,' Enzo commented in a clear effort to soothe his wife's concerns. 'Never a hint of a scandal about him, definitely *not* a Casanova with women—'

'Well, if he protects his privacy with NDAs there wouldn't be,' Skye chimed in, less impressed than Alana had hoped she would be by that accolade.

'I like him, I respect him and I trust him,' Alana heard herself say in a sudden rush. 'But you can't ever tell anyone that I said that about him!'

And her tiny sister, several inches below Alana in height, burst out laughing at that admission.

'OK, kid sister. I'll trust you to know what's best for you this *one* time, but the moment you doubt this decision or need help, we're here for you,' Skye proclaimed, gathering Alana into a warm, reassuring hug, and all Alana's fears that she might damage her ties to her family by marrying Ares drained away at that same moment.

The next morning, Ares glanced at Alana's delicate profile in the helicopter, noting the tense set of her soft pink lips and edgily recognising her nervous tension. She had signed the contract. Everything was organised, nothing left to go wrong. But any woman could get cold feet about marrying, couldn't she? Furthermore, plans made for his original bride candidate, Verena Coleman, were not a good fit for Alana Davison.

At least, in Ares's opinion, if not in his legal team's opinion. They had seemed almost bewildered by his attitude when he'd pointed out the many differences.

How could he possibly dump Alana in an unfamiliar city, expect her to buy a suitable wardrobe for herself and live alone in an apartment? Had she ever lived alone? Thanks to that background check, he knew that she had not. He didn't think her time spent as a maid living in hotel accommodation worth considering. Leaving Alana without family in London would be like dumping one of the babes in wood straight into the witch's cottage, he reflected with deep unease. His chief lawyer, Edwin, might believe that it was acceptable to treat Alana the same way as Verena, but Ares saw such assumptions as belonging under the heading of 'expecting too much'. Alana was years younger, less experienced, less confident, less an awful lot of things, he framed in his own quick and clever brain.

Naturally there would be *some* drawbacks to his choice of Alana as a fake wife and this was one of them. He would need to make more allowances until they reached the married phase and he let her sink or swim on her own. For now, he had to be supportive to ensure the success of their pretence *after* their marriage, he reasoned, and he relaxed at that conviction because that made perfect good sense to him. That also fully explained to his own satisfaction why he had been stressing out—something he *never* did—about leaving her and returning to his usual routine.

'We're going shopping…*together*?' Alana surveyed

Ares in astonishment as they walked at a fast rate of knots through the London airport, shielded on all sides by his security team. 'But I thought we weren't going to do *anything* together—'

'Do you know what kind of clothes you need to choose? Do you even know what wealthy women wear at formal occasions?'

Alana winced. 'Well, no, but—'

'That's why you need my assistance,' Ares decreed calmly, satisfied that all his concerns during the flight were now proven.

'But why would I need clothes for formal occasions when you're not planning to take me out anywhere with you?' Alana asked in a hesitant tone, because she had already discovered that Ares seemed to have a definitive answer for absolutely every question.

'There's a benefit in Athens being held by my charitable foundation in a couple of months. I have decided that for the purpose of authenticity we should make at least one public appearance together.'

'I understand,' Alana declared although, in truth, she didn't. What she had originally understood was that Ares was planning to leave her in some city apartment where she was to concentrate on kitting herself out as a credible Sarris bride at his expense. It was true though that she wouldn't have had a clue what sort of clothing to buy. The life she had lived until now had not included any need for formal apparel.

Barely more than an hour and a half later, Alana found herself modelling a floral dress and jacket that she believed would do very well for the civil wedding. She and Ares had contrived in the politest and chilliest of terms to fight quite a bit over her clothes selections. Unopposed, Ares would have shoved her into fashion far too old and staid for her tastes. She suspected that Ares socialised with women around a decade older than she was, for that classic tailored look was rarely what the average young woman in her early twenties sought.

Initially seated with Ares in the opulent private viewing room while svelte models strolled out in front of them on the little catwalk to show off garments, Alana had had a couple of glasses of the complimentary champagne brought to them. She could feel that faint buzz in her bloodstream and it made her feel a little more daring than normal as she strutted out on the catwalk in her bright dress, doffing the jacket like a professional and whirling round to let the skirt flip out round her slender legs. Ares stared at her as though he were transfixed, those stunning eyes of his amber gold as a predatory jungle cat's aglow below the lights.

'You have the most amazing eyes,' Alana told him chattily from the very edge of the catwalk, which was the closest she could get to him without stepping down to his level and in the very high heels she wore she didn't trust her balance.

Ares canted up a satirical black brow, cool as ice, not even a hint of a smile, and Alana just laughed.

'What?' Ares queried levelly while he thought that in all his life he had never seen a more gorgeous woman than Alana in *that* dress. He had insisted that it was too flamboyant and too short when she first showed it to him. Although he had not withheld his strong opinions, she had pretty much ignored his advice, which had disconcerted him. Yet in the flesh, clad in that dress she reminded him of a glorious bouquet of tropical flowers and she did have the most stupendous legs to show off. The golden sheet of her hair had fallen untidily round her flushed face when she twirled, lighting up green eyes like stars and a rosy pillowy mouth that was almost more temptation than he could withstand in that instant.

'I know we're having a register office do with no frills,' Alana continued. 'But this looks kind of bridal in a very *small* way.' As she held up her hand and two fingers measured the very tininess of that bridal element to minimise it for his sensitive benefit, she lurched at the edge of the catwalk and, before she could fall and hurt herself, Ares lunged up out of his seat and caught her in mid-air.

'How the heck did you move that fast?' Alana gasped in amazement. 'I mean, you were in your seat and then you grabbed me—'

'I saved you from tripping,' Ares slotted in a touch raggedly, endeavouring to make his arms lower to put her down on her feet, but that amount of help wasn't happening when his gaze was locked to hers. Not when the desire he saw in her eyes was the exact same as the lusty pulse roaring through his big, powerful body. He knew he shouldn't touch her. He knew he should put her down...but he *didn't*.

'Just do it,' she said simply, and he knew he shouldn't be listening either but when she tilted her head back a little and her velvety soft lips parted in clear invitation, any logic and restraint Ares retained simply tanked. He bent his head, and he kissed her. He took his time about it too. If there was only ever likely to be one single kiss, he fully intended to make a meal of the experience.

Ares had looked at her as though she could walk on water. Alana loved it. No man had ever looked at her like that, as though she were beautiful, special, and insanely sexy. Her heart was hammering so hard at the strength of the arms holding her against his lean, muscular frame that she could hardly breathe. He was so strong, so fast on his feet, so totally amazing when his stunning dark golden eyes held hers fast. Just at the moment when she was afraid her heart would pound the whole way out of her chest, he brought his mouth down on hers and steadied his hold on her, moving somewhere. Right at that point, she didn't care where he was moving, only that he did what every greedy cell in her body demanded and kissed her.

Ares sat back down in his seat and kissed her. She tasted so good, it blew his mind. He didn't usually kiss women. It was too intimate, too romantic, too personal. He did everything else but he didn't kiss, a little private quirk, he had often smoothly excused himself when taxed with that aversion. But when he cradled her cheekbones and held Alana imprisoned in his arms on his lap, Ares was for once unruffled by breaking his own code of rules. There were so many rules in Ares's life. He did *everything* according to the rules. He kept himself safe that way. He protected his assets that way. He ensured that he would never ever be vulnerable to another person again.

He knew how to kiss, he knew how to kiss so well that at first contact with the hard brush of his lips across hers Alana's head spun as though she were on a merry-go-round. It was incredibly, smoulderingly sexy when his lips gently, firmly parted hers and his tongue invaded with precision, sending a shower of fireworks cascading wildly through her body and lightening up pulse points she had never felt before. In fact, she had never felt sexual hunger like it, so it was an enormous shock when Ares, without the smallest warning, brought that kiss to an abrupt end. He dragged his mouth from hers, flipped her upright and stood her between his spread thighs as if she were a doll.

'We're not doing this,' he breathed hoarsely, a faint dark edge of colour scoring his cheekbones. 'Not you and me together. That *can't* happen...do you understand?'

Shell-shocked by the speed at which that moment of closeness had been severed, Alana nodded numbly. No, she didn't understand, she didn't understand at all, only that Ares looked tense, angry, and unhappy and she didn't like that either. It made her feel guilty, like some fatal temptress who had somehow lured a man into doing what he did not want to do.

'I'm sorry,' she said automatically.

'You didn't do anything. It was *all* me,' Ares asserted, his wide sensual mouth now taut with disapproval. 'I took advantage. You don't let me do that ever again. You say *no*.'

'I say no,' Alana repeated obediently, keen to say anything that would bring the mortifying lecture to an end. 'Got it.'

Ares watched her back away from him as if she were retreating from the lion's den and he expelled a shuddering breath. She was flushed and tossed, her award-winning mouth swollen, her eyes wide and dark with distress and, for the first time in his life since he had become an adult, Ares felt seriously bad for something he had done. Way too young, way too innocent for him, he reminded himself fiercely.

'I messed up your hair,' Alana warned him belatedly. 'You should tidy it.'

'Try on the next outfit. That dress is a definite buy,' Ares told her, prodding her back into role in the hope that while she was changing he would somehow magically work out why he had succumbed so easily to temptation.

'Alana…?' He spoke quietly before she could disappear from view.

She turned back, eyes evading his, no longer lit up like stars, he reminded himself crushingly. 'Yes?'

'Are you a virgin? I know it's a very personal question, and I apologise for asking, but I really would like to know,' Ares murmured in an undertone.

Alana froze and felt her face burn like a bonfire

but, now that he had kissed her, she didn't see why she shouldn't answer. 'Yes.'

As she vanished from view to change, Ares breathed in deep on that confirmation, assailed by a variety of very particular reactions. Virginity should be the equivalent of a suit of armour on his terms. It should mean that he would never touch her again, he assured himself resolutely. No honourable male would do anything less when there was no possibility of their relationship going anywhere.

Theos…how had he contrived to *do* this to himself? An own goal of outrageous efficiency? Saddle himself with the one woman he could barely keep his hands off? He should let her go; he knew he should, but he also knew that he couldn't face doing that either. She was safer with him, he told himself, especially now that he *knew*. He would never take advantage of her again. He might be ruthless in business, but he would not be unscrupulous in his private life. It crossed his mind then that, until Alana had thrust herself into his company on that Italian lake front, he hadn't *had* a private life. Occasional, perfunctory, invariably forgettable sex didn't count, and he had no family either.

'It's lovely here. I'll be fine,' Alana declared a couple of hours later as she surveyed the view of the Thames from the balcony, her back turned to him.

Ares had delivered her like a surplus parcel to a beautiful luxury apartment, fully furnished and with a kitchen already stocked with food. She didn't mind being on her own, of course she didn't.

'What about Christmas?' she asked him abruptly, half turning round. 'It's next week and I'm not staying here alone.'

'I don't do the festive season,' Ares parried without any expression at all.

'I'll go home, then, for a couple of days, play the gooseberry for Enzo and Skye,' Alana replied cheerfully, refusing to give way to disappointment. 'I can't miss seeing the children.'

Ares didn't want her leaving London before the wedding. He didn't want to spend any more time with her either, however, lest his once legendary discipline slip again. He forced back his distinct unease at the prospect of her being that far away from him as opposed to being just across the city and jerked his chin in acknowledgement without comment. It was the lesser of two evils, he told himself squarely.

Alana studied him. He revealed nothing. His classic bronzed features could have been carved from ice, his beautiful eyes veiled and narrowed. The kiss had definitely been a mistake. She felt vaguely as though she had a force field around her because he had kept his distance with such pronounced care since then.

'Is there someone else in your life?' she asked baldly, needing to know, refusing to back off to the extent that she didn't dare even ask.

Ares expelled his breath in a slow measured hiss. 'No. But *us*—this is business and you know that.'

'You're the one who broke the contract,' Alana reminded him with unhidden satisfaction. 'If it's business then let's be sure that we *both* stick to business boundaries.'

Ares could not recall the last time anyone had confronted him with a mistake. Not only did he rarely make a mistake, but also most were sufficiently intimidated by him not to mention it if he did. Why the rock-solid detachment and gravity he wore like a defensive shield didn't work on Alana Davison he could not comprehend.

'Obviously,' he agreed, refusing to rise to that bait that she had tossed out, hoping, he guessed, to involve him in an argument. He wasn't that predictable, at least, he *refused* to be that predictable. 'I'll text you the time and place of the ceremony. If there is anything more you require—relating to the contract—you can contact my lawyers or me but I'm very busy.'

Alana heaved a sigh. 'I'm unlikely to contact you before the wedding. I need nothing and I have nothing to say.'

Ares allowed himself one last lingering look at her. She wore one of the new outfits, a short full skirt teamed with a dusky blue sweater and a leather jacket, complete with knee-high boots. He couldn't even steal a fleeting glance at her without imagining himself pinning her to the nearest surface, be it horizontal or vertical, he wasn't fussy. On the drive to the apartment the amount of erotic imagery that had engulfed his normally disciplined brain had appalled him. It felt horribly as though she were infiltrating him in some way and he detested it. He was walking in the other direction, doing what he knew he had to do to be logical, and only for a split second did he contemplate the reckless option of diving head first into trouble with her. He was too clever for that, he assured himself, too sensible…

Ten days later, Alana contemplated her reflection in the mirror. The dress was very pretty, very flattering. It was her wedding day and she had no nerves. Why would she have? It wasn't a real wedding in the bridal sense. It was a fake, a pretence, nothing more. She had hardened her heart against Ares Sarris. He had closed her out, backed off, spelt out his indifference. *Not even a text?* Well, she would show him that nobody could be any more indifferent than she could be.

The kiss? She had lain awake a few nights recalling how she had felt and then she had shut that down fast. It had been a mistake. For him and for her, a blurring of the firm lines between them. But it tickled Alana pink that *he* had broken their contract first. He wasn't supposed to touch her in any sexual manner and he had smashed his own rule with raw enthusiasm. Put that in your pipe and smoke it, Mr Sarris, she thought childishly, her head swimming a little.

'Are you sure you're feeling well enough for this today?' Skye pressed from her seat on the bed. 'I wish you'd gone to the doctor as I asked you to do—'

'It's just a cold, Skye, not pneumonia.' Alana sighed, her throat aching like her head and she had a bit of a cough. Her muscles were aching a little too. That was all though, certainly not sufficient reason to cancel the wedding that she was being paid to show up at and participate in.

In any case, she wanted the wedding bit done and dusted and then she believed she would feel better, feel more like herself than she had of recent. Her spirits had stayed low even over Christmas with Skye, Enzo, and the kids, when she was normally on top of the world. She didn't know why she was feeling down and continually reminded herself that that ghastly debt was gone now and that soon she would be able to move forward in her life again to a future full of exciting possibilities.

Skye, in full maternal mode, leapt up to rest cool fingers on Alana's brow. 'You're *definitely* running a temperature.'

'I'm OK,' Alana insisted, leaving the bedroom. 'Let's join Enzo. We're getting boring in here.'

'You look great,' her brother-in-law told her carelessly, visibly as certain as a man could be that this was no normal wedding. 'We should leave. Traffic might hold us up.'

Alana suspected that Ares would not be expecting her to have brought guests, but she didn't much care. In any case, her relatives were leaving as soon as the ceremony was complete because Enzo had an important dinner to attend in Italy and he and Skye and the kids were all flying there together. Enzo was so attached to her sister that he took her virtually everywhere with him and Alana admired their closeness as a couple.

That was *her* blueprint for the future: finding a guy for herself who would treat her the way Enzo treated Skye. Or even as her stepdad had treated her mother, she thought absently as Enzo's limo nosed through the morning traffic, although she didn't want a man with a gambling problem. She realised that she was finding it difficult to concentrate and her mind was drifting aimlessly.

There was a crush of people in the foyer of the register office. Most of them appeared to belong to Ares's security team and she recognised Edwin Graves, the older man, who was Ares's senior lawyer. She saw the top of Ares's silvery fair head towering over everyone else's and refused to let herself even look in his direction. Let him find out what it was like to be shoved out in the cold and ignored!

Ares scrutinised his bride. Long blonde hair bundled up in some dignified topknot. It didn't suit her. She was just a little bit too thin as well, he decided, noting the almost gaunt aspect of her facial bones. Even so, nothing could dim the loveliness of her face, he conceded, thinking, though, that she had rather overdone it with the rouge. He knew he was being deliberately critical because in some indefinable way he had missed her. Missed that bright novelty freshness that could be so inexplicably appealing. He couldn't explain that oddity to his own satisfaction when he barely knew her and had only recently met her. He tensed in surprise when Enzo Durante appeared in front of him.

'Thought you might appreciate a couple of family

witnesses,' Enzo drawled casually. 'But don't worry, we're not staying. We're flying to Italy as soon as this is done.'

Ares's spine tightened. Sixth sense warned him that Enzo knew it wasn't a real wedding. He wasn't even trying to hide the fact. Alana had talked, he was convinced of it but, unusually, he found that he didn't much care. Enzo was no gossip and the bridal family's presence at the wedding did lend validity to the proceedings.

'Look after Alana,' Enzo murmured coolly. 'She's very precious to my wife and her siblings.'

'Alana will come to no harm,' Ares stated with finality, getting really antsy as he looked past Enzo to see his bride *still* not looking at him. Was she trying to make some point? Sulking with him? Offended for some reason? And why did he care either way? Why was he even wondering?

'It's time,' Ares declared, stepping forward to place his hand on Alana's wrist.

'Is it?' She shook her arm free and stalked ahead of him through the doors being held open for their arrival.

In front of the celebrant, he was close enough to Alana to see that what he had assumed was rouge was in fact high colour in her cheeks and it was so obvious because she was deadly pale. He grasped her hand to thread on the wedding ring, a plaited diamond-studded platinum circle that was too large for her, he registered in exasperation, knowing that that was a detail he had overlooked. She hooked her finger round it to keep it on and laughed and then she started coughing and dug out a tissue and he watched her slender shoulders shake as she struggled to stop coughing.

'You're unwell,' Ares said as they walked back out again and she had virtually no memory of the ceremony, merely the drone of a voice in front of her and the stupid ring threatening to fall back off her finger again.

'I'm fine.' Her voice was muffled by the embrace of her sister, who was muttering apologetically that she and Enzo had to leave.

Enzo hugged her as well and Ares thought that was too familiar now that Alana was his wife. A family interaction, he censured himself, the kind of platonic affection he had no experience of being around.

As the other couple departed, Alana slung him a surprised glance. 'You're *still* here?'

Ares froze at that provocative sally.

'Goodbye, Ares,' Alana framed, holding her head high, barely knowing what she was saying because she was feeling so dreadful, weak and sweaty that she wanted to melt into the floor beneath her and vanish.

Before he could even react, she turned away and moved a few steps and then she just dropped into a crumpled heap of bright floral fabric.

'My goodness,' his highly conservative lawyer, Edwin, commented. 'I suppose we'll have to drop her off at some private clinic. At least she made it through the ceremony though.'

Ares stooped and snatched up his unconscious bride

from the floor in a hasty movement and locked both arms securely round her. 'I'm not dropping her off anywhere.'

Edwin's brows rose high. 'But—'

'If Alana's ill, she's my responsibility until she's well again,' he announced and, angling his head at his security team, he strode out of the register office onto the pavement, unconcerned by the stares he was attracting for the first time in his life.

CHAPTER FOUR

IT WAS A NIGHTMARE. Even asleep, Alana knew she was having a nightmare. She was trapped in a strange house with endless rooms, and she was running and running and something terrifying was chasing her. Her heart was pounding, her muscles burning as she cried out in fear.

'It's only a dream,' a deep, dark voice murmured soothingly.

Alana felt heavy and unspeakably exhausted and her eyelids were too weighted even to lift. She wondered dimly what was wrong with her but it didn't feel important enough to mention when her brain was a swamp.

A hand grasped her limp fingers where they lay splayed on the cover. 'You will feel better tomorrow,' the voice assured her with impressive confidence. 'It's your temperature. You have a fever. It is probably causing the nightmares.'

And she knew right then that the voice belonged to Ares. Only Ares would give her that much detail when she was beyond caring and yet the very knowledge that he was with her was a comfort because somehow she *knew* that he would deal with any problem with the utmost efficiency. 'I'm ill,' she mumbled as a more pressing need made itself known to her.

'You have influenza.'

You say flu, she wanted to tell him, but she didn't have the energy and she simply sighed as she shuffled her legs across the bed to find the edge, wondering then why Ares was around when she was in a bed, of all things. She attempted to roll her heavy body.

'What are you trying to do?' Ares demanded, sounding tried beyond measure, making her feel guilty.

'Bathroom,' she said curtly, mortified by that necessity.

Ares gazed down at her with impatience, pushed back the duvet and scooped up her slight body. He had got used to carrying her around and now it cost him not a thought to do it. She weighed far less than she should. The doctor had spelt that out to him in rather accusing terms, as though it were his fault that his wife was so skinny. Maybe she had assumed he was one of those men obsessed with having only a very thin partner. Well, he wasn't, he thought, tucking in one pale slender arm with great care as he strode into the adjoining bathroom and settled her down.

In astonishment at having been lifted in such a way, Alana opened her eyes for the first time and she focused dizzily on a tiled floor and her own bare feet. Her hands slid down over fabric and she studied it in amazement. She was in a nightdress, she who never wore nightdresses, who was a vest and shorts girl, and all she could think about then was how she had got out of her clothes and into a nightdress when she didn't even know where she was.

'Where am I?' she mumbled.

'My home where you are safe.'

She lifted her head enough to focus on bare brown male feet, nicely shaped feet too, she acknowledged abstractedly, noting the hem of jeans visible. Ares in jeans? She really wanted to see that because he was always in a suit and she could imagine him going to bed in a suit like a vampire retiring to his coffin. 'My brain's dead,' she complained of that piece of nonsense.

'Because you're ill.'

Not so ill that she wanted a man in the bathroom with her, she thought fiercely. 'Go! Close the door. Leave me alone.'

'You're not well enough to be left alone,' Ares informed her stubbornly.

With immense effort, Alana threw her head back and finally focused on Ares, barefoot, sheathed in faded jeans and a shirt hanging open on a bronzed torso worthy of a centrefold and a thousand camera flashes. It was to her credit that she didn't get sidetracked by the view and still hissed, 'Says who? Get out of here!'

As soon as the door closed on his exit, Alana slumped and slowly took care of herself, crawling across a cold floor to lever herself up by a cupboard to a sink. As she clumsily washed her hands, splashed water on her hot face and buried her face in a towel, she remembered that they had got married. She looked at her hand but her finger was bare. Oh, heavens, had she already lost that ring that had looked as though it had cost a king's ransom?

As she began to open the door, it opened for her and Ares scooped her up again as if it were the easiest thing in the world to lift a fully grown adult woman. He settled her back into the bed, fixed the pillows, tugged the duvet over her while her green eyes clung to his hard bronzed features in a daze. 'I've lost the wedding ring.'

'It was falling off. I removed it and I'm having it resized,' Ares explained, lifting a glass of water with a straw to angle it at her helpfully for her to drink before retreating to an armchair within a few feet of the bed.

'What time is it?'

'It's the middle of the night. Go back to sleep.'

Her troubled gaze rested on him. It might be the middle of the night, but Ares Sarris radiated energy just the same as usual and betrayed not a hint of emotion. 'I'm being a nuisance,' she began uneasily.

'You're my wife. You're my nuisance for the moment,' Ares retorted crisply.

'You've got no tact,' Alana framed drowsily.

'And you're *surprised*?'

'You still look like an angel,' she whispered, almost mesmerised by the light from the lamp that gilded his hair and threw his perfect features into an intriguing mix of exotic peaks and shadowed hollows.

Even if Alana was plainly still feverish, Ares was relieved that she was opening her eyes and talking again. Unconscious, Alana had panicked him just a little. Until the doctor had reassured him, Ares had been deeply concerned...*obviously*. Married one day and a widower the next might not have fulfilled the will and it would be outrageous to go to such lengths as matrimony only to be thwarted by a dying bride. On another level, impervious to the ruthlessness of that last thought, Ares watched her sleep, scanning the silky golden hair tangled across the pillow, the curling lashes separating her determined little nose above the peachy softness of that mouth he had tasted with such forbidden pleasure. He almost smiled as he opened his laptop, deeming it safe to work now that she had made what he viewed as her very first step in the recovery process.

A nurse in a uniform greeted Alana when she wakened later the following day.

'I'm your nurse, Fay,' she said cheerfully with a smile.

'Where's...er...?' Alana framed, lying still as she realised she felt too weak to push up against the pillows.

'Your husband? Probably sleeping, Mrs Sarris. From what the staff told me, he was so worried about you that he sat up all night with you.'

Alana's lips rounded into a soft 'oh' of surprise, but her heart warmed. Ares had worried about her. Presumably, that was why he had been in her room when she'd surfaced in the middle of the night. Even though it was only a dose of the flu, she could understand why he had been concerned when she had fainted the way she had, wincing at what a show she must have made of them collapsing like that in a public place.

Fay asked her if she would like some breakfast.

'I'm not hungry—'

'Dr Melrose is concerned that you have missed so many meals and that you still have little appetite,' Fay said. 'It would be great if you could try to eat something. Toast?'

Alana nodded absently.

Living in at the hotel, she had got thinner, she conceded, probably because she worked long hours and, when she wasn't working in what was often a very physical job, she ate whatever was cheapest and quickest to prepare in the small kitchen in the staff quarters.

'Who's Dr Melrose?' she asked.

'She's very nice. Your husband brought her in to check you over yesterday. I arrived about the same time and I put you to bed.'

Alana sank back into her huge bed and dully surveyed a bedroom the size of a football pitch. If this was Ares's home, he lived in incredibly opulent style. At least he hadn't dared to undress her and put her into the gothic nightdress. Last night she had been so pale and washed out in appearance she had resembled a corpse in her white shroud. Luckily, she was still feeling too unwell to care what she looked like.

Fay switched on the giant television on the wall and brought her the controls. 'This is the most fabulous house I have ever been in,' she confided in some excitement, but Alana was already sliding back into sleep again, exhausted by her time awake.

Over the following couple of days, there were times that Alana didn't know whether she was asleep or in a waking dream but slowly, far more slowly than she would have liked, she began feeling better. There were glimpses of Ares in her recent memories and she didn't know whether they were real or imagined. She had an image of him gazing down at her from his great height, dark golden eyes troubled as she tossed and turned. She had another image of him working at a laptop while he sat by the window and looking up, finding her staring, he had said, 'You should eat something.'

'Not hungry,' she had told him hoarsely as he'd brought the straw in the water glass within reach of her parched lips.

'Some women would eat just to please me,' he had told her with assurance.

Her nose had wrinkled. 'Not that desperate,' she had mumbled and he had laughed.

Had that exchange really happened? she wondered now that she felt stronger and her appetite had returned. Breakfast arrived very soon after Fay had ordered it by phone. It came on a trolley as though she were in a hotel and two servers accompanied it, one carting a lap tray, which was unfurled for her use and soon furnished with flowers and cutlery, the other showing off the choices on the trolley. A lot more than tea and toast had been prepared. There was oatmeal, eggs, toast, pastries, fruit and, like Fay, everyone was so patently keen for her to eat that she duly took the eggs even though she couldn't eat very much. Soon after that, the female doctor called in, a serious young woman, who talked to her about good nutrition.

Having slept the afternoon away, Alana felt well enough to try out the rainwater shower in the bathroom with Fay nearby in case she became dizzy. Refreshed, she was disconcerted when the nurse informed her that the dressing room off the bedroom was packed with her clothes, which had arrived two days earlier. Alana discovered that her new wardrobe and her own small stock of clothes were now combined. Ares must've had the apartment she had been using cleared and her possessions transferred to his home. Clad in shorts and a vest, her hair dried at Fay's insistence, she felt better.

Skye phoned her from Italy. 'Good to know that you're making Ares Sarris work at this marriage,' her sister said teasingly.

'What on earth are you talking about?'

'You bridegroom was on the phone to me the day before yesterday for almost half an hour—'

'What did he phone you for?' Alana exclaimed with a frown.

'He's contacted us every day since you fell ill. He's been asking questions and not about business. He had to know what sort of books you read, what sort of movies you like, what you like to eat, what your favourite colours are… Oh, there's no end of detail to what Ares feels that he *needs* to know!' Her sister punctuated that comment with an appreciative giggle. 'So, I haven't worried too much about you being ill, not with your personal doctor and nurse on call, and Ares ready to go to superhuman lengths to ensure that you're well looked after.'

'I'm amazed,' Alana responded honestly.

'I was as well. I thought he was a total iceberg...but underneath there's definitely a thoughtful guy trying to break out. Enzo thinks it's very funny. He used to think Ares was a total stuffed shirt and a grinch and now he's wondering.'

A knock sounded on the door and Fay answered it. Two staff members carried in a table and placed it beside the window. A third brought a dining chair.

'I believe your husband's planning to join you for dinner,' her nurse told her in an *Aren't-you-a lucky-girl?* tone.

Alana forced a smile. Fake new bride, she reminded herself anxiously. Ironic though, she thought wryly, that Ares had still contrived to spend their official wedding night with her. Presumably his visits were for the benefit of his staff and he was doubtless resenting the hell out of that necessity. After all, the plan had been for a separation immediately after the wedding ceremony. She was already falling down on her *fake* wifely duties, she reflected ruefully. It would be natural for Ares to feel annoyed when she had fallen ill and he had not felt it possible to walk away.

But what was the actual purpose of the bogus wife charade? she finally stopped to wonder with intense curiosity. What could make a male as strong as Ares Sarris resort to such a tactic? That fascinated her.

Alana went into the bathroom to brush her hair, pinch her pale cheeks and use her lip gloss and every step of the way she told herself off for doing so. So, she was attracted to him. No big deal. Adolescent crushes had taught her that a girl didn't always get what she wanted, especially if he was a teen idol in a band. That was life and Ares Sarris had more choice of female company than most, not to mention the fact that he preferred to abide by their contract and was determined not to break it. Even though he already *had* in a small way with that kiss? Alana went pink, recalling that surge of wicked uncensored hunger that had flooded her and squirming at the recollection. She was less impressed remembering Ares's cool retreat in the aftermath.

Ares strode through the door and her nurse studied him with glazed appreciation written all over her face. Yes, he was very, very good-looking, especially with a five o'clock shadow of stubble enhancing his strong jawline. Even Alana was riveted to her pillows, just taking in the whole vibrant vision of her warrior angel. Silvery hair ruffled over that classic hard-boned face, dark deep-set eyes with a hint of gold, a dark formal business suit perfectly tailored to his lean muscular frame. She watched him dismiss her nurse, barely breaking his stride, and then the food arrived along with what appeared to be deliveries, which were settled onto the foot of her bed.

'What's all this?' she asked in the midst of the chaos of food being served and Ares sinking fluidly down into his chair emanating that calm, controlled assurance that was uniquely his.

'I bought you some stuff,' he imparted with an eloquent shift of one lean brown hand. 'You won't be up and about for a few days yet, so I asked your sister what you enjoyed.'

'And what did you get me?'

Ares arose again to tip out a bag of books, bright cover designs catching her eyes, and she almost shrieked in dismay, her fingers clenching round one at the sight of a half-naked male with wings and a sword. Heat burned up from the centre of her and flushed her entire skin surface.

'Angel romance,' Ares said unnecessarily, trying not to smile, trying not to linger on the recollection of what she had said to him while still feverish. 'A niche concept but, according to your sister, your favourite—'

'I like fantasy books,' Alana acknowledged flatly, averting her gaze from the colourful risqué covers as she crammed them all back into the bag with clumsy hands. If a woman could die from embarrassment, she would have died there and then right in front of him.

'There's a tablet there as well and it's loaded with digital copies. I forgot to ask your sister your reading preference.'

'This is so kind of you. Thank you,' Alana voiced her gratitude between gritted teeth.

Ares lifted another bag. 'And you like to knit…'

Knit? Alana hadn't knitted anything since her school art exam had demanded she produce a handcrafted item. She looked into the bag at beautiful shades of wool and needles and several patterns and her tummy flipped. My goodness, he must think she was a really exciting young woman with her angel romance and her stupid knitting! Couldn't Skye have lied and invented more exciting, glamorous pastimes for her benefit?

'There's other things there.' Ares indicated the bags and sat down at the table where the first course of his meal awaited him. 'I thought if you were feeling up to the challenge, I would take you out of this room for a while.'

'I would love that.' Alana smiled warmly, lifting her knife and fork.

'We'll have our coffee downstairs,' Ares decreed as he leant back in his chair. 'Have you a robe?'

Alana pushed away the lap tray and slid out of bed to head for the dressing room.

'There's a new one here,' Ares divulged, rising to indicate the big shallow box still lying at the foot of the bed.

Alana returned to the bed and bent down to open the box. 'Why would you buy me something like that?' she asked uncomfortably.

'I didn't know what you owned in that line.'

Alana went pink, recalling that she had modelled neither the nightwear nor the lingerie for him, merely choosing sufficient to meet her needs behind closed doors. She shook out a slippery silky robe in a soft shade of green.

Ares was welded to her every move, his attention roaming from the full firm mounds of her breasts swelling above the vest neckline to the pert curve of her bottom before scanning the surprising length of her slender legs. The swelling at his groin was immediate and intense and his expressive mouth tightened. It annoyed him that he could still be so susceptible, and it struck him as a downright unforgivable response while she was still recovering from illness.

Alana tied the sash on the robe and walked to the door.

'Slippers?'

'I don't have any. Didn't think of them.'

Ares opened the door and then bent down to lift her up into his arms.

'What on earth are you doing?'

'It's a lengthy walk and you're not that fit yet,' Ares told her levelly.

'I'm fine.'

'Your sister admitted that even if you were on the brink of death you would still insist that you are *fine*. I'm not listening,' Ares declared, walking down a wide staircase with her firmly clasped in his arms.

'You're too bossy and pushy for me,' Alana protested, striving to hold her own and act as casually as he did and as though the intimacy of his hold were not a trial to her.

But then possibly he was less sensitive and self-conscious than she was. But she could *feel* the heat of his broad chest all along one side of her body, smell the faint tang of his cologne and was almost within touching distance of his outrageously perfect mouth. As he strode through an echoing hall, she breathed in deep, ashamed of the prickling sting of her nipples and the surge of heat between her thighs.

'This is the orangery,' Ares informed her as he laid her down on an upholstered chaise longue in a large room walled with lush indoor plants and a line of windows overlooking a lit winter terrace. 'My housekeeper is bringing coffee for me and hot chocolate for you.'

'Skye must've talked her head off to you.' Alana sighed, colouring. 'But I'm almost on my feet again, so you must be relieved about that—'

'You can't leave until your health is fully restored,' Ares slotted in quietly.

'I feel like *your* responsibility now,' Alana gathered. 'And you take your responsibilities very seriously.'

'That is a trait I am proud to possess.'

'But I'm not your responsibility...well, at least only on paper,' Alana reasoned, stiffening when Ares raised a dark brow of silent disagreement. 'It's not as though we are a genuine husband and wife,' she added in a whisper, mindful of the risk of being overheard.

An older woman appeared with a tray.

Alana cradled her ornamental china cup of chocolate in one hand while nibbling at a tiny truffle cake. 'Skye told you about my love of truffles as well,' she groaned. 'And you're spoiling me.' As if she were a sick child, she thought in powerful chagrin.

'You deserve to be spoiled after the experience you have had.'

'No, I don't!' Alana argued with sudden vehemence, green eyes wide. 'I let you down. I caught the flu and forced you to change all your plans.'

Ares watched her stretch out on the sofa, little pink

toes extended. She had tiny feet, tiny hands, dainty narrow wrists and ankles. The sash on the robe had loosened, parting the edges of the robe, treating him to a view of pointed nipples indenting her flimsy top. Ares tensed and addressed his attention to the sickly-sweet treats that had vanished from the plate at speed and again he tried hard not to smile, he who so rarely smiled. She amused him, that was all. There was something so essentially feminine about her. He couldn't quite work out what it was or why she exuded incredible sex appeal without making the smallest effort. He only knew that he resolutely refused to succumb to that appeal.

'Ares?' Alana said. 'You didn't answer me—'

'It's not your fault that you fell ill,' Ares slotted in drily. 'But we won't be revisiting my original terms in the contract until I believe that you have fully regained your health.'

'Is that so?' Even to her own ears, her tone sounded tart but he made her speak like that, she conceded wryly. He was such a know-it-all, really couldn't help being like that because she reckoned he was accustomed to being the cleverest person in most rooms. And she could live with that, kind of understood it. What she couldn't live with was the way he tried to act as though the attraction between them didn't exist.

That drove her insane. For her, it wasn't simply physical attraction and she knew that. Alana had never hidden from her own feelings. Ares Sarris mesmerised her as thoroughly as a snake charmer did a snake. When he was around, she couldn't take her eyes off him and her heart pounded as though she were running. And the whole time in the background of her brain she was experiencing this wild edge-of-the-seat excitement she couldn't quell just because he was with her. She supposed it was an infatuation, but she wasn't a kid any longer and she suspected she was falling in love for the very first time and that scared and thrilled her in equal proportions.

A slanting grin slashed Ares's lean bronzed features without warning, chasing the air of studious gravity he usually wore. 'I think we both know how much I enjoy being what you call…er…bossy. But I do have a surprise for you—'

'Everything you do is a surprise!' Alana told him truthfully, still reeling from that sudden almost boyish grin and a level of charisma that blew every rational thought right out of her head.

'I believe you're strong enough to travel now. We're flying to my property in Abu Dhabi tomorrow, where you will enjoy some winter sun and complete your recovery process,' Ares informed her smoothly. 'After that, we will return to fulfilling our contract as it was written.'

CHAPTER FIVE

ONLY TWENTY-FOUR HOURS LATER, Alana chattered to her sister on her mobile phone while resting back on a lounger on a sun-drenched terrace lapped by the turquoise waters of the Persian Gulf. It was idyllic. From indoors, Ares was absently listening to that tone of bubbling energy and pleasure that he most enjoyed hearing in her voice. Delighting Alana gave him a kick and he didn't know why.

'It's the most amazing house. It's right on a private beach and it's built of wood and stone,' Alana was carolling. 'And it has this bathroom with a circular bath that overlooks the beach. I can't wait to get into it! Ares has such amazing, good taste. He designed it. Can you believe that? He designed it himself!'

Ares stopped listening and smiled as he worked. She was happy. When she had been ill, she had been miserable, that soft mouth down-curved, those bright eyes dull and lifeless. He had felt guilty about that. He had wanted to see her smile again and she hadn't stopped smiling since his private jet had landed in the UAE. She had been leaning out of windows, pointing at stuff, talking him to death by asking constant questions, basically showing off how youthful she still was with her enthusiasm for everything, he conceded ruefully. It was cute, *she* was cute, but basically only the way a puppy or kitten was cute, nothing more personal than that, he assured himself confidently.

'Sometimes you're very quiet,' Alana complained over dinner after her fifth conversational sally had crashed and burned. She wanted to slap him because her temper was on a hair trigger. All day, Ares had tuned her out as though she were a television playing in the background. It drove her mad. How could he *do* that? How could he ignore the chemical attraction that lit her up inside like a light installation when they were together? How could he behave as though it weren't happening? And yet when he looked at her directly, every time she *knew* that he wasn't indifferent to her. It was just there in his eyes, the curve of his lips, the tilt of his head. He couldn't hide *everything* from her.

Alana didn't understand what that stupid contract had to do with anything in the *real* world. That contract was primarily to protect Ares's wealth, that was what she had read in all those weighty paragraphs of legalese that she had ultimately only given a cursory read because it would genuinely have taken her hours to properly go through such a long document. At the heart of that contract, however, they were still two adult, single human beings, both of them surely free to do as they liked. Only Ares flatly refused in any field of his life to do as he liked if he believed that doing so would be unwise. Sadly, when it came to her, Ares had a will as strong as forged iron.

Ares contrived to smile across the table at the air of exasperation stamped on her lovely expressive face. 'When I have a business problem, I tend to be very quiet while I consider it.'

Having finished eating, Alana sprang upright. 'Well, you should have explained that sooner!'

'It's antisocial to be like that but I've *always* been like that,' Ares admitted levelly, neither apologising nor soothing her ruffled feathers, because he was who he was.

'Well, I've used up *my* day's allowance of sociability,' Alana countered squarely. 'You had your chance to be company and you blew it… I'm going for a bath!'

'I'll see you tomorrow, then.' Ares's dark golden eyes glittered with ferocious appreciation as he watched her stalk sassily out of the dining room. He liked her cheek. In the past ten and more years, nobody but her had ever dared to be cheeky with him. Possibly it would've surprised her to learn that he found her incredibly entertaining and stimulating company. After all, it had surprised *him*. She sizzled and boiled with emotions like a miniature volcano and displayed it all on her beautiful face. She was his polar opposite in personality.

In the bedroom next door to Alana's, he peeled off his suit, resolving to put on shorts and a T-shirt the next day before Alana criticised him again for failing to relax his dress code. He froze. Why was he taking account of *her* preferences? Ares had always moved to his own beat, stubbornly opposed to meeting other people's wishes and standards. He fell still and then dropped his shirt with a chuckle. Obviously, he was *humouring* her, the same way people indulged children and pets, he told himself.

The shriek that broke the silence cut through the wall between their bedrooms and acted like an enemy air-raid siren on Ares. In his boxers, he raced out of the room and into hers and straight into the bathroom… where she was bouncing around stark naked and sobbing and clutching at her foot.

'My toe!' she gasped tragically.

Ares averted his gaze from her nudity, but not quite before he had appreciated that the richer protein-based diet in his London home had made her a touch less slender. He snatched up a giant towel and wrapped her in it while she continued to try and hop around like a frantic one-legged bunny rabbit being chased by a shotgun. In frustration, Ares lifted her protesting body out of the bathroom and sank down on the edge of the bed with her on his lap. He smoothed her foot with a firm hold and soothing stroking fingers over her stubby little toes.

He touched her with a gentle kindness nobody who looked at him would be aware he was even capable of demonstrating, Alana conceded. He had been so good to her while she was ill and when they had arrived at the fabulous villa, it had felt ridiculously like a honeymoon destination and as if they were normal newly marrieds.

She blinked back the tears that had engulfed her and started to apologise for the fuss she had made. And then, she thought, *No, I'm not doing this, I'm not doing fake when I've finally got his arms round me again.*

Her hand stretched up to slowly push her fingers into his tousled silvery fair hair and hold him fast. Her other hand found its own path up to the sensual fullness of his lower lip and scored along it.

'What are you doing?' Ares asked icily.

But Alana knew that icy detachment he called up at will was only superficial, certainly not anything that she believed she needed to worry about. His stunning eyes locked to hers. 'Alana—'

'You're faking disinterest,' Alana muttered. 'Stop it! Stop acting like I'm assaulting you! You want me just as much as I want you. I'm not so stupid that I can't see that. I don't know why you're doing it. I don't understand why you're pushing me away yet keeping me so close...'

And within a split second, Ares caved in to the sheer temptation of her because he didn't understand either and he really, *really* didn't want to talk about it and if he kissed her, at least, she wouldn't be asking him for answers he couldn't give her. His mouth claimed her parted lips while she was still talking and every atom of the raw hunger he had suppressed flooded through that first kiss like a dangerous storm warning.

Alana surfaced dizzily to find herself prone on the

bed. She went back into the kiss after a necessary in-take of oxygen and every skin cell was screaming with joy that Ares had finally dropped his walls and surrendered to their mutual chemistry. She knew that she was encouraging him but she also knew that he had started it all with that first kiss. Until then, she had held back, she had suppressed her response to him but that first kiss had set that attraction free and Alana had never been too timid or afraid to go after what she wanted.

It was one of those very rare occasions when Ares wasn't thinking, indeed he was refusing to think. He *knew* that if he started thinking he would stop and come up with all the very good reasons why he should *not* become intimate with Alana Davison. He arranged her on the bed with precision and great care and he looked at her, lying there, letting him look with that intoxicating smile of hers and not a hint of shyness. He enjoyed that view so very much that for the first time ever he understood why lovers took naked photos of each other, an act that had previously struck him as the worst and lowest of aberrations.

'Why are you staring at me? Is there something wrong?' Alana gasped, emerald eyes suddenly anxious.

'You're a fantasy,' Ares framed, not entirely convinced that that *was* him speaking, but she was smiling again, so it really did not matter if he had turned into some Jekyll and Hyde twin-natured creature who didn't know what he was doing or saying. He liked it when she smiled. It was that simple.

And then Ares claimed her lips again and Alana

was in heaven because Ares was incredibly good at the art of kissing. Certainly, no other male had ever got her so stirred up with kisses and she had never let any other male go travelling with his kisses across the rest of her body. But when it was Ares, everything was different. Every inch of her craved Ares's touch and when he paused to suck at a straining nipple, her hips left the bed and she made a squeaky sound that made him glance up at her in surprise.

'I liked it,' she told him hurriedly, lest he desist in the belief that she hadn't. 'Just lost my voice.'

A wicked grin illuminated his dark features. 'You're very vocal… I like that, *asteri mou*.'

And Alana was discovering that she seemed to like absolutely everything that Ares did to her. Her body no longer felt under her control. Her heart was racing and jumping, her muscles jerking taut. A lean hand stroked her thigh and she was convinced she was about to spontaneously combust. There was a buzz inside her like a battery revving up, but it was a buzz that had been building for days every time Ares looked at her, touched her, spoke to her—her sense of connection to him was that intense. That Ares was finally acknowledging the same reactions felt miraculous and wonderful.

He traced her fine bones and the glorious curves of her with a sense of discovery that was new to him. The creamy smooth skin, the bright green eyes, the soft silky strands of hair. It was just sex, his brain chimed in without warning, and there was never anything remotely special about sex. He *knew* that. He had seen that from his earliest years and the darkness of those times had ensured that he was more careful than most not to attach any deeper emotion to a physical act. That thought cooled his heated blood and he fell back from her, suddenly questioning what he was doing, why he was smashing down barriers that he had always respected, why he wasn't weighing up the potential costs of such unusual behaviour.

'What's up?' Alana lifted her head off the pillow, chilled by that revealing withdrawal, the black lashes lowering to veil his dark eyes to a narrow golden shimmer. 'No, not now,' she muttered, her finger splaying across a satin-smooth bronzed shoulder. 'Don't you dare go inside that head of yours and start brooding and questioning and doubting. I won't have it.'

A reluctant laugh was wrenched from Ares. 'You won't?' he scoffed.

'No because this is *my* big sex scene, not yours,' Alana countered, teasing him in a way she had never imagined she would tease a male, but there was something about Ares's reserve that made her bold. 'Your only responsibility is to make it amazing—'

'Could be a challenge for a man with a virgin,' Ares parried, his dark deep drawl shaking slightly because in a handful of words she had somehow banished the darkness inside him with her own weird gift of light and made him swallow back laughter.

'Am I the first one you've been with?' Alana asked jealously.

'Yes.'

'Then you don't know what you're talking about, so keep quiet,' Alana urged, small hand travelling down over his indented muscular torso in an appreciative caress. 'Lie back. I want a live anatomy lesson—'

Ares grinned and caught her tiny hand in his and gently eased her back again. 'You're not running this show. I am, *asteri mou*,' he assured her, and that shadowy instant of almost stepping back from the brink was conquered by her appeal and forgotten. 'Tonight is for you, *only* for you.'

'I'm not going to be a selfish lover,' Alana objected.

Still smiling, Ares gathered her into his arms and kissed her breathless, revelling in the taste of her, the silky soft delicacy of her skin against his. Alana quivered as he rubbed gently over her prominent nipples, nurturing the sensitivity there to send a dart of heat down between her legs. She squirmed as long skilled fingers traced the damp core of her, gently teased the entrance, delivering a cascade of unfamiliar new sensations that parted her lips on a moan.

His tongue dallied with hers and she writhed as the intensity of sensation gathered like a hot liquid pool low in her belly. He rested her down and kissed and licked a trail down over her quivering length, sliding her thighs further apart. He used his lips on the sensitive bundle of nerves that controlled her and from that point on, everything he did to her was off-the-charts *hot* and so exciting she gasped and writhed and simply lived in the moment. The tension at her core built and built until her climax flamed up through her, leaving her limp in the aftermath.

'That was amazing,' she told him chattily.

'That's my line,' he censured.

'So far, the fun has all been mine,' Alana pointed out.

Ares laughed, dark golden eyes smouldering. 'I don't have fun. I'm a very serious guy.'

She wanted to tell him that he wasn't going to get away with being serious twenty-four-seven with her around, but she wasn't yet sure that he would give her the chance to *be* with him. It was like being on trial, she acknowledged nervously, waiting to see how he reacted to her, what he would want…perhaps, he wouldn't want a repeat or anything else. After all, theirs was not a real marriage, she reminded herself, and it was on paper a marriage without a future.

But from that first kiss, Alana had been entrapped and she had turned off her critical thinking. Instead, she was taking a risk and Ares Sarris was very much an unknown quantity. He was so generous with everything but information. He didn't tell her anything about himself, his life, his background, his feelings. All of it was a closed book and she hated that because she was frantic to know him better and learn exactly what drove him aside from an evident need to make mountains of money.

'We've only begun, *asteri mou*,' Ares husked, leaning over her, dark stubble accentuating his beautifully sculpted pink lips. His narrowed gaze, thickly lined with black lashes, was stunning that close, eyes burnished by every shade of gold just like that night by the lake.

Her heart skipped a beat and she lifted her head and found his mouth again for herself. He released her reddened lips and trailed his own down over her cheeks to her throat and she shivered with reaction, nerve endings awakening where she had not realised they existed.

'I'm not expecting rainbows and kittens,' Alana told him with innate practicality.

'Is that supposed to encourage me to sink to the level of your low expectations?' Ares enquired lazily as he lowered his lean hips, sliding between her thighs, and she felt him hard and ready at the heart of her. 'That's one challenge I won't be accepting.'

The tender tissue at the heart of her was so wet, he slid against her and a ripple of arousal ran through her afresh. He tugged back her knees and settled her into a more favourable position, rocking over her, grinding down with his hips, stimulating her clitoris with every movement until the hunger began to heat and course through her veins again. He entered her slow and steady and she tipped back more as he spread her knees wider. As he pushed deeper, there was a slight burn that was bearable and then he glided out and into her again, pushing forward, punching through the barrier she had not even guessed still existed. The sharp pain made her rise up and cry out, gritting her teeth hastily on any further noise, chagrin filling her as Ares stilled.

'I hurt you… I'm sorry.' He murmured something

in Greek and brushed his lips across her brow in a surprisingly tender gesture .

Well, not so much a fantasy woman any more,' Alana reflected ruefully as he stilled. 'Don't stop,' she urged unevenly. 'It's not hurting now.'

And in a smooth shift of his lean hips he withdrew and then drove into her again and a jolting thrill gripped her, the pleasure receptors at her core reacting to that raw invasion. Her hands rubbed across his strong shoulders and stroked down his smooth, muscular back to grip him. Now she was finding out what sex was all about, not those first moments after all but much more was to be discovered in what followed. His every powerful thrust made her clench her inner muscles round him and the friction sent her excitement racing up the scale. Heart thundering in her ears, she gave herself up to the intoxication, rising up against him, frantic for his driving pace to continue and when she reached the ultimate peak and convulsed again in what felt like a million glittery pieces of drowning pleasure, she was shaken but satisfied as he too shuddered with completion.

Happy, she wrapped round Ares like an octopus.

'I love being close to you like this,' she whispered.

It had been years since anyone had dared to touch Ares without permission, even in bed. He didn't cuddle, he didn't snuggle. Alana's easy affection cut through the drugging glaze of his physical satisfaction. It reminded him that she had none of his emotional damage, that she was *whole* and that he had nothing whatsoever to offer such a woman. She would want love and affection and a family and, not only was he not equipped to meet such needs, but he also knew that he would never seek out such binding ties. In that acceptance of his fatal flaws, Ares dropped instantly from what felt dimly like the heights of some unnamed emotion to rock-bottom reality and, a split second later, he pulled free of Alana and sprang out of the bed.

From the doorway, he looked back at her and momentarily stilled, his powerful bronzed body taut. 'This was wrong for *both* of us,' he told her grimly. 'I'll leave early in the morning and you'll stay for the rest of the week as planned. Next week you'll move into Templegreen, my country house in Surrey.'

'I don't understand *why* it's wrong,' she declared defiantly.

'I won't answer that,' Ares countered tautly.

Alana didn't say anything more. In that moment there didn't seem anything to say that wouldn't invite an even greater humiliation. As the door thudded closed, she was pale as death and chilled to the marrow. She huddled into the cocoon of the sheet and shivered, no longer feeling brave, bright and happy. He had rejected her, indisputably rejected her. There would be no coming back from that. He didn't want what she had to offer and really, when all was said and done, what did she have to offer a male as sophisticated and spoilt for choice as Ares Sarris? It wasn't as though the fact that they were married counted in the balance because Ares had never intended it to be a real marriage. And obviously in the seductress stakes she had struck out badly as well.

She wanted to call her sister and spill her guts in the hope that that outlet would take away some of the anguish building inside her. But some stuff, she acknowledged heavily, wasn't for sharing. She couldn't empty her heart to her sister when Enzo and Skye knew Ares and Enzo did business with him. That wouldn't be fair to Ares when she had been a fully participating partner in everything that had happened between them. Never mind that stupid contract that had already been broken by their intimacy, but she *had* promised not to talk about him, *had* agreed to protect his privacy. And privacy meant more to Ares than to most men. He didn't deserve a punishment for the mistake of having had sex with her, did he?

He was entitled to have sex with a consenting partner and then walk away afterwards if he chose to do so. It was a free world…for Ares, if not for her. That meant that she wasn't entitled to chain him up in a dungeon somewhere and torture him until he agreed to be hers and *only* hers. They were only husband and wife on paper and she didn't have any of the rights of a wife.

What Ares did next was none of her business. He could be with other women if he chose to be with other women. He didn't have to be faithful to her, although *she* had to be faithful to him. Yes, she had read those parts of that iniquitous contract and appreciated that, while he remained essentially free, she remained bound to consider appearances and the onus was on her to conduct herself as the wife of Ares Sarris should at all times. And that meant she was not to do anything that might attract publicity or be seen out in public in the company of other men. Not that anyone but her immediate family and his lawyers even knew that they were married as yet, but she presumed that over time their marriage would become more widely known.

On the score of her behaviour, however, Ares had already contrived to turn her right off the prospect of any sort of involvement with a man. Just then, Alana felt horribly responsible for her own downfall. *She* had wanted Ares from the very first moment she saw him. Admittedly, that had not been why she'd offered to be his fake wife. She had done that because she was in debt and saw no reasonable way of clearing that debt unless she chose to hurt her sister by telling her the unlovely truth about the stepfather she had adored. Whichever way she looked at the current situation, it made her feel guilty. After all, she had married Ares, secretly armed with foolish hopes and dreams that she had next to no chance of fulfilling.

Before they had had actual sex, he had attempted to back off and she had argued him out of that decision, insanely convinced that intimacy would bring down his barriers and give her a chance with him. But all she seemed to have achieved was that Ares had built his walls even higher and was now asserting that anything between them was a mistake. It might not have been a mistake for her but clearly it was for Ares. And that was life, she told herself with helpless self-loathing. You didn't always get what you wanted and people didn't always react as you wished. She had made her best effort and lost. He didn't want her. He was walking away untouched while she felt torn apart and desperately hurt.

And what were these feelings that he had thrown back in her face? No, she wasn't travelling any further down the road of regret. She had had a one-night stand and she had always wanted more for herself, had always hoped that when she finally had sex, it would be within a meaningful relationship. The last laugh was on her for being as naïve as to believe that she could share anything meaningful with Ares Sarris.

At least she hadn't run the risk of getting pregnant, she consoled herself, thinking of the contraceptive pill she had begun taking a couple of years earlier for her painful periods. Just at that point, she froze in dismay and jumped out of bed in haste to retrieve her handbag and check on her pills. When had she last taken one? It was an effort to concentrate and the answer was not reassuring. It had been *before* the wedding and she had taken none while she was ill, forgetting about them entirely. Even worse, she had changed handbags and come away without the packet.

Apprehension filled her. She assumed that Ares had taken precautions of his own and then she frowned because she couldn't recall any evidence in that field. If they had both been careless, and she was challenged to believe that *he* would have run that risk, where did that leave her? In a stupid panic of ever-increasing worries, she scolded herself. It was foolish to fret about what she couldn't change.

But the damage had already been done. Blinking back stinging tears, Alana lay sleepless most of the night. She finally drifted off out of sheer exhaustion but only after she heard a helicopter arrive and then depart again. She knew then that she was now alone in the villa, aside from the staff.

CHAPTER SIX

ARES FLIPPED VERY slowly through the photos sent by Alana's protection team, magnifying most of them and scrutinising all of them with careful attention to detail. His wife had been enjoying the hell out of herself since his departure. He had never seen any woman smile so much. If he had assumed she would simply rest back on her sunlounger and work on her tan while taking the occasional break to shop until she dropped, he had been very much mistaken. And if he had worried that his sudden exit could have upset or hurt her, he had been equally misguided.

There she was on Saadiyat Island, soaking up the culture at the Louvre Abu Dhabi, stocking up on art supplies from the Manarat al Saadiyat and strolling along a shaded pathway in the garden city of Al Ain. She was perfectly dressed in respect of local mores, chino trousers hugging her long legs, a simple cotton top screening her delectable curves from the heat, but that river of honey-blonde hair and that perfect pouty mouth were unmistakeable even though he couldn't see her eyes because she wore sunglasses below a stylish beaded trilby hat. She had spent hours in the Al Qattara Arts Centre, exploring the archaeological finds on display there and participating in a pottery class.

His wife…and wasn't it strange how the moment he'd *left* her, he began to view her as his wife? And his wife, it seemed, had no problems playing the tourist. There she was, driving an SUV and trying to climb dunes in the desert—far too dangerous, he had warned her security team, furious they hadn't prevented that. She was also happily getting friendly with Saluki hounds, having her hands and feet painted with henna designs and dressing up in traditional Arabic dress for a photographer. She was having a terrific time without him and she was thoroughly enjoying herself. And hadn't he planned those activities for her amusement? Hadn't he instructed a private tour operator to satisfy her every wish?

As the week stretched on, inexplicably feeling like the longest week of Ares's life, he saw snaps of his wife kayaking in the Mangrove National Park, sailing, snorkelling and scuba diving. She was fearless and athletic and what her shapely curves did for a modest black swimsuit should be outlawed. He hadn't liked the idea that her protection team had seen her so lightly clad and he was ashamed of that obvious streak of sexual possessiveness, which he had never experienced before. But the acknowledgement that lingered longest with him? Not once did Alana do what any other woman he knew would have done in Abu Dhabi when furnished with a bottomless bank account. She didn't enter a single designer fashion or jewellery outlet.

In the course of the week, however, Alana had made her presence known in Abu Dhabi without ever mentioning to anyone that she was *his* wife. She had been very discreet yet word of her solitary presence at his villa had still leaked out onto the local grapevine. In London, Ares had received two approaches from Arabic businessmen offering to send their wives and daughters to his wife's aid to entertain her and offer their hospitality. That had made him gnash his teeth and he didn't know why. He had politely refused the offers. Was it because he had felt guilty that he wasn't there with her? Was it because she was clearly having a spectacularly good time without him? Whatever, he knew he would be relieved when she moved into Templegreen, and he no longer felt the need to constantly check up on her.

'Your bride is working out very well,' Edwin Graves pontificated at the end of that week over a private business lunch. 'Apart from that initial hiccup with her health, she seems a perfect match to your requirements.'

'Yes,' Ares agreed between gritted teeth because he now knew that somewhere in that list of requirements, he had got something very badly wrong. Self-sufficient? Hadn't he wanted a wife with that quality? Why was it that a quality that Alana clearly had in spades was now an irritant?

Was it because Alana was too young, too beautiful and too sexy? Was it because she had tempted him beyond belief and he had fallen at the first fence and destroyed all appropriate boundaries? Or was it because he had said goodbye to his mistress of several years' standing as soon as he'd realised that Marina mysteriously no longer attracted him, and that had been quite a while before his wedding?

Ares was unsettled and restless for the first time in years and he hated it. He wanted his life back to normal. He wanted to stop thinking about sex all the time as well. His fake wife should have occupied only a tiny slice of his life, out of sight and out of mind as she should have been, yet instead she had hogged ninety per cent of his attention while she had been convalescing in Abu Dhabi.

Alana flipped the page in her sketchbook again. The robin outside the window had *moved*. Now she saw that, regardless, the lines weren't right and that her bird outline was too static to be realistic and that drawing anything sooner than draw Ares's sculpted features was not an effective escape from the dark thoughts that possessed her. Fizzing with frustration, she cast aside her sketch pad—regrettably full of incomplete charcoal drawings of Ares. She stood up and stretched, her slender figure lithe in the scarlet yoga pants and cropped top she wore, and honed by the gym activities and the running she had taken up since her arrival at Templegreen.

This was her new life, a life cocooned in luxury against a backdrop of grandeur far different from any she might have hoped would one day be hers. Templegreen was a Georgian mansion of extraordinary style and classic elegance. After her busy week of exploration in Abu Dhabi when she was bent on proving to Ares that his departure had meant nothing to her, she had arrived at his country house to be ushered into the palatial master bedroom like a queen and to dine every evening in solitary splendour in the grand dining room. Whatever, she was out of her depth and drowning. She was the lady of the house, who didn't know *how* to be the lady of the house. The housekeeper visited her at the start of each week with a selection of menus. The estate manager came to her to ask if she had any special requests.

And if there was any special request she could have made it would have been for company, because the one thing Alana had not foreseen was how alone she would feel pretending to be Ares's wife in a world that was so foreign to her, a world in which expense was unimportant and in which ease and idleness were taken for granted. She couldn't ride the horses in her husband's fancy stables. She had toyed with the idea of hiring a riding instructor but decided not to bother as her future was unlikely to include horses and the leisure time to ride them. There was no point getting too comfortable with a luxury lifestyle that was only temporary. Exercising, making use of the excellent gym facilities and the pool at Templegreen had seemed a sensible way to fill the empty hours.

Keeping relentlessly busy had also given her something else to focus on other than the fact that her period was late. She shivered, suddenly cold at that acknowledgement. After the way she had stopped her pill, it was hardly surprising that her menstrual cycle would be unsettled and she never had been regular, she reminded herself soothingly. If her cycle didn't kick in soon, she would do a pregnancy test, indeed she already had one awaiting her in her bedroom. That she wasn't making use of it immediately could be put down to her determination not to frighten herself into a panic. After all, she didn't want to risk a false result by doing the test too soon.

Enzo, Skye and the children had visited for a day soon after her arrival. Once again Alana had had to resist the temptation of confiding in her sister. If she was in a mess right now, it was her own fault. Why would she stress Skye out with her anxieties? That would be selfish and unfair when she had made every decision that had put her in her current predicament without asking for her sister's advice.

The sound of a helicopter sent her over to a tall window to peer out. Her shoulders hunched. She knew that she was only looking because the estate manager had mentioned that Ares only ever visited by helicopter and that he was overdue a visit. It made her wonder if the many properties Ares owned were only for investment as he didn't seem to make much personal use of them. He ensured his various homes were kept in order but rarely went near them, it seemed. She had only picked up such little titbits listening to the staff talk. When the noise of the helicopter became louder rather than receding she went rigid, craning her neck for a better view, and she was just in time to see the unwieldy craft landing on the helipad.

Barely a split second later, a tall male vaulted out and she knew immediately that it was *him*. Only Ares moved with that feral, prowling, outrageously sexy grace, luxuriant silvery fair hair blowing in the breeze, broad shoulders squared, back straight as an arrow as he strode across the lawn, disdaining the path. Alana literally stopped breathing, smoothing down her exercise outfit and flushing in dismay and wishing that she had opted for something other than comfort when she had emerged from her early morning shower. At that thought, her chin came up at a mutinous angle. She was doing exactly what she had been paid to do, living in his home and keeping her head down. But wasn't she also supposed to be *behaving* like a wife? On that thought, Alana sped out through the French doors and raced across the immaculate lawn to greet him.

Ares didn't quite know what he had expected from Alana, but it had definitely not included Alana flinging herself at him in an enthusiastic welcome witnessed by all the household staff. He found himself with an armful of fragrant woman and she smelled of sunshine... and sex? No, no, that was his imagination, which was currently drowning in such base thoughts. Thoughts that ran on a continuous torturous loop inside his head.

'Relax, Ares,' Alana urged, soft and low, as the tension in his big powerful body thrummed into hers. 'It wouldn't look like much of a marriage if I didn't make a fuss of you when we've been apart for weeks.'

Ares had to admit that she had a point. Wasn't he visiting Templegreen for the same reason? And hadn't he decided in his usual cool, logical way to straighten things out between them? There would be no room for passion or temptation once he told her a little about his background. She was a bright girl. She would quickly realise that no woman would want a future with a male like him. It wouldn't hurt her feelings either, so, on his terms, that was a definite win-win when her co-operation was essential to his plans.

He eased her slowly down onto her own feet again, feeling the slight brush of her slender, curvy figure against his clothed length and hypersensitive to that awareness. Of the softness of her breasts, the brush of the slim thighs he had spread. *Theos*, he was hard as a rock. A long arm clamping to her spine, he walked her towards the house, his dark features rigid because he was determined to stay in control.

On the steps of the imposing entrance, his estate manager awaited him, only to be dismissed by him in a handful of words distinguished by a clipped-off, 'Later.'

'You should've let me know you were coming,' Alana murmured flatly, stiff as a walking stick below that controlling arm.

'It was a last-minute decision,' Ares admitted. 'I'll be gone again soon enough.'

A stark pang of disillusionment cut through Alana

and she hated herself for being so vulnerable. Coping with rejection was much harder than she had ever realised. Doing it with dignity was even tougher. She wanted to shrug and walk away and yet she couldn't. That contract had deprived her of such face-saving displays. Behaving like a conventional wife with Ares was a huge challenge. She had no idea what Ares would do next. She had expected him to immediately take off with his estate manager, keen to escape her company, and he *hadn't*, which only confused her more.

'A light lunch *now* would be convenient,' he informed his housekeeper as he walked past.

'Did you give her advance warning of your visit?' Alana asked.

'No.'

'Don't you think that was inconsiderate?' she asked soft and low.

'No,' Ares answered without hesitation. 'I pay my staff three hundred and sixty-five days of the year, but I am only here a handful of days in that year. Expecting the kitchen to provide a light lunch on short notice should be a doddle.'

Alana swallowed hard, taking his point as he strode into the long gracious drawing room and offered her a drink. Mindful of her concern that she might be pregnant and paling at the prospect of that challenge with a male like Ares, who took nothing for chance, she asked for an orange juice.

'Make yourself comfortable,' he advised, seemingly

unaware that his very presence ensured that she could not relax.

Yet she still watched him while he poured the drinks. He was breathtakingly eye-catching in that instant, his carved, classic features illuminated by the sunlight flooding through the windows. He was exquisite, bronzed and extravagantly handsome in his perfection, every line of his lean, powerful body balanced and fluid and outlined by his designer tailoring. Heat simmered low in her body and she looked away again hurriedly.

Ares watched Alana from below black lashes that carefully cloaked his expression. *Theos*, he was burning up for the sweet release of her hot, tight body. There she was, minimally clad, lush breasts barely contained by a crop top, pointed nipples on view and then those pants, hiding nothing, not the bouncy full swell of her pert derrière or the faint but definable cleft of her sex.

The pulse at his groin was positively painful. Just looking at her roused the most primitive instincts and the most powerful memories but he was not planning to surrender to those urges again, he reminded himself fiercely. He was going to do what he should have done in the first place: explain to her why there could never be anything deeper between them. Possibly she didn't even need that explanation, possibly she had already moved on, labelling their brief encounter in Abu Dhabi a mistake just as he had. Surprisingly, that suspicion was not as welcome to him as he had believed it would be.

Alana carried her drink into the dining room, almost bemused to find two places set close together at the vast polished table where she normally sat in solitary state. 'Why do you have this house when you hardly use it?' she asked as he strode up to join her.

'I used it as a conference centre before I bought the London house.'

'You should use it for relaxing at weekends,' Alana told him.

Ares collided with misty green eyes, reading the softness there and retreating from it in haste because it made him uncomfortable. He was very still while plates were slid in front of them and then he lifted his bright head and said wryly, 'I don't really do weekends or relaxation.'

'That's not healthy,' she pronounced, embarking on the colourful chicken salad with its tangy dressing. 'You need downtime like everyone else.'

Ares sipped his wine and set the glass back down again with the hint of a crack. 'You asked me a question that I chose not to answer in Abu Dhabi. You asked me *why* I thought we were a bad combination.'

Alana stiffened defensively. 'Those weren't the words I used.'

Ares lifted and dropped a broad shoulder in dismissal of that protest. 'What I meant was that I couldn't offer you what you would want and expect,' he intoned flatly. 'I don't do attachments. I'm not from a normal background.'

Alana's chin came up. 'I don't think that sort of a thing matters.'

'Let me try to explain. My father impregnated my mother when she was only eighteen. He didn't support her and she ended up on the streets. She was a drug addict and eventually she moved into a brothel,' he explained grimly. 'I spent my formative years in a cathouse. My mother abandoned me there when I was four. She took off with one of her customers and I never saw her again because she died a few years later in a car crash. Her co-workers in the house looked after me for six years until the authorities learned of my existence and intervened...'

Alana stared back at him, unable to hide her shock at those impassive revelations. He had spent his early years in a place where women, including his mother, sold sex to survive? His mother had then deserted him? She was appalled and she lost colour, her tummy giving a queasy lurch at the image of any child being subjected to the damage of such an environment.

'As a result of that background, sex for me is a transactional exchange bereft of finer feelings...and it could never be anything else.'

'You mean...' Alana hesitated in confusion. 'You mean, you...you go to hookers for—?'

Ares shot her a dark look. 'Never!' he rebutted with a fierce frown. 'I would never choose to *be* with a sex worker. I saw too much of that lifestyle growing up and I would never take advantage of such women. But in recent years I did choose to keep a mistress solely for sex. She would fly out and join me wherever I was when I wanted her and in return I supported her financially. It was a discreet arrangement and caused nobody any harm. There is, however, no current mistress in my life.'

A combustible surge of reaction overtook Alana. She was relieved that there was no other woman in his bed but saddened by the dispassionate choices he had made. 'That seems a very cold, emotionless way to live.'

'It was practical. It would not be practical for me to be with you. I can't give you what you would want from me—'

'You don't know what I want,' Alana whispered shakily. 'Maybe I simply want to *be* with you.'

'A romantic wish I have no doubt died the moment I told you about my disgustingly sordid background,' Ares assumed with a sort of grim satisfaction that chilled her.

'No...' Alana framed slowly. 'Your background has no influence at all on how I feel about you. I am sad and hurt on your behalf that you should have endured such a terrible childhood, but it doesn't change anything for me. You rose above all that and became who you are today. That is even more impressive after such a humble and challenging start in life.'

Colliding with the surprisingly shining eyes now locked to him, Ares flinched and thrust his empty plate away to spring upright. 'You can't mean that—'

Alana stood up as well, pretty colour flooding her cheeks. 'I meant every word of it. I don't look at the world through rose-tinted glasses, Ares. But I do try not to judge other people because I'm not perfect either and neither is my background or my parentage.'

Ares drew close, staring down at her with intent black-as-night eyes that glittered. 'You're full of idealism and I'm trying not to hurt you.'

'Let me worry about me being hurt,' she advised breathlessly.

'Without heels, you're too small to talk to standing up,' Ares censured, startling her as he planted big hands to her hips and lifted her up to set her on the table, nudging her knees apart to stand between her thighs.

Her breath feathered in her throat, her entire body suddenly on alert at the intimacy of his stance. The intangible scent of him that close stole into her nostrils, warm and masculine and unbearably familiar, starting up a sensual hum between her legs and a terrifying craving.

Looking into those bright eyes, Ares ran a knuckle lightly across her delicate collarbone. He saw the pulse flickering like crazy there and it lit a roaring fire of desire inside him that he could not suppress.

'Go upstairs and wait for me in the master bedroom,' he murmured huskily as he lifted her carefully back off the table again.

So, she didn't care about his humble beginnings. She wasn't thinking it through though, still wasn't seeing him for what he was. But just how far was he supposed to go in keeping her at a safe distance? He wanted her, she wanted him, so far, so simple, only a male of his ilk knew it wouldn't be that simple. Even so, with his zip biting into his erection, Ares was in no mood to waste time quibbling. He wasn't her knight on a white charger and he never would be, and sooner or later she would wake up and realise that she could have so much more with another man. Unfortunately, the thought of Alana with the younger, more idealistic male who would be a better fit for her made Ares grit his teeth together in sudden rage.

Her cheeks red as fire, Alana glanced up at him, uncertain, charmingly disconcerted and still so innocent. And *his*. His *for the moment*, Ares qualified, satisfied with that amendment. The prospect of having Alana under him again momentarily struck him as all the Christmases he had never benefited from coming at once, turning his head with crazy glitz, potential and anticipation. He would reconsider the contract, have it adjusted to reflect their new agreement, but the instant that idea came to him, he discarded it again. For once, he would keep the lawyers out of it, run that risk and accept that self-indulgence always came with a price. And there was nothing more self-indulgent than Alana in his bed for the foreseeable future.

Encountering a burning glance from eyes that shimmered like gold ingots, Alana only hesitated for a split second before turning on her heel and leaving the room. *Wait for me in the bedroom?* That was so hot that it made her feel flushed all over and breathless. Why had nobody ever warned her that the desire for sex could reduce her to a mindless puddle of longing?

She walked upstairs. He had tried to push her away again by telling her a little bit of the ugly truth he hid from the world. But she had told the truth back. She didn't care what he came from, who his parents had been, how he had spent his early years or even his later ones. But she wouldn't tell him that *his* truth had almost made her cry with hurt on his behalf or that she was keen to learn more to understand what had made him so wary of other people and emotion of any kind.

Ares wouldn't want to hear any of that. It would hurt his pride. He would interpret her interest as pity or crude curiosity. He wouldn't want to know that she was falling in love with him either because he wasn't ready to offer love back. And maybe he never would be, she acknowledged ruefully. She had to be realistic too. In the bedroom, she peeled off her pants and crop top and walked into the bathroom. Heavens, she looked a mess, hair in a tangle, not even a scrap of make-up. He had to be sex-starved to still want her when she was so unadorned. And maybe he was, she considered, when there was no mistress in his life. All she had to do now was persuade him that a wife could be a lot more entertaining.

And she wouldn't achieve that goal by telling him now that she suspected that she could be pregnant. That would be a step too far at this early stage of their relationship. That would shock Ares, make him batten down the hatches as he saw the threat of serious complications cloud his horizon. No, she didn't want Ares to feel pushed into what he didn't want, so she would

stay quiet for now and not forewarn him, let their relationship develop without that limitation.

Ares strode into the bedroom and wondered where
he would sleep that night. He would use the room next
door, he decided, his intent gaze welded to the slight
bump Alana made in the big bed. He liked that she
was there already, that for once she had done exactly
as he asked, that she had grasped that he wasn't in
the mood for any kind of game. He stripped off his
jacket, wrenched loose his tie, kicked off his shoes.
He had never undressed at such speed, never wanted
any woman with the fierce hunger that she inspired.
And for once, he wasn't overthinking his reactions.
He was going with the flow, no matter how much that
went against his nature.

Ares wrenched the sheet back and slid in beside her,
stark naked, bronzed and muscular and hugely aroused.
When he simply grabbed her, Alana crumpled into
helpless giggles.

'What's so funny?' he demanded.

'You missed me?' she teased.

'Yes, I missed *this*. I only had you once and it wasn't
enough, could never be enough,' he husked against the
ripe promise of her soft lips. 'I hope you're ready to
spend the rest of the day in bed.'

'My…you've got that much stamina?'

'Try me,' Ares challenged.

'Oh, I intend to,' Alana confirmed, wriggling out
from under him to push him back against the pillows.
'And there's to be none of that growly "you're a virgin

and I'm in charge" stuff this time. This is my show this afternoon.'

Wildly disconcerted, Ares looked up at her with a frown, thickly lashed dark eyes narrowing. Her golden hair was tumbled round her slight shoulders and her green eyes danced with mischief and warmth. In a sudden movement, he kicked back the duvet and lay back again, his big powerful body relaxed and yet tense with arousal. 'Make yourself at home,' he urged thickly.

'Tell me anything you don't like. Can I tie you up?'

'No...well, at least not this time,' Ares breathed in a driven undertone, not wishing to squash her aspirations even though he could never ever see himself agreeing to trust anyone to that extent. 'Would you let me tie you up?'

Alana grinned. 'I think that could be something I might like to explore eventually,' she confided, small hands spreading to glance up over his ribs, a possessive vibe lancing through her as his hips surged, telling her exactly what he wanted. 'There's a lot I'd like to try, if you think you'd be up for it—'

'I'd be up for it,' Ares growled as strands of blonde hair trailed enticingly across his powerful hair-roughened thighs. 'Experiment all you like.'

'You're not going to get bored,' Alana promised, exploring warm little fingers stroking, shaping, making his flat stomach contract, sending an unmistakeable shiver through his big body. 'But you're not allowed to interfere unless I do something you don't like...'

And then she proceeded to tease and torment with a confident sensuality that was totally unexpected. It was the most erotic experience of Ares's life.

CHAPTER SEVEN

'WELL, THAT'S THAT COVERED,' Alana pronounced as the last slivers of satisfaction pulsed through Ares.

His ridiculously long sooty lashes lifted. 'Is there a checkbox you have to tick?'

She grinned. 'There could be, but that's for me to know and you to wonder.'

Ares reached up and dragged her down to him. 'Now it's my turn,' he told her thickly. 'And I may have a checklist too…'

He flipped her over and claimed her reddened lips in a passionate kiss, revelling in the responsive rise of her slender body below his. He shaped her straining nipples and a little whimper of sound escaped her. His tousled silvery head came up. 'Too delicate?'

'It's near that time of the month,' she muttered. 'They're always more sensitive.'

And it was true, perfectly true, she reminded herself, because her breasts were often swollen and tender coming up to a period. That there could be another explanation this time was her business until she had done that pregnancy test and she was determined not to do it too soon and risk a false result. A few days and then she would know one way or another.

'I'll be gentle,' Ares promised, dropping his mouth to the distended pink bud with less haste and more care and dallying there until little quivers were shaking her and she was arching up to him, having discovered that that same tenderness could also translate into greater arousal. 'We need to consider contraception,' he continued. 'I'll take precautions.'

That information lightened Alana's worry. If he was that careful, it was unlikely he had been irresponsible in Abu Dhabi, she reasoned. Just because she hadn't noticed him using anything didn't mean he hadn't, because she had been too caught up in the thrill of the experience to be observant. In fact, it challenged her to believe that Ares could be careless in such a field and most probably she was worrying about nothing. If only she had asked him at the time...but if she were to ask him now, he would surely guess *why* she was asking.

A blunt forefinger scored a flushed cheekbone. Brilliant dark eyes held hers fast. 'You're a hundred miles away in your head,' he complained.

Alana was taken aback that he was sufficiently attuned to her to have noticed that she had withdrawn. 'You're like that most of the time—'

'But not with you,' Ares contradicted, lowering his head to run his stubbled jaw over the soft, smooth slope of her breasts.

That roughened sensation made her shiver and he smiled down at her with sudden brilliance and then he kissed her, gathering her back into the heat of him, making her aware of every hard line of his long muscular body. His big hands roamed over her with the assurance that accompanied everything he did, and she could feel the heat rising between her thighs as he tugged at her swollen nipples and gently traced circles round her clitoris. A finger slid between her slick folds, teased at her entrance before delving inside her and she squirmed back into him, helpless in the grip of that flood of sensation.

'You're so tight and wet.' He savoured the words, pulling back from her and reaching for something.

He tore it open with his teeth, angled back his hips and deftly donned the condom before flipping her over, laughing at her gasp of surprise as he arranged her on her knees and straight away plunged into her, stretching her tight depths without hesitation.

'My goodness,' she burbled, eyes wide at the new tidal wave of sensation as her body initially struggled to adapt to take him.

'My ambition is to make you say a rude word. You never ever curse.' Ares pulled out of her before driving back into her yielding sheath with greater force. 'It's cute but unsustainable.'

'Not up to a conversation right now,' Alana wheezed, all concentration banished, her body now awash with the surge of sexual reaction. Dangerous little eddies of breathtaking need were gathering low in her belly with the sensual friction of his invasion.

Ares rearranged her with firm hands and angled

deeper into her, speeding up as breathy little sounds started to escape her. Excitement grabbed her in a blinding rush, her body jolting to the pounding thrust of his until she felt insanely out of control. Her heart sprinted inside her chest—thump…thump…thump— as the torturous pleasure climbed and climbed and it became harder and harder to breathe through the sheer exhilaration of her response. The ache of hunger and need was unbearable until finally a starburst of heat flared at her core and radiated out in shock waves of drowning pleasure.

Breathing hoarsely, Ares watched her collapse down on the bed like a puppet with its strings cut. He laughed, turned her over, dark golden eyes running possessively over her hectically flushed face and the drowsiness etched there. 'Don't go to sleep. I'll want you again.'

'Stop being so bossy.'

'Stop being so lazy,' Ares quipped, sliding an arm beneath her and lifting her.

'What are you doing?'

'Taking you for a shower…a wake-up shower,' he extended, carrying her across the room and kicking the door of the en suite bathroom open.

Once the water was streaming, he walked her under it and began to wash her with a cloth. 'I'm beginning to feel like a doll,' Alana protested.

'*My* doll…*my* wife,' Ares countered with a quirk of his sensual mouth. 'But way too feisty to allow me to do anything you don't want.'

The cloth moved over her skin in gentle soapy sweeps. It was the first time that Ares had referred to her as his wife as though she were a real wife and she liked it, she liked it way too much. It was a huge shower and he sat her down on the bench and did a very creditable job of shampooing her hair. 'Now you'll smell like me as well,' he remarked.

'What is this?' she framed warily.

'The prelude to shower sex. I assumed you'd be keen to tick that box too,' he teased.

'I didn't think about it—'

'You don't need to think. I'm very inventive when I need to be. I'm in Switzerland next week. You can join me and the week after we'll be in Greece together,' he reminded her.

He was finally letting her into his life, Alana thought on a wave of intoxicating happiness. Shower sex suddenly seemed a very good idea, particularly when she had never seen Ares act so relaxed. She watched the water stream down over his well-developed pectoral and abdominal muscles and stroked her hand in the same direction, touching him, appreciating him. She looked up at him, connected with smouldering dark gold enticement and her heart hammered afresh and her mouth ran dry. He lifted her and took her lips with hungry urgency, long, drugging kisses that left her mindless. Before she had regained ground, Ares had her backed up against the wall and he was slamming into her again hard and fast, making her feel every inch of him, rocking her world with such ease that it left her breathless and moaning through another seething climax.

Ares slotted her into a giant towel and patted her dry, wrapped her hair in a smaller one and laid her down on the bed. 'Have a nap. I'll see Rothman, the estate manager, and get up to date with some other stuff and we'll dine when I'm free.'

Green eyes verdant as a forest glade opened wide. 'Even my naps have to fit into your schedule now?'

'You said you wanted to be with me,' Ares reminded her bluntly.

'And it's all in or all out?'

'Pretty much,' he confirmed.

The moment he left the room she got up and went back into the shower to condition her hair because it would dry into a rat's nest without it. While she decided what to wear for dinner, she questioned the sudden shift in their relationship. Had she let herself down by admitting that she wanted to be with him? No, no, she refused to believe that. She had never been the kind of young woman who sat around waiting for anyone or anything and she had taken her future into her own hands to shape it. Why shouldn't she be upfront about her desire to be with him? That had cut through the shell of his reserve as nothing else could have done. She didn't know why or how her attitude had achieved that miracle, but she wasn't about to question it when it was so obvious that Ares wanted her too.

Of course, there was a chance that it was only sex for him, but given time she would see how much of his life he was willing to share with her. She wasn't about to quit at the first hurdle, she assured herself.

Ares rushed through his meeting with his estate manager and settled into work, immediately sidelining or delegating anything that wasn't urgent. In the midst of that exercise he found himself questioning that laid-back approach, which was so out of character for him. Why was he behaving in such an irresponsible way? Why couldn't he stop remembering Alana's breathy little moans of pleasure? Or the dreamy expression on her face post-orgasm in the shower? Why was he still reliving the raw excitement of having sex with her again? It was sex, it was simply sex, nothing more, nothing less, nothing he needed to stress about. He was allowed to step off the eternal grind of the business wheel and enjoy life occasionally, wasn't he? And that was what Alana was for him, he recognised reflectively, pure honest enjoyment.

Inevitably it would stop being enjoyable and he would get bored, but he would have to let her down lightly. Of course, possibly *she* would get bored first. He batted that idea back and forth in his brain and discovered that he didn't like that idea, that suspicion that in a very short time she might want to spread her wings and fly free without him. She was young, a lot younger than he was, he conceded grudgingly. The contract only tied her to him for a year at most, and by then he might well be glad to see her leave his life. In the short term, however, he would have to keep her amused, and never in his life before had Ares had to make an effort to hang onto a woman's interest.

Alana came down to dinner in a strappy scarlet dress that fell to just above her knees. The lacing at the bodice and the pale full swell above attracted Ares's gaze. 'You look outrageously sexy. When I see lacing, I want to unlace,' he breathed huskily.

Still a little shaky in the unfamiliarity of high heels, she sank down in the dining chair across from him.

Dinner was very much a special occasion, it seemed, because there were candles lit and evidently the chef had really pushed out the boat for Ares's benefit because there were several very tasty courses and Alana ate with appetite. Ares made light conversation and was rather more sociable than she had expected. Coffee was served in the drawing room in front of the log fire and it reminded her of their meeting at the Blackthorn Hotel.

'You're lonely here, aren't you?' Ares guessed, his sculpted lips compressing. 'You can invite your sister and family down here to stay any time you like.'

'Skye travels with Enzo whenever she can. She's rarely at a loose end.'

'Come here…' Ares invited, stretching out an expectant hand. It was an unplanned move because for a split second he had been on the very brink of suggesting that she join him in London. That such a thought had even occurred to him shook him inside out. He liked his own space. He had always liked his own space and he fiercely guarded his privacy. Next week she would be waiting for him in Geneva. Presumably he was capable of waiting a week? On the other hand, when his hunger was at such a height, having her available on the spot would pay dividends as well.

Alana went pink and slowly rose to her feet.

'Take off the shoes. You're not comfortable in them.'

With a sound of relief she kicked off the shoes and came to him barefoot. His hands clasped hers and he drew her down onto his lap. 'Relax,' he urged lazily, the faint accent in his husky tone sending a little shiver down her taut spine. 'You're a walking dream of a temptation in that dress, *moraki mou*.'

Alana tried to play it cool while his fingertips toyed with the lace bow and then gently tugged it loose. 'Ares—'

'Hush,' he said softly, tugging down the bodice to bare her breasts and bending his head to capture the swollen crown of one peak between his lips, toying, teasing, so that her pulse raced and her head fell back, her lips parting on a helpless moan of compliance.

His other hand smoothed up a slender thigh and disappeared below the skirt of her dress, flirting with the lacy edge of her knickers and stroking across the taut silk between her legs to start a hum of deeper arousal low in her belly. He tapped a fingertip against her clitoris and her back arched and then he tugged away the silk to play with her hot, damp core. Within minutes she was helplessly engaged in muffling her cries against his jacket.

He tugged her head back into the shelter of his arm and rested back in his armchair with a wicked smile. 'I suppose this is what you call the honeymoon phase. Tell me if I'm being too demanding.'

'No…er…' Alana fell silent again, fighting to organise her confused thoughts. She hadn't known that she could hunger for someone the way she did for him, nor had she realised that it would be a constant hunger that was never quite sated.

Hours later, when Alana lay in an exhausted heap in her bed, Ares began to pull away to go to the room next door. He never ever slept with anyone. He never ever shared a bed. But Alana moved closer in her sleep and flung both an arm and a leg over him, as if even sleeping she could sense his restlessness. Almost groaning out loud, Ares rested his head back again. She was like a little wriggling octopus in bed, at least one limb cleaving to him at all times. He didn't want to wake her up. She deserved her rest when she had been more than generous in meeting his quite insatiable demands. He had never had sex that often in such a short space of time and he had never spent so much time with any woman.

Unhappily for him, he didn't wish to hurt her either and that was an unfamiliar new limit in his world that equally disconcerted him. After all, she would survive wounded feelings. But the need to return to his own normality triumphed when he wakened at five the next morning and he eased very, very slowly away from her snuggling body. He texted his driver, showered in the room next door, dressed and headed out to the airport to fly back to London. He would text Alana later and he would show his appreciation with some splendid gift. Emeralds to match her eyes or diamonds to reflect her sparkling personality? Why not both?

Within twenty-four hours, a magnificent necklace and drop earrings arrived for Alana at Templegreen. She studied the river of glittering diamonds and the big central emerald in wonderment and read the gift card that suggested that she might want to wear the jewellery set in Athens. In other words, the pressie hadn't arrived on such terms that she felt she could rationally refuse to accept it. It was reasonable for Ares to give her the kind of fancy jewellery that people would expect a billionaire's wife to be wearing at an exclusive charity ball. At best, it could be viewed as a prop for the wife role. At *worst*?

Well, the wages of sin and all that...

Doubtless he would be surprised if he realised that staying to have breakfast with her or even leaving a note would have been more welcome to her. Her pale face took on a painful flush when, the following day, a superb set of designer luggage arrived and, on the next, a diamond and platinum watch. In the luxury gift department Ares was keen to spoil her rotten. Encouraged by such gestures, she was soon counting the hours until her trip to Geneva.

She travelled by private jet and limousine in the utmost comfort and arrived at a penthouse apartment in an exclusive hotel. Ares didn't actually show up until it was too late to make the theatre trip he had promised her. His business negotiations had gone on later than he had assumed they would. Alana didn't complain. Hadn't she promised herself that she would give him a chance to do stuff *his* way? She had sworn not to judge, not to make demands.

Result?

Ares spent an hour on the phone after his final appearance while his busy staff milled around him and she sat in a corner like Cinderella all dressed up with nowhere to go. She retired to bed. Five minutes later, shorn of his phone, Ares dragged her into the shower with him, wrecked her carefully straightened hair while enjoying a passionate bout of sex with her...and then someone came knocking on the bedroom door and he retrieved his phone and began chatting in a foreign language again while he got dressed.

Alana? Alana ordered a meal from room service and returned to bed. At some stage of the night Ares joined her in that bed, explained the sudden business crisis in unnecessary detail before expressing further apologies and soothing himself and her with more spectacular sex.

But the last straw for even Alana's forgiving nature?

That was when she woke up alone again and registered that Ares had slept in the room next door. While she ate her solitary breakfast in the lounge, she pondered her predicament and blamed herself for misunderstanding the rigid boundaries of the neat little drawer Ares had now put her in. He wasn't lifting his ban on relationships, he wasn't revising their marriage contract either, he was simply using her as a sexual outlet. Or maybe she was using him? No, it would have saved her pride to think that, but she knew that she had only flown to Geneva with the goal of achieving greater closeness to Ares and winning, if not his love, at least his respect and appreciation.

Instead she had met up with a guy who put business first and wouldn't even share a room with her, a guy who placed his privacy above her feelings. How had he imagined she would feel waking up alone after the disappointments of the evening before? Had he thought such shabby treatment was enough for her as long as he sent her expensive gifts in consolation? Was that why he had mentioned a trip to New York in two weeks and a return to Abu Dhabi the month afterwards? He was scheduling her into his calendar as a mistress within a marriage that was no marriage at all!

'You're leaving now...' Ares gathered, noting the luggage stacked by the door, sending his keen gaze circling back to where she stood in a turquoise coat teamed with turquoise suede-fringed cowboy boots, an outfit that was so Alana, it made him smile. He liked the weird way she often slotted a quirky note of individuality into her outfits. He noticed, though, that her usual smile as bright as the sunshine was markedly absent.

Alana let her attention linger on him. Heavens, Ares was beautiful. Complex, frustrating, infuriatingly lacking in emotion and dynamite in bed. But also, indisputably beautiful with his classic bronzed features and stunning dark golden eyes.

'Yes, I'm leaving.' She conceded the obvious in a flat tone since her departure time had been as regimented as her arrival time and nothing whatsoever to do with her.

'I'll see you next week in Athens.' Ares frowned, now wondering what was wrong.

'Hold the sex, though,' Alana advised as the front door opened and her luggage was whisked out by efficient hands.

Ares elevated a level dark brow. 'Meaning?'

Alana moved closer to ensure that she was not overheard. 'You made me feel like a call girl last night,' she admitted starkly.

Ares froze as if he had heard a hurricane warning, his lean strong face snapping taut, and he caught her wrist between his fingers to prevent her from turning away again. 'What did I do?'

'What *didn't* you do?' Alana slung back bitterly. 'And I can't say that you didn't warn me, can I? But when you get out of a bed you're sharing with me to find another one in the middle of the night it's not acceptable and, what's more, it's hurtful—'

'Hurtful,' Ares repeated, shaken that that should be her main complaint about an evening that had been a car crash from start to finish. Not that they hadn't made the theatre, not that he had had hardly any time to spend with her. No, she was complaining that he hadn't spent the night in the same bed. Crazy woman!

As Alana tried to pull away, he caught her free hand in his as well to hold her there in front of him. 'I'm not used to sharing a bed,' he framed awkwardly.

'No, it's not that,' she whispered shakily. 'It's that you don't *want* to, it's that you can't face even that amount of closeness with me, it's another barrier you're determined to keep up to shut me out… yet when it comes to getting down and dirty, gosh, there's no holds barred with you!'

Ares almost laughed at that final comment, but he held it back because there was a glossy sheen to her bright eyes that he recognised as tears. No, she hadn't been joking when she utilised that word, 'hurtful'. 'I can change,' he heard himself say doggedly, even though he thought he couldn't.

'Maybe the contract is a safer bottom line for two people as different as we are,' Alana muttered shakily.

'I'm sorry,' he breathed unevenly, something clenching tight inside his chest as he watched her fighting back the tears and he felt very much to blame.

Five minutes with her and he felt fantastic, but it didn't seem to work the same way for her. He didn't know how to fix what he had broken either. He didn't know what to say to remedy the situation.

You made me feel like a call girl.

He had misjudged everything. He had assumed she would understand, overlook and pardon his workaholic ways because she was usually very accommodating.

But then she had complained about his preference for sleeping elsewhere, he reminded himself grimly.

'And to give us both a completely clean page I will share my only secret with you to give you fair warning. I've been worrying for a while now that I could be pregnant after our first night together.' Alana lifted her chin in a decided challenge as she made that admission. 'And I'm going back to Templegreen to do a test.'

Pregnant! It was as if a field of too-bright lights lit up Ares's brain, stunning, blinding, preventing any kind of thought process. In short it was an overload. Very pale, he stared down at her in disbelief.

Alana flinched in the rushing silence of his visibly aghast reaction. 'Even worse, as I'm sure you're aware, that development is not covered in that dreadful contract of yours.'

Ares then found himself staring into empty space. She had slid out of the door, taking advantage of his shock. Alana was pregnant? His brows knitted. He could see Alana with a baby, but he could definitely not see himself.

CHAPTER EIGHT

'I'VE BEEN ASKED to warn you that there will be a delay, Mrs Sarris,' the stewardess on Ares's private jet informed Alana as the jet sat on the tarmac.

Alana had a magazine open on her lap although she wasn't reading. In reality all she could still see was Ares's appalled reaction to the prospect of her being pregnant. He hadn't said a single word but maybe that had been the saving grace of her being on the very brink of departure. For better or for worse, she had warned him. She should have done the test at least a week earlier but she had wanted to meet him in Geneva first.

Why? How could she ever have been naïve enough to believe that having sex with Ares would miraculously lead to him attaching feelings to the sharing of that act? How stupid was that? Tears burned at the backs of her eyes, and she blinked them away angrily.

Quick steps sounded on the metal airstair and there was a chorus of greetings from the air crew. Her self-loathing session interrupted, Alana glanced up and her eyes widened in dismay on the disturbing sight of Ares striding down the aisle towards her. The jet was not delayed, she registered, the jet had merely been waiting for its owner's arrival. Ares had also changed since she last saw him. He wore a black designer suit, probably Armani or Brioni, the expensive cloth faithfully tailored to every inch of his big powerful body, a dark blue roll neck hugging his bronzed throat. No shirt and tie? She was surprised and unnerved when he sank down in the leather seat right opposite her and spread his muscular thighs, fine cloth pulling taut.

'I thought you were staying on here—'

Ares canted up a sleek ebony brow. 'After what you shared with me?'

Alana went pink. 'I only said that there was a risk of that development, not a certainty.'

'We'll have certainty very shortly after we land,' Ares declared. 'I've organised a doctor to do the test. Isn't that test a little overdue?'

Alana could feel her face getting as hot as a bonfire and guilt squirmed inside her. 'I wasn't in a hurry to find out,' she acknowledged between the clenched teeth of mortification.

'I am,' Ares admitted.

'A doctor isn't necessary. I have a simple test waiting at Templegreen,' she pointed out.

'A simple test that you could have used sooner,' Ares qualified crushingly.

'It's not your body, it's mine!' Alana shot back at him angrily. 'It's easy to be judgemental when it's not your life being potentially derailed. I was nervous, I was *scared*… OK?'

'OK.' Ares compressed his lips at that admission, feeling like a bully. He didn't think it was the moment either to point out that his life would also be derailed if she was carrying his child.

'And while you're sneering at me about taking too much time to do that test, does it occur to you that *you* are the one to have neglected contraception?' Alana hissed, her emotions all over the place and violently stirred up by his unnecessary comments.

'I assumed you were on the pill at the villa. But I'm aware that nothing other than celibacy is full proof.'

'I'm afraid not,' Alana confirmed in a curt, driven voice.

'It doesn't much matter how it happened if it's happened,' Ares remarked drily. 'Bestowing blame will not fix anything.'

'Oh, stop being so pedantic about it!' Alana flared back at him, her temper rising in spite of her efforts to tamp it down.

'The likelihood of conception is—'

'Don't say another word,' Alana warned him furiously. 'We don't need some mathematical take on the probability right now!'

Ares breathed in slow and deep. How did he get across to her that she didn't need to think and behave like a terrified teenager facing single motherhood? Alana was his wife. Suddenly, it seemed, his *real* wife because only a genuine wife could be giving him a child, he reasoned hesitantly. Yes, she was upset, he conceded, but his own brain wasn't exactly functioning at its usual speed either.

It wasn't that *he* was upset. He didn't do messy emotions, he reminded himself. Of course, he wasn't upset. Possibly a little shocked, he conceded, but definitely not upset and it was presumably shock that had given him the irrational urge to simply drag her into his arms in an effort to provide comfort. Irrational, out-of-character, foolish behaviour that such a pointless act would have been.

'You should have shared your concern with me the moment you suspected the possibility,' Ares murmured in a tone of finality.

'That wouldn't have changed anything,' Alana pointed out defensively.

'No, however, you would not have been worrying about this alone and getting all worked up about it—'

'I'm not worked up!' Alana flared in furious rebuttal, putting her hands down to release her seat belt as the whine of the engines kicked higher and the jet proceeded to race down the runway.

Ares was up in a flash, big hands engulfing hers to secure the belt again. Alana felt as though she were about to explode with rage and she closed her eyes then, rested her head back and counted slowly to ten, praying for the seething emotions that were so close to the surface to simmer down again.

When she finally opened her eyes they were airborne and Ares was ordering coffee.

'Herbal tea for me,' she intervened stiffly, because she knew that some people avoided caffeine during pregnancy and she didn't want to risk anything.

'I'm excellent in crisis management,' Ares intoned softly.

Alana almost rolled her eyes at him. He was so clever but he just didn't *get* it. Her baby, if there was one, was not a crisis to be managed. Her baby would be a little part of her and a little part of him and she already felt hugely protective of that tiny potential being.

'And I'm very calm, which would appear to be a useful skill in the present climate,' Ares remarked.

And that fast Alana wanted to hit him again. She set her lips firmly together. She lifted her magazine and commenced staring blindly down at it again while recalling how wild and passionate Ares was in bed. How did she equate that passion with the chilling detachment of the guy she was currently dealing with? Of course, that was sex, not the emotional relationship stuff that appeared to terrify the life out of him. Yes, she understood that he had had a ghastly early childhood and that that had scarred him, but did that mean that he had to regiment his entire life like some frightening genius robot and feel absolutely no warmer thing for anyone? Evidently to Ares, it *did* mean that, she thought with a sudden flood of compassion that infuriated her even more. Why was she feeling sorry for him? Was she truly insane?

Ares was relieved that it was such a short flight. He didn't like Alana being silent and still. It made him uncomfortable. It made him start wondering what would make her happy and then it worried him even more that he didn't know. And yet he was trying, he really was *trying* to be what his brain told him she needed. Supportive, strong, unselfish. Only as he handed her into the limo collecting them in London to take them to the doctor he had engaged, she was *still* silent.

The silence in the medical surgery was profound. The middle-aged female consultant chatted inconsequentially to the nurse and the ultrasound technician since she could barely squeeze a word from her new clients.

'There...you see,' she remarked, pointing to the screen. 'Eight to nine weeks.'

Ares stared transfixed at the screen. It was a tiny blip the size of an olive. That that tiny bunch of cells could grow into an actual human being within a few months struck him as a fact worthy of wonder and fascination, but then he was primarily a scientist and he wasn't sure that that take would be welcome to the mother of his child.

Alana studied the screen with a trembling lower lip. *Her baby!* Her poor, poor baby, with a man who would never truly want him or her, who would simply go through the motions of fatherhood in a logical, dutiful way. Unnoticed, she shot him an unhappy glance. Her eyes stung. She blinked rapidly.

The consultant discussed the blood test that could tell them the gender of their baby. Ares was all on board for that and failed to even consult Alana as to her preference. He took charge, the way he did with everything, she reflected resentfully. It was her body, her baby, but the way he was behaving, you wouldn't have thought so. And there he was suddenly being a positive chatterbox with the consultant about the hormonal effects of pregnancy. Now he would begin treating her like a basket case. How dared he nod knowingly like that when the doctor mentioned the possibility of mood changes?

'Lunch is waiting for us back at the house,' Ares announced as she clambered back into the limo.

'It's a long drive,' Alana muttered.

'I was referring to my house here in London. I can hardly maroon you at Templegreen when you're pregnant. I hope I am more considerate than that.'

Alana could feel that mindless rage building inside her again and sensibly said nothing.

Ares gave up and switched his phone back on. Did she really resent the idea of having his baby that much? She would be a young mother. A lot of young women would not be pleased to find themselves pregnant at her age. Especially when she had only signed up in the first place for a brief fake marriage that had now become…*what*? He attempted to quantify what their relationship now was and failed. He was lost without that contract. There were no rules, no guidelines. But the contract had become a bad joke after he had broken it in Abu Dhabi and the baby was a consequence of that irrational act. Yet strangely enough he wasn't feeling remotely annoyed about that baby. Ashamed that he had lost control…*yes*. Ashamed that Alana, whom he should have looked after better, was clearly distressed…*yes*.

It felt like a hundred years to Alana since she had last stepped into Ares's palatial London house. She had been ill and newly married, she reminded herself. She had also been naïve and foolish and utterly mesmerised by the male by her side. That had been when she fell in love with him, she surmised, when he had demonstrated how amazingly caring he could be. A sniff escaped her and Ares flashed a glance at her from his shockingly beautiful dark eyes, a concerned glance. And it was that last proverbial straw all over again!

Ares saw the storm coming and he guided Alana into the vast drawing room and closed the door in his surprised housekeeper's face. 'What can I do?' he asked quietly. 'To make you feel better?'

'Nothing!' she wailed on the back of a sob.

He helped her out of her coat, urged her down into a comfortable armchair and hovered. 'There has to be something—'

'Tell me the truth.'

'About what?' Ares frowned.

'How you *really* feel about the baby!' She gasped. 'Because so far you have faked everything you have said and done and you haven't given me one honest reaction to this pregnancy of mine. I want the truth. I can *stand* the truth. I'm not a kid!'

Ares thought very hard. 'I don't really know how I feel yet. It's all too new and fresh. I never expected to have a child—'

Like a hare scenting a fox, Alana sat forward in her seat. 'And why's that?'

'I planned to never have one,' he admitted grimly. 'It was a decision I made many years ago—'

'But why?' she persisted.

'I think it was my idea of revenge...*not* to carry on the family name of Sarris, to let it die out with me,' he clarified tautly.

Revenge? Alana was shocked by that explanation. Ares, who on the surface seemed so calm and rational, had harboured so primitive and passionate a desire?

'And how do you feel now that we've managed to conceive a child?' she almost whispered.

Disconcertingly, Ares laughed with what appeared to be genuine amusement. 'That the revenge idea was a leftover piece of my adolescence and something I should have left behind me a long time ago. After all, it is a melodramatic concept and I am a logical man. Why would I let my ugly past control my entire future?'

'Yes,' she agreed, relieved by that concession, feeling calm again, not even understanding why she had almost lost her temper.

'I can adapt to new circumstances,' Ares commented with decided pride.

'Yes...' Alana smiled. 'And outside the boundaries of a legal contract.'

'We don't need one now, but without one we have no framework,' he added wryly.

'How do you feel about the baby?' she almost whispered.

'I'm still considering that. You're very impatient,' Ares censured as a knock sounded on the door and he turned his head to issue an invitation. 'That will be Edith offering us lunch.'

Lunch was an oasis of calm after the emotional storms of the morning. Ares chatted away about the latest app he was developing, not seeming to worry about the fact she only understood a tenth of what he was explaining. And then he surprised her right out of the blue by asking how she felt about her birth father, whom she had never met.

'I asked your sister when I called her while you were ill, but she didn't want to talk about him.'

'There's really nothing to talk about because we never knew him. Him and Mum were sixteen when she got pregnant. Her parents threw her out and his parents took her in and after Skye was born he managed to get Mum pregnant again...which was me.' Alana rolled her eyes. 'They were just teenagers with no sense. Ultimately, he went off to an oil rig to work and basically never bothered with Mum or us again. He didn't even help to support us. He wasn't interested, so why would I be interested in him?'

'I can understand that. My father...' Ares grimaced as he voiced the term. 'I suppose I should really call him a sperm donor. I sent him a letter when I was ten years old and went to his office in Athens in the hope of meeting him. He had me thrown out by security—'

Alana paled. 'Did he know you existed before the letter?'

'Yes. My mother approached him when she was pregnant and he denied any knowledge of her as well.

He had a one-night stand with a college student and, I'm afraid, it came back to haunt him. If he had had anything to do with it, my existence would never have been acknowledged.'

'That's appalling,' she muttered, thinking in honest horror of the mother who had abandoned him and the father who had rejected him. It was another little piece of the jigsaw of early damage that Ares had suffered. 'I was only able to shake off my birth father's indifference because I had a loving, kind stepfather, who treated Skye and me as if we were his own daughters.'

'Hence your loyalty to him, but I still can't overlook that debt he lumbered you with,' Ares breathed harshly. 'That nasty little gangster he left you indebted to was an accident waiting to happen. Fortunately he's now in custody and he won't be trapping any other young woman the way he trapped you—'

'In...*custody*?'

'I used a private investigation firm and presented a file of evidence about his activities through my lawyer to the police. He's now awaiting trial for a number of offences,' he completed quietly.

'I never thought you would take the trouble to do anything like that,' Alana confided with warmth and admiration in her eyes. 'I'm really pleased you did though. I was very scared every time I went to make a payment to him because he was always dropping hints that there were *other* ways to pay.'

'That's how men of that ilk operate. Get you in debt, get you on drugs and then put you out on the street to sell like a product. It's what happened to my mother,' he imparted grimly. 'The charity benefit next week is in aid of the homeless, addicts and women like her.'

Alana was interested in the charity and would have liked to ask him more about his childhood but sensed from the tension etched in his lean, strong face that he had shared enough for one day.

Ares went off to work in his study and Alana was moving through the hall when the housekeeper intercepted her and offered her a tour of the house. Alana smiled, thinking of how much had changed between her and Ares and that she was now being recognised as his wife in his actual home in London, and that cheered her up a good deal.

The house was huge with three wings built round a courtyard with a very pretty central garden. The basement contained a pool and a sauna and a gym. Upstairs she walked into the master bedroom for the first time, enjoying the sight of her luggage being unpacked right next to Ares's, and she strolled through numerous bedrooms before Edith, the housekeeper, was called away to answer a query. Alana paused at a door at the foot of a corridor and, when she tried to open it, found it locked.

'What's in here?' she asked the older woman once she had returned to her side.

Edith dropped her gaze and became rather flustered. 'It's just another bedroom, Mrs Sarris,' she said with obvious embarrassment.

'Then why's it locked?' Alana enquired.

The housekeeper shrugged awkwardly. 'Oh, there's some stuff in there that hasn't been collected yet.'

Her brow furrowing, her curiosity huge, Alana decided to leave the matter there for the moment and continued the tour while knowing that, one way or another, she intended to get into that locked room. Ares had made it very clear to her that this was now her home.

Ares went out to a business dinner that evening and Alana ate alone, wondering if they had really made a fresh start or whether she was just looking on the bright side and kidding herself. He wasn't likely to change his routine and habits overnight, she scolded herself. Expecting too much too soon from him would be a recipe for disaster, but she could see that he was *trying* with the separate-bedroom issue now behind them.

Later that evening, she was just climbing into the vast emperor-sized bed when Ares appeared and began to undress before striding into the bathroom. She lay there listening to the shower running and when he reappeared, she said nothing even though her heart was pounding and her tummy was full of butterflies. The mattress moved a little as he got in and then doused the lights. He didn't speak, so she didn't either but every muscle in her slim body was taut with the expectation that he would reach for her. Only, he didn't. Maybe he thought she was asleep. Maybe he found pregnancy a turn-off. Maybe he was only trying to be caring. It was a long time before Alana slept.

Almost the instant she wakened she was propelled at speed into the bathroom to be ingloriously ill. She was relieved that Ares had already left the room, presumably to make one of his ridiculously early starts to the new day. Freshening up, she wondered if a poor night's rest and her nerves had contributed to her finally experiencing the nausea she had expected to feel sooner. She pulled on jeans, discovered they were already too tight for comfort and grimaced. By the time she got downstairs, Ares was long gone.

The pattern repeated all week. He left early, returned late, ate precisely two dinners with her and made inconsequential conversation. It made her feel like an invisible presence in his home. As for that shared bed? Zilch...*nada*. He wasn't touching her any longer either. As the days wore on, frustration currented through Alana like a live wire. Was it the baby she was now carrying? Was that a passion killer for him? Or was he merely playing a difficult situation the only way he felt he could? Or even, was Ares just bone-deep stubborn? There was no contract now. He had only ever wanted her on a temporary basis. Was keeping his distance how he expressed anger at feeling trapped? And why couldn't he just talk about how he felt and if he was incapable, why not let her sort it out?

'Are you annoyed with me?' Alana asked in the darkness of their bed the night before they were to fly to Athens for the charity benefit.

Ares froze. 'No. Why would you think that?'

'You avoid me—'

'I work long hours,' he contradicted.

'Because you want to, not because you *have* to.'

'Working hard is in my DNA.'

'Being avoided and deprived of sex is not in mine.'

The minute those frank words left her lips, Alana almost groaned in annoyance because she had not intended to be quite that blunt. No, she had started out planning to be subtle even though she wasn't sure that subtle would get her anywhere with Ares.

In the darkness, a sudden surprised grin of unholy amusement flashed over Ares's taut features as he lay with care on the far side of the huge bed. *'Deprived?'*

Alana sniffed. 'I'm sure I have marital rights too. How am I supposed to feel? You hand out such mixed messages. One minute you're pouncing on me as if you haven't had sex in months and the next I'm in the same bed and it's like I have a physical force field around me.'

Ares was smiling. 'I accept that that would be confusing. I didn't quite see it that way though. I know you haven't been well most days—'

'How do you know that?' Alana demanded, taken aback because she had believed she had successfully hidden her attacks of nausea from him.

'Edith mentioned it. You should have,' Ares added.

'It's no big deal. I'm pregnant. At this stage pregnant women sometimes throw up,' Alana told him breezily, not wishing to sound like a sick person, an invalid.

'You're going through a lot right now. I didn't want to make assumptions and I didn't know what you wanted—'

'You could have tried asking,' Alana pointed out with audible impatience.

'You make it sound so simple. It didn't feel that simple to me.'

'But that's because that's you. You make a four-course meal out of every potential problem even if there isn't one that I can see!' she complained with spirit.

Ares laughed out loud, wondering why he had never met anyone like Alana before, why no other woman had ever dared to challenge him with such fearless honesty. He rolled over the bed, across the boundary he had carefully respected, and closed both arms round her slight frame, pulling her close. He was as hot and hard as he had been every night sharing the same mattress. Even at a distance, scenting the lemony scent of her hair products, sensing her tiny movements only feet away and hearing her breathy little sounds, he had loathed the belief that he shouldn't touch her any more.

You made me feel like a call girl, she had told him in Geneva. That statement had hit him hard and chastened him.

'So, do I have marital rights?' Alana teased.

'Of course you do, but after what you said in Geneva—'

'Let's not get into that again. I was upset.' Alana shifted into a state of quivering anticipation as he disposed of her pyjamas and brought his sensual mouth down hungrily on hers, sending every pulse in her body racing. Her fingers slid into his hair, possessiveness licking through her like a river of lava rushing along her veins, lighting her up inside with white-hot energy.

She couldn't get enough of him and he didn't seem able to get enough of her. It had only been a week since they had last been intimate but it felt like one heck of a lot longer. They came together in a tempest of passion as he sank into her with a hungry growl and the pace was frantic, feverish and spectacularly sexy. She reached a peak fast and her climax drove his, plunging them both into hot pleasure and gasping satisfaction.

'I'm never going to move again,' Ares swore raggedly into her tumbled hair.

'That was incredible,' she framed a little smugly, hands smoothing over any part of him she could reach.

'It was…and now you have to sleep. You need your rest,' he reminded her.

'When you get bossy, I get irritated,' she warned him.

'Go to sleep, *moraki mou*. Tomorrow will be a long day.'

Alana drifted off in a blissful haze, everything right again in her world, and awakened to breakfast in bed without Ares, who would apparently meet her when he joined her flight in Paris.

Hours later, groomed within an inch of her life by the stylists who had arrived at her husband's penthouse apartment in Athens, she walked down a red carpet into a blinding blitz of flashing cameras with one hand daintily anchored on his arm and an overwhelming sensation of being out of her depth. Yet she knew she looked her very best. The extravagant emerald and diamond necklace was round her throat, an embellishment to the designer white beaded sleeveless gown that swept down to her toes, highlighting her curves but essentially showing nothing. Ares had chosen it on that shopping trip before their wedding and it looked amazing, she had to give him that. He had added to her sophisticated appearance with a diamond tiara that very evening.

'It belonged to my grandmother, Katarina Sarris,' Ares had imparted, intervening to direct the stylist to put her hair up and personally anchoring that glittering crown of flashing diamonds into her upswept hair. 'It's a shame that she's no longer alive to see my wife wearing it.'

And there had been an odd dark tone in his deep voice that persuaded her *not* to ask for an explanation just at that moment when they had an audience.

'Did your grandmother pass away recently?' she asked instead in the limo on the way to the benefit.

'Yes.'

'I'm sorry—'

'No need to be. I never met her.' Expressionless, Ares glanced down at her. 'Tomorrow, we'll be visiting the ancestral home of the Sarris family. I've never set foot there before either…something to look forward to—'

'Gosh, you're suddenly letting all these cats out of the bag when I least expect it,' Alana gasped, stretching up to whisper in his ear.

'No need for secrecy now,' Ares intoned with quiet mockery. 'And it is *why* I married you, *moraki mou*.'

Shock shivered through Alana's taut frame as they were ushered through the glamorous cliques of bejewelled, designer-clad women and elegant men, every eye welded to them as they made their entrance and were shown to the top table. A welter of introductions followed and everyone stared her up and down, seething speculation in their every smile, sally and glance. Who was she? Where had she come from? Ares Sarris's *wife*? Her cheeks were flushed by the time they finally had the peace to sit down.

'Why did you tell me that now?'

'You'll have to mull over it before you confront me with it,' Ares retorted with amusement. 'I was surprised that you haven't demanded an answer sooner.'

Alana flushed to the roots of her hair and then paled, annoyed by his nonchalance. But he had hit the facts dead on target and she was ashamed that she had stopped asking questions. When had she become so involved in their fake marriage that she no longer worried about why he had needed a pretend wife in the first place?

'That's why I told you,' Ares advanced smoothly. 'Heading off a complication in advance.'

'You actually haven't explained—'

'This is neither the place nor the time.'

Grudgingly accepting that reality, Alana sat back in her seat to watch the famous celebrity currently treating the guests to her latest song. With a parade of such world-class acts to entertain them the evening went past at speed and by the time Alana drifted off to the cloakroom, she was no longer as tense.

Ares was teasing her. Sometimes he did that. Having noted her revealing omission, he had pointed it out. Did he realise that she had far from contractual feelings for him now? Had she exposed herself to that extent? It was perfectly possible, she acknowledged ruefully. She didn't hide anything. She didn't play hard to get either. Maybe he had already worked out that she was in love with him.

Emerging from the cloakroom into an alcove with a comfortable sofa, Alana sat down and dug into her tiny beaded purse to extract a lipstick.

'The Sarris bride?' an English voice queried from the bar nearby. 'She was so incredibly young and unsophisticated I couldn't believe my eyes. Has to be the last woman I would have paired with Ares Sarris!'

'Beautiful, though—'

'Still not his type. If it's true that he was cosy for years with Marina Vasileiou, the violinist, his renowned preference lies with older, sophisticated brunettes.'

'So, he married a youthful blonde and festooned her in jewels worth a king's ransom. Sadly, there's nothing new in a very wealthy man falling for a fresh pretty face,' her companion remarked cynically.

Marina, the violinist? Who was she? Alana's sensitive tummy turned over sickly. The former mistress he had briefly referred to?

Alana went searching on her phone and found pictures of a tall, gorgeous brunette in her thirties, all long black hair, classic features and endless legs. A famous soloist, who looked like a supermodel. She swallowed hard, deleted the search and rose from her seat to return to the function room, refusing to even look in the direction of the chattering women. She didn't listen to idle gossip, did she? And she wasn't about to question Ares either. She had more pride than that, she assured herself.

CHAPTER NINE

FIRST THING THE next morning, the London consultant contacted them with the results of the blood test. They were having a little girl, news that enthralled them both, with Ares even beginning to consider names, which Alana had told him was premature.

'So, this is where...?' Alana asked once they were arriving at the Sarris property, having left the penthouse with their luggage.

'Where I would've grown up had I been born legitimate,' Ares filled in as the limousine swept them up a long driveway screened by carefully tapered cypresses planted like sentinels to cast long thin shadows across the sun-baked gravel.

'And yet you've never been here before?' Alana checked uncertainly because, as yet, she really didn't know what Ares was about to unload on her. It was not as though he was likely to fill in the blanks beforehand.

'You know that my father wouldn't acknowledge me,' he reminded her flatly. 'After he turned me away from his office, the local priest went to his lawyers' office and told them about me instead. They ran DNA tests to confirm the blood in my veins because they accepted that if I belonged to the family line, that would have repercussions for the family trust. After long discussions with my father, they reached agreement that I would be sent at his expense to be educated at an English boarding school under a fake name to protect the Sarris reputation—'

'But illegitimate kids aren't as big a deal in today's world,' Alana argued in surprise. 'Why all the secrecy?'

'My parentage disgusted my father's family, particularly my grandmother. A mother who was a hooker?' Ares grimaced.

Alana's hand came down on top of his where it was braced tautly on the leather seat between them. 'Only a hooker because your father refused to step up and support her when she was pregnant,' she reminded him fiercely. 'Don't let that embarrass you—'

'I don't,' he asserted.

But he did. Alana silently cursed the Sarris family roundly for forcing Ares into hiding as a child. Exiling him to a foreign country for his education, his Greek family had ensured that he was imbued with the conviction that he was something to be hidden and ashamed of. Abandoned by his mother and denied by his father. Her heart literally bled for what he had been forced to endure.

'I was a very bright child and fortunate to receive a first-class education,' Ares added almost argumentatively. 'The lawyers did their best for me.'

'But, essentially, you were an orphan,' Alana reflected. 'So where did you go at holiday times?'

'Supposedly, my uncle's, my father's brother. By that time my father had married and produced his first legitimate son and I was still very much the dirty secret. Naturally, my uncle and his family didn't want to be lumbered with me either. Why would they have?' Ares asked grimly. 'I was his brother's mistake, *not* his. I only went to my uncle's home once and he passed away from heart disease soon afterwards. After that, I went to friends' homes but sometimes I just stayed on at the school. That's when I learned to work so hard. I was determined to succeed in life so that nobody could ever treat me the way they did again.'

'Completely understandable,' Alana murmured as the limo drew to a stately halt outside a huge porticoed entrance. 'So how did you come to inherit when they wouldn't even let you visit this place?'

'A terrible tragedy. My father, his wife and my two half-brothers died in a plane crash several years back,' Ares volunteered harshly. 'And even though from that moment on my grandmother, Katarina Sarris, knew that I would inherit she still refused to meet me.'

'Even allowing for her grief, that was pure bitterness and bile,' Alana told him, enraged on his behalf. 'She must have been a very mean-minded woman. You were still her grandson even if she didn't approve of your background and you deserved a more generous response. Nobody should punish a child for the adults' irresponsibility.'

'Which is why *our* daughter will never suffer for one moment believing that she was unwanted,' Ares swore in a raw undertone as he closed his hand tautly over hers. 'That is *very* important to me.'

Alana's heart lifted high at that adamant assurance and no longer did she have to wonder at his unquestioning acceptance of their accidental conception. Ares was so determined to do everything differently for *their* child that she could only be filled with relief and hope for the future. Whipping round in her seat without the smallest hesitation, she reached for him and laced her fingers into his silvery blond hair and kissed him. Ares reached down and unclipped her belt to drag her straight into his lap. He ground her down on him with a muffled groan of desire, crushed her pink lips hungrily beneath his and let his tongue slide in for one urgent sweep before pulling back from her.

'Sex in the limo is sleazy,' he informed her.

'Never had it but could be convinced otherwise,' she mumbled shakily, all flustered and pink, and then she glanced out of the tinted window and saw the assembly of people awaiting their arrival on the steps of the substantial house. 'Who the heck are all those people?'

'Lawyers, domestic staff. A big moment. The last Sarris arrives,' Ares remarked drily.

'The only one with any courage or honour!' Alana quipped almost aggressively, so protective of him at that instant that she was almost in pain because of what he had suffered growing up: the cruelty, the humiliation, the shame. Sometimes Ares wound her up like a clock and she didn't know what to do with all the emotion he could send sloshing around inside her.

'When did you end up taking my side?' Ares asked with a wry smile.

'When I fell in love with you,' Alana told him bluntly without even thinking about that declaration, because she knew that he needed someone to believe in *him*, not his wealth, not his power, all the other much more important stuff that made him the guy he was. 'And no, you don't have to reciprocate—'

'Don't think I know how,' Ares slotted in gruffly, stunning dark golden eyes locked to her lovely heart-shaped face in sheer wonder at a creature so different from him that she might as well have been an alien being. 'You don't hide anything at all, do you?'

'Guess I walked into that one,' Alana conceded as she scrambled off his lap to vacate the car, dazed by what she had revealed and yet knowing deep down inside her somehow that Ares had needed that support from her. Arriving at the Sarris ancestral home as the new owner, finally acknowledged for who he was, *was* a very big deal for him.

Alana loved *him*. Ares was in shock as he swung out of the limo. Was she crazy? Didn't she know how damaged he was, how impossible it would be for him to be what she deserved in a man? And yet with that unequalled generosity of hers she had given him that pledge regardless of all his faults. She was giving him a level of trust that left him breathless and shaken.

They were ushered into a vast entrance hall like

visiting royalty. Alana felt overpowered by the sheer grandeur of the building but stood tall for Ares's sake. The last thing he needed right then was a wife cringing by his side as if she didn't feel good enough for such fancy surroundings. In a library walled with old books, two older Greek men, the lawyers whom Ares was already clearly acquainted with, set out documents on a polished desk for his signature. It was a surprise to her when Ares urged her forward to add her signature to his. As a celebratory glass of champagne was proffered, Ares waved hers away on her behalf and requested something non-alcoholic.

An older man approached them in the hall just as Alana was about to ask why her signature had been required. 'This is Dmitri, head of Household Sarris,' Ares imparted. 'But we don't require the official tour. We'll explore on our own.'

Alana sipped her juice as Ares strode through another grand doorway and she followed with less assurance. She had never ever in her life entered a property built and furnished on such a magnificent scale. Everything she looked at seemed to be antique and the paintings on the walls were huge and imposing.

'Are these your ancestors?' she whispered.

'No, this is the classical collection of art which the family used to show off on very occasional open days to the public,' Ares told her. 'I've read everything written about this house. I could probably show you around it blindfolded.'

Alana had to blink rapidly in response to that admission of knowledge about a property he had been forbidden to even visit. 'The family' he referred to had been *his* family, but of course they had deprived Ares of ever believing in that blood bond because they had refused to recognise his existence. Even the death of most of that family hadn't altered his mindset.

Did you attend your grandmother's funeral?' she whispered curiously.

'No. She left instructions making it clear that she did not want me to do so,' he told her.

'Nasty old shrew,' Alana mumbled, aghast that anyone could be that bitter about an illegitimate grandson even on their deathbed. 'So, why did I have to sign those documents?'

'My grandmother, Katarina, found a loophole. Ultimately, she couldn't stop me from inheriting this place because there is a legal trust that prevented her from doing so. When I was still a teenager I gave an interview boasting about how I would never marry, which was, indeed, my mindset for more years than I care to count,' Ares conceded in a wry undertone. 'So, Katarina played a blinder. In her will she passed it all on dutifully to me with three little extra words: *and his wife*. To claim my inheritance *without* a wife I would've been forced to prove my identity in an open courtroom and that would have dragged out all the dirty laundry. It could have been done. There was no way I could be denied what is mine by right of birth but I was reluctant to face that courtroom exposure.'

'Of course, you were,' Alana agreed, reaching for

his hand, squeezing his fingers. 'It would have embarrassed you and why should you be embarrassed all over again after what you've already had to rise above?'

'That's pretty much how I felt about it as well,' Ares admitted, his wide sensual lips compressed into a flat line. 'So, that's why I was looking for a wife, who *wasn't* a wife—'

'And ended up with a wife, who *is* a wife…or *am I*?' Alana heard herself ask in sudden helpless dismay.

'I imagine the jury is still out on that one,' Ares countered with his usual innate caution, while wondering how the hell a guy was supposed to handle a woman who was so open and impulsive and just hung everything out there when, all his life, he had kept everything hidden and locked down until it was literally forced out of him. 'It's early days for us.'

So, what am I, then? Alana questioned herself anxiously.

A *trial* wife? A wife only until she had given birth? Was that the date that Ares was truly awaiting? Once their child was born, would he then be counting on a divorce? What else could she be expected to think after such a careful statement? Her heart sank to the level of her shoe soles.

Ares strode into the portrait gallery, a space optimised to show his ancestors, including his father.

'That has to be your dad,' Alana guessed, scanning the silvery blond male in the modern suit. 'You're better looking…he's got a weak chin. It figures, a guy who couldn't cope with hard reality—'

'Yes,' Ares conceded, struggling to respond in English, disconcerted by that blunt appraisal that fitted the man surprisingly well. A man who couldn't deal with an unexpected pregnancy or a little boy, of whom he was the father, a man set on denying the truth until the day he died. For the first time, it struck Ares that that sperm donor of his hadn't been much of a man at all. He had been a coward, a total wimp when decency demanded that he should step forward. It had taken the lawyers to remind his father that Ares could not be ignored, that it would be too dangerous to leave an heir to the Sarris trust uneducated and unpresentable.

He had been taught at boarding school how to speak, how to dress, how to behave in polite company. It had been shell shock of the strongest kind for a street kid brought up simply to worry about his next meal and survival. His IQ count had been his saviour, allowing him to fly in every subject while the less fortunate floundered. But he knew, indeed, he fully recognised that had he been less clever he would've failed and sunk like a stone in such a challenging environment where even the language and the culture were unfamiliar.

'It must've killed them,' Alana whispered, scanning the line of portraits. 'What did your half-brothers look like? Were they blond like you?'

'No, dark-haired like their mother.'

'So, it would have annoyed them even more that you were an almost exact copy of your father, of the family Sarris trait of that very fair hair and dark eyes.' Alana's tone was celebratory. 'They denied you, but you were so much a Sarris from birth—'

'Never thought of my colouring quite that way,' Ares admitted, once again taken aback, gazing down at her, so little and so cute and so very much herself even in the medieval Sarris palace of sophistication and dignity. Ironically, she was very much more comfortable than he was.

'Of course, you didn't. You would've been far too busy concentrating on all the negative aspects, never looking for the positive ones,' Alana condemned with conviction. 'You never ever look on the bright side, Ares—'

'Except when I'm with you,' Ares allowed tightly.

'Did you inherit money with this place?'

'Not a drachma. There wasn't much left of the Sarris wealth. They lived high, earned small and this house needs a lot of money spent on it and the upkeep is costly. What little money there was after Katarina's death went to charity.'

'Such idiots to ignore you when you could have saved them all as a money-maker,' Alana pronounced with huge satisfaction. 'You were exactly what this family needed when their fortunes were on the wane, but they were too snobby and precious to recognise your worth as a tycoon. You were well rid of the lot of them.'

'How do you make that out?' Ares demanded, shocked by such a declaration when all his life all he had thought about was his rejection, his humiliation, the knowledge that he was only an embarrassment to his late father and family.

Alana viewed him in surprise. 'Well, if they'd been friendly, they'd have hung on your sleeve for sure because they undoubtedly needed your money and drive. You had the brain and the get up and go which they clearly lacked. I don't know what your father was like in business but, I assume, nothing to write home about if your grandmother died without leaving much money. They probably resented you going from strength to strength while they fell by the wayside, *yesterday's news*,' she framed with emphatic satisfaction.

Before Ares even knew it, he had wrapped his arms around his wife and backed her up against a bare stretch of wall.

'What?' she said in astonishment.

'Sometimes you're the slow one,' Ares growled, ravishing her parted pink lips without further ado.

'Ares…?'

'I never wanted you so bad as I do right now,' Artes hissed, wrenching up her elegant narrow sheath dress with a ruthlessness that led to the sound of ripping fabric, because it had surely not been designed with the possibility of receiving such brutal treatment.

'Is that so?' Alana couldn't have cared less had he stripped her naked because her heart was racing and her whole skin surface was tingling with sensual awareness.

Ares had that molten golden glow in his gaze and it melted her from inside out like heated honey. He was a very sexual male with a high libido, her perfect match. She liked to be wanted, she *needed* to be wanted when it was the guy she loved. It might be the lowest common aspect of a relationship but she would settle for what she could get while she built on other things. No, she didn't expect everything offered upfront like some women, yes, she was willing to work for a stronger bond.

Everything she wore below the dress was ripped, shredded, cast aside. Ares in a certain mood blazed with passion. He kissed her breathless, his seething hunger setting her alight like a flame on dry straw. To be desired to that degree was an aphrodisiac. It fired her up like a blazing star flaming through the heavens. She was yanking at that silvery hair, hauling at his shirt, clawing at his smoothly tailored shoulders, fully on board for every electrifying moment of that sexual connection.

Ares lifted her up against the wall and sank into her slick depths in one single, utterly thrilling moment and she shrieked his name in ecstasy as he stretched her to the limit. She needed him as much as he needed her and that was all right as far as she was concerned. Powerful pleasure consumed her from her pelvis up through her entire body as he pounded into her at a crazy rhythm. It was wild and exciting and she climaxed in a rush of sheer joy that wiped her out.

Swallowing a curse as the best sex of his life still rippled through his shuddering frame, Ares lifted up his wife and carried her into the nearest bedroom—

that mental floor plan really did come in handy at that moment. He laid her with apologetic care down onto a gilded four-poster bed and studied the tatters of the dress he had ripped, wondering where the lingerie had gone. Recalling in a surge of X-rated imagery, he stalked back out to the portrait gallery to retrieve the evidence. His pregnant wife, and he had gone at her... like a rutting *animal*, he conceded in shock and shame, unable to explain that behaviour, appalled by it. There had been just that instant where everything inside him got to be too much and nothing would do him but he possessed her again.

'*Theos*... I am so *very* sorry,' Ares framed raggedly, staring down at her in shattered disquiet.

'Why are you saying sorry?' Alana looked up at him with tranquil green eyes bright as stars, blonde hair wildly tousled round her lovely face. 'That was absolutely freaking *amazing*!'

Ares stared down at his wife, his incredible sex fantasy of a wife, in wonderment. No, she was the amazing one. Every time he was with her, he was reminded of that fact, that she was totally unlike any other woman he had ever been with, and it blew him away. With her, he was the kind of mindless he had never been.

'But I've ruined your clothes,' he mumbled thickly.

'You said we were spending the night here,' she reminded him calmly. 'We bought luggage with us.'

Ares glanced around the room for the first time, saw the cases as yet unpacked and let some of his extreme tension escape. They were in the master bedroom, double doors off the arch at the end of the portrait gallery, his brain reminded him once again of that all-important floor plan.

'I was rough…you're pregnant—'

'Still enjoying the passion,' Alana interposed. 'Not an invalid. Doctor said it was fine as long as I'm healthy and I am. Did you miss that statement?'

'Was probably still studying that screen with the baby blip,' Ares confided.

'Yeah, not much to see there yet.'

'But her heart is hitting one hundred and eighty beats a minute and her brain is functioning in the blip,' Ares informed her expansively. 'And the wrists, the elbows and the knees are forming. The legs and arms are longer too.'

'Right.' Alana nodded and smiled sunnily, relieved that he had relaxed enough again to be back to normal and telling her all the things that he knew and she didn't. He was also displaying a level of interest in their daughter's development that delighted her.

'It's really fascinating,' he confided, flopping back on the bed. 'I'm tired.'

'Course you are. This was a challenging day.' Alana sat up, tugged loose his tie, began to wrench him free of his jacket and unbutton his shirt and since she had sent a few of those buttons flying on the gallery that wasn't much of a task. 'And you gave me incredible sex on top of all that, so you've done astonishingly well, hit every Ares Sarris target, in fact.'

'Really?' Ares canted up an ebony brow, watching

her take care of him as no woman had ever taken care of him and wondering how she could be so casual, so relaxed when what was happening to him felt so very visceral, so very *intense*.

Alana slid off the bed to finish stripping him, drowning in those glorious dark golden eyes like the addict she was. Shoes and socks went flying along with his tailored trousers. She wrenched back the fancy silk cover on the museum-quality bed and pushed him flat. 'Now you sleep. You need rest.'

'I just arrived!' Ares objected, flying upright again.

Alana pushed those big brown shoulders back down firmly again. 'You're knackered but you won't admit it. You didn't sleep last night. Don't think I didn't notice you up in the middle of the night working on that laptop! Anyway, we need to rest before we get up for dinner in this palace and act like we belong because we *do* belong here because this is *your* home now.'

Ares computed those plain facts, lay back and sighed. When it came to the ordinary things, she knew what she was talking about. She saw stuff in a different way from him, but it amazed him how good she could be in that line, how wonderfully, brilliantly practical.

As Ares fell asleep, his phone was buzzing. Alana scooped it up before it could wake him and the name flashed across the screen, *Marina*, and her stomach turned over sickly as she switched it off. His ex, his mistress? She didn't know, didn't really want to know after what she had heard about the lady, but she didn't like that she was still calling Ares after he had got married. Why were they still in touch with each other? Wasn't that suspicious?

Was wondering that even her business now? Where exactly did she stand with Ares? What did the marriage, which should have been wholly fake, now consist of? Her accidental pregnancy, she answered inwardly and cringed. That was no basis for a proper marriage. Her own intelligence warned her of that reality.

She hovered, just watching him sleep. Heavens, he was still her warrior angel, so unappreciated by those who should have loved and admired him for all that he had grown into as a man in spite of his tormented beginnings. And exquisite from that ruffled silvery hair to the long black lashes fanning his model high cheekbones and the perfect pink pout of those movie star lips of his.

He was hers now but for how long? Could she really expect to continue holding Ares's interest when it came to a temptation like that gorgeous sleek brunette she had seen online?

CHAPTER TEN

'*PREGNANT?*' ALANA'S SISTER Skye gasped as though it were the worst news she had ever heard, her eyes huge.

'Thought it might be heading that way,' Enzo remarked wryly. 'Reckon the way that business contract went off the rails so fast shocked the hell out of Ares!'

Alana frowned. 'How did you work that out?' she asked her brother-in-law.

'Know him, know you…it was obviously going to be a car crash—'

'Thanks,' Alana said tightly.

'A car crash in a *good* way,' Enzo rephrased with amusement. 'Never met a guy who needed to live a *real* life so badly. There he was inhabiting his billionaire safe bubble and then he met you. Not car-crash territory, I agree, but certainly a massive wake-up call. So, Ares is going to be a father.'

'He's quite…happy about that,' Alana said carefully, thinking of Ares's fascination with their daughter's development. A scientific experiment on Ares's terms? She inwardly shrank.

'He's accepted it, then,' Skye remarked, looking a little less panicked.

'Ares is amazingly adaptable,' Alana proclaimed with pride.

'Which he's basically *not*…in the slightest,' Enzo chipped in, unhelpfully. 'So, that means that he has to be crazy about you.'

'I don't think so,' Alana contended worriedly.

Her brother-in-law shrugged with elegance, all Italian cool. 'Well, what would I know?'

Her family had only been making a fleeting visit en route to a flight to Berlin but Alana was relieved to have seen her sister and told her a little more about her mystery marriage. Maybe eventually she would tell Skye everything but just then it had felt like much too soon to reveal the complexities of her relationship with Ares. Ares, the guy who only followed transactional rules in relationships, who hadn't ever been in love, she assumed. There was no straight path to reach a male of such intricate challenge. He knew she loved him. She thought he believed her, but he wasn't likely to ever say it back and she wasn't ever going to say those words again lest it make Ares feel trapped by expectations he could not fulfil. Nothing would chase him from her side faster or kill his desire for her quicker than that kind of unwelcome pressure.

In the short term, Alana preferred to keep her own counsel and concentrate on the positives in her world like Ares and her baby, rather than the disappointments. There was no such thing as perfect, neither in people nor situations, she told herself firmly, refusing to be cast down and constantly fretting about what she couldn't have.

One little secret, however, she did have the power to control, she reasoned with determination as she searched out Edith to request the key for that locked room. The London house was now *her* home. Hadn't Ares made that clear every time he got the chance? In fact, Ares was so fond of employing the word 'our' when it came to any kind of ownership of his vast pool of possessions that Alana sometimes laughed on that score. He had urged her to use his fabulous cars, throw out furniture she didn't like or find comfortable, redecorate wherever she liked. So, yes, she definitely had the right to see inside the mysterious locked room!

Once again, she noted the housekeeper's discomfiture but there was no hesitation about handing over the key. Edith did not, however, offer to accompany her, which once again persuaded Alana that the contents of that room were purely personal to Ares. And she had no plans to go rummaging through any of his private stuff without him, she reflected wryly, because she wasn't one of those women who refused to respect that a guy could have boundaries too. Whatever she discovered she would decide on her approach afterwards.

The first acknowledgement that struck Alana as she stepped over the threshold of that bedroom was that it was not a mere guest room, it was an overwhelmingly feminine room still littered with a woman's clutter. That knocked Alana straight off balance. Somehow she had been mentally prepared only to see an unfurnished room full of sealed boxes belonging to Ares. She was not at all prepared for what she actually found.

A woman's room?

Her disconcerted gaze locked to a large glossy photo of… *Marina*! And really, after that, there were no doubts to be had whatsoever as to who had once made use of the room. Alana's stricken gaze shifted to glamorous photo after photo of her husband's former lover. Marina in evening dress, Marina walking red carpets, Marina performing with her violin on stage. And the woman was gorgeous, there was absolutely no denying that fact. Overall, the room bore a closer resemblance to a shrine than a bedroom, she thought sickly, and she only anxiously tugged open one drawer on sets of daring wispy lingerie before retreating back to the door in shock, wondering what other intimate items might still be packed away and truly *not* wanting to know. She yanked the door shut, locked it again and walked away.

Curiosity killed the cat, she repeated inside her head, marvelling that it had not occurred to her sooner that the housekeeper might be embarrassed at her queries because she had assumed that no wife would wish to walk into such a room in her own home. So, why was it still all there in situ? Alana swallowed hard. Was Ares expecting Marina to come back into his life? Was he unable to quite make the break with Marina that he had insisted he had? Was it some sort of sexual obsession? Or was he now realising that he was fonder of the woman than he had ever appreciated?

Unhappily, Alana could fully imagine Ares being that blind to his own emotions and reactions. He lived very much in that world inside his own head, superb at developing technical stuff and solving business problems but barely more sophisticated than a toddler when it came to the more subtle, delicate promptings of his own feelings.

So, she told herself squarely, she was married to a guy who retained a bedroom for another woman. She could handle that. She could deal with that. Of course, she could, she told herself. After all, theirs wasn't and never had been and never would be a *normal* marriage and it was time she stopped pretending otherwise. Getting mushy and sentimental and wittering on about love was unlikely to solve the problem. But what *would*?

An hour later, Alana climbed into a limousine to go shopping. She had looked online but some stuff needed to be personally selected to fit and, what was more, she had been keen to seek out the most exclusive outlet possible. Heaven forbid that she wore anything on her body that might remind Ares of any other woman, never mind one particular glam, glossy giraffe-legged possibility. She had even gone back into that wretched room to check labels and she was ashamed of herself. How could she be so weak, so vulnerable that she changed herself to meet a man's apparent needs? She had never believed that she could ever be that sort of a woman and now she very much feared that she actually *was*!

In reality, aside from a couple of special occasions, like her wedding day, Alana was a white cotton granny-pants sort of girl under her clothing. She liked flexible and comfy and had not the smallest desire to climb into lacy bits of suggestive nothing or erotic corsets and suspenders.

But now it seemed obvious to her that that was the kind of stuff that Ares enjoyed and it would surely only be a very confident wife in a secure marriage who chose to ignore that truth. Alana was neither confident nor in a secure relationship. She did, however, have a black credit card and she wielded it like a secret weapon at her destination. She would get over her discomfort at the prospect of packaging herself for a man, even for a husband's benefit, she assured herself righteously, emerging from the bathroom, barely recognisable to her own gaze when she caught a glimpse in a cheval mirror and swiftly looked away again.

Ares was due home and he was a guy with a routine. He strode through the front door, went straight upstairs for a shower and there he would find her waiting. Simples, she told herself, no big deal, just another step in the right direction for the sake of their baby and the marriage she wanted to last. Did she also need long black hair and perfect features and legs as long as a rail track? Maybe she was overreacting to that room. Was that possible? But she was always reading that men were kind of basic when you got down to the bones of them and there was certainly nothing more basic than what she was doing, was there? Steeling herself, Alana arranged herself like a sex bomb—she hoped—on the bed.

Ares came through the door wondering where Alana was and found out. It was the nastiest surprise his bride had ever given him. He took one stunned look at the outfit and hurriedly looked away again. It had never once occurred to him that she would get done up like that and think he would like it because she wasn't that sort of woman. And he liked that she wasn't that sort of woman, and catching a glimpse of her done up as though she were being filmed for some porn site shook him rigid. He lost colour, hovered and looked everywhere but at her.

'What's happened?' he asked, striving to understand what on earth could have prompted her into that sleazy seductress mode that ran so much against her character as he knew her.

Equally taken aback by the brooding silence, the tautness of his lean, darkly handsome features, Alana sat up in consternation. She hadn't been expecting him to start stripping where he stood because Ares was never that predictable, but she certainly hadn't expected him to treat her to one stricken appraisal and look away as if there was something rather indecent about her attire, because he was not prudish in bed.

'Nothing's happened,' she said defensively. 'I just thought that maybe you would…er…like—'

'No,' Ares sliced in. 'I *don't* like, *moraki mou*. I became far too used to seeing scantily clad women when I was a child. That sort of thing takes me back to times I would sooner forget.'

And that was the moment that Alana registered how

crass she had been, to not even think of that possibility, that she was married to a male who had spent his early years in a highly sexualised environment and that such an outfit could be a kind of trigger for him. 'I'm really sorry,' she whispered shakily. 'But I wish you'd told me—'

'It never crossed my mind that *you*—'

'But it was all right when *she* did it, was it?' Alana gasped on the back of a choked sob of humiliation, because she was discovering that going out on a limb to try and make someone love and want her more could be a deeply wounding exercise and a mistake.

Disconcerted by that comeback, Ares quirked an uncomprehending brow at the identity of 'she' voiced with such venom. Alana kicked off the ridiculously high heels, snatched up a robe and, hugging it to her, vanished into the bathroom. The door slammed. The lock turned.

Ares breathed in slow and deep. Perhaps he should have mentioned that aversion sooner. Perhaps he should have kept quiet and faked pleasure even. He hadn't meant to hurt her feelings. She was sensitive, very sensitive, and she had clearly made a singularly weird but commendable attempt to be sexy for him. It was not her fault that he hadn't found it sexy. It was not her fault that he had frozen like a statue in the middle of their bedroom and found it too much of a challenge to even look at her. It was entirely *his* fault, because a *normal* guy would have been thrilled, turned on, delighted to discover a wife who made that much effort, particularly when she was pregnant and coping with all sorts of horrible side effects.

He knocked on the bathroom door. 'Alana!'

'Go away!' she wailed. 'I'm not speaking to you.'

'I'm sorry—'

'Not as sorry as I am!' she slammed back, studying her red face and anguished eyes in the vanity mirror. She had made a fool of herself. Rise above it, her brain instructed her firmly.

Alana stripped off the lingerie, peeled off the stockings, bundled it all into a heap and put the robe back on. She washed her carefully made-up face clean as well. Well, if he preferred ordinary, he might as well get ordinary in spades, she thought bitterly.

Barefoot, she emerged from the bathroom. 'You cut me off, made me feel stupid.'

'That wasn't my intention. I was just…shocked,' he finally selected.

'Wasn't really me, was it?' Alana muttered. 'I felt so fake—'

'It wasn't you. The last thing you are is fake,' Ares asserted, trying to close an arm round her before finding that she had retreated several steps to make any such comfort impossible. 'I apologise for upsetting you—'

'It was that locked room that set me off!' Alana condemned.

'What locked room?'

'Don't be so dense. *Marina's room!*'

Ares frowned. 'I stopped seeing Marina long before we got married. Why would she have a room here now?'

Fed up with what she interpreted as deliberate masculine evasion, Alana closed a small hand over his and dragged him to the door. 'Ares!' she snapped when he proved resistant.

'You are behaving oddly,' he pointed out, and then he looked as if he wished he hadn't said that and, without further protest, he followed her down the long corridor to the very foot where she wielded the key and flung the door wide on Marina's lair.

'Theos mou...' Ares framed in seeming astonishment. 'She did like her publicity photos, didn't she?'

'This is *your* house and this is *her* room, so presumably you've been in here before—'

'No, I haven't been. I said she could use a room for storage because she travels a lot and it suited me. We met up at hotels, not here. This is my home,' Ares stated quietly. 'But why hasn't she cleared all this stuff out?'

Satisfied that she was receiving explanations, Alana shrugged. 'Not my problem. Your housekeeper kept this room locked until I requested the key—'

'Maybe you were hoping to find the equivalent of Mr Rochester's mad wife locked in here,' Ares remarked with sudden inappropriate amusement.

'Marina was phoning you only a couple of days ago when we were in Athens.'

'Yes. I've blocked her now. She kept on phoning to chat.' Ares frowned. 'We never chatted before. Why would I want to now? But I'll tell Edith to box up her belongings and contact her to collect them.'

His dispassionate response made her turn to stare at

him. Stunning dark golden eyes framed by black lashes met hers levelly. 'You don't care about her, do you?'

'That wasn't part of the package. I wish her well, of course,' he breathed in an ironic lie because right then he was wishing he had never met Marina and never made her his mistress. Her very existence even in his past was causing waves in his marriage and distressing his pregnant wife. Alana's peace of mind was much more important to him.

'Why do I feel sorry for her now?' Alana mumbled. 'Just an hour ago I was hating her.'

'You're a very emotional individual. I'm not, but I do very much admire the way you just put everything out there,' Ares admitted, pushing himself to talk, recognising that he had had a narrow escape from a ghastly misunderstanding that had hurt and upset Alana. 'I should think Marina left her possessions here because she was hoping to reanimate things with me, but then I doubt if she even knows I've got married since I haven't announced our marriage the way I should've done.'

'You admire that about me?' Alana had already moved on from the topic of Marina, content to credit that the other woman was a mere shadow from Ares's past and not likely to figure in the present in any guise. She understood the whole situation now, thanks to Ares's honesty. Edith had simply locked the room because Marina was an ex, who had yet to pick up her stuff.

Ares extended an arm warily and slowly closed it

round her slight shoulders, greatly relieved when she didn't pull away. 'I admire a lot of things about you.'

'How come you've never mentioned that before?' Alana asked suspiciously.

'I don't talk much about stuff of that nature but I'm trying to change,' Ares admitted steadily. 'For you, I mean. Be less of an island, less solitary. I was thinking today that inviting Enzo and Skye and the children to visit us as a family rather than only seeing you would be a good idea.'

'Oh, yes, I would prefer that!' Alana carolled cheerfully. 'It always feels as if you're being left out—'

'Alana… I've spent many years deliberately excluding myself from everything *but* work. That has to change for your sake and for our daughter's,' he intoned calmly.

Alana was bewildered by that declaration. 'When did you decide that?'

Ares compressed his sculpted lips. 'Well, I would very much like to say that I realised that the day I first met you, but it took a lot longer for me to work out what I *should* be doing…which turned out to be what I *wanted* to do, so it wasn't that big a stretch.'

'I'm not sure I understand what you're saying.'

'I'm less than proficient when it comes to expressing emotion, but I can learn!' Ares hastened to assure her. 'When you told me you loved me in Greece I didn't know what to say, which was wrong of me. I should've said how happy I was with that gift of yours, shouldn't I?'

'You think being loved was…is a gift?'

Ares urged her back into their bedroom. 'What do you think? Nobody has ever loved me before. I'm not the world's most loveable male—'

'Yes, you are. You're *very* loveable,' Alana told him chokily.

'You're not allowed to cry when I tell you that I love you,' Ares warned her. 'It can't be the right reaction, surely?'

'You love me?' Alana fought to keep her voice level and not bounce round the room like a maniac in celebration and gratitude.

'Don't you know that? I thought you would have already worked that out for yourself and that you were telling me first to make me brave enough to say it back,' Ares contended in some surprise at such ignorance. 'I only realised when you told me that you were pregnant and I *liked* the idea. But I should've guessed in Athens because you were such a tower of strength there in that Sarris palace that I… I just adored you for that—'

'Did you?' Her voice was small but her heart was swelling like a dawn chorus inside her chest. 'I love you so much, Ares.'

'I don't know why though. That worries me. You're everything I'm not. Open and sunny and free and I love all that about you, but it only reminds me that I'm older and set in my ways and kind of boring beside a woman like you—'

Alana's hands framed his high cheekbones, green eyes alight. 'You are *not* boring—'

'Even when I'm droning on about algorithms?'

'You leave me behind sometimes, but I'm not bored,' she declared with confidence. 'You fascinate me. You did from the first. I fancied you something rotten from the minute I first saw you at the hotel. I know you didn't notice me then, but that's all right. You're not the type of guy who perves on lowly employees and I'm glad you're not. I thought you looked like a warrior angel.'

Ares dealt her a slashing, almost boyish grin. 'Oh, I picked up on that when you were ill and I was... I was mesmerised by you seeing me like that. All that emotion just shining out of you. You were so tempting and I tried really hard not to take advantage of you and then I *did*...and it was horrible walking away again after being with you. In fact, that week I left you alone in Abu Dhabi was one of the worst of my life,' he confided, serious again. 'I wanted so badly to still be with you but I thought it would be the wrong thing to do for you. You deserved more than I believed I could ever give you. You were so young and bright and full of life and I was scared I would dim that light of yours, because what did I have to offer aside from my wealth?'

Her eyes stung. 'I didn't understand that that's how you felt and thought.'

'But you still gave me your heart and wanted my baby and that was...that was amazingly generous of you,' Ares intoned huskily. 'You don't care about my background. You love me in spite of it. You forgive my mistakes. You even make excuses for me when I get stuff wrong—'

'Yes, you really do love me,' Alana concluded with a misty smile, holding back the tears lest they freak him out.

'Madly, fiercely, *for ever*,' Ares stressed. 'I need to know you're planning on staying married to me until the day I die because I'd go crazy without you in my life. I'm sorry I was clumsy when I saw you got up in that outfit you wore this evening. I didn't intend to hurt your feelings. I hate hurting you. I love it when you're happy. I love *making* you happy.'

'I'm never going to leave you…but you do know you'll now have to celebrate Christmas and Valentine's Day and all those sorts of occasions. I'm a sucker for all that sentimental stuff and I want a dog and maybe a cat too,' she warned him anxiously.

'I'll cope,' Ares assured her with a wide smile, his lean bronzed features more relaxed than she had ever seen. 'What I couldn't cope with is being without you. You're more important to me than anything else in this world.'

Alana could feel herself standing as tall as a sky-scraper. He was hers and far more hers than she had ever dared to dream. She tugged at his tie and he got the message fast. Off came the business suit, the gold cufflinks, the shirt. He lifted her up and kissed her with hungry urgency, telling her how much loved her, how he couldn't wait for their daughter to arrive. Indeed, now that he was finally talking to her, he was talking too much and she hushed him, which made him laugh. They repossessed each other slowly, both feeling so much more than ever before and no longer hiding it.

'I love you, Ares,' she mumbled drowsily. 'Goodness, we never had dinner.'

'We'll go down and find something when we feel like getting up, and that won't be any time soon,' Ares forecast, holding her close, simply enjoying that moment of perfect peace with her in his arms, safe and secure and his. He labelled what he was feeling as happiness and felt that he was becoming an emotional man. Once he had believed that that was dangerous, but it no longer bothered him because all that truly mattered was that Alana be happy with him. And she was.

Five years later

Alana tucked her daughter, Clio, into bed in the Sarris home in Athens. Her little brother, Lykos, was still snug in his toddler bed at the age of two. Both children had inherited their father's silvery hair and their mother's green eyes. In spite of a father as driven to work and succeed as Ares, they were remarkably easy to handle, even of temper and relaxed. Ares claimed that that was his calm nature coming out in their genes, but Alana thought it was hers.

It was their fifth wedding anniversary, but it wasn't the same date as their original civil marriage. While Alana was still pregnant with Clio, Ares had suggested that they hold a blessings ceremony and that was now the date they honoured. The ceremony had taken place at the same hotel where Enzo and Skye had enjoyed their nuptials because that was, after all, where Ares and Alana had first properly met. In truth that blessings celebration had borne a closer resemblance to a second wedding in which Alana, finally, got to wear a bridal gown and her sisters and her triplet niece, Gianna, got to dress up as bridesmaids. Skye's boys, Luka and Gaetano, had been far too active at the age of three to be entrusted with the role of pageboys and Enzo and their nanny had spent much of the day trying to keep them in control.

That very same night, Ares had dragged Alana down to that lake front and done what he had admitted he had wanted to do that first night when she'd asked him to marry her. He had tugged her into a passionate clinch on the beach before racing them both at an indecent pace to their room to celebrate in privacy.

Those days of emotional and physical restraint that Ares had once imposed on himself were now far behind them, Alana reflected happily. Their children had taught Ares how to relax. Add in a rescue puppy called Loopy and a black tomcat called Misha and theirs had become a busy household. They spent most of the week in London and weekends in the country or visiting Skye and Enzo abroad.

Alana had chosen to finally tell her sister about her stepfather's gambling debts. She had told Enzo first to get his advice and he had reckoned that Skye had moved on enough from the past to handle the revelation that their stepfather had been imperfect. Sharing that secret had allowed the sisters to return to their close relationship and now it was Alana rather than Ares chatting on the phone late at night, to her sibling when their children were in bed.

The Sarris home was still a very grand property. Over time, Alana had also become a little grander. This evening, she wore a sleek red designer gown with diamonds at her throat. Earlier that day she had worn a very smart suit to give a short speech at Ares's charity foundation, which she was now involved with. Raising money for good causes kept her busy, well, that and ensuring that she and Ares spent little time apart. Once she had teased him about being possessive and now she didn't dare because the longer she was with him, the closer they became and the less tolerant she was of being without him.

Now, Alana strolled down the superb carved staircase to move out to the imposing terrace where their anniversary dinner was being served. Just the two of them, just as she preferred. Ares emerged from the house to join her, resplendent in a dinner jacket, and she studied him with pleasure. But there he was, still her warrior angel, who made her heart pound and her mouth run dry while a tiny little hum awakened low in her pelvis.

She walked towards him, and a flashing smile of tremendous warmth swept his lean, strong face. 'You look amazing in that dress,' he told her, linking both arms round her to draw her close.

She didn't tell him that he always looked amazing,

because he got embarrassed when she mentioned his good looks. Instead, she quietly revelled in the knowledge that he was hers.

'You also make me amazingly happy, *moraki mou*,' Ares confided, reluctant to cloud the evening with the truth that he didn't think he had known what happiness was until he met her. Yes, they had had their ups and downs until he had learned how to appreciate the gift he had been given, but right now in the moment he knew that he was holding the woman who was the centre of his world.

'I love you,' she murmured, gazing up at him with her clear green eyes.

'We're dropping the children off with Enzo and Skye in Italy and spending a few days in Abu Dhabi.' Ares revealed his surprise gift.

'You're taking time off again?' Alana gasped.

'Again,' he emphasised with quiet pride in that sacrifice of working hours, because making Alana happy was always his goal.

Alana locked both arms round his neck in her enthusiasm. 'I love you ten times more than I did a minute ago!'

His sensual mouth claimed hers with hungry brevity and when she would have continued it, he closed a hand over hers to walk her back to the table and pull out a chair for her. 'You're the most wonderful woman I've ever met but you still need to eat to fuel your energy.'

A languorous gleam in her gaze, Alana dealt him

a smile of anticipation, sparks of excitement dancing through her bloodstream like glitter.

As assured as ever, Ares sank down in his seat and shook out his napkin. 'I love you, Alana Sarris. I love the children you've given me. You've turned me inside out and upside down with emotion and I even love that.'

'I'm such a great influence,' Alana told him irrepressibly.

* * * * *

CROWNED FOR THE KING'S SECRET

KALI ANTHONY

MILLS & BOON

To my darling Daisy dog.

I miss your zoomies and your long, cold, wet nose
of love under my arm as I tried to write.

Run free.

PROLOGUE

ONE NIGHT. THAT was all Sandro wanted.

One night to be a man and not His Majesty Alessandro Nicolai Baldoni, Ruler in Exile of Santa Fiorina. A country he hadn't seen since the night of his uncle's midnight coup twenty-five years earlier, when life as he knew it had ended. Dragged from his parents' arms, as a weeping nine-year-old. Their last words to him had been, *'Be good, Sandro...'* and to his godparents and other faceless minders, *'Keep him safe...'*

He'd been good ever since, his conduct impeccable, making himself a small target for his enemies. Every moment trying to live up to his parents' memory, to the role he would now play in his country's future.

Tonight was for him. To be selfish and throw caution to the four winds.

Sandro sank back into the plush chair in an opulent room of a private club, the clink of glasses and the soft, ambient music washing over him. From the outside, on this dreary autumn evening, there was no hint of what lay behind the walls of the Georgian terrace located on a quiet London street. Inside was a rarefied place where people could only enter if vetted and checked till their lives were laid bare. Where money talked, but it wasn't the only language spoken here. Paupers with power and influence or in need of a safe haven could open doors in this place just as well.

For a long time he'd understood poverty, of resources and spirit.

But tonight shouldn't be for thinking about his homeland, which after so many years spent in England felt distant, unfamiliar. Even though by the end of the week it would be distant no longer. The weight of that realisation was almost too much to contemplate. He'd have returned triumphant, the rightful monarch on a throne stolen from his father, and, by extension, from him, negotiations complete to remove his pretender of a cousin from the throne he'd had no right to, other than by an illegitimate uncle's midnight coup.

Alessandro took a sip of the rich, dark red wine in a fine crystal glass. It soured on his tongue. His return was no triumph. Others had fought for the country's freedom. For his return. His name and face a figurehead for their struggles, whilst he'd been protected at all costs in a foreign land. He'd never led an uprising, or an army, against his bastard relatives. Only partly blood. Instead, the name of his family drove his people to free themselves. He may have worked in the background with relentless diplomatic and legal efforts. But others had risked their lives in his name whilst he remained protected. Safe. The realisation that he'd been complicit in this enforced cowardice sat bitter on his tongue.

No more. Those bleak thoughts had no place here.

He wanted a thrill. A chase. The risk of rejection, rather than one of the women he'd kept company with over the years who understood he could never offer them anything but his body, and who were happy with the exchange of their own. Mutual pleasure free of obligation, for a few breathless hours. Tonight, Sandro craved a flirtation where there was no certainty of an outcome. Only hope. And, living in hope, because for many years hope was all that had been left to him, he'd booked a suite here. He had a few condoms in the bedside drawer, champagne on ice and a sliver of excitement so sharp and shocking he could almost taste the coppery tang of blood as it sliced through him.

Sandro lifted his glass to take another sip of his wine, to find the glass empty. It didn't matter. Tonight he could have another. Tonight wasn't about denying himself, or maintaining control. It was about living. Yet he didn't seek intoxication in a bottle, but in the form of soft, perfumed skin and heady sighs in the arms of a woman.

One night. Glorious. Anonymous.

There were several women gracing the club tonight with bare legs, ruby lips and miraculous curves, all beautiful. Perhaps available. His gaze slid over them, snagging on a lone figure at the bar. Perched on a stool with legs crossed, black skirt riding up her thighs. The sliver of lace peeking out from under the hem hinting at stockings rather than tights. His heart thumped like a kick in the chest.

She lifted herself from the seat a touch, and shuffled the skirt back down, tugging at the hem to cover the stocking tops. He almost moaned in regret as she smoothed slender hands over the sleek fabric of her skirt. Sandro couldn't see her face, only the tumble of blonde hair down her back, looking tousled as if she'd walked through a whipping breeze to get here. She had barely any skin on display. Her white blouse was fitted but with billowing, sheer sleeves adorned with tiny black polka dots. She lifted a hand and tucked a strand of hair behind her ear. He was transfixed as she toyed with the glass in front of her, raising it to her mouth in a long, slow sip.

His own empty glass was an opening. He rose, walking over to either have the night of his life or be shot down in flames, even though when he played it was always to win. A decent put-down would be interesting in its own way. He'd never had one before, and tonight was all about new experiences. He moved in beside her and caught the briefest whisper of vanilla scent, like some delectable dessert. He desperately wanted a taste.

Alessandro looked over at her. Would have tugged at his tie if he'd been wearing one and felt strange not to be, but tonight he wasn't a monarch in waiting, he was simply a man and had attempted casual, as much as a bespoke Savile Row shirt and trousers would allow. Her face was hidden by the curtain of her hair. She hadn't acknowledged him, not yet. He'd speak first and see how the game played.

'You look like you're running dry.'

For a heart-stopping moment it was as if she ignored him and then she turned, raising one perfect eyebrow. Golden hair fell about her shoulders in soft, whimsical layers he wanted to stroke from her face, run his hands through, grip. She was arresting, rather than classically beautiful. A strong nose dominated her face but with an upturned end which gave her a cuteness. Then her eyes fixed on him, the beautiful grey-green of old stone. There was something about them, as if they'd seen too much. Eyes you could dip into, the emotion ran so deep…sad eyes. It was as if a fist reached in and clenched the heart of him.

He brushed the sensation aside.

'Perish the thought I should shrivel into a husk,' she said, her voice all glorious, rounded vowels of the aristocracy here, but hers with a raw tone as if flavoured with whiskey and smoke. A voice that spoke of sultry nights and one he wanted whispered breathless in his ear. Every part of him tightened with desire. She pulled the toothpick from her glass and toyed with it, poking at the perfectly curled lemon rind in her drink. Then she raised the rim of the glass to her shell-pink lips and drained the remains in one swallow.

Now was the time to introduce himself. He should use the name agreed upon with his security, who sat at their own table, keeping their distance. A false name, to protect him. Sandro didn't want fakery, he wanted truth. For his real name to spill from her lips at least once before tonight was over. Even better, screamed loud. He held out his hand.

'Alessandro Baldoni.'

What did it matter? In a few days he'd be gone from here, a distant memory. He'd been in England long enough for everyone to lose interest, anyway. Keeping a low profile, not filling the tabloids with his exploits. Not like his cousin, who'd seen fit to run Santa Fiorina into ruin with his excesses. Continuing what his father had begun. Sandro gritted his teeth. Later, he'd think about that task ahead of him to rebuild his country. Not tonight.

The woman placed her cool, slender hand in his. He marvelled at the touch, how it sparked through him.

'That's quite a mouthful.'

His heart stuttered for a beat, and his eyes dropped to her lips. Oh, the things he wanted her to do with that full and generous-looking mouth. Those rampant thoughts were the stuff of dreams. He cleared his throat.

'Then call me Sandro.' He hadn't been called that name since childhood. His advisors and staff used Your Majesty or Sir. The last people who'd called him by his diminutive were his parents, and for some reason he needed to hear her say it. *His* name. A man's name. Not a king's.

The corners of her lips curled into an enigmatic smile. She squeezed his fingers then slipped her hand away from his. He felt the loss as if it were something physical.

'Sandro it is.' She didn't disappoint, saying his name as

if she were tasting it. By the look on her face, the shimmering spark of silver in her cool gaze, she enjoyed the sound. 'I'm Victoria... Astill.'

The hesitation was unmistakeable, almost as though she was trying out a new name for size. Something chill pricked at the base of his spine. A warning. He'd learned to listen to those feelings. They could mean the difference between life and death. Of course, there'd been no attempts on his life since childhood. Still, he'd been forced to tolerate many things during his exile, but duplicity would never be one of them.

'Are you sure?'

He kept it light, but he needed to know what was going on. The thumb of her left hand rubbed over her ring finger. It was unadorned but even he couldn't ignore that she was toying with the place where a wedding band would have sat, as if something was missing.

'Married?' he asked.

They were both adults. She could do what she wanted and knew that people came here to escape many things, but he refused to be the vehicle for infidelity. He had cold, hard experience of what that could do. The sins of his grandfather had set Santa Fiorina into darkness for a quarter of a century. An illegitimate uncle who'd never accepted his position in the family hierarchy, below that of Alessandro's father. His ambitious wife with dreams for her son's own succession, encouraging him. Taking what they wanted with violence and bloodshed. These were the things Sandro knew. They'd been inscribed on his soul with his parents' blood since the night he'd lost them for ever.

He would never do that to any other family, even if the consequences wouldn't be so dire. Victoria, if that was her name, looked up at him, her eyes taking on that sad, distant look again. One that spoke all kinds of truths he wasn't prepared to delve into. She shook her head.

'Not any longer.'

Sandro exhaled, muscles relaxing. He hadn't known how much he wanted her to give that answer, because there was no one else here he had any interest in. She toyed with a tiny black button on her blouse. One of myriad down the front, disappearing beneath the waistline of her skirt. His eyes were drawn to her cleavage. The tracery of her lace bra under the silken fabric. All giving him mere glimpses and hints of the temptation lying beneath. He couldn't wait to undo her slowly, if she'd allow him the pleasure.

He motioned to his own glass. 'Would you like another drink?' The bartender had been watching them, leaving them alone till it was clear Sandro wanted something more. He joined them now with a professional smile.

'Same again, sir?'

Sandro nodded. The French red was a spectacular vintage and drinking now, when he had no interest, was a waste, but he doubted the woman before him would drink alone. He motioned to her. She didn't look at the man behind the bar, but at Sandro, in a way that scored right into his heart.

'Vodka martini, dirty, with a twist.'

The blood rushed straight from his brain to much, much lower in a roar of pleasure. He wanted to grab her, leave now so they could start the rest of the night together. Instead, he employed the infinite patience he'd required during his exile.

He knew from personal experience that waiting made the ending so much sweeter, and he didn't want this night to end too soon. This was an old game they played. One that thrilled him, more than tearing down a polo field at speed on horseback.

He couldn't help the corner of his mouth curling up in a slow smile of ego-driven pleasure.

'How dirty do you like it?'

She fiddled with the toothpick in her glass, brought it to her mouth and nibbled, almost as if thinking. He counted the seconds in his thumping heartbeats. Then she drew the pick from her mouth and placed it in a napkin on the countertop.

'Seven out of ten.'

The words slid through him, swift, neat and red-hot.

'I have a suite here,' he said in a voice that sounded rough and alien to his ears, as the bartender walked away to make drinks Sandro didn't give a damn about and was sure Victoria didn't want either.

'And what's in your suite?'

He leaned forward, to get closer. Caught the delectable scent of her again. Their knees brushed and the pleasure of that barest of touches shimmered through him.

'Everything we need.'

Sandro thought he heard her breath catch. Then a look came over her face and all the expression melted away till what was left was blank and fresh and unreadable. Except her eyes, those sad eyes that caught his attention and held. She nibbled on her lower lip, looked down into her lap. Hair tumbling in soft strands around her face as she smoothed her hands over her skirt again.

'That's not something I…do.'

She glanced up at him through veiled lashes, as if it was important she told him that. As if gauging his attitude in case he'd judge her. The only person he judged was himself, constantly. And now he realised that he might have overplayed his hand, forced something fragile too soon. Still, he was used to the seemingly impossible becoming reality. In a few days he was taking back the throne of Santa Fiorina, something on his darkest days he doubted he'd ever achieve.

'Neither do I,' he said.

That was the truth. Whilst he'd dallied a little at university, he'd always been too closely protected, everyone around him vetted and known. This situation was as new for him as it seemed to be for her. Victoria's eyes widened a fraction as she took in his words then she threw her head back and laughed, the sound earthy and raw. Heads turned and all the men in the place looked at her with envy, coveting the precious woman he would make his tonight if she deigned to give him more time.

'That, I don't believe,' she said, her voice containing the warmth of the smile now barely contained on her lips.

Even though exiled, Alessandro knew he'd led a privileged life. But he'd never felt more privileged than with Victoria now, these moments fresh, new and like a storm washing away the tired dust and detritus from his past years.

'Why?'

He enjoyed this, the banter. The chance that at any moment he could fail horribly tightening his gut and ratcheting the anticipation.

She waved her hand up and down in his general direction. The move seemed as regal as her royal name. 'Looking like you do.'

'And how do I look?'

'Now you're fishing for compliments.'

Their knees brushed again, the hint of that feeling an electric shock right through him. 'You still haven't answered.'

'You look…' She huffed out a breath, which fluttered her soft fringe. Revealing her gaze as she eyed him up and down, long and slow. He felt every second of that gaze on him like a touch '…like you're not real. Almost too good to be true. And in my experience, someone like that often is.'

An intensely satisfying thing, his pride, uncurled and stretched like a tiger in the sun, basking in her comment.

'I could say the same,' he said, allowing himself a slow perusal of her, taking in things he hadn't noticed before. The hint of freckles across her nose, the perfect shell of her un-pierced ear. She toyed with the buttons of her blouse again, drawing his attention to the shadow of her small, perfect cleavage. Even in the soft light the blush of pink bled up her slender neck and coloured her cheeks, almost as if his appraisal was unfamiliar.

Who wouldn't constantly tell this woman she was beautiful?

'I'm no fake.' He wanted to take her hand, place it on his chest, assure her he was all flesh and blood. He didn't.

'Aren't we all fakes, in our own way?'

Not tonight. He hoped tonight that he could be more real, truer to himself than he had been since childhood. He wanted *only* the truth. A man, a woman. Two bodies sharing pleasure together.

'You could touch me, to prove to yourself I'm real. I won't bite.'

She cocked her head, almost as if surprised. 'You'd like that, wouldn't you?'

'I think you'd like it too,' he said.

'I think I might.'

The sounds of the room faded away. It was just soft lighting and the possibility of something magic shimmering in the air. Alessandro took the chance.

'Come to my room.'

Victoria picked up the toothpick from her martini glass with its speared olive and pulled the olive from the pick delicately with her teeth. Chewing with deliberation before swallowing. So much went on behind those cool eyes of hers, as if the secrets of the universe were held there. His heart sped up in anticipation as she grabbed her clutch bag from the bar. Yes. No. He wasn't sure. A thread of uncertainty wound through him.

He'd wanted many things in his life. In this moment, he'd never wanted anything more than Victoria Astill.

'All right.'

Two simple words and anticipation flooded through him, hot like a slug of spirits. He stood, told the bartender to put the drinks on his account. His bodyguards watched with caution as he and Victoria walked out of the bar to a bank of private lifts leading only to the Royal Suite. Their instructions were clear. There'd be no interference, although by now his people had probably vetted her. Whilst privacy was everything in this club, she'd still had to place her name at the door and his security were always zealous with his safety. He was his country's future, after all. The weight of that expectation and responsibility hung heavy on him.

The gleaming, golden lift rushed them to the suite. In a few moments he'd be unlocking a door to the room and hopefully to the rest of tonight. Because tonight he could be a man.

Tomorrow, he'd revert to being King.

Victoria took a steadying breath as the lift slowed to a whispered stop and the doors opened. It didn't really help the flurry of butterflies in her belly or the thready beat of her heart which she told herself was anticipation. The man next to her stood to the side, let her pass. She caught a hint of the scent of him. Spicy, warm, like mulled wine on a winter's evening. And like mulled wine, she was sure too much of him would scramble her senses.

But wasn't that what she wanted? To lose herself and yet find herself all at the same time? Now she wasn't so sure. She'd felt so sophisticated downstairs, yet she was a woman schooled in pretending. The reality of what she'd agreed to crashed into her with each click of her perilous heels on the cream-coloured marble of the suite's entrance foyer. Her husband had never liked heels because they made her taller than him...

Enough. That man had ruled her life for five long and painful years since the marriage brokered by her parents had begun with naïve innocence on her part. She'd hoped it would bring happiness. Children. But she'd quickly realised that her wants and needs didn't matter. Her marriage hadn't been a partnership, but a dictatorship. When she'd begun asking for more, the vicious put-downs made her stop asking for anything. Then her accident, and heaven help her when she couldn't give her husband what he'd wanted on demand.

If he hadn't died in a fall from his horse, she didn't know where she'd be now.

A shiver ran through her. This evening wasn't for dwelling on her past. It was for starting her future, which she'd decided to grasp with greedy hands when she'd received the letter from the proprietors of this place on fine, embossed paper, saying she'd inherited her husband's membership should she wish to take it, with the club's compliments and condolences.

Vic wondered what tonight was about for Sandro, who claimed this was something he didn't do, when a man like him could have any woman he wanted, with his imposing height, which made her feel strangely small and safe, and his powerful build. Broad shoulders, strong biceps hinted at under the sleeves of his shirt. Thick, dark hair swept back from his high forehead. Eyes so deep and blue a person could happily drown in them…

Those butterflies in her belly began whipping about again as the door to Sandro's suite closed with a quiet snick behind her. His presence was so close goose-pimples sparkled down her spine. Her heartbeat raced. Thrilled, terrified, she couldn't be sure but she'd embrace any emotion after the numbness of her past life. Vic rubbed her thumb against the ring finger of her left hand, where her wedding ring had sat. Once a mark of ownership, all that remained now was a strange sensation of emptiness, of finally being free.

'You keep doing that,' Sandro, said, nodding to her left hand. His voice deep, warm, with the barest hint of an accent. She craved to immerse herself in the sound as if she were sinking into a freshly drawn bath. Washing herself clean of the taints of the past. Learning how to live again. 'Is it recent?'

'Yes, but I don't want to talk about it.' Her deceased husband wouldn't occupy any more of her thinking time, not when there was living to do. She'd been dead inside long enough. The corners of Sandro's full, tempting mouth tilted in the hint of an empathetic smile.

'I understand.'

Once, she would have said nothing but she refused to silence her voice any longer. Silences were liminal spaces where darkness and dreadful secrets hid. She cocked her head and met Sandro's vibrant gaze.

'You don't want to talk either.'

It wasn't a question. She knew deep in her heart that tonight was as much about running from reality for him as it was for her. His shoulders rose and fell as a long breath eased from him.

'I find that everyone has their cross to bear. It's no use comparing the wood and the nails.'

Something about that statement seemed distant, almost like a reflection. Then it was as if he shook himself out of the moment. Sandro walked to a side table and held up an empty crystal flute in long, elegant fingers. 'Would you like some champagne?'

She shook her head.

'No, I don't want to be numb.' She'd been numb for too many years already. 'I want to feel what it's like to be alive.'

'I can help you with the living,' he said. Sandro's words were weighted, like a stone dropped into a pond. He put down the champagne flute, walked towards her with a fluid gait, his long legs closing the space between them.

'I need to kiss you,' he said, his pupils wide and dark. 'Get my hands on your skin. Taste every part of you.'

His voice was rough and raw, and it lit something inside her that she'd thought long dead, now burning wild and insistent.

Desire.

'What are you waiting for?'

He cupped her jaw, the palms of his hands hot against her skin. Dropping his head till his mouth grazed across hers, her lips tingling at the touch. She melted into him as he took her slowly. Their tongues touching. The kiss slick and lush and indulgent. She slid her hands up his powerful chest, resting there. In her fantasies she could imagine his heart beating fast in his chest, matching her own. He broke the kiss for a moment.

'Do I feel real now?'

'Oh, yes. *Yes.*'

'I told you.'

He reached out his hand and swept the hair over her

shoulder with a gentle brush of his fingers against her neck. His mouth soon followed, his breath gusting warm across her tingling flesh. Slow, soft kisses that lingered. The tip of his tongue touched her skin, tasting her as he'd promised.

Where else would that tongue of his seek out before the night was over? His beautiful, full lips skimming every part of her. She needed it *all*.

Something changed then, became more insistent. She moaned as he pressed himself into her. His body so hard and uncompromising, his arousal obvious, yet his touch a gentle contrast. Slowly breaking down the bricks of a wall she had built so high, so carefully, that she wasn't sure what she'd remake of herself once this night was done.

'*Please*,' she whispered.

He swung her into his arms as if she weighed nothing. Cradled in his embrace like a bride on her wedding night. Desired, cherished, as Sandro strode through the suite to a room lit with low lights from a lamp in the corner. He carefully set her down at the end of the bed, reaching out with long, elegant fingers to slip one tiny button at the front of her blouse through a loop. Then another, and another. Was that a tremor in his fingers? She trembled herself, almost mindless with need, with a desperate emptiness that she hadn't realised she'd held on to for most of her life. One that she needed him to fill.

It was if she were burning alive. Burning for him. His nostrils flared as her blouse parted over her breasts and a rumble came from him. Deep, primal. He took her left breast in his palm. Teasing, toying with her nipple through the lace of her bra. It tightened in pleasure, the lightning shock of it spearing between her legs. Her breaths gusted out of her in short pants. She moaned.

'So beautiful. So responsive.' Sandro stepped into her

body, his lips at her neck again, murmuring against her skin. 'Close your eyes. Enjoy.'

'If I close my eyes, I'll fall.'

'I'll catch you.'

For tonight, she'd trust that he would. Victoria dropped her head back as he kissed and nipped at her neck, a free hand snaking round her body to undo the clip at the back of her skirt, slowly bringing down the zip, brushing his hand under the waistband so that the fabric slid down her legs to the ground. He cupped her backside, drew her hard against him, his arousal bold and obvious through his trousers.

'What you do to me.' His voice was thick with so much unsaid. The wonder of it. Then he stood back, his vivid blue gaze fixed on her thighs where the lace of her stocking tops encircled them. 'Perfection.'

'Careful,' she said, trying to regain some equilibrium. 'Your words might go to my head.'

'Who wouldn't tell you constantly that you're beautiful? You're a goddess who deserves to be worshipped.'

Sandro walked forward and began backing her into the bed. She stepped out of her skirt, propelled in a slow dance with him till she couldn't go any further. He slid his hands into her underwear and began slowly slipping her panties over her hips. Down, down until he was on the floor, looking up. It was an intoxicating thing because she believed him in this moment. How could she not when such a powerful man was kneeling on the carpet before her?

'I can't wait till these magnificent legs are wrapped round my waist.' She began to lift her foot from her shoe to step out of it. Sandro gently gripped her ankle and she stilled. 'No. Leave them. I want those heels digging into my back as I thrust into you.'

Her body went up in flames, insecurities forgotten. He

made her feel like an immortal with the way he treated her with such reverence.

'I seem to be at a disadvantage,' she said, her voice unlike her own. Lower, huskier. Provocative. 'I'm wearing far fewer clothes than you.'

His pupils dilated wide and dark as he shut his eyes and brought his lips to the skin of her stomach. Kissing. Inhaling her. Goose-pimples peppered her skin. He pulled back.

'You have *all* the advantages over me. Lie back and let me show you.'

Victoria smiled, the power of that statement coursing through her veins like wildfire. She turned round, wanting to be bold. Crawled up the bed on her hands and knees. Sandro's heavy exhale as she did was a reward of itself. As she reached the head of the bed she stretched out on the luxurious coverlet. Lay her head down on the plump, down pillows and rolled over onto her back, arching like a cat in the sunshine. She smiled at the hiss leaving Sandro's lips.

Sandro began unbuttoning his shirt, exposing the slice of tanned skin on his chest. Then he shrugged the fabric from his broad shoulders and her mouth dried. His body was the stuff of midnight fantasies. The defined muscles of his chest, the ripples of his abdomen, the shadows heightened in the low light of the room. His narrow waist, the curve of his biceps. She didn't know where to rest her gaze, until it snagged on the tempting vee running from his hip bones beneath the waistband of his trousers. He stood there with one eyebrow raised, an element of cockiness she couldn't help but admire because he was entitled to it.

'Like what you see?' His voice was a low rasp choked with need.

'I'd like to see more.'

He chuckled deep and low. The sound like a threat and a

promise. 'You'll have everything of me tonight, *bella*. It's all yours.'

Sandro loosened the belt of his trousers, slid it through the loops and tossed it onto the floor. Kicked off his shoes, socks. Undid the top of his waistband and pushed down his trousers and underwear.

He might have claimed she was a goddess, but naked, he was a god. Every part of him perfect. Large in a way that made her mouth water and her body soften.

'*Oh.*'

The breath rushed out of her with an audible exhale. Sandro's vivid blue gaze turned dark, like hectic storm clouds over an afternoon sky. He knelt on the bed and it dipped under his weight.

'Open your legs.' His voice was a command that she couldn't disobey. 'Now say my name.'

'*Sandro.*'

He put his hands on the bed and moved forward towards her. 'By the end of tonight I'll ensure you never forget it. I'll have you chanting it like a prayer by the time I've finished with you.'

He was so close. His lips caressed the tops of her thighs, her stomach, his breath gusting over her skin, his tongue licking and tasting her. Then lower, and lower till his breath caressed between her open legs and she moaned. His tongue gently traced her flesh as the burn built inside her, his touch light, teasing till she was writhing and panting under his ministrations. Never giving her enough to tip her over the edge.

This man would be her end, but she craved to be the end of him as well, for just tonight. And she vowed that she would be. They'd end each other and wipe their slates clean. Starting anew.

'Sandro.'

Her voice came out as a whine, a plea. She propped herself on her forearms so she could watch him, on the bed, between her legs. He looked up at her with a wicked grin. He knew what he was doing and she loved and loathed him for it. How he could play her body with such finesse.

'Goddess, lie back and let me worship you.'

He dropped his head again and she collapsed on the bed once more. This time there was no teasing—he was relentless till she broke and flew, as he turned her into the goddess he'd promised.

CHAPTER ONE

Twenty-one months later

Victoria looked down at her little boy, Nicolai, banging at a small drum with enthusiasm, and giggling as he did so. She knelt on her floor mat, leg forward, relishing the burn of a hip-flexor stretch as her son played.

Who on earth thought giving a toy like that to a one-year-old for his birthday was a great idea? She sighed. An absent father, that was who. One who didn't understand parenting at all. Though even with her own personal disappointment in Sandro, try as she might, reminders of the night Nic was conceived still intruded. The indescribable pleasure, the floating bliss. Whispered caresses in the darkness of two people she believed were trying to find themselves that night.

Even a broken condom hadn't worried her.

Why should it? She dropped onto her back, crooking her foot over her knee into a gluteal stretch, working out tightness from her long-ago injury and more recent effects of pregnancy and then childbirth on her body. After years of trying to have a baby with the man she'd married, she'd resigned herself to supposed infertility.

'I can't get pregnant.' That was what she'd told Sandro before they'd both collapsed into each other's arms, exhausted after a long night of lovemaking.

She'd been almost proud of herself when she'd left him in the bed, deeply asleep, the next morning, with only the pink imprint of a lipstick kiss on the club's notepaper and a scrawled *Thank you* as a final reminder of what they'd shared, because she didn't have the words to explain.

Pregnancy had been the last thing on her mind in those heady weeks afterwards when she remembered the evening as the chance she took on life and on herself when she'd spent so many years trapped in the iron cage of her marriage.

She hadn't thought much when her period didn't come because it was notoriously irregular. Until she became sick with what she though was a stomach bug and her doctor gave her a gentle suggestion, and a pregnancy test. She'd laughed in disbelief and joy. The pregnancy was an unexpected blessing. There had never been any question she'd tell Sandro—what need was there to hide it? And when in excitement and some trepidation she'd searched his name on the internet she'd found…

A *king*.

Vic hadn't known what she'd expected when she first contacted the palace with the news. Though deep in her heart she'd hated that she'd hoped, hoped for some contact from Sandro. Another glimpse in real life of the man who'd changed her for ever, for the better.

Even now, her heart skipped a few beats thinking about him, the way his gaze had pierced her soul, the way his touch undid her, then stitched her back together. It had been like some miracle. Until a palace envoy insisted that all future contact go through him. She must make no attempts to contact *His Majesty*, ever again. Monthly reports were to be provided about the child, which would be given to the King for his perusal. In exchange, Nicolai would be supported financially, with her in control of his future. This was put to her as the only choice if she wanted to maintain any connection to Sandro and Santa Fiorina, for the sake of her baby.

So she took it.

It was the offer of money that made her feel strangely grubby. She didn't need it. Whilst her husband's family estate went to the new earl, she'd inherited most of the rest, so was comfortable. Anything Nic's father deigned to give her was locked away in an account, untouched. Her son could decide what to do with it when he was old enough.

She moved into a plank. Her core was still not as strong as it had used to be before her pregnancy, and she needed that strength if she was to stay relatively pain-free. She didn't want to end up in physical therapy again or, even worse, craving the strong painkillers that had once ruled her life after her injury. Not now she had so much to live for. Her muscles trembled as Vic counted down the seconds she held, with every one of Nic's drumbeats.

Her little boy wanted for nothing. She'd made sure he had all the love and care she'd missed out on as a child. It didn't really matter that his father didn't want to see him. Her own brother, Lance, had transformed himself from London's wildest billionaire to the UK's finest uncle, through marriage to his beloved Sara. If Nic ever needed a male role model, her brother was perfect. If Sandro didn't want to know his son, even on his birthday, then that was his loss.

How her life had changed. She smiled. People might have thought once that things were perfect for her, when she'd been married to an earl, went to glamorous parties. Socialised. All the beautiful clothes and trappings that hid the cracks of a person breaking apart. It had all been fakery. This was glorious, messy reality.

Nic continued banging away at the infernal drum, his

favourite birthday gift. Except now the drumbeats became irregular, fractious, and he dropped his drumsticks. She finished her exercises then crawled towards her tired little boy. He smiled, loving when she got down on the floor with him.

'Come on, darling. Time for your nap.' She stood, then swept him into her arms as he protested, twisting, crying, and reaching for the drum. 'Even birthday boys need their sleep.'

As she held him in her arms she rocked from side to side, taking the chance to do a few final stretches. She hadn't been as vigilant as usual recently and her back and hips would give her trouble if she didn't keep up. She accepted she'd never really be the same even four years after the accident, when one of her rescue horses spooked whilst she was in its stall. The pregnancy had been hard on her too. She was only now getting back to normal.

Nic's head dropped to her shoulder as she rocked him and held him tight.

'Let's get you some milk, Little Prince,' she said as she went to the kitchen and warmed Nic's bottle, then took him to his room.

The nickname was closer to reality than she'd initially liked. In her and her solicitor's research about Santa Fiorina they'd discovered something unusual for a monarchy, that there, illegitimacy wasn't necessarily a bar to succession. All a king or queen needed to do was to acknowledge their illegitimate child and that child could theoretically take the crown. She'd held her breath for months when she'd discovered that quirk of succession, until Sandro's minion arrived on her doorstep with his employer's demands and an assurance that no formal acknowledgement would come. She had full custody, parental responsibility and decision-making rights, although she'd ensured in their agreement that Sandro could visit whenever he wanted. Whilst he hadn't yet, she'd left the door open.

She'd never deny Nic's father access to his child.

Vic placed Nicci in his cot and waited a few moments whilst he settled, snuggling into his blanket, eyelids drooping. Her heart did a funny little twist, the way it always did when she looked at him, with his shock of large, dark curls and eyes slightly paler than his father's, a curious mix of his and hers. Her joy, her miracle. Vic smiled as she left the room, closing the door gently behind her and going back to the lounge, hoping he'd sleep for a while. She had a grant application to write for the charity she supported for women escaping domestic violence.

Vic sat and opened her laptop, working through the complicated forms to get funding for a much-needed service— caring for women's pets when they fled the family home. As she knew so well, what to do with their animals and fears for any pets left behind was often a huge barrier to women leaving. This grant and her other fundraising efforts could help. Her passion for the project made the words flow easily.

The soft chime of her doorbell cut through her peace. She wanted to ignore it, and not have to deal with the person on her doorstep, but if whoever was there woke Nic right now there'd be hell to pay. Vic hopped up and checked the video feed on the baby monitor. Still asleep. The doorbell rang again, and he stirred a little.

'Coming, coming…' she said a little too loudly as she approached, yanking the door open with a whoosh.

Her heart did something similar.

Standing on the step was the man who had interfered with too many of her dreams and fantasies of their night together, even after he'd sent a palace representative to her door with the offers of money and a cold, yet silent, acceptance of the birth. She'd been disappointed for Nic's sake, but she was horrified at the realisation she'd been disappointed for herself too, because she'd wanted to see him again, with a craving that itched and pricked at her. Still, she was sensible enough to recognise that her feelings weren't reciprocated. If they had been, he had the perfect excuse to visit and rekindle what they'd shared…

In the end, Sandro Baldoni was like most men, a disappointment. But, as Lance said, it was far easier not to have a king in your child's life. And that this cold arrangement was better for her and his nephew.

Now Vic realised the wisdom of Lance's words.

'*Victoria.*'

That voice. Soft, deep, a low rasp. A voice that had haunted her dreams. After all this time she hadn't expected to see him again and yet here he was, dressed unlike a king in casual trousers and an open-necked shirt. Although the trousers were obviously tailored to his powerful form, and the shirt was bespoke. She'd lived around fine tailoring enough to be able to tell.

Today he wore sunglasses. She was thankful for that. On their night together she'd believed he could peer right into her soul and she'd enjoyed the sensation of being…*known*, far too much. But what if he took off his sunglasses right now? Vic gripped onto the doorjamb lest she fall, or flee into the house, locking the door behind her, because this man was a risk to her equilibrium…

No.

She wasn't that person any more. She'd hidden before, smothering her sorrows and her physical and emotional pain in prescription medication and an uncaring façade that had hurt herself, and the people she'd loved. She wasn't doing that now. Fight, not flight.

'What are you doing here?'

The corner of his perfect mouth kicked up in the barest of movements at her less than welcoming greeting, though what did he expect? Still, a traitorous whisper of warmth slid through her. That mouth of his had been a revelation, exploring her body in every way. Soft, coaxing. Hard and relentless. He'd given it all to her and she'd craved more. She'd never wanted it to end.

Enough.

'I came to see my… Nicolai. For his birthday.'

She loathed the hesitation in Sandro's voice. The chill. The complete lack of acknowledgement of Nic's place as Sandro's son, whilst accepting it all the same.

In the months after the custody arrangements had been finalised, she'd welcomed the lack of that formal acknowledgement from Sandro. All she'd wanted for Nic from the moment of his birth was a happy, normal life not weighed down by expectation that she knew the aristocracy, and most certainly royalty, carried with them. Her brother had suffered enough and by extension her, and he'd been a duke. She could only imagine the pressures on a king and his heir. And selfishly, she didn't want anything taking Nic away from her. She also didn't want him dragged back to a country once torn apart by a civil war in which Sandro had lost his parents and a country he had been exiled from for years.

Even now that knowledge had made her heart break a little, for the boy this man had once been. Who'd lost everything. As a mother she simply couldn't imagine it. Learning about her son's father and the man with whom she'd spent one blissful night had been a shock and a revelation. What he'd survived, what he'd achieved. But even with the catastrophic loss of his parents, he hadn't wanted to know his own son, share his heritage with his little boy. She'd been responsible for all of that, for trying to ensure that even as an infant Nic knew who his father was, and what his country looked like. She'd never understood Sandro's reluctance, but then, she accepted after her disastrous marriage that she'd never much understood men at all.

'Nic's sleeping right now, but thank you for the gift.'

'The gift…'

He probably had no idea what had been purchased. He'd have staff to buy presents for his illegitimate child. She should be thankful that he'd arranged for anything to be purchased at all, though she knew gifts didn't mean that people cared.

Two people seemed to melt from behind Sandro, a man and a woman, casually dressed although wearing jackets even on this warm summer's day. There was nothing casual about their demeanour, the way they scanned the street. They murmured something in what sounded like Italian, Santa Fiorina's official language. She tried to peer around Sandro's impressive form to get a better look at them.

'Please excuse my personal protection,' he said, his voice a little more accented than when she had first met him. 'May I come in?'

An uncomfortable sensation pricked at the back of her neck. The male security operative smiled at her as the female continued monitoring the street. They loomed rather than seemed intimidating, yet why did she feel the electric sensation of a threat? Of course. She had a *king* on her doorstep. Nothing about this situation was normal. She gripped the door harder. Sandro smiled at her too, with not the warm, seductive smile of a night that seemed so long ago, but something sharper, more brittle.

She supposed you didn't keep royalty standing on the doorstep, even if they had arrived unexpectedly.

'Of course.'

Vic stepped aside as Sandro came through. The whole entrance hall seemed to shrink in his presence. His height, his breadth. Once, his size had made her feel small and safe. Now, it was as if the air had been sucked from the space. His security detail followed, and she shut the door behind them. Why did she feel trapped all of a sudden?

The man spoke this time. More Italian. She'd been trying to learn for Nicci, in case one day he wanted to travel to Santa Fiorina. Mr Falconi, the palace representative who seemed to be a constant and unnecessary visitor, had offered to teach her, but that man's presence made her skin prickle uncomfortably. The way he looked at her. The personal disclosures, like telling her he hadn't been able to have children of his own, as if that was somehow meant to bring them closer, when he was an intermediary and could never be the man she still wanted in a visceral kind of way. So she'd politely declined his assistance and stuck with phone apps instead.

'My apologies,' Sandro said, bringing her back to the reality pressing down on her. 'My security would like to look through your house. They're zealous about my safety.'

Sandro removed his sunglasses, her breath hitching at the way his vivid blue gaze caught her. How many times had she recollected his heated looks, his eyes the colour of balmy summer days? Their shared passion? Now there was no heat. Only something like the open ocean. Cold, remote, unfathomable.

She could say no. This was *her* home, somewhere warm and welcoming she'd set up, away from the inner city. A place to quell the vicious memories that still plagued her at times. Where she could make a simple life for her and Nic, do her charity work. Try to make a small difference.

But she understood, Sandro wasn't a normal man as much as she'd liked to pretend that he had been. She'd wanted to ask why—why that one night, why her? But she supposed the answer didn't really matter when there were so many other questions that were more important.

Such as why he wanted nothing to do with his son when he'd lost so much himself.

Vic turned to the woman. 'You can look through the house and garden, just don't go into the room upstairs with the closed door. That's Nic's and he's sleeping.'

She nodded, and disappeared into the house with her colleague, leaving Vic and Sandro awkwardly alone with the hallstand, umbrellas and coats. He raised one strong, dark eyebrow in an imperious kind of way.

'Would you like to come through?' she asked, wondering where her manners had gone. He nodded as she led the way to her lounge. The sensation of him close behind, tingling between her shoulder blades. 'I can offer you tea, coffee, water...'

'No...thank you.'

Everything about their conversation seemed like an afterthought, as if he was waiting for something. She wasn't sure what. She motioned to the sofa but he remained standing, looking about the room.

To Sandro, the space probably seemed like a mess. To her, the room was warm, comfortable. Lived-in. A home. Yoga mat on the floor, toys scattered about. Laptop open on the coffee table. Scrapbooks she'd made about Santa Fiorina, words in Italian. Others might have seen her efforts as a waste when she could buy perfectly good picture books, but it was fun adding her own drawings and writing. Trying to connect herself to her son's heritage, as much as connecting him to the man she'd always wanted Nic to know was his father. She wouldn't keep secrets from her son; that was where pain lay.

She tugged at her T-shirt and her cheeks heated a little. Acutely aware that she stood here looking all too under-dressed compared to Sandro's casual, assured elegance, she didn't know now what he'd ever seen in her when he approached her at the bar. But what did it matter? That was well in the past. Her life was focused on the present. Her son, her charity work. That was all she could control.

The security guards returned, murmured something to Sandro and left them alone. Seemingly taking up a station in the entrance hall.

'You can take a seat if you like,' she said to Sandro, but he stood resolutely at the centre of the room, as if the universe should spin around him. She supposed in his own country, it did. That didn't mean she had to jump to his tune. As it was, she was running on empty. Nic's teething made him unsettled, waking him some nights as many times as a newborn.

'Well, this is a surprise. Has your son finally reached the top of your royal to-do list?' she asked. Sure, it was Nic's birthday, but after the twenty-one months of silence, something about this seemed strange. Perhaps it was just surreal to have a king standing in her home, but there was more, a brittleness about him. A wariness that had no place here.

Sandro's hands clenched then flexed. His jaw was tight, everything about him on high alert. She didn't understand why. It wasn't as if he was walking into the enemy's den here. She'd been open with Sandro about seeing Nic any time he wanted, because it was the right thing to do.

'My life has been full of surprises of late. Now was the right time to come.'

That comment rankled, as if she had nothing better to

do than sit around and wait for him to arrive. 'It might not be the right time for me.'

Sandro's eyes narrowed and something about that look pinned her to the spot, like a rabbit being eyed by a fox. 'You think I shouldn't be here.'

Interesting that it was a statement, not a question.

'I have a life.'

Sandro cocked his head, looked about the space. At the wrapping paper that Nic had enjoyed playing with left on the floor, the toys. Was he judging her, when being a mother had been her *sole* priority? Was that why he was here? In a moment of weakness Vic had told the palace representative about Nic's teething, how tired she'd been, and he'd suggested a nanny. Was Sandro looking at the place and questioning her ability to care for her own child? She gritted her teeth. Not here, not now, not ever. 'And you're in my house. I don't need to work to the whims of someone who's dropped in unannounced. Maybe you can come back another day? When Nic's awake.'

Sandro ran his hand over his face, pulled it back, and it was as if he was a changed man. The brittleness went the way ice melted away in spring. His gaze became smokier, more intense. More like it had been on a single night an age ago when she became totally wrapped up in him and believed he'd become totally wrapped up in her too. He still had that hold over her, but she knew what it was: desire. A chemical thing that wasn't rooted in any kind of reality.

'I can't come back tomorrow. I'm leaving…tonight. This isn't going how I planned.'

Her heart rate kicked up a few beats. 'How had you planned it?'

'I've spent over a year reclaiming my country. Now there

are things which are important and have been left for too long.'

Sandro walked round the room, almost as if he couldn't stand still any longer. He stopped at a bookshelf adorned with photos. Of Nic, Lance and Sara on their wedding day with her in the wedding party, smiling and happy for them yet not happy in herself. A picture of Sandro she'd taken from the internet, putting it in a decorative frame with *Daddy* written on it. Some people might think it a strange addition, but she'd been determined to ensure Nic always knew who his father was.

To her shame, she'd never been able to forget the man.

'That's…me,' he said, his voice strangely quiet, almost shocked.

'Nic needed to know his father.'

It had been her wish when she first signed those custody papers, and hated that the desire might have been more for her own benefit than her son's.

'He seems important to you.'

'What kind of bizarre statement is that?' she said. Only important? Nic was everything to her. 'He's my *son*.'

Through the monitor Nic snuffled. Victoria checked the video feed. He rolled over and began to stir.

'He's my son too.'

Her breath hitched. As if that was any answer when the world was full of deadbeat dads. She wanted to say so. To say if he really cared he would have been there from the beginning.

'There's more to it than simply providing the genetic material.'

'As I'm painfully aware,' he replied, almost through clenched teeth, as if there was a world of hurt he was holding in.

She supposed there was. Her research had turned up a terrible family history but still, that was no excuse. Her history was no rose garden either. As he'd said to her that night, *'Everyone has their cross to bear...'*

'Which is why I have a special gift for him.'

Sandro's words dragged her out of recollecting an evening which should have been relegated firmly to the past.

'Isn't that enough?' Vic nodded to the drum kit on the floor which she was sure would be the bane of her existence for the next few months till Nic bored of it.

Sandro frowned. Right. Further proof, if she needed it, that he hadn't cared enough to choose a gift himself. She sighed. 'Okay. What gift are you planning to give him?'

'It's a...surprise.'

'I'm his mother; there are no surprises for him at this age. Why couldn't you bring it here?'

'Security reasons. It's the greatest gift that I can physically bestow on him for now.'

Something chilled in her blood. What could a king possibly bestow on his child? An important gift, a *great* gift. 'Are you officially acknowledging him?'

That would mean Nic was his heir, would mean that maybe Sandro would try to take him away from her.

'Would you like that?' His voice was soft, almost expectant. Somehow all the more deadly for it.

Except, why would he need security for something like that? And they had a custody agreement. It was unambiguous, official, through the courts. She knew all about the Hague Convention, to which Santa Fiorina was a signatory. Her solicitors had told her that as well. Still, she narrowed her eyes, tried to give him her most frosty glare. She was no pushover, not any more, and royalty had a knack of getting their own way, irrespective of international conventions and legal documents. She needed to remind him of what they'd agreed.

'You should well know the answer to that question.'

He turned his back on her, shrugged. 'I'd like you to join me at my hotel for the afternoon.'

In the video feed Nic rolled over again. She willed him to stay asleep, then Sandro might simply *go* for now. Till she could stitch herself back up, somehow make herself immune to him.

'Maybe if you came another time.'

'It's difficult for me to leave my country at this delicate stage.'

Mr Falconi had said as much when she'd confronted him over why Sandro didn't want to see his son. Why reports and photographs were not enough.

'Things are precarious in Santa Fiorina.'

He'd also mumbled something about public knowledge of an illegitimate child making the situation worse should news come out. Perhaps that was true. She'd never lived anywhere pulled from the brink of civil war before, and didn't want anything she did tipping someone's homeland into war again.

'Perhaps we could have afternoon tea?' Sandro continued. 'Spend some time together before I fly out? My chauffeur can drive us. Then he'll return you home.'

'You have a car seat?'

He smiled, and that smile was warm and lit up the whole room. 'Yes. I was hoping you'd join me and we could talk about Nic on the way.'

Tempting. *Too* tempting. She couldn't help remembering that other night, where they'd made love, ordered room service, feasted on each other. That drizzle of awareness, that desire. It hadn't gone. A horrible sense of rightness settled over her, seeing this imposing man in her now humble home. She tried to shake it off. Kings didn't just turn up on your doorstep bestowing gifts, they made appointments and involved lawyers. This was unexpected. She didn't much like surprises.

'Where are you staying?'

'Why?'

Vic took a deep breath. 'If I'm to go with you I'd like to know where that is and to confirm you're booked there.'

'Of course,' he said, sounding sincere enough. But the corner of his mouth kicked up in a smirk that seemed almost…knowing. He mentioned the name of a boutique London hotel, a place well known to be frequented by royalty and celebrities. 'I'll be happy to call them for you, so you can confirm with the manager.'

He took his mobile and appeared to look into his contacts, rang a number.

'Mr Arnold…' She heard the murmur of a voice on the other end. Sandro looked at her. 'My stay has been perfect… Yes. I'm considering having a visitor to my suite this afternoon. She'd like confirmation of a few details…'

He handed the mobile to her, warm from his hand. What could she say? *I don't trust His Majesty, so can you please confirm he's booked to stay with you?* That might be the truth, but she'd never admit it publicly because her fear gave him power over her.

'Hello, this is Victoria Astill.'

'Lady Victoria,' the man said. She'd met the manager only once before, in what she considered to be her old life. One she'd left behind. It was strange to hear her honorific being used again. That time seemed so distant now, but her brother was the Duke of Bedmore and still notorious. Not for his antics any more, but for the grand love story with his beautiful wife. 'How may I help you?'

She had to make up something that sounded plausible.

'As His Majesty told you, I'm thinking of visiting this afternoon for a meal and of bringing my son, who's one year old... I'm assuming you're able to cater for him?'

'Of course...' the manager said. They discussed whether Nic had any allergies, likes, dislikes. At least she could be assured Sandro was telling her the truth. She thanked the manager and hung up.

'I hope his answers were to your satisfaction.'

'Yes, but I still—'

A cry sounded from the monitor. Nicci was sitting up in his cot, tugging at his ears. Poor little man. His teeth might be the end of her. Sandro looked to the monitor as well, then at her. She'd run out of options, for now at least.

'I'll just go and get him—wait here.'

She walked to Nic's room, her heart pounding. She was terrified at the thought of Sandro meeting him, as if it would steal something of her son from her. But that wasn't fair to Nic. She'd never deprive him of the father who now seemed to want to get to know him, even if she remained unsure of travelling to central London. The dread of what a surprise might mean, although who knew? He might simply be wanting to give Nic a pony, or maybe even some kind of heirloom, like a...a...crown. She laughed in a mildly hysterical way at that as she opened the door.

'Hello, little man, are your teeth giving you trouble?'

Nic sat there, tugging at his ear with one hand, other thumb in his mouth. Vic lifted him up and he snuggled into her arms. She gave him an extra-long hug, burying her nose into his hair and kissing him on his head.

'Come and meet your daddy.'

The words sat strangely on her tongue now that Sandro was in the house, as if the reality of it all carried such weight. Victoria checked his nappy, which was still dry, and clutched him tight as she walked down the stairs to her lounge, where Sandro stood, flicking through the scrapbooks on the table next to her laptop.

As she entered the room he wheeled around. Walked up to her slowly, eyes wide, as if he almost couldn't believe what he was seeing. Nic turned his head, and she whispered to him, 'That's your daddy, darling.'

'He looks like I did as a child. I only ever had one photograph of myself.' Sandro's tanned skin looked paler. His Adam's apple rose and fell in a swallow. She wondered what it would be like to see herself truly reflected in her child, because the minute Nic had been born she'd known she would be reminded of his father for ever. Every day, looking at her son was a vivid reminder of the man standing before her right now.

'You gave him my middle name, my father's name.' Sandro might have been speaking to her, but he didn't look anywhere bar at Nic. Fixed on the little boy in her arms. 'For that I should thank you.'

The words sounded bitter on his tongue. Perhaps it was self-recrimination for staying away so long—she couldn't tell. When she'd proposed the name her palace contact tried to dissuade her, suggesting other names that didn't resonate. Deep in her heart she knew the name she'd chosen was right. She'd read about Sandro's father in the research she could find. He sounded like a good man, and what better way to connect her son to the countries of both his father and mother than name him after two fine men? The paternal grandfather his people seemed to love, and the maternal uncle who'd remade himself into a loving husband and philanthropist.

So, Nicolai Lance he had become.

She should offer Sandro the opportunity to hold him, but she didn't want to relinquish her little boy to anybody. Not yet. The silence then was heavy. Almost as if something momentous was about to occur. Nicci lifted his head from her shoulder to look at the man she had no doubt he would someday grow to look just like, watching Sandro with his big grey-blue eyes. She knew her resolve weakened as she witnessed this silent meeting. Sandro looked as if he'd seen a ghost, the myriad emotions flickering across his face real and impossible to hide. He was affected. This was a child he wanted to know. So why had he stayed away?

Then Nic reached out his little hand, spreading his chubby fingers. Opening and closing it as if he was trying to grasp something just out of reach.

'Da!'

And Victoria knew from that moment that her life had changed for ever.

CHAPTER TWO

SANDRO DIDN'T KNOW who to look at, his son, or the woman who'd become his downfall in so many ways. The one he'd craved, the memories of a perfect night overtaking him in quiet moments, his moments of weakness. So much so that when his secret trip to the UK to negotiate better security and trade ties was being arranged, he'd held illicit fantasies about meeting up with her again for one more night, to see if they could rekindle a few moments of magic before he went back to the brutal reality of what it was to rule a broken country.

In that moment of weakness, he'd asked his head of security to find her. To ascertain whether she remained single, whether she might welcome his getting in touch.

What they'd found was his own personal nightmare. The words *'Your Majesty, we have a problem...'* were still ringing loud in his head. She'd had a child. There were reports that his deposed cousin was a regular visitor to her home, that she'd been receiving money. Then the birth certificate, naming him as the father... Could it be true, or was it an elaborate ruse? He'd been filled with cold dread at what another illegitimate child could mean for his country, especially one in the power of his cousin and a scheming woman. Santa Fiorina had been almost destroyed by another illegitimate member of his family and a wife so ambitious, she'd been an accomplice to terrible violence.

It was Sandro's obligation never to allow that to happen again.

He'd promised himself as a young man that he would never revisit the sins of his grandfather, leading the country into destruction. A pretender and his wife murdering his family and stealing the throne. Then there'd been *her*. A broken condom. His acceptance of a woman looking at him with her sad eyes, telling him not to worry, that she couldn't fall pregnant.

Lies, all lies.

The burn of bile rose to his throat. In that moment, in that suite in a private club he hadn't visited since, his past had been forgotten, as had his future. All he'd wanted was a moment to be Sandro, not King Alessandro Nicolai Baldoni. He and Victoria had crashed into each other, destroying themselves on the jagged rocks of their passion. Nothing had mattered to him, caught in the maelstrom of it all. For that night, he'd never wanted to escape.

It had been a profound disappointment to wake in the morning to find her gone, with only a note and a kiss in lipstick left for him.

Thank you.

He'd held on to those thanks for nearly nineteen months before he'd heard the news. That he had a child who'd been hidden from him. From that moment on, his security team had worked tirelessly to strip Victoria's life bare, finding payments to her from an offshore account. Likely money stolen from Santa Fiorina's treasury by his cousin before his exile. They had begun putting together a retrieval plan for the child who may not be his, but who Sandro would *never* allow to fall into the evil clutches of his bastard relative, to be used as some puppet in a game Sandro was sure was some effort to regain the throne.

'*Da!*'

It was a repeat of what he'd said only moments earlier, but was more strident now. Nicolai's eyes were wide and blue, his plump little arm outstretched, grasping for something…or someone.

Him.

'What's he saying?' Sandro asked, his throat closing over at the emotion of seeing a child he knew even without DNA testing was his. A clone of the one photo of himself he had as a little boy. One of the only photographs his godparents had saved the night they fled in the darkness.

Victoria took a step forward, then hesitated. Looking up at him because, whilst he'd remembered her as being tall in heels, without them he still dwarfed her. Her skin pale and waxy. Wearing an old T-shirt that moulded her upper body. Black leggings encasing her legs leaving little to the imagination. Yet there was a fragility about her, until he looked at her eyes and all he saw there was tigress, a resolve that he was tasked with breaking today. He'd promised his security he would do it, before more expeditious methods were used to reach their ultimate aims, assuring his team that he could still influence her, not knowing why he retained that almost unshakeable belief, when recent events showed he really understood nothing of her at all.

The heat rose in him then, sliding through his veins, all temptation, till it was replaced by something sharper, harder. A blazing fury at the indefinable something this woman still held over him. Yet he couldn't allow that fury to overtake him. He was required to be pleasant, bland. Acting a part that had been planned from the moment they'd uncovered Nic's existence.

'That's his word for Daddy.'

It was as if something cracked inside him. His cold, dead heart broke then was stitched together again with a bright thread, golden and new. From this moment on, he'd be changed for ever. He knew one day he'd be required to marry, have children to protect his line, the line of Nicolai Baldoni, true King of Santa Fiorina. It had all seemed cold and academic. There was nothing academic about this. To hell with the DNA test; this child was his. Conceived when he'd been told it was impossible.

Nicolai leaned in his mother's arms towards him. Still grasping at the air. He didn't know what to do. The plans of the day were all frozen by his paralysis in the face of this. So much bigger, more affecting than he'd ever expected.

'Would you like to hold him?' Victoria's voice was quiet, rough. He might have thought it clogged with emotion, but he didn't trust this obvious schemer and any crocodile tears she might shed. He nodded and Victoria held the little boy out. He came into Sandro's arms easily.

Nic regarded him, son to father. Raising his hands and patting Sandro's cheeks, testing to see whether he was real. To Sandro he was lighter than expected. Solid, less…breakable than Sandro knew humans could be. Whatever might come next, Sandro silently vowed to protect him from any person who'd use this child for their own aims.

'Happy birthday, *il mio piccolo principe*,' he murmured. He wanted to take him now, leave, ensure he was safe.

'I call him Little Prince too. That's what it means, doesn't it?'

He turned his attention to Victoria. Those sad eyes back again, the ones that had captured him from the first moment she'd turned them on him. Yet she held a gentle smile on her face.

'Yes. It's what my father used to call me.'

He didn't know why that memory assailed him then or even why he told her, but ever since he'd been given the news of Nic's existence, memories of his own long-lost family had returned with a vengeance.

Her shoulders seemed to soften. 'If we're going to go to your hotel for a meal, I suppose we should get moving.'

He nodded as relief flooded over him. Soon Nicolai would be safe. Then he'd deal with his son's duplicitous mother. Except as he looked at Victoria, he realised she didn't seem like the villain in this saga, simply a woman who was tired. The whole tableau here—the room full of toys scattered in a haphazard way, her, him—seemed so *ordinary* he could have laughed had he not known what was at stake.

'I'll just need to get dressed. Give me Nic and we'll get ready.'

He didn't want to relinquish his child, not even for a moment. His grip tightened. 'I can hold him.'

Victoria glanced to the door which led to the front hall, where his security stood, waiting for his orders.

'I'm sorry, I—I'm not leaving him with strangers. And he'll need a nappy change.'

Sandro wanted to shout at her. *Who made my son a stranger to me?* But didn't. This morning was all about patience and he had infinite amounts. He'd waited twenty-five years to take the throne of his country—what was another half an hour in the scheme of things?

So long as Nic was safe.

The boy went to his mother easily, as Sandro reluctantly handed him over, missing the weight of him in his arms. Nic snuggled into her neck. At least his son appeared to love his mother. He recalled his own parents. Their love had been a constant beacon. Memories of being taught how to ride, of laughter. Until the memories intruded of a tear-stained, dark night when he'd lost everything. He shut those thoughts down. That time in his life had passed. Here, now, was all he had.

His whole body rebelled as Victoria left to do what she needed, taking Nic away from him. It would *never* happen again. Sandro's security entered the room, ever-present. He knew they'd been listening. Everything about today had been carefully choreographed.

'Your Majesty.'

'Any threats?'

'None so far. Though we need to move quickly. As we discussed, there are more efficient ways to carry out this exercise.'

He well knew what they meant. Today had been planned down to the last minute, the only variable being what happened in this house, and they'd made very clear what *efficient* meant: a forced extraction rather than this. Something about him had rebelled at the suggestion because to do that to a woman and child would be terrifying. Whilst he considered Victoria with certain enmity, he was no monster.

'As you can see, there's no need. Her mobile and computer are here with us. You advised she had no landline. What's she going to do? I assumed you have the perimeter monitored?'

They nodded. Their job had been to secure the house and the street. He'd promised he could get Victoria to come in the car with him, and, whilst he'd played his hand poorly in the beginning, the shock of seeing himself in Nicolai, of seeing *her* again, overwhelming, he was on track again.

He hadn't known what to expect from her. A fight? More shock, even some fear? Yet in the end all his presence had seemed to garner was weary acceptance. Strange, given the circumstances, yet he didn't have time to dwell on it. Not yet. He pinched the bridge of his nose, a familiar pressure building behind his eyes. Sandro tried to will and hope away the headache he feared was to come, a brutal reminder of the car accident almost a year earlier that his security now believed was a hastily planned assassination attempt.

His cousin Gregorio, The Pretender, as his people had called him, hadn't let go of the throne as he'd promised to. Nic was simply another part in what appeared to be his plan to regain it. Sandro would never allow him to succeed. His father had never had the measure of his half-brother, who overthrew them in the midnight coup. Sandro wouldn't make the same mistake.

A voice sounded from a monitor on the coffee table. Soft, lilting. He moved to the screen. Victoria held Nic, chatting to him in her light, laughing voice. The whole of him tightened as she moved around the room, in and out of the frame of the monitor's camera. Speaking with her son as she readied him, changing his clothes, his nappy. Grabbing who knew what and putting it into a bag, not ceasing her narration to Nic about what she was doing.

'Your daddy says he has a present for you. Let's go and see what it is. I hope it's better than a set of drums, but that's your favourite thing so far, isn't it?'

The drums? She'd mentioned them before. He had no idea what she was talking about. Something else to catalogue for later, when he had time.

She slung a large bag over her arm, and picked up Nic.

'Let's go, Nicci.'

His security moved to the front hall once more, leaving him alone. A few moments later, Victoria swept into the room with Nic perched on her hip and his breath seized. She'd changed into jeans, some soft blouse in swirling blues that reflected the colour of her eyes. Her hair up in a messy style, a slick of gloss on her lips. Her cheeks pink as if she'd been hurrying. She looked vivacious, beautiful, and he loathed how his body reacted to her in a way that was totally out of his control.

'I just need to turn off my laptop,' she said, more to herself than anything. She placed Nic on the floor, where he crawled to a set of drums and began banging away, each beat of that drum jolting through Sandro like some timer. He stiffened as she moved to her computer. Yet all she did was close out of some screens, shutting it down as she'd promised, before grabbing her phone and a smallish book from the table, dropping them into the front pocket of her oversized bag.

'Okay, I'm ready. W-would you like to carry Nic out?'

He smiled as he picked up his little boy, the first almost genuine smile he'd given since he'd walked into this house and had to pretend not to rage. He led her outside to a car that he knew had only just sped into place. Everything was going to plan, finally. *Finally*. Then Nic was buckled into the recently installed child seat between himself and Victoria, she handed Nicolai a toy he began chewing on vigorously, and it was almost over.

Half an hour or so, given traffic, and they'd be done. On the way to Santa Fiorina.

Safe.

As they moved off and began to drive away a security vehicle pulled out in front of the car and he knew another would pull in behind. He still had a job to do, a role to play, but for now he sat back, closed his eyes for a second. The pressure in his head began to ease.

'Is everything all right?'

Her voice was gentle, kind. It caught him by surprise. He opened his eyes, looked at her. 'Yes. It's been a busy few months.'

What he thought would be a secret trip to the country

that had supported him, and which he'd called home whilst in exile, had morphed into a retrieval mission.

'I suppose being a king in your circumstances would be. I can't imagine.' She looked out of the window. 'I thought we'd be going the other way...'

'There appear to have been some roadworks. My security doesn't want me stopped in traffic.'

Keep her talking had been their only suggestion once they got her into the car, and he was good at small talk. Sometimes that was all you had to work with as a king.

'I'd assume having a young child would be a busy role too.'

Vic took her eyes from the road, back to Nic, her gaze morphing into something warm. A look of love, if he'd been asked. He questioned whether anyone who would throw their hat in with his cousin had the capacity for the emotion. Though perhaps she'd been fooled. Except the money... no. She'd been complicit. He hardened his thoughts against her once more.

'It is. Exhausting, challenging. Incredible. There's never any switching off, but it's all I've ever wanted.'

'No nanny?'

She frowned. 'I didn't want to subcontract parenting to anyone. I have my brother and sister-in-law and they love Nic. There's a university student who comes to help at times if I'm working. But no nanny. I'm surprised you didn't know that.'

He didn't understand—what should he know? He'd only found out about his child recently. Nic threw his toy on the floor of the car and Victoria picked it up, gave it back to him. He threw it down again. She rustled in the bag next to her and pulled out something, unwrapped it and handed it to Nic.

'Do you want a rusk, darling?'

His son grabbed what she handed him and began chewing. She looked out of the window again. He didn't want her to realise they were going in the opposite direction to London. Whilst any histrionics would be contained now they were in the vehicle, he'd prefer none. Not yet, anyway.

'Has he been a…a good baby?'

He'd never been around children; he didn't know what to ask. Victoria raised her eyebrows. Sighed.

'So you haven't read the reports. What a surprise. *Fine*. He's teething now and that hurts him, so it's lots of restless nights and exhausting. As a newborn he was always happy. Smiling. Though the witching hour in the early evening was horrible and he'd cry and cry, plus he had a bit of colic, but as for the rest of the time he was an angel.'

Sandro didn't know what the witching hour was and all he knew of colic was from his horses, so it sounded painful and dangerous. A cold chill ran through him at the thought of this child in pain. Of how much he'd missed because of this woman.

'The traffic's bad this afternoon and Nic isn't usually good in cars.'

He needed to get her talking. He didn't want her focused on the outside of the car, but on the inside.

'Milestones?' He'd been told this was important, and frustratingly, whilst his secret service could find out a great deal about Victoria, Nic remained a mystery.

Victoria frowned again, such a disapproving look. As though he'd in some way mortally failed her.

'All normal. I kept a book of them if you'd like to actually read something about your child when we get back home… Though I suppose you won't be joining us.'

He was interested in that book, but a tiny stab of guilt pricked at him. The dark rings under her eyes, the slightly worn look to her, as if she needed to put her head down and sleep. Obvious tiredness that wasn't hidden by the touch of make-up she'd put on. He didn't know why that worried him so much. Why her health meant anything to him at all.

'How was the pregnancy and the rest? I hope it was easy.'

She looked at him. Her eyes cool, like granite. 'You *really* want to know?'

All he was trying to do was continue the small talk. But secretly, he did want to know. He nodded.

'A little morning sickness. I was tired all the time for the first three months. They say the second trimester is the best but it wasn't for me, and the third was hell. I had a lot of pain. Moving about was difficult. Things are still… *Anyway*…'

The *anyway* seemed to carry so much weight. A heaviness he had trouble comprehending. Nic continued chewing on the hard stick of bread. Making a mess. He held it out to Sandro.

'Da!'

'I called my father Papa,' he said. That thought came out of nowhere. A burn stung at the back of his nose. He breathed through it. The memories distant, as if he were seeing everything through mist. Only snatches. Occasional weekends in the country. A pet rabbit on his sixth birthday. So much he'd missed with his parents…

All those tender, soft memories and feelings had no place in his life. Not any more. They made you weak, prevented you from doing what you had to do. He'd already missed a year of Nic's life. He'd lose no more. He had a responsibility to his son and would think only of that. Of the boy he needed to protect with his considerable powers as a king. Nothing else.

'You are sure you're okay?'

There was that concern for his welfare again. He didn't know why she kept asking him. Part of him softened, warmed. Began to question…

No.

He knew how deadly a woman could be. His aunt had been co-conspirator in his parents' deaths. Some claimed, an active participant. The evidence against Victoria was incontrovertible. His son, who'd been hidden from him. His cousin's visits to her. The money going into her account. There was nothing more he needed to know. He refused to mull on the prickling doubt.

'Yes, why wouldn't I be?'

'You lost your parents young, Sandro. I—I well know how having a child can bring a lot of things to the surface.'

How he had come to be exiled was well known. Had she looked him up, it was all there on the internet. Given who she was involved with, he was surprised she'd mention it.

'That's in the past.'

'Trust me when I say, it's really not.'

They were close to the private airport now. By special arrangement they'd been allowed to drive straight onto the tarmac. Talk of threats to his life in the right ears meant that it had been arranged seamlessly. England had been home for so long, its ties to Santa Fiorina were strong ones. The advantages of power and money were on display today. Soon his son would be away from any risk, whatever evil scheme his cousin had concocted thwarted.

'Venti minuti.'

His head of security. Twenty minutes. A narrow window to get onto the waiting private jet and leave here.

Victoria looked out of the window as the airport came into view.

'Where are we?'

An error. Since they'd left her home, he'd tried to keep her focus on him and Nic. He shouldn't have been thinking about himself and his past when he had a job to do here; he should have kept her talking. She'd know now that they weren't anywhere near a hotel in London. Although it was better than expected. His security had thought it would take far less time for her to realise things were not as they seemed. He didn't answer because it didn't matter. The course was inevitable; there would be no deviation.

'Sandro?'

He turned to glare at her. There was no need to hide his feelings now. They were allowed to be on full display.

'It's *Your Majesty.*'

Her eyes widened, then she paled. The glow she'd had in her home before they'd left drained away. He knew that look. *Fear.*

In other circumstances he might have felt guilty. Not today. She'd kept his son from him, linked up with the man whose parents had murdered his family. Yet she didn't stay fearful for long. One deep breath later and Victoria straightened her spine, narrowed her eyes.

If looks could kill, he'd have expired in the back seat. Nothing could have saved him.

'Not. Bloody. Likely. Where the hell are we?'

The entourage slowed on a bitumen road, some gates opening to let them through.

'I would have thought it self-evident. We're at an airport.'

Sandro's voice was as cold and brittle as fresh ice over a pond. Stupid, stupid, stupid. How could she have allowed this to happen? Because she'd believed in him. Because she'd hoped that he'd wanted to see their son. And perhaps, deep in her heart, she'd wanted to trust him. To share the joy of their little boy, the miracle that they'd made together. Then when Nic had reached out, recognised his father, wanted to go to him... She was always going to get in this car. Even on the journey, the questions which she should have been suspicious of, given she'd been supplying his envoy written reports of Nic's progress, the feigned interest…she'd soaked it up like the little fool she'd always been. She should have known she meant nothing to Sandro. That night she'd never been able to forget clearly not memorable for him. Now he'd come to…what? Take her little boy away?

Never.

If only she could call someone. They hadn't taken her phone. Lance. He was a duke, he had contacts. She grabbed it from her bag, yet there was no signal. She tried to call. Nothing.

'My phone. It's not working,' she whispered, more to herself than anyone else.

'No.'

One simple word from Sandro and she knew it had been deliberately disabled somehow. Then the real fear began to seep in, cold and choking. She could barely breathe but she had to try to hold it together for Nic, because she was the only one who could protect him now, and hopefully save herself at the same time.

'Why are we at an airport?'

She wasn't a foolish woman, but she wanted to hear him *say* it. To admit what he was doing. There was a jet sitting on the tarmac. A flurry of activity. People she presumed were security getting out of the SUV in front. She turned, and there were more behind in their own identical vehicle. The door on Sandro's side opened for him.

'We're leaving for Santa Fiorina,' he said, and got out of the car. She hurled her own door open and got out as well, leaving it open because it was a warm day, and she wasn't removing Nic from the child seat.

Victoria stalked around the back of the car towards him.

He stood talking to one of the many men in black suits surrounding them and she knew she only had one choice. For most of her life she'd been meek, taking what life had thrown her. Now she had a child to protect and she'd decided the day he'd been placed damp and squalling in her arms that there would *never* be a time she'd be silent and simply take it, ever again.

'No,' she said, perhaps too quietly. Sandro and the rest of the people ignored her. She wouldn't be ignored, not now.

'What if I *refuse*?'

One of his security team leaned in to him. '*Quindici minuti.*'

It sounded like a countdown. If she could just keep the plane on the tarmac maybe they'd miss their window… Sandro looked at her, blank and unrecognisable.

'That would be inadvisable but, no matter what you decide for yourself, Nicolai will be coming with me.'

'You can't.'

'As you see, I can and I will. He's been kept from me long enough.'

'Kept from you?' His arrogance and entitlement astonished her. 'You've had no personal interest in your child throughout my pregnancy or for the first twelve months of his life other than receiving reports you haven't even read. Now you think you have the right to just take him?'

Sandro's eyes narrowed, and he seemed to hesitate. 'It's a compelling act, but an act none the less.'

'Had I refused to come with you in the car this afternoon…' if Nic hadn't reached out to this man and said *Da*, meaning she wouldn't deny her son getting to know his father '…what would you have done?'

'Every contingency was planned for.'

The clinical way he spoke almost froze her to the spot. All

that conversation was to keep her occupied so she wouldn't notice what they were doing. Bile rose, burning in her throat. The incontrovertible fact was that she'd wanted more from Sandro. The sad little girl who had never been loved, studiously ignored for the most part by her own father, desperately wanting Nic's father to give him the attention she'd craved as a child, so he didn't always wonder what he'd done wrong, as she had.

'*Dieci minuti.*'

'I speak with my brother most days. He might not be a king but he's friends with one and he'll be looking for me.'

'As of this moment your brother's been informed that you're planning to take a brief holiday with Nicolai on my royal yacht in the Mediterranean.'

Her mouth went dry; no words would come. The planning this would have involved… This was no whim…

Sandro turned away from her and leaned into the back of the car. Was he going to unclip Nic from his seat? No. He wouldn't touch Nicolai ever again. She grabbed Sandro's arm. Immovable. As strong and muscled as she remembered.

'You will not touch my son,' she hissed.

The crowd of men in dark suits collectively stilled, then stiffened. Her sense of threat ratcheted up. There was complete silence, only the warm breeze over the tarmac giving her any sense that the earth hadn't stopped turning. A few of Sandro's security moved forward. He held up his free hand and they stilled.

Sandro turned and stared at her hand gripping his arm. 'You have no friends here.'

She released him.

'I'll fight you to the death to protect Nic! Can you say the same?'

'Yes.'

That word again. Chilling and calm. In the back seat, Nic let out a wail.

'Get out of my way,' she spat.

Without thinking she pushed past Sandro and leaned in, unclipping Nic's harness. He'd have heard raised voices. Having lived a life with no conflict, only love, he'd be scared. She'd failed him in every way. He came into her arms, crying. She wrapped her own around him, rubbing his back as he buried his head in her neck.

'It's okay, Nicci. It's okay.'

It wasn't. She knew she had no chance here. They could take Nic and be gone and she'd be simply…left.

'*Cinque minuti.*'

'Are you happy with what you've done?' she said.

Sandro seemed to grow in stature. At her home he'd seemed large but it was as if he'd been holding something in, something back. Making himself…less. Not now. She couldn't help seeing how tall he was, how broad. How he had her under his total control, and always had had.

He tore his phone from his pocket.

'What *I've* done? Look. *Look* at this.'

He thrust the screen to her face and it contained what appeared to be a grainy photo in black and white she had trouble understanding. Were those piles of crumpled clothes? Then there were pools of dark behind. Something a bit charred. Was that…an arm? Then it dawned on her. That grainy picture looked like a crime scene. Nausea twisted in her gut as saliva flooded her mouth. She swallowed it down.

'My God, what is that?'

She didn't understand any of this. It was too horrifying to contemplate. She held Nic tighter and he squirmed. Was Sandro…threatening her? What sort of man would keep photographs like that on his phone?

'This is what was left of my parents. My father's half-brother did that to them when he stole the throne in a midnight coup.'

'Why are you showing me that photograph? Why do you have it?'

Her words sounded faint to her own ears. Sandro slipped his phone back into his pocket. The people in black on the tarmac kept their distance, some moving to the plane, others getting things from the car. For the first time in a long time, she felt inconsequential.

Sandro's jaw clenched, his mouth a hard and brutal line.

'It's a reminder, whenever I forget what my uncle and cousin are capable of. Do you think that he won't do the same to you? You brought his attention to Nic. Every time he visited your home, he was likely scheming how to get rid of you and use my son to return to the throne. You may have thought to gain money and power by contacting him, but if you don't get on this plane there's no place safe for you and Nicolai. You'll be seen as an impediment to be disposed of. My son will be a pawn in his sick game for ever.'

Her head spun. She gripped the car door to steady herself. The only representative ever to come into her home was the one from the palace. Wasn't he? She didn't know what Sandro was talking about, but Nic and her in danger? She'd thought the danger was here. Now it seemed as if it was everywhere.

'I—I don't understand.'

'It's simple, Victoria. I'm your only chance of survival.' He fixed her with his cold, hard gaze. 'You should have done better research before getting into bed with a murderer.'

CHAPTER THREE

SANDRO PINCHED THE bridge of his nose as their entourage made their way through the halls of the palace. He'd downed painkillers on the plane, and they were barely holding back the headache he knew was to come could he not find a few hours of peace in a dark room. At least there had been silence on the journey here. As he'd expected after his show-and-tell on the tarmac, Victoria had boarded the private jet in quiet mutiny. He hadn't wanted to show her that photograph, so deeply painful and private as it was. Yet it'd achieved its aim. Keeping Nic safe.

Victoria followed them now, as silent as she had been on the plane. Still holding his son, as she'd done during their trip. Narrating their journey with fake excitement to keep him calm during take-off. Rocking him to sleep in her arms in the back seats. If he hadn't known who she was and what she'd done to hide his son from him, it would have made a beautiful scene. Like Madonna and child. Yet she was no innocent here.

They arrived at the suite Security had chosen for her, one of the few they'd made habitable after what had been done to the palace during the twenty-five years of his uncle's and cousin's reigns. In the areas they'd resided they had replaced the palace's most well-loved treasures with their own idea of what it meant to be king. All gold and gaudiness. Turning the castle from what had been a seat of power, a work-place and a home into a bordello that would take years and money he doubted the country could afford to repair.

'This is where you'll reside,' he said, opening the door. She walked inside the large space, seeming to be dwarfed by it as she wrapped herself around Nic, who looked around wide-eyed. In this imposing room it was as if she was some-how weighed down by it all. A sensation prickled uncomfortably in his chest. Sandro rubbed it away.

'There's some clothing in the wardrobe,' Sandro went on. Photographs of her taken by Security in their surveillance had been enough for a personal shopper to put something practical together quickly, given it was a mystery request from the palace.

Victoria said nothing, just turned in a slow circle, the smallest of frowns on her face.

'A nursery is through that door.' He pointed but she didn't look. He wanted some reaction. Outrage, anger. He didn't know why he found the lack of it troubling, just as he couldn't understand why he'd found her fury on the tarmac so satisfying. Then she fixed her eyes on him, and they were the colour of stone chips, sharp and hard.

'I'd like to speak with you about this farcical situation.'

'I'm listening.'

Though he knew what she'd say. She wanted to go back to England. Whilst she might speak, he'd do nothing she requested. She was here, and she needed to get used to it. Unless she wanted to leave his son and fend for herself.

He looked at Nic, snuggled into her arms, sucking his thumb. So peaceful. *Happy.* As much as he loathed it, his child needed her.

Victoria nodded to his security detail. 'Alone.'

'They're interested in my safety.'

'They didn't seem to be at my *home* when they left you alone with me. Of course, what was I going to do, run you through with a child's drumstick? And what am I going to do now? Brain you with a box of rusks?' Her gaze narrowed as she looked right at his head. 'Tempting as that might be right at this minute.'

'I'm sure my personal protection could list any number of risks to my safety from you.'

Though perhaps not his equilibrium, however much he'd never admit that to anyone. She still affected him. No matter what she'd done, his reaction was the same. Heat. Need. Wrapped up with his anger at her duplicity, it was an explosive mix. Like nitric acid and glycerine.

'Fine.'

A dangerous word, to be sure, said with venom. She bent over with a sharp gasp. Hesitated for a moment then placed Nic on the floor. He sat there, blinking at everyone standing around him. She took a book from her bag and opened it to a page with a picture of animals cut out and pasted in, and hand-inked lettering spelling the animals' names in Italian, then English. Similar to other books he'd flicked through on her coffee table, it looked handmade. Had she done that for Nicolai? Like the photo he'd seen of himself, in the blue frame with the word 'Daddy' in bright colours, he didn't understand it.

'Look at the *leone*, Nicci. You love lions.'

She straightened and arched her back in a stretch. Seemed to wince, before turning on him.

'You've accused me of things, and I don't know why.'

He snorted. She couldn't possibly deny what they knew.

'What, Sandro? I gave you everything that was asked for, which admittedly wasn't much. You showed no interest—'

He slashed his hand through the air. 'You kept him from me.'

The words were said calmly, because Nic was sitting on the floor and he didn't want to make his child afraid, or worse, to cry again. His tears had scored deep wounds to Sandro's heart. Still, Victoria took a step back and he immediately regretted the show of emotion. He didn't want to terrify anyone, unless that fear kept them safe from his enemies.

'I called the palace.'

Sandro took a deep breath, reining himself in. 'There is no record—'

'You, you...*ignoramus,*' she hissed.

'What did you call me?'

Behind him someone coughed, which might have been mistaken for a laugh had he been convinced that none of his staff would laugh *at* him. Still, it was better they did not witness her attempts at his excoriation, no matter how calm each of them pretended to be. He asked Security to leave and they filed out. They'd be waiting outside the closed door should they be required.

'Oh, so you don't want your staff hearing this? Afraid they'll hear the truth? I called you what you *are*. Try and deny it to justify what you've done, holding me prisoner—'

'You're not a prisoner here.'

Not exactly. She was...*contained.* For that, he held not a shred of guilt.

She shook her head. 'I might not be in a jail cell, but you know exactly what you've done.'

The pressure in his head returned, began to increase. He pinched his nose.

'What I've done? You're being paid by my cousin.'

'I receive payments for child maintenance, from *you*. Which I put into an account for Nic to decide what he wants to do with when he's older. You need to listen to me.' She spoke slowly, as if he might not understand what she was trying to say. As if he was truly the ignoramus she claimed him to be. 'I called the palace when I discovered I was pregnant. A man came and arranged for a DNA sample. When it proved Nic's paternity, my solicitors and yours negotiated a parenting and custody agreement. Part of that agreement dictated I wasn't allowed direct contact with you. I provided monthly reports.'

He hesitated. Victoria looked him in the eye, her posture open, as if she was being truthful. But what she said was impossible. Of course, she might simply be a fine actress...

'There has never been an agreement negotiated with me. The first I knew of a son was two months ago, when I was advised of his existence.'

She stood silhouetted against the windows, the light from them overly bright. He wished she'd move but she stood as if frozen. Her mouth dropped open.

'That's a lie.'

As the light from outside scoured his eyeballs, he manoeuvred till the wall was her backdrop instead. She tracked every move as Nic sat babbling on the floor, looking through his picture book, opened now at another picture Sandro recognised. The castle, bedecked with flags and garlands celebrating Santa Fiorina's national day. The first national day after he'd returned to his throne. A moment of triumph till an accident had almost ruined everything.

'I'm not the one telling lies,' he said, pinching the bridge of his nose. He needed to go. Since the accident, or what they now expected was an assassination attempt, his life had been one of careful control and routine to keep the post-concussion migraines at bay.

Nothing about this situation with Victoria was careful or controlled.

'I need a working phone, or I need a computer.'

'Why?' he asked. 'To seek Gregorio's help? This conversation is taking us nowhere. I need to leave, and you need to accept the situation in which you find yourself.'

'I don't know who Gregorio is. You think I don't have evidence of everything I'm talking about? I'll give it to you, but I need access to technology to do that. I also have to know what's happening because none of this is clear. You're saying my life, Nic's life, is at risk. I need some clarity, because right now, our biggest risk seems to be you.'

It had been forty-eight hours since she'd arrived in Santa Fiorina, speeding through the city from the airport in an armoured car. Staring out at the beauty of the vineyards and golden countryside she'd seen in photographs of the place as she'd researched for Nic, then onto the pockmarked desolation of a place scarred by civil war. It was such a contrast. Now she was a prisoner. Oh, sure, she'd been assured she wasn't, but when she opened the door to her suite to see if she could make up a bottle for Nic there'd been two burly men outside. She'd tried talking to them but they didn't talk back, so she didn't go any further, calling on a phone she'd been told only carried an internal line to ask for some hot water.

It had been a humiliation. She was entirely reliant on that one phone for everything, not even having her own clothes, but a walk-in wardrobe full of new items which miraculously fitted. As though the people here knew everything about her, right down to her bra size, when she didn't know anything about them.

Her only visitor had been a doctor who said he was taking Nic's DNA for a test. She didn't understand that at all. Wasn't one DNA test enough in her son's lifetime? And since their arrival, Sandro hadn't even visited the son he professed so strongly had been kept from him.

That told her all she needed to know about him. He only pretended to care.

Victoria yawned, exhaustion bearing down on her. Last night, after a magnificent pasta dinner she barely ate and a thoughtfully prepared smaller serving with vegetables for Nic, she'd tried to sleep. It had been near impossible, the anxiety she'd thought she'd put behind her returning with ferocity, guilt riding her hard that she'd failed her little boy.

Nic had picked up on her emotions, was unsettled as well. Fearful he might be spirited away from her during the night, she'd tucked him into her bed and he'd fallen asleep as she stared at him, allowing tears to fall before collapsing into a fitful slumber herself.

This morning, she'd waited on Sandro. He'd stalked out those few days before, taking the name and contact details of her solicitor, and hadn't returned. Victoria guessed, it still being the weekend, that her lawyers wouldn't be in the office, but she expected *something* from Sandro at least. Not this fretful silence. She loathed feeling powerless. It reminded her of those dark days in her marriage where there was nothing within her control. Sandro's refusal to believe her when she was telling the truth felt a lot like all the times Bruce alleged she was imagining things, such as when she'd confronted him about the women she'd suspected he was seeing. The way he'd gaslit her daily. Those thoughts creeping back now, crushing and oppressive.

In this suite, everything weighed on her. The atmosphere, dour and depressing, amplifying the negative feelings she thought she'd left behind with her marriage. Vic had loved the home she'd made with Nic. Had she been allowed to train and get a job, interior design was what she'd have chosen. Making a space warm, comforting. One that invited you in and made you want to stay in, not leave. So unlike this, where she itched to get out, even to the uncertainty of what was beyond these four walls. She looked around. Heavy mahogany furniture in some places, dainty items in others, which didn't fit. The whole placed mismatched, as if it had been cobbled together as an afterthought.

Except Nic's room. It was an explosion of colour and light. Books, toys, top-of-the-line nursery furniture. Everything perfect for the son of a king. Of course, she knew then. The afterthought in this place was *her*. Unwanted, unneeded.

No.

Nic needed her. He always would.

She went into the nursery where Nicci had been catching up on some sleep. He stood at the head of his cot, trying to reach the animals on the cot mobile. When he saw her he smiled, and she bit her lip to stop herself falling into floods of tears again. Did Lance believe the fiction she was on Sandro's yacht? That they'd miraculously reconciled? Or was he suspicious of the story, and using his considerable resources to find her? She knew she'd been a constant worry to him whilst she was married, especially after her accident. During those dark days when she'd tried to numb the world and in the course of that was cruel to those she loved who'd tried to stop her. His constant worry had almost ended his engagement with Sara…

Enough.

She wasn't that person any more. The one who didn't fight back. With therapy and time, she'd found her voice. Her courage. She'd find it again. Except at home, she had people who supported her. Loved her. Here, she had no one.

Apart from Nic.

She picked him up and the gnawing referred pain in her side from her old back injury plagued her. Too much stress, not enough of her stretches. Yet another thing to worry about. After changing him, she carried Nic to the window and looked outside onto a walled garden. Rambling and wild with gravel paths, it looked like a beautiful place to visit. She craved to get outside, breathe the fresh air. Sit in the sun and allow herself to feel hopeful again. Movement caught her eye. A flicker in the undergrowth, then out onto one pathway tumbled one kitten, then another.

'Look, Nicci,' she whispered. Part of what had kept her going during the bleak years of her marriage were the animals she'd fostered. Of course, she'd only realised much later that they'd been a trap. One of the things keeping her there because she'd feared for their safety. She missed it, but she'd soon come to realise the only baby she could care for was her own, so she'd worked with charities instead. Still, watching the kittens brought back memories of her small triumphs.

Nic squealed and she smiled. Maybe they could go into the garden and feed the little ones? She couldn't see the mother, but they looked happy. At least from a distance. She stared at the joyous frolicking, lost in it all, when a knock jolted her back to the present. Would it be Sandro with some news? Maybe he'd end this charade and she and Nic could go home?

She moved through to the sitting room as a woman walked in, having been allowed through by Security. Tall. Short, dark hair. Wearing weathered jeans and a T-shirt, with toned, muscular arms. She was free of make-up. Naturally beautiful. She smiled and, although that smile seemed genuine, Vic had the sense this woman wasn't someone you'd toy with.

'Signora Astill.' The woman walked forward, holding out her hand. Vic took it, the handshake firm and strong. 'My name is Isadora Fiorelli.'

'And who are you?'

'I am Nicolai's nanny.'

Her replacement.

No. Way.

The inertia that had seemed to be overtaking her was burned away in an instant. She saw this for what it was, another attempt to sideline her. To show that she wasn't necessary to her own son. Never again.

'I don't need a nanny.'

'His Majesty—'

'Can say whatever he wants to. Look around.' She swept her arm wide, indicating the room. 'It's not as if I'm socialising or spending my days at tea parties. This suite is the sum total of my existence.'

The woman might have looked sympathetic. The thoughtful expression, the understanding nod. 'And yet, I have my instructions. I'm here to help.'

'Can you get me on the first flight home?'

Stoic silence. Victoria was sick to the brim with it. Reminding her of all those times Bruce had pretended to listen, to be sympathetic. Undermining her sense of self, her confidence. She wanted to *scream* at everyone's condescension and yet she had Nic on her hip, and every shred of the emotion that wanted to spill out she had to turn inwards. It simply rioted around inside her instead.

'Right. Well, if *His Majesty* was going to employ a nanny, I'd expect it to be discussed with me, given I'm the *mother*. Since he seems to have missed that step, let's do it now. Where is he?'

She'd test the theory that she wasn't a prisoner here. She stormed up to the door of the suite and flung it open.

'Do you want to go and visit Daddy, darling?' she said to Nic in an excited voice. They'd both been dragged here because Sandro seemed to have finally found some kind of fatherly feelings, no matter what he said about risk and danger.

'Da!'

That was as good an encouragement as any from her son.

'Right, let's go!'

She bounced him on her hip, absorbing the ache of her muscles as he giggled. The security detail outside her room simply looked at her in their noncommittal kind of way as she stepped outside.

'Where's His Majesty?' she asked them. 'We need to talk.'

They said nothing, and her heart rate picked up. She took a deep breath. Time to be brave and step into the void.

'Well, I'm going to find him.'

She began to walk, with the security detail and Isadora trailing behind. In truth she had no real idea how she was going to locate Sandro, but she had some inkling of the way they'd come through long halls when she'd first entered the palace.

'Isadora?' she said.

The woman moved beside her, stride long and confident. More like the security guards than a nanny. 'Yes, Lady Astill?'

'Oh, none of that. I'm sure Sandro meant us to be *great* friends. Please call me Victoria. You said you were here to help, so help with something I'm sure you can answer. Where is he?'

Isadora glanced sideways at the men who followed along in this ridiculous entourage.

'If you don't tell me, I'll start calling out for him like I'm looking for some lost puppy. Trust me when I say that there is *nothing* beneath me right now. If I'm to be treated like an errant child instead of an adult, then I'm happy to start acting like one. I'm sure it'll entertain Nic no end seeing his mummy being silly.'

The woman stared at her with assessing brown eyes, as if she was coming to some decision. 'I believe, Victoria, that His Majesty is in his office.'

A win. Small, but she'd take it. Vic gave Isadora a smile. Her first true smile in days. Isadora returned it, though her smile might have been wry and resigned, rather than truly happy.

'Well, then,' she said, to herself more than anyone else. 'Let's go.'

CHAPTER FOUR

SANDRO'S ADVISERS ARGUED amongst themselves. He'd assembled seven of his most trusted confidants for this meeting, as around Victoria he recognised that he had little perspective. She claimed not to know what was going on, yet the cold, hard evidence sat in a dossier in the top drawer of his desk. Could there be something in what she said? He didn't know, though the doubts began creeping in. Whispers that she was an innocent in all this. That he'd made a mistake. He shut them down.

When similar whispers had come to his father's ears about his half-brother, Sandro's godparents and guardians told him his father had ignored them. Accepted denials that the man and his wife were plotting to take the throne. Anyone involved with that blighted branch of his family needed to be treated with scepticism. So he sat back, silent, absorbing the conversations about how to solve the problem that was Victoria Astill.

'Pay her off. She can leave the child here and go.'

'Money isn't the issue. She has enough of her own to keep her comfortably wealthy for life.'

'Then what does she want? Power?'

'He could have promised her marriage, the throne as consort to a regent. It's not like she entirely lacks respectability. She's the daughter of a duke, the sister of a duke, the widow of an earl. Her pedigree is good, and she was bred for the role.'

Sandro stilled. Something about those comments caused a revolt deep inside. 'Lady Astill is *not* one of my polo ponies whose breeding is vital.'

He didn't know why he took such offence. It was as if some instinct deep inside shouted that Victoria was more than that. So much more.

'With the greatest of respect, sir, in matters of royalty, everything is about bloodlines and breeding.'

Had she been promised a marriage to his cousin? He didn't understand why the roar of incandescent rage began to build inside him. No, that pretender would *never* get his hands on her. Anyway, she professed not to know who Gregorio was, even though the man visited her home on a regular basis. His security had been keeping track of him before Sandro's visit to the UK. They hadn't put together Victoria's importance until he'd asked them to find her...

'She says she doesn't know him,' he said. 'Security is still looking into her claims that she contacted the palace. She's given us the name of her solicitors.'

What if she wasn't lying? He'd driven his people hard to get answers. The frustration built that he still didn't have them. Until then, they hadn't wanted to return her phone or allow her anywhere near a computer. He pinched his nose, the pressure of all the unknowns building behind his eyes.

'Occam's razor.'

Another of his advisers. The newest, perhaps the most shrewd and insightful.

Sandro turned to him. 'Your meaning?'

'The simplest answer to a question is often the correct answer.'

That statement began another round of discussion

amongst the assembled team that he barely paid attention to, fixed as he was on those words. What was the simplest answer to all of this?

Outside there were raised voices. Some kind of commotion. He stiffened. Someone pushed the door open.

Victoria. Nic on her hip. Security detail behind her. The only way she could have found his office was to be directed here. She glared at him, a vicious, entirely fake smile on her face. There was no pretence with her, not today.

She was magnificent. Full of fire. Fury. As ferocious as a mother lion. Standing there in casual clothes. Cargo pants. A simple T-shirt. Hair piled on her head in a messy bun. Why did she look more enticing than if she'd been wearing a revealing evening dress? His heart thumped hard, every part of him running hot and rich. The way she affected him was pure, undiluted chemistry. Inexplicable and intoxicating.

She gave a quick and disdainful curtsey, delivered with all the disrespect he was certain she meant.

'I'd like a word.'

'Of course.' He then addressed his staff. 'We'll continue this discussion later.'

Victoria moved aside as they left the room, some smiling at Nic, others stony-faced. He motioned to one of the many seats in front of him and she sat down with a slight wince.

'Are you all right?' he asked. 'You seem in pain.'

Her eyes widened, a slight flush bleeding over her cheeks as if she was surprised and pleased someone might have asked after her welfare.

'Old injury. Not been doing my stretches. But I'm not here to talk about me.' Her gaze hardened and he knew his concern was being dismissed.

'You engaged a nanny without talking to me first. How dare you?'

Her tone sounded bland enough, falsely polite, no doubt given Nic's presence, but he knew the words were tossed at him like daggers. He needed her to understand.

'It's in everyone's interests—'

'Don't give me that. I know what it's like to be sidelined. Your interests and mine don't align. Do you seriously want your child cared for by a stranger?'

Nic sat on her lap and sucked his thumb, blinking at him with his huge blue eyes. So much time he'd missed. Time he'd never get back.

'That's what has happened for twelve months.'

Her mouth tightened. 'I'm not a stranger, I'm his mother. I feel like you're blaming me for an old and well-worn story. Two people attracted to each other spend a night together, and contraception fails. Well, I wasn't the one who handed you a condom that had been sitting in a wallet for who knows how long, after we ran out. That isn't my fault.'

'You said you couldn't fall pregnant.'

Those sad eyes of hers, looking up at him from a dishevelled bed when she told him. He'd believed her.

'Not that it's any of your business, but I'd tried for years. Every time, I failed. I was told I was probably infertile, and it almost crushed me. You want to see my medical records along with everything else? Go right ahead. But I'll never regret Nic, ever. If you do, then I don't want you to have anything to do with either of us, because you don't deserve him.'

'That's not what I said.'

She shook her head. 'It's like I'm in an alternate universe. You talk to me as if I should know things when I don't. Have you been in touch with my solicitors? Your aide organised—'

'He's not my aide!' Sandro refused to allow any link between himself and Gregorio to go unchallenged. 'The man who you've been speaking to regularly, from whom we believe you've been receiving payments through a complicated series of companies and trusts, is my cousin Gregorio. The pretender to the throne of Santa Fiorina. Whose father murdered my parents in a coup.'

He was standing now, glaring down at her. He couldn't even remember getting up from his seat.

She paled, white as the paper on his desk. Had she not been sitting down he would have helped her to a chair. Nic looked up at him, blinking. Sandro took a deep breath to calm himself. Whatever might be going on between him and Victoria, Nicolai would never suffer for it.

'No. His name was Guido Falconi. He said he was your representative. He had a letter from your office saying he was acting for you.'

So she claimed, but he knew all about lies. As much as he desired to, he still didn't have it in his heart to believe her when so much was at stake. He wouldn't be the first man taken in by a beautiful and accomplished actor.

'I'm sure he was most convincing.' He wasn't so sure at all. 'However, we know who we saw during surveillance.'

The knowledge of that man anywhere round his son was a bad thing.

'You were watching me… That's how you found out about Nic?'

How could he admit that he'd wanted to see her again? Revisit their night together? That would be a weakness he could never share.

'Gregorio made certain promises on leaving the country. My security needed to ensure they were being kept, given I was visiting the UK. You were incidental.'

Lies. She'd always been the main game. A look washed

across her face, a fleeting burst of something that seemed a lot like hurt.

'Nice to know where I stand,' she murmured.

He wished he could have taken the words back. In his role as King there was no room for doubt. The wounds of his country were deep and needed strength to heal. With Victoria, all he did was doubt himself.

'As for Isadora,' she said, 'Nic needs *me*, he doesn't need someone else to look after him. Especially someone I don't know.'

'Dora is an aunt to six, and part of my personal protection team. I've trusted her with my life on more than one occasion and I trust her with Nic's.'

Victoria's eyes widened, the stone-grey turning dark and troubled as if she needed reassuring.

'I promise you can also trust her with yours. She knows the importance of looking after the mother of my child. It might also allow you some time to do your stretches.'

Her eyes seemed to become a little glassy and overbright. She ran her hand through Nic's curls. Nodded.

In a litany of recent failings, he took it as a win.

CHAPTER FIVE

'COME ON, NIC, let's go and see if we can feed the kittens. Remember how we say it? *Gattini*.'

Victoria reached down and picked Nicci up, grabbing a bag with some toys and a little packet of cooked chicken. She'd made friends with the kitchen staff a few days earlier after an introduction from Isadora. Vic had hated simply calling down for warm water so she could make up some formula, or when she felt like having a snack. The first time she met them, she took Nic with her and they'd all crowded around her son, smiling, loading him with attention. Today they'd asked her to promise to bring Nic back for a visit.

She left her suite, asking Security for directions to the walled garden. One led the way, another followed till they reached a door which opened onto a cloister with carved columns, leading to the gardens beyond. They stayed in the shade because she'd told them she didn't want them scaring the kittens away.

The air brushed her skin. Warm, and scented with the fragrance of flowers and herbs. The space was ramshackle and overgrown, looking like an unkempt kitchen garden with citrus trees and undergrowth intermingled. Butterflies flitted lazily from one bloom to another. It was as if she could finally breathe again, being here, being outside in nature. She took a gravel path through the tangle of plants and found a bench under a gnarled olive tree, where she and Nic sat, waiting.

She'd known that mid-morning was the time she'd most often spied the cat family. She tossed a few pieces of meat in front of them as an encouragement whilst Nic played with a toy beside her.

It didn't take long.

She caught flashes and a rustling in the undergrowth but she guessed the smell of cooked chicken was too much of a temptation. From under a fat basil bush sneaked a tiny calico kitten. It looked at her then crept forward and ate some of the meat. Soon, another three kittens followed.

'Oh, you little darlings,' she whispered. Nic giggled and the kittens stilled, but Victoria tossed more meat to them, and hunger overtook their fear. She wondered how they got in, though the walls around the garden seemed to be crumbling in places. Plenty of room for a cat to get through, and safe enough from predators, she supposed.

As she sat, the mother began creeping through the undergrowth.

'Hello,' she whispered, and she threw her some food.

She reminded Vic of the stable cats she'd tried to tame as a child. Sitting for hours till she could feed them by hand, stroke them. Never understanding why her parents let them run wild, uncared for.

They're working, they're doing their job.

Vic realised now that that was all her family had been interested in, whether something could do the job they'd assigned it. Even her. She'd managed to sneak one cat she'd tamed inside. Astill Hall staff had taken pity on her and fed it, but she spent so much time in boarding school whilst her parents travelled with Lance that she'd had to leave it behind. In the end, the household staff said they'd given him to someone, since he wasn't welcomed in the barn any more by the other cats. Vic was never sure that was the truth.

She didn't know why that thought struck her now, why it made her sad to think of that little cat, these kittens here. The sense of melancholy that overtook her...

It was because she'd had no place. Not with her family, not in her marriage, not here. The only time she had was in her own home with Nic, working with her charities saving abandoned animals and women fleeing from domestic violence. She had purpose raising money, which she was *good* at. Something she was proud of after coming out of the haze that had been numbing her sorrows with prescription medication, and from the brutality of her marriage. Along with being a mother to Nic, these were achievements that made her feel as though she had some value, for the first time in her life.

If nothing else this could give her some purpose. Maybe she could tame this little cat family. Get them spayed and rehomed. The mother gorged on the meat she'd brought. An animal that never knew where its next meal would be. She'd been like that with Sandro, she realised. So starved for affection and attention she'd gorged on him the night they first met. Not knowing when such attention and affection might come again. She'd fooled herself to believe that he felt the same.

The crunch of gravel behind her made the cat and kittens freeze. Then they darted into the bushes. Nic squealed as they ran away.

'*Gatt!*'

'We'll come back tomorrow and feed them again, darling,' she said as an imposing shadow fell over them.

Vic didn't need to turn round to see who it was. Her senses were attuned to this man, a tingling thrill down her spine whenever he was near. Sandro moved in front of her and she looked up as he was framed by the vivid sky above them, as blue as his eyes, dressed in a dark suit and looking perfect as ever.

'You scared them,' she said.

'I'm sorry, I didn't mean to chase them away.'

She shrugged. 'They'd finished the meat, anyway.'

Seeing his father, Nic quivered in excitement. He slid down from the bench and tried to wobble over to Sandro, who scooped him up.

'Did you enjoy the *gattini, il mio piccolo principe*?'

'I think he did.'

She smiled. The one thing she was certain about was that Nic had a huge capacity to love, and loved his father. 'He was almost as excited about them as he was to see you.'

The look on Sandro's face took on a strange intensity. 'You have a soft heart.'

She shrugged. Once, she'd hated that heart of hers. The way she expected the best and was always served the worst by people. Thought it made her weak, especially during her marriage, when she'd tried so hard in the end to make herself cold and unbreakable.

She wondered if that held true with Sandro too. He stood there in the warm sunshine, almost gleaming, such a perfect specimen of a human it was as if he had been gifted to the earth by the gods. His lips curved up, not quite in a smile but in a way that burnished off the edges of his hardness. It had been a few days since their conversation about Dora, and every evening he now came to her rooms to say goodnight to Nic, carrying that same whisper of a smile on his face. As if he wanted to be happy and couldn't.

He'd still given her no word about contact with her solicitors. Such a strange limbo to be in. It was difficult to believe he didn't know about Nic, but he was adamant he'd had no idea. As adamant as she'd been that she'd told the palace. She was telling the truth, so could it be possible he was, too? She wanted to challenge, to confront. To demand to know what he was doing to fix this mess that had her and Nic in his palace, cut off from the outside world. What if that had been his aim all along, and he was lying to her? Men lied all the time. She'd lived through it in her marriage…

Her thoughts spiralled.

Vic blew out a slow breath. Nic was here, having fun. Even if she kept any conversation about this civil, he'd pick up on the vibe. She didn't want Nic to become the silent victim of his parents' conflict. She took a few slow breaths. In, out. Counting. Her thoughts eased. She tried for neutral conversation.

'Before Nic, I was involved in animal rescue. Seeing the kittens, I couldn't help myself. I thought they'd need feeding. I wondered whether I could tame them? Perhaps pay for a vet and find them new homes?'

'You could try. I know staff here feed a number, though there are many strays in Santa Fiorina. The civil war and the years since made it difficult. Some people couldn't afford to feed their pets as the country descended into ruin.'

She remembered the disrepair as they'd driven through the city to the palace. Beautiful old buildings, pockmarked with bullet holes. How she'd thought then that there appeared to be so much need here.

'Do you have rescue organisations?'

'Yes, although they haven't been as well-supported as they should. We've had some international organisations here too.'

Nik grizzled in Sandro's arms. She checked her watch.

'He probably needs some milk. I'll need to go to the kitchen. You want something?'

'I'll come with you.'

Strange, after his distance, how he wanted to spend time with them now.

'Don't you have meetings? Busy, kingly type of work to do?'

'Nothing's more important than this,' he said as they walked together through to the cool stillness of the cloister and then the palace. Those words warmed her almost as well as the sunshine outside. Though Nic was probably the one who held the importance, not her. They arrived at the doors of the kitchen. She reached out her hand to push through.

'I'd like you to have dinner with me tonight,' he said.

She stopped, pulled her hand back. Heart beating a little faster than she would have liked.

'Why?'

'There are things we need to discuss. Come after Nic's gone to sleep. Isadora can look after him while you're gone.'

So far she'd not left Nic alone with Dora. Mainly, she just tried to teach Nic Italian, and was a bit of company for Vic when she became lonely.

'I'm not—'

Nic grizzled again. He'd be getting hungry. 'Okay, little man.'

She briefly knocked, then pushed through the double doors and walked inside ahead of Sandro. The staff greeted her like old friends, full of warmth for her as a few asked whether she'd had success in the garden. Even the chef, who had terrified her at first because he'd made crystal-clear this room was his domain. Then they noticed Sandro, and the silence was striking. Everything stopped, the same as those kittens in the garden, except his staff had nowhere to run. Victoria turned to look at him as everyone curtseyed, bowed. There was a tightness around his eyes, his mouth, as if he was uncomfortable with the attention.

He held up his hand in a stop motion, and everyone did indeed stop. 'There's no need. We've come to prepare some formula for Nicolai.'

The staff began to bustle about, getting everything ready whilst Sandro stood in the middle of the room holding Nic, looking uncomfortable and out of place.

'Please,' he said. 'We can manage. I'm sure you have better things to do than wait on us.'

'There's no higher privilege,' said the chef.

'Your lunch was magnificent as usual,' Sandro replied. 'You're wasted on me.'

'Give me a proper state dinner, Your Majesty. *Any* dinner. Then you'll see it's no waste.'

Sandro laughed, as did the rest of the staff. That sound rumbled through her, warm. Genuine. 'As soon as I can, I'll grant your wish.'

Nic began to complain again.

'And as soon as I can,' she said, as an apprentice handed her the sippy cup on a little silver tray that she'd never seen before, but no doubt was for Sandro's benefit, 'I have to give Nic his milk or there will be tears.'

'For dinner I've made him something special, what my *nonna* made me as a *bambino*.'

'Thank you. I'm sure he'll love it.' With more thanks and smiles they left the kitchen. She turned to Sandro. 'He really is an incredible cook.'

'He ran his own starred restaurant before my cousin ate there and decided he wanted that food cooked for him each day, so compelled Michel to work for him on threat of imprisonment.'

Victoria gasped. 'That's terrible.'

'That's typical of my cousin.' His eyes darkened, to the colour of a stormy sea. She knew it was another warning, to never forget the danger he claimed she was in.

'Yet Michel is still here.'

'I offered him his freedom, offered to reinstate his restaurant. He refused. I've never understood why.'

His look of confusion seemed genuine enough. Yet she couldn't understand why he didn't realise that one of his subjects might want to work for the real King. The King they'd waited for so long to return. It was a tiny vulnerability that made her pause. She reached out for Nic and Sandro hesitated, then handed him over.

'I have to put Nicci down for his sleep soon, but… I'll have dinner with you.'

Any fleeting uncertainty on his face melted away to be replaced by something harder, more determined.

Ah, *hello again, Your Majesty.*

He nodded, reached out his hand to the kitchen door, no doubt to give Michel the good news that there was a dinner for two he'd cook tonight. 'I'll collect you from your room at eight.'

As Victoria strolled off on the way to her rooms, she tried not to think of the butterflies fluttering about in her belly like the ones she'd seen in the walled garden.

Victoria waited, strangely nervous. Like she was going on a first date. Like the first night Sandro had walked up to her at the bar, and spoken to her in the deep, warm voice of his that reminded her of dark winter nights in front of a fire, that had sent a shiver of pleasure tripping down her spine. There was nothing pleasurable about being spirited away from your home. Thrown into a former war zone.

Being accused of terrible things; that you were consorting with a murderer, had hidden a child from his father. Being told your life was in danger. Yet she couldn't help the giddy sensation inside, as if she'd drunk too much champagne. It needed to stop, because Sandro wasn't that man and she wasn't that woman. They hadn't known each other, back then, and they were both different people now.

Victoria checked the time. Almost eight. She went through to Nic's room, where Isadora sat, reading him a book, his eyelids drooping in his cot. Her heart dissolved, seeing him lying there, all sleepy, tucked into a blanket. She still wasn't sure about relinquishing his care tonight, but Dora had been shadowing them both, so it wasn't as though she was a complete stranger.

'If there's any problem, please get a message to me. He can be unsettled if he wakes up.'

'Of course,' Dora said. Then she smiled in a knowing way. 'Enjoy your meal.'

Vic took a few more moments watching her little boy then left before she called off the whole evening and stayed in the room. As she did there was a gentle knock at the door. Her heart skipped a beat, part anticipation, part nerves. She walked to the door and opened it. Sandro stood outside, looking as devastatingly handsome as ever. Dark trousers that fitted his narrow hips and strong thighs far too well, a matching jacket with corresponding perfect fit. A blue and white striped business shirt which amplified the colour of his eyes. How could he still affect her this way? The breathless feeling, like a teenage crush… It had no sense to it, no reason. As she stood there, his lips lifted into a slow smile.

'You look beautiful.'

Sandro looked at her with an intensity that almost cut her off at the knees. She ran her damp palms over the front of her simple dress—a soft, flowing silk of blues and greens, like the ocean—basking in his appreciation, although this wasn't a date and she shouldn't care that he thought her beautiful or otherwise. Still, she'd been taught to have manners.

'Thank you.'

He looked over her shoulder to the closed door of Nic's room. 'Is Nicolai asleep?'

'When I left, almost. Did you want to say goodnight?'

Sandro nodded and they went to the nursery together. When they entered, Dora made to stand, probably to curtsey.

'Your Majesty.'

'No, please,' Sandro said. 'There's no need for formality.'

He went to the cot where Nic lay sleeping, and smiled again. Something warm, almost wistful this time. Untarnished affection shining on his face.

Love, if she was asked to name the emotion.

'Buonanotte, mio piccolo principe. Sogni d'oro,' he murmured.

The whole of her softened at the scene. Had she ever had anything like this as a child? All she recalled was cool indifference most of the time. Lance had always garnered more attention from her parents, because he was the heir. But she'd taken affection from the nannies who'd cared for her. In the main, they had been good. But they weren't what she'd wanted, which was parents who cared. It was why she never wanted a nanny for Nic. She'd never allow him to feel as if she hadn't wanted him.

Sandro turned to her.

'Are you ready for dinner?' he asked.

Ready as she'd ever be. She nodded and they left Nic's room. 'What did you say to him?'

Sandro glanced back towards the nursery. 'I wished him golden dreams.'

Something warm and soft swirled in her belly. This was a man who seemed to care, for his son at least. She couldn't deny it, not the way he looked at Nic, the things he said. Calling him *my little prince*. Wishing him golden dreams.

At least she knew her son would be cared for. Her? She couldn't be so sure.

They walked together in silence through the palace halls. The place was a strange mix of ostentation in areas and neglect in others. Not so far from her own suite, Sandro unlocked a door then walked through into an entrance foyer of what looked like an opulent apartment, taking her through to an elegant, comfortable lounge area. The whole place seemed warm, inviting with its creamy, soft carpet, and rich autumnal tones. There were antiques, but no overblown gilt that made them look as if they should never be touched. Instead, they were handsome and refined.

She stopped, her heart hammering in her chest. These were his rooms; she was sure of it. Not some neutral corner of the palace. Memories flooded back of going to another room, of shared intimacy that when she was around him she found almost impossible to ignore.

'Where are we?' She *knew*, but she needed him to say it. To gauge whether he had ulterior motives. Something about him seemed to be softening, warming, but he'd fooled her before. Instead of remembering their one night together, she should instead remember the day he had visited her home. Convinced her to travel with him under the ruse of an afternoon tea, when all along he'd planned to spirit her and Nic out of the country.

She should *never* forget that.

'My apartment. I thought we could have a meal on the terrace.'

'Couldn't we have had dinner in the dining room?'

He stiffened, the slightest tension entering his pose. 'Some of the palace was allowed to fall into disrepair over twenty-five years. Much of it needs extensive renovation, and we're still finding some of the original furniture in the cellars.'

She didn't move. 'Why your *suite*? Your private rooms? It's not exactly neutral.'

He narrowed his eyes. Tilted his head to one side. 'There's a problem?'

'Can I trust you?'

He reared back, before collecting himself. A look passed across his face, almost like a flinch. There was a pain there, and a tiredness too, a heaviness about him, as though the world weighed him down.

'After what's happened, I understand why you wouldn't. Trust is earned, and I know I've broken yours. I'm trying to make amends. If you're not comfortable, we can go to my office. Ask my staff to bring the dinner there. It would be a shame to miss the meal Michel was excited to cook for us, because I didn't consider how you might feel in less than neutral territory.'

What he said seemed real, genuine. His stance was open, his posture as relaxed as she'd ever seen it.

'There's no real neutral territory in the palace.'

'Perhaps I should have flown you to dine in Switzerland instead.'

She couldn't help herself, she laughed then and so did he. A tiny moment of humour breaking the pressing tension, giving her more clarity. If he was trying to make amends, then didn't it make sense for her to hear what he had to say?

'Michel would have been devastated if you'd done that. I'd hate to disappoint him. We can eat here.'

Sandro nodded. 'Thank you. Please. Come through.'

Sandro motioned to large glass doors, sheer curtains in front of them drifting from a breeze. He led her through to a large marble terrace, overlooking some expansive gardens lit up with beautifully placed lighting. Huge pots of olive trees and flowers adorned the space. Candles flickered about the terrace, and along the balustrade. The scene it all set was intimate, as if it was arranged for seduction rather than practical conversation.

Sandro looked about the area, eyes widening a fraction almost as if he was surprised. On a small, intimate table for two sat what looked like a luscious antipasto platter. Her mouth watered. She hadn't eaten much all day. A staff member in a neat black uniform appeared from the shadows.

'Would you like a drink? Champagne? Red wine? Something else?' Sandro asked.

Around him she didn't want to let her guard down.

'Do you have some sparkling mineral water?'

She was handed an icy cold glass and took a sip. Sandro asked for a red wine. As they sat at the table, the staff member bowed and left. She picked up some of the meats and cheeses for herself. The night wrapped round them, quiet and dark, the candles and carefully placed lighting painting everything in a warm glow.

'Nic seems to like Isadora,' Sandro said.

'She is very good with him.' Which in many ways Victoria loathed, but no one could ever take away that she was Nic's mother. Although that old insecurity rose again. 'But she's not me. I never wanted to subcontract the care of my child to another person. I know what it's like to have that happen. It's…lonely.'

'You were raised by nannies?' Sandro took a long sip of his wine, pinned her with his intense blue gaze.

She took a deep breath. This wasn't something she really wanted to talk about. He'd invited her here with things to say and she'd come here to listen. She wasn't supposed to be telling her story. But still, he'd asked a question, and it might make him understand why she'd been so resistant to Dora's presence in the beginning.

'At times. My father was Ambassador to many countries, primarily Lauritania. My brother travelled with them. They said it was important that he learn about other places, diplomacy. My father always said Lance would be prime minister one day.'

'Did he want to be?'

She shook her head. 'Never. He rebelled in his own way.'

He'd become a complete rogue, for the tabloids at least. To her, he was her beloved big brother who'd tried to help her pick up the pieces of her life, as much as she'd tried to protect him from it. Was he worried about her now? He'd tried so hard to help her get back on track, and she had promised herself after Bruce had died she'd never give Lance anything to worry about ever again...

Vic stopped, took a slow, settling breath. A sip of sparkling water. They were thoughts for later, and she tried to concentrate on now.

'What about you?' Sandro asked.

'I led a different life. Shunted to boarding school, where I stayed. Sometimes even over the holidays. So I know *all* about leaving the care of your child to others. That's not something I ever wanted to do to a child of mine. Why have one, if you're going to send them away?'

She wondered why her parents had had another child at all. In the end, the only conclusion she could come to was that they'd wanted another boy, and that her gender had been a disappointment.

Sandro nodded. 'Dora was never meant as a replacement

parent. You needed close security, and I thought another female might make you feel more comfortable.'

Victoria relaxed a little more. Maybe her persistent fears of being replaced were misguided.

'You are...' The low light of the candles flickered over him, painting him in gold. Her breath caught. He was such a magnificent man. And she stupidly wanted to hear what he thought of her, as if it mattered at all. He took another sip of his wine. 'A wonderful mother. That book, with pictures. The Italian and English words. You made it?'

She nodded.

'Many people would have taken no interest in Santa Fiorina, but you showed Nic his heritage. You didn't ignore this part of his life. When he recognised me... I never expected him to know me.'

'I'd always wanted him to know you because I knew what it was like not to have my parents around or caring. I *never* wanted that for him. I was always prepared for you to see him, even though I had sole custody.'

Sandro looked out over the palace gardens.

'I know.' His voice was quiet, as if he didn't want to really say the words.

She hesitated. Did she hear that correctly? 'What do you mean, *you know*?'

'This is what I need to say—'

Some staff made their way onto the terrace. Whisking away the remains of their entrée, replacing it with a chicken dish rich with the scent of garlic and herbs. They topped up Sandro's glass, refilled hers too. She didn't want food at this moment, she wanted to hear what he had to say. Yet Sandro cut into his chicken and began to eat, as if avoiding the conversation.

'What do you need to tell me?'

The question came out more harshly than she liked, but she didn't care. This was her life, *Nic's* life, being toyed with over political machinations she had no interest in.

'That… I'm sorry. You always told the truth. My security team have found evidence you contacted the palace.'

CHAPTER SIX

SANDRO WASN'T SURE how Victoria would react to the news. She had every right to be furious. The ground he had to make up now was vast. The distance was something he didn't believe could be breached easily, but he had to try. He had a child with a woman whom he'd grossly misjudged.

This morning watching her with Nic in the garden, mother and son, it was so…wholesome. Bringing forth sensations that he couldn't explain. He'd been transfixed at the pure joy of it all, leaving him with an ache in his heart. Had he ever experienced such simplicity as a child? If he had, he couldn't remember much of it, those happier days clouded by the memory of being torn away from all his support, from the people he *knew* loved him. Yet here was a woman who loved her child fiercely, and he'd torn her away from everything she'd loved too.

He needed to reset because of what his security had discovered. Because of what he was furious they'd allowed to happen in the first place, because they were his eyes and ears and should have known.

The risks weren't hypothetical any more. Not mere suppositions and guesses. This was what was imperative for her to understand.

She put her knife and fork down carefully, deliberately, her eyes narrowing.

'You mean, more evidence than my phone records, the details of my meetings with your representative, my legal agreement regarding Nic and our custody arrangements?'

It was *so* much more than that. Much worse.

'Yes. Knowing the date you contacted the palace made it easy enough to find the staff members on the palace switchboard that day. All calls are usually logged. Yours wasn't.'

'So you believe me? That proves I'm not scheming with your cousin. I can go home now.'

Sandro put his knife and fork down with a clatter. He wanted to shout, *Never!* Yet he'd been clear that she wasn't a prisoner here. Instead, he reined in any emotion, refusing to examine why he was so happy when she'd shown an interest in Santa Fiorina's animal-rescue organisations, in caring for the kittens in the walled garden. It suggested something longer-term…

'No.'

'What do you mean, no? Wasn't this whole thing…' she waved her arms about, vibrant and expressive '…because you believed I was scheming with your cousin? You can, I don't know, interrogate this staff member. That'll prove everything and I can go back to England.'

He shook his head. 'It's not so simple. The woman who we believe took your call resigned a month after Nic was born, to travel overseas. She died in an accident—'

'That's terrible.'

'In suspicious circumstances. She'd received a strange windfall of cash. Told her family it was a work bonus, but she was *never* paid one by the palace. We believe my cousin eliminated the only other person who knew of Nic's existence, whom he couldn't control.'

Victoria's skin paled. The warm spring breeze took on a cold chill.

'What does that have to do with me?'

'Whilst my cousin is free, you're in danger.'

'My brother—'

'Is a duke. I know. He's a man of means, and I'm aware of his resources.'

He hadn't told Victoria that Lance had contacted the palace, perhaps not believing the ruse his staff repeated to him when he called, that Sandro, Victoria and Nicolai were holidaying together. The Queen and King of Lauritania, Santa Fiorina's first fresh ally when he'd returned to the throne and friends of Victoria's brother, had also made representations to the palace about her welfare.

'Then you know he'll keep us safe.'

Not the way I will, because Nicolai's my son.

'He's not a king. He doesn't have the weight of a country behind him. He's also married. The moment he protects you, he and his wife are at risk too. Don't ever underestimate the things my cousin might do to get to Nicolai.'

Her mouth opened. Closed. As if she had things to say and couldn't get the words out.

'He wouldn't…would he? I mean, why now? I thought he'd left the throne by mutual agreement.'

When the country was falling apart around him, that man hadn't had the courage to fight for it. He'd only thought of himself.

'He had no interest in caring for Santa Fiorina. When people began to rise up in the cold of winter because they had no money to keep themselves warm, I suspect he believed it was too hard. He was happy to put down the occasional uprising; however, he was in a difficult position if he wanted a life of laziness and pleasure-seeking. And he had no heir. Even though he'd been married, his wife failed to produce a child.'

Victoria looked down at her lap. Toyed with her napkin sitting there.

'He told me he couldn't have children. I thought he was mentioning it because it was something he thought we had in common.'

For Sandro, the pieces of the puzzle began to fall into place. They left him frozen to the marrow.

'We extracted promises he would exile himself, with no further interference in the country. I believe we underestimated his cunning and desire to return to the throne. Did he ever try to get closer to you?'

'He suggested we could go for lunch once.' She shuddered, as if the memory was an unpleasant one.

He was now sure his cousin thought he could ingratiate himself. Marry the mother. Dispose of Sandro. Become Regent for a child he'd control, a child whose blood was royal.

The horror of that plan.

'It must have been hard to let him go after what happened to your family,' she said.

He'd wanted that man prosecuted and convicted with no hope of leaving whatever prison he'd been left to rot in. His advisers cautioned that Gregorio wasn't responsible for the sins of his father, that the people of Santa Fiorina came before the desires of one man. Sandro chose to be the King his country needed, and swallowed the rest like poison.

'In the end, there was little choice to make. We exchanged the reality of a protracted civil war where many in my country might have died, for the certainty of a peaceful transition. That was good for Santa Fiorina. But with a father like his, I should have realised, I ought to have fought harder.'

'What do you mean?'

How could he admit his failings to her? That he might have worked tirelessly on the diplomatic front, making rep-

resentations which would place financial pressure on his
cousin, asking former allies of his father to impose travel
bans, financial constraints, so his cousin's life became unbearable. But he'd always been safe. Protected for ever because his loss was considered a loss for the country. He
hadn't fought beside his people, some of whom had died
as they waited for his return like the prodigal son from the
wilderness. *All* of that felt like a failure, not a triumph.

'You need to understand. My half-uncle seemed to be a
loving family member. Would sit me on his knee, claimed
to support my father. All the while he plotted against my
family…he plotted for *years* before executing his plan. My
parents were shown no grace, no mercy. That's why you
need to stay in Santa Fiorina. I can't stress enough that I
will protect Nic, I'll protect you, with my life. I won't let
anything happen to either of you.'

She wrapped her arms round herself, her eyes gleaming
in the low light, as if with unshed tears.

'One of your own staff hid Nic's birth from you. It feels
like we're surrounded by the enemy.'

He ran his hands through his hair. 'She's the one we
missed. But I have a core of people who kept me safe when
I was in exile, others who worked to return me to the throne.
They kept me alive.'

'How did you get away? How did you escape?'

These memories were ones he never wanted to revisit.
One of the most painful nights of his life. However, if he
was truthful about their getting to know each other better
for the sake of their child, it was a story he'd tell her.

'My parents sent me away with my godparents and most
trusted courtiers. I was spirited across the border and then
to the UK, which offered me safety. They were betrayed.'

'Sandro, I'm so sorry.' She reached out as if to touch his hand, pulled back. 'I can't imagine.'

He shrugged because he'd long had to accept what had happened to him, his family. It was a dreadful, bloody part of the tapestry of his life.

'I was saved, and it was always my job to return to the country as King.'

'If you were so well protected, how did you end up at a private club with me? I could have been anyone.'

He smiled. That was one memory he could take pleasure in.

'It was two days before I was to leave for Santa Fiorina. I wanted one night to myself.' To take a chance, because his whole life he'd taken none. 'The Asteria Club is renowned for its safety and security. I was offered membership the moment I turned eighteen with the promise that it would be a safe haven if I needed it. It's one of the places my security and I trusted the most. You were my one moment, when I was allowed to be selfish and simply want.'

She stared at him, her eyes brimming with sympathy. So beautiful in the low light, wearing the colours of the ocean, her hair falling around her shoulders like cornsilk. Victoria shook her head.

'How did you survive it? You were only…what? Around nine?'

Sandro took another draught of wine. 'Because I had no choice. Because I had a purpose.'

'But you've spent more time in England than you have in the country of your birth.'

To his shame, in his teens he'd wondered where his home truly was. Santa Fiorina seemed so distant. Like a dream. 'I was reminded of my past constantly, of where my future lay.'

She frowned. 'I can't imagine that, not for a child. You would have been grieving.'

He rubbed at a tightness in his chest. All those years in a foreign land, wondering if he had a true place in the world.

'I had my godparents. My parents' most trusted friends and courtiers to look after me. I wanted for nothing.'

'Apart from your mother and your father.'

He'd been told he had to be strong, because that was what they would have wanted.

'Of course. They were…' His voice caught in his throat. Fleeting memories of happiness clutched at his consciousness, but they were so distant, remote, it was hard to hold on to them. Then she reached out and finally placed her hand over his. Something about it was solid, grounding, when all he had of his past seemed so ephemeral.

'They would have been irreplaceable.'

'I had so little to remember them by.' That had been the cruellest thing for a child, how the memories faded till he was unsure whether they were real or simply dreams. 'We left without any pictures of them. Their royal portraits were destroyed. Their memory seems distant now, like a faded photograph. I've moved on. My responsibilities are greater than a single man's grief. I have to wear my country's as well.'

Victoria's eyes still gleamed, overbright with unshed tears. He didn't need her sympathy. He drew his hand from underneath hers. He'd learned long ago that his strength was all he had.

'You have one picture of them. Why is that?'

It was as if he'd been plunged into a winter sea. He could hardly breathe. All he could recall was a dark day in his early teens, when he'd told those protecting him that he didn't want this any more. There was no hope. No point pretending he would one day be King in the memory of people long dead.

Then he was brutally reminded why it was necessary.

'It's irrelevant.'

He didn't know why the words were so hard to get out. Why this felt like an evisceration.

'Did anyone really love the grieving little boy you once were?'

'They all loved me; I was their future ruler.'

'That's not what I mean. That picture. It's not the sort of thing I found on the internet in my research about Santa Fiorina about your parents. So why do you have it? Who gave it to you?'

'It doesn't matter who gave it to me. All that matters is that it was a reminder.'

It was his godfather. His father's best friend. Tossed it before him as a raging teenager, to remind him of what they were all fighting for. After seeing that photograph, he'd fought for his parents every day since, without question or complaint.

'How could they do something like that?'

'They loved me, they wanted me safe. Wanted to make sure I took no risks, that I knew the enemy I faced and how evil they were.'

Victoria's eyes narrowed, her lips a thin line. 'I'm questioning who the evil ones are here.'

'They did it out of love.'

She shook her head slowly, pressed her hand to her heart. 'Oh, Sandro. Can't you see? I know all about control being wrapped up in the illusion of love. I've lived it. What was done to you was abuse.'

'Never, they—'

'So, if anything happened to you or me it would be fine

for the people who were tasked to protect Nic to do this? Not to find a picture of us as living and loving humans so he could remember us like that for ever, but a photo of us destroyed, that would likely destroy him too? That's okay with you? As a father?'

He pushed his chair back with a scrape but his legs seemed weak. They wouldn't allow him to stand. 'No!'

That's not what it was like. He was here, he was alive because of the tireless efforts of many people over the years, who deserved his thanks, not his disapprobation. Yet why couldn't he get enough air, as if he'd run some terrible race? Why did it feel as if the whole of him was being crushed under a weight so heavy he might never survive it?

Victoria left her own chair and moved to stand in front of him.

'Then why was it okay to have it happen to you?'

It was as if something in him broke.

'That's different.' His voice was hoarse, the words difficult to get out.

She cupped his cheek with her cool, soft hand, the tenderness and care on her face almost cutting him off at the knees. It was the same way he saw her look at Nic.

'I'd like you to explain to me how. I'd like to know who cared for the terrified little boy who was torn away from his parents and taken to a foreign country. Who truly loved him, protected him the way they would have wanted? Not as a future ruler but as a child. Tell me, Sandro. Who gave that little boy who'd lost *everything* a hug?'

His skin was feverish under her palms. She looked into his eyes and saw the pain there because she'd seen it reflected in her own in the mirror too many times, and some days still did. He might have survived the ordeal, but did he truly thrive? *Allowed* to do things? As a child maybe, but as an adult, had anyone ever asked him what he wanted? She'd bet the answer was no.

Her heart broke for the little boy he'd been, the one who'd needed someone to love him the way a caring parent would. Not just teach him about duty and taking back the throne, as commendable as those things were, but allowing him to be a child who could grieve. No wonder he looked exhausted now. She knew how hard it was not to have somewhere soft to land in the place you called your home. She'd lived like that for most of her adult life, particularly in her marriage. A wash of tenderness flooded over her, the emotion filling all the cracks. This complex man was getting to her and she couldn't help herself, so she didn't try to.

'I'm here,' she murmured as she dropped her lips to his because he needed so much. 'I'll give you what you need.'

Their lips brushed and he didn't move apart from the cool rush of his sharp inhale. She hadn't known what to expect, but she had so much emotion to spare she could fill him with it. Try to bring back the tender man she'd witnessed that night back at the club. The man she knew he could be because he transformed around their son.

'I'm sorry,' he murmured against her lips.

Then he groaned, a guttural, pained sound, and thrust his hands into her hair, surging forward, standing and hauling her to him. He overtook her completely. Consuming her. She gave right back to him. Their mouths fused together, teeth clashing as if they were warring with one another. The glory of it. Heat roared over her. A tearing kind of passion that threatened to rip her apart. There was no gentleness here in this moment, and she knew without question that he needed it. That she did too.

She poured her pain and anger into the kiss as he tightened his arms round her, all of him hard and uncompromising, aroused, as she ground into his erection. He dropped one arm to her waist. Another held the back of her head as if he was afraid she'd try to escape, but there was no running from this. The storm of it. She craved to be whipped away into the turmoil of sensation flooding her. She thrust her own hands into his hair and raked her fingernails through it, a moment so heady it was as if she'd lost all common sense.

He pulled his lips from hers, both of them panting. Vic gave a tremulous laugh. 'This is probably a mistake.'

The look he gave her could have cut her off at the knees. Pure, undiluted desire. 'I don't care, do you?'

She didn't. Not one bit. She shook her head.

He picked her up then, no gentle swinging into his arms. This was an abduction. She didn't care. She craved him in a way that didn't make any sense. She wanted this wildness, this barely controlled passion, to take all of him for her own because this cool, controlled man had lost the last vestige of control to her. The sense of her power overwhelmed her as he stormed through the suite, the only knowledge of where they might be because rooms changed from light to dark to light again as their mouths were fused. She hardly knew where they were going.

They reached a space where she could tell the light was soft, muted. The kiss softened, stopped.

'I need you,' he said, his voice rough and low. 'I need you and I can't—'

She placed a finger over his lips. 'I'm here. For you.'

Something changed then. He placed her gently, reverently, on the bed and climbed up next to her. Lying side by side, they faced each other. Sandro stroked his finger tenderly down the side of her face, drifting to her breast. Caressing her nipple through the fabric. He brought his lips to hers once more, teasing her mouth with his own. Their breaths mingling. She began to unbutton his business shirt, smoothing her hands over the strong, sculpted muscles as he moaned into her. He shrugged it from his shoulders, tossed it to the floor. Reached round the back of her dress, slowly pulled down the zip. It was as if she could feel each notch. The sleeves fell from her shoulders and he skimmed his lips over the side of her neck.

She lay back as he lifted the dress from her body, looking down at her in her lacy underwear of blues and greens to match the dress, his eyes the stormy colour of the deepest ocean. Victoria stretched like a cat under that worshipping gaze.

'Beautiful,' he murmured as he stood and she took him in. His body was leaner than she'd remembered from their night together. Harder. Her mouth watered at the sight of the carved and chiselled muscle, the highlights and hollows in the golden light from the lamp on the bedside table. Sandro dropped his trousers and underwear, his legs strong and muscular. His erection impressive. She needed him inside her, with an ache so deep she knew only he could conquer it, desire so overwhelming it fogged her brain. He moved to the bedside drawer, sheathed himself and crawled over her, hooking his hands into her underwear and gently dragging her panties down her legs. Then he dropped his head to the centre of her. Kissing her stomach, then lower.

'I want to taste you,' he whispered into the skin of her thigh, pressing soft kisses closer and closer to where she needed him most. Then his tongue found her. The perfect spot. Teasing, tantalising. She tilted her hips up to meet him.

'I need you,' she said, her voice breathless, almost stolen by the pleasure as he sucked and her back arched from the bed, the pressure between her legs building and building.

Then it stopped. She moaned in protest and he smiled, something wicked and at the same time joyous. Moving to her bra. Undoing it. Casting it aside. Taking her left nipple into his mouth and lavishing it with attention till she writhed in ecstasy.

For a few moments she believed she could die from pleasure. It could all end, right here and now. She was so close, and then he was over her, arms propped either side of her head, their noses touching. The blunt sensation of him between her legs.

'Whatever you need, *bella*, I will give you.'

She tilted her pelvis up, and he slid inside in one long thrust that stoked the ache inside, all the while easing her. A contradiction of sensations. Then he stilled and they stayed there, his forehead to hers, their panting breaths mingling. She slid her hands round his narrow waist, resting them on his buttocks, the muscles taught and tense. As if it took all his will not to move. Then he began rocking, the slow thrust in and out. His lips teasing hers in feather-light swipes. Keeping up the gentle, remorseless pace. She gripped as his muscles under her palms bunched and released with each move deep into the heart of her. Till she stopped caring and their breath and lips and bodies fused in perfect synchronicity. The glorious slide of him winding her tighter and higher. In a slow and perfect burn that caught, and roared over her as she sighed his name breathlessly onto his lips.

She surrounded him, with her scent, her slick body. It was all he could do to hold on till the spasms subsided and he gloried in her again. He could lose himself in this woman, as she curled her legs round him and gripped tight, still moving with him. Such a wonder. The care she showed to him…her seemingly boundless capacity to give. Sandro never wanted it to end.

The feeling built, prickling at the base of his spine, curling and winding harder and tighter as he kept the slow, steady pace, her gasps and moans driving his arousal tighter and further. How he wanted to thrust hard into her body and end this torture, yet he kept going, because of her, the grip and release of her hands furtive and desperate and he was sure she was close again. Then the desire became too much to bear as he ground into her, swivelling his hips, the exquisite feel of her hot, wet body against his own, and the sensation ripped through him, tearing him apart, putting him back together. Then she followed, pulsing around him once more, her nails cutting into his buttocks as another orgasm overtook her. He'd be happy if they drew blood as wave after wave of sensation followed.

He slid out of her, rolled onto his back and carried her with him. She lay there limp, breathing heavily. Skin damp. Her hair a tangle across his chest. The rightness of the moment settled bone deep. The wonder of this moment bright, like a beacon. How Victoria gave and gave. To their son, and especially to him, when he was the one who least deserved it. Sandro was humbled. She was a woman who was owed tender care. A soft place to call her own. He owed her so much, but after tonight?

His debt was greater than ever before.

CHAPTER SEVEN

SANDRO SAT IN his office, waiting. He'd invited Victoria here for an important discussion, on neutral territory. Since their night together a little under a week before what he hadn't expected was the constant incandescence of his desire. It was unrelenting. Bleeding into every spare second of the day. It addled his common sense.

Sandro had no idea what was happening to him.

That night…they'd both acknowledged in the moment that it was a mistake, but try to convince his body, which craved her. He'd had to enforce some distance. He'd visited Nic, of course, but otherwise remained cool. Perhaps a little aloof, however much he was sure Victoria hadn't cared. After a few days, she'd seemed just as aloof too, though he didn't know why that was an annoyance, like a burr in his shoe. It was a relief that they could remain practical about the situation in which they found themselves.

Instead, he'd immersed himself in long days of meetings. About security, safety. The future… All this meant he'd not had enough sleep, had drunk too much coffee, changed the strict routines imposed since his concussion. Those things did not bode well, given the tenuous nature of his health since the accident. Whilst he was still in the recovery phase it was as if he'd taken a backward step with Victoria's presence in his life. The constant worry, the fears in the dark of night when he recalled the loss of his parents. The photos. How fragile humans were. How small his own child was…

Yet he mustn't think about any of it. The past was behind him, and the future required his full attention. Sandro pinched the bridge of his nose, feeling…he wasn't sure. His headaches usually gave him some warning, enough to find a dark room and hide himself away till they passed. This was different, an ever-present weight he wasn't sure how to shift.

Probably tiredness. The past few months had been enough to try the strongest of men.

He checked his watch. Of all the meetings he'd held recently, this was his most important in many ways. A solution to protect his son, and Victoria. The only sensible approach, especially now that the second DNA test had confirmed Nicolai was his.

Marriage.

Given her clear interest in doing everything possible for Nicolai, he knew she'd agree. It was the only thing that made sense.

A knock sounded at the door.

'Enter.'

His private secretary ushered Victoria into the room. His breath caught as he saw her, even though today she was dressed practically for running round with a little boy. However, there was something about seeing her in the clothes he'd arranged to fill her wardrobe that gave him a kind of perverse satisfaction—jeans that hung slightly low on her hips, a simple black T-shirt that hugged her body. Her blonde hair was done in another messy topknot. She looked fresh, casual.

Beautiful.

She looked even more beautiful with that hair spilled out over his pillow. Head thrown back, gasping his name…

He tugged at his tie. No, those thoughts had no place here. Perhaps they could discuss intimacies after they'd come to an agreement. Together, they were blisteringly compatible. There were natural consequences of a marriage. Should Victoria want to, they could enjoy the considerable pleasures of a physical relationship. It made perfect sense…once he'd won this battle. He motioned to a seat in front of him and she sat but there was no deference in any move she made. No curtsey for the sake of a member of his staff. Nothing. He didn't know why he enjoyed it so much.

'Coffee? Tea?' he asked.

Victoria's face was impassive. Not a hint that she was other than entirely unaffected in his presence. Unlike him in hers. It was a humbling moment. She nodded.

'Tea, please.'

'How do you like it?'

'White, with no sugar.'

His assistant left with the order. Sandro smiled.

'Sweet enough?'

It was a quaint phrase his English nanny had used to use when she asked him if he wanted sugar in his tea as a child. A drink he'd come to enjoy so much in his time in England he'd had his favourite blend imported to the palace.

She looked at him, spearing him with her stony blue-grey gaze. 'I've never been accused of being sweet.'

He could see it. She carried that edge to her. Tart and refreshing as a lemon. Never sweet.

'How's Nic?' he asked, keeping the conversation on safe ground.

'Well, as ever. Settling into a routine. Were you planning on visiting him tonight?'

Her voice carried an almost sing-song quality, with a bite. As if she was mocking him. Holding back something she had to say. No doubt there were several things each of them would want to discuss today.

A tightness squeezed at the back of his neck. He rubbed the area. Negotiations needed to begin. Sensible steps to secure a marriage that would stabilise his country and ensure Victoria and Nicolai's welfare. Yet how to start when he was used to commanding those around him and they acted without question?

'My team and I have been discussing the best way forward.'

Victoria frowned. The moment was interrupted by a knock at the door and tea and coffee arriving. After taking hers with thanks, she sipped, levelling him with her granite gaze once more.

'The best way forward for what?'

Sandro attempted a benevolent smile. 'You and Nicolai.'

Her eyes narrowed. 'And what were your conclusions?'

'We had a number of ideas, but one stands out as obvious.'

'Nice to know,' she muttered into her tea.

'Your safety is paramount, which is why it's clear we must marry.'

Indeed, it was the only solution. The simplest answer. He'd always accepted he'd need a wife one day and to have children as soon as possible. However, he'd decided he should take at least a year or two to stabilise Santa Fiorina before doing so. Victoria's presence in his life fitted the timeline. When contemplating marriage, he'd assumed it would be arranged with a suitable candidate. He'd never experienced romantic love and he didn't expect it as part of his life, so its lack here wasn't an impediment. As for the attraction that exploded between them, the way they were in the bedroom together...that was a windfall. A bonus for both of them. He tried not to think of it, how she felt in his arms, how he lost himself inside her. Those thoughts were for a later time…

Victoria froze, her cup part-way to her mouth. She placed it back on the saucer with an emphatic click. Her eyes took on the coldness of a glacial lake.

'Well, there's a proposal for the ages. They'll be writing poetry about it. *Tragic* poetry.'

Not exactly the reaction he was expecting. A tightness gripped his head again. Sandro pinched the bridge of his nose.

'There is nothing poetic about our situation.'

'No kidding. What about me, specifically, makes marriage the answer to this situation?'

'You're the mother of my child. You're the daughter and sister of a duke. I need a queen.'

'So I fit the criteria,' she hooked her fingers and made quotation marks in the air, 'for a queen. Did you think perhaps I might have been involved in these discussions? Since, I don't know, they involve *me*?'

'You're being involved now. You must see it's a practical solution.'

She crossed her arms, her mouth a thin line. 'I don't see that at all. Practical would be taking me home, talking to my brother about your concerns and organising security with him. This? I don't know even what to call it. Comedy hour, perhaps?'

'There is nothing comedic here.'

'Oh, I know that, Sandro,' she hissed through gritted teeth.

'You would have the weight of a country behind your safety. Nic would be protected by my blood, by the crown. Think of him if nothing else.'

She leaped from her chair, began to pace. '*Think of him?* I've done nothing but think of him from the *moment* he was conceived. Don't you *dare* try to use him against me. You were nowhere in this scenario and now you swoop in to try and take control. I've been married once and I never want that again. Been there. Know what it's like. Over my dead body.'

At those words, she stopped her pacing, placed trembling fingers over her mouth as if trying to shove the words back in. The most terrifying thing was that it might have come to that. He'd put nothing past his cousin. Nothing at all.

Victoria seemed to come back to herself. 'Is that what the other night was about? The romantic dinner for two. The…the…sex. Were you trying to butter me up for this? A proposal?'

Now it was his turn to stand. The sudden motion caused a stab of pain behind his eye. He flinched. Paused. The unfairness of that accusation struck him.

'Never! Why would you say that?'

'I don't know. We have sex, then this farce. What did you think? That a few orgasms might make me happy enough to say yes? Lucky me. Except you probably shouldn't have given me the cold shoulder because that sure let me know where I fit into your life.' She gave a sharp and bitter laugh.

'You are not taking this situation seriously.'

'Not taking…the *hide* of you. I was all but kidnapped—'

'You came willingly. To protect Nic.'

She snorted. 'Don't you dare rewrite history as a panacea for your guilty conscience. I remember what you said. *"Every contingency was planned for."* Tell me now, what did that mean?'

He shook his head and grabbed the desk to steady himself as an aura prickled the side of his vision. Not here, not now. This was *not* the time. He had to finish this discussion.

'I was trying to keep you safe. You didn't care when I told you what my cousin was capable of.'

'Showed me, don't forget. And how could I forget that photograph? Tell me, Sandro, how does it feel to use your parents' deaths to manipulate a woman? Do you think they'd be proud?'

He reared back. No one spoke about his parents other than in hushed tones and reverence. *'Enough.'*

He couldn't take more of this. This conversation that had skidded out of control. He had no sense of finesse here, all he was filled with was anger and pain. The signs were unmistakeable now. He'd had too many of these headaches over the past month. The vision fading in his periphery. The tightness in his head like an iron band. Sandro knew what was coming and it was something he couldn't control. There was no continuing the conversation, not like this. He required his doctor, a dark room, some hours to himself.

He moved from behind his desk, his legs still steady but might not be for long. The whole world was contracting in on him, crushing him like a vice. He pinched his nose.

'This conversation is over.'

Victoria crossed her arms, glowering. 'Why? Can't you take the truth?'

He could not let Victoria see him like this, because there was only one truth. If she discovered it, she would never trust him, and never stay. He was a man who, in these moments, was weak.

A man wholly unable to protect her or Nicolai.

Victoria checked on Nicci, quietly asleep in his cot. She watched the rise and fall of his chest. The warm wash of love, spiked with something sharper and more jagged—fear—ran over her. In the end, Sandro was right. It was all about their son. Her life had changed. There was no going back. She had to keep Nic safe.

Yet this morning, with Sandro…those old hurts creeping into her consciousness. The sex, then his aloofness. His attempt to control. It all brought back memories of her marriage, those triggers which still haunted her. Her reaction had been her way of self-protection. She'd lived a life of emotional unpredictability, with a man running hot and cold, passionate then cruel, till she was left little more than a husk of a person. She could never go back there again.

Now, watching Nicci sleep, she had time to reflect. Sandro's passion for her on their night together in his suite hadn't seemed feigned. That whole night it was as if they were both possessed by something shocking and out of control. They'd also both confessed they thought it was a bad idea. Would he have said that if he was trying to manipulate her? Or would he have made her promises of love and adoration instead?

She didn't know. What she did know was that she'd been unfair to bring up his parents today. Victoria had experienced cruelty and she'd also once meted it out to the people who cared for her. Acting like one of the trapped animals she'd so often fostered. Afraid to take any kindness in case the person turned on her and hurt her the way she'd so often been hurt in the past.

Was that what had happened today?

She wasn't sure, but regretted what she'd said. How her words had struck Sandro almost like a mortal wound. He'd flinched as if he'd been slapped. How pale he'd become, almost pained. That pinch round his eyes. Gripping his desk, as though the world were tilting on its axis. Almost as if he didn't seem well.

She'd done that to him, which meant she had the power to

hurt him. She'd never had that in her marriage. In a similar situation, Bruce would have acted with aggression. Sandro had walked away, which meant he wasn't like her husband, and she needed to apologise, explain. Because if she knew one thing, it was the power of words. How they could hurt as much as heal.

Vic called Dora, asked her to look after Nic, which she seemed happy about. When she arrived, Victoria left to find Sandro. She had no luck at his office. His private secretary said his diary had been cleared for the afternoon, and suggested the gymnasium or his suite. She'd try his suite first.

She picked up her pace to his rooms. Tapped softly on the outer door. When there was no answer, she cracked it open and looked around. The curtains were drawn and the room was dark, as if the whole space was covered in a shroud. She couldn't see anyone, but there were murmured voices coming from the bedroom.

She padded across the thick carpet and listened.

'You need to take greater care, Your Majesty. Keep to your routine. We've spoken about this.' A man's voice. One she'd never heard before. Tight with concern.

'I can't. You know why. Today I need this to stop. Tomorrow we can talk further management. Changes.' Sandro's voice ground out, rough and hoarse. She crept up to the door. It was wrong of her to spy. She knew it, but something was going on here and the feel of it was all too familiar. The darkened rooms, the pained voice.

Pain.

Her old foe. It had taken years of rehabilitation to get to where she was now—drug-free, and mostly pain-free if she was careful. Kept to her routine, just as the stranger with Sandro said. But this wasn't about her. Sandro was hiding something. And secrets meant danger. She peered through the crack in the bedroom door, which stood ajar. Saw a man she assumed to be a doctor, dressed in a suit with syringe in hand. Sandro sitting on the bed, in nothing but boxer briefs, head in his hands.

'We need to. The medication is for acute pain.' Vic couldn't see what was going on, but she knew. The man took the now empty syringe and dropped it into a sharps container. 'This isn't a long-term solution. I'm concerned they're increasing in frequency and—'

'Quiet. Please.' The tortured sound of Sandro's voice strengthened her resolve, heart pounding at her ribs. This scene was a familiar one, so close to her own history. The agony after her accident she never thought she'd survive. The fleeting, floating escape opiates gave her. How her pain melted away. Physical, emotional. Till the medication stopped working and she needed more and more to escape. She'd learned a terrible lesson—that what had been given to help her in the beginning, ultimately harmed. Controlled. Sandro's words were what she constantly told herself, that she'd stop *tomorrow*.

Then tomorrow came, and she took the pills again.

An insidious slide into addiction that it had taken physical and psychological therapy for her to overcome.

Nicci would be the victim here, having an addict as a parent. She would not put him at risk. She clenched her fists. Her jaw. Stormed into the room.

'What the hell's going on?'

The man she presumed was a doctor whipped round. 'Leave at once. I'm attending to my patient. If you don't go, I'll call Security.'

She didn't care about him. It was Sandro she focused on. The lines on his face were etched deep. Except his eyes were blank, as if he barely cared. She remembered that feeling, where nothing mattered at all.

'Try it. I'm not leaving till I get an answer.'

There was only silence.

'Fine. You won't give me answers, I'll find them myself.'

She stalked into Sandro's en-suite bathroom, driven to protect Nicci, because she *knew* what she'd find. Opened his medicine cabinet and there they were, an array of plastic bottles. She pulled them out, one after the other, pills rattling angrily as she read the names. Some medications she recognised like old enemies. Others weren't familiar, but it didn't matter. Vic had seen enough.

She took a deep breath, went back into the bedroom. His doctor greeted her.

'His Majesty needs to rest.'

'His Majesty needs to start telling me the truth.'

She walked to Sandro and stood in front of him. He sat hunched over, not meeting her gaze. She should have sympathy, but right now all she wanted were answers. He'd promised to keep them safe. Yet how could he, when he was keeping secrets from her? What more was he hiding?

'You say you're protecting my son but you're his biggest danger, aren't you? Deny it!'

She opened the drawer of his bedside table, rifled through. A few more pill bottles, though these weren't prescription. She searched further, till her fingers touched a slip of paper with the shape of lips in pink and the words *Thank you* in a familiar hand, because it was her own writing…

Everything stilled. The note she'd left him when she'd walked out early in the morning after a night of passion like she'd never experienced. A night that changed her. Created Nic. He'd kept that note all this time.

What did it mean?

'Sandro,' she whispered, not knowing what to do, what to say, the conflicting emotions churning inside her. But that note in his drawer was like a punctuation. A full stop to the worst of her fears in this moment. She dropped it back into its place. Whether he'd seen her find it, she didn't know.

'Tell her.'

Sandro's voice was the barest whisper. As if he was asking for his greatest shame to be admitted.

'Sir, you're in no state to make a decision like this when—'

'Tell her.'

He lay on the bed then. Stretched out. This vital man was clearly suffering, his arm flung over his eyes as if to block out the last vestiges of light. His doctor glared at her, walked about the room, switching off the en-suite light, ensuring there was no crack in the curtains, till the room was cloaked in darkness.

'Come. Let him sleep.'

They went into the sitting room and Victoria shut the door to the bedroom with a soft click. Sandro's doctor rubbed his hand over his face.

'I don't like this.'

'I'm the mother of his child. I deserve to know what's going on, and he's your king. He was explicit in what he wanted.'

She walked to the curtains and opened them, letting some light in, taking slow, steady breaths, trying to stop the trembling, to evict the memories of what she'd gone through in her own struggles from her head. One good thing she could say, was she didn't react to seeing the medication as she once had. The cravings had gone. Her fears now were all for Sandro.

The doctor pushed his glasses up his nose.

'Six months ago, His Majesty was in a car accident. He suffered post-concussion syndrome, which left him with migraine-like headaches, particularly when he is under significant stress.'

Which would be all the time, given he was a king trying to rebuild his country. But she suspected that their earlier conversation was a trigger too. How pale he'd become. She recognised now that he'd been in physical pain when he'd left his office so suddenly.

She blamed herself.

'Who cares for Sandro when he's like this?'

'Me. There's no one else he trusts. You need to understand, he demands this be kept secret. He fears the instability—'

Vic held up her hand. 'I understand. I'll stay with him. Leave your number, and if I'm concerned I'll call you.'

She looked at the closed door of his bedroom. Her presence, Nic's presence in Sandro's life would be a stressor too. His drive to marry made more sense now as well, to fit everything into neat boxes of solutions so he could wrestle control of his life again.

Nothing about their current situation was neat or ordered.

The doctor pulled a card from his pocket and handed it to her. 'He'll sleep. When he wakes he's usually well again. Tired, but pain-free. If he's not, I need to know.'

She nodded, and the man hesitated for a moment, then left the suite.

Vic turned, and gently opened the door to Sandro's room, letting her eyes adjust to the dark. He lay sprawled on the bed. Even unwell, his body was powerful. She hated that he'd been felled like this, how it must make him feel, a man who always tried to project strength, perfection. Vic moved closer. His breathing was slow and steady, but she knew this type of sleep wouldn't really leave him feeling refreshed. Already she could see a sheen of perspiration gleaming in the dim light. She gingerly sat on the edge of the bed, taking care not to wake him. A lock of hair had fallen across his damp forehead, and she reached out her hand, swept it away. He shifted under her touch.

'Shh. Go to sleep.' Vic gently slid her fingers through the hair. He exhaled in what sounded like a pleasured sigh before he settled again and was still.

She was sure that he wouldn't want her seeing him like this but suffering in hiding was where the problems began. She watched him in his slumber, and placed her hand on his cheek, the skin warm to the touch.

She wouldn't let him hide any longer.

Sandro gripped onto the snatches of consciousness that were as ephemeral as mist. How long had he been out this time? He clawed his way back from the haze that had been a blessing but which he loathed. It left him vulnerable, weak. There was no room in his life for it and yet he was still a slave to the injury he'd suffered six months before.

Even worse, there'd been someone else to witness his infirmity. The moment this news escaped his inner circle everything was placed at risk, and Victoria was the biggest risk of them all because he couldn't control her. He opened his eyes, lids still heavy. It would take a little while for him to wake fully. The headaches always left him feeling scraped out and a little raw. He needed a coffee, a shower. Sandro rolled over onto his side to sit up. There was movement from an armchair in the corner. A shadow bleeding out of the surrounding darkness. His doctor, who always stayed. The only person he ever allowed to see him so vulnerable.

'How long have I been out?' His voice was rough and thick with the leftovers of a drugged sleep. He *hated* it.

'Lie back down.'

That voice. It wrapped round him, as cool and soft as a river of silk. His body reacted the way it always did around her. He was half hard in an instant. He dragged a sheet over himself. Victoria was the last person he wanted to see. That sense of something shameful slicked over him like a coat of filthy oil.

'What time is it?'

'Early evening.'

He'd been out for hours this time. Victoria rose from the chair and walked into his en-suite bathroom. The light flicked on in there, illuminating his bedroom in its soft glow. The sound of water ran briefly before she came back with something in her hand.

'I know what it's like to wake up after one of those shots. It takes a while to feel normal. Lie back down.'

He obeyed. Her voice was so gentle and soft. A temptation, to fall into it and settle there, even though he had no room in his life for comfort and complacency.

'You were hot, but I didn't want to wake you.' Victoria reached out and smoothed a damp, cool flannel over his skin. He almost groaned at the pleasure of it.

'How long have you been here?'

'Most of the day.'

Plenty of time to witness his humiliation. 'Where's Nic?'

'Isadora's looking after him.'

He shut his eyes as the cool cloth swiped his face. His body. He relaxed into the bed. Not in a drugged stupor but in true pleasure. The pleasure of being cared for, for once. He wanted to purr like one of those kittens, quietly being tamed by her.

'Your doctor told me you have post-concussion migraine. I've seen what's in your bathroom cabinet. I know what the doctor gave you.'

That doused the pleasure like cold water tossed onto a freshly lit fire. He remembered the pain, as if his head were being torn in two, her words, *'What the hell's going on?'* and in that moment of desperation for silence demanding that his doctor *tell her.* What had his doctor said, and what did she think of him now?

'My doctor's been explicit about the risks versus the short-term benefits. I'm only using it as a last resort.'

Victoria shook her head. 'You're playing with my old enemies. I thought I was in control of it too, till I wasn't.'

She continued to smooth the flannel over his sensitised skin. Victoria wanted to talk, that was clear. Perhaps she had admissions as difficult for her as his own were for him.

'What happened?'

'It was with a horse I rescued. She spooked and I was crushed. Back injury. Pelvis. It was agony. And whilst everyone told me my body had recovered, the pain didn't go away. And then my doctor gave me something he said would help. It did, short-term. But it didn't just take away my physical pain. It took away *everything.* Every problem I had ceased to exist, for a few hours at least. Then one day, I found I couldn't stop. I never believed I could become an addict, till I was.'

He looked at Vic, sitting on the edge of the bed, so earnest. He ran his hands through his hair because all he wanted to do was to touch her. Take more of her caring, because she shouldn't care about him at all. She should revile him and yet here she was.

'How did you overcome it?'

He knew the reports his team had put together on her.

Bland documents about a sanitorium in Switzerland that did not reflect this beautiful, vital woman who seemed to have borne so much and yet won her struggles.

She gave a bitter laugh. 'I realised that I was tired of people controlling me. That the only way I was going to escape was to escape the addiction.'

'People?'

'I was encouraged to take the medication by my husband. He liked the way it made me calm, quiet and accepting of things I wasn't happy about: my life. My marriage, which was a cold, dark place to live. When I had the accident *he* became the victim and martyr. I couldn't fall pregnant. He blamed me for that too.'

She seemed so fragile in that moment, these admissions of hers allowing herself to be so vulnerable to him. When had he ever had the luxury of the same, to show all of himself to another human being?

One night, that was when, in bed with a woman on his last night of freedom. Then he'd been true to the man he was.

'It takes strength to recover, Victoria. It's something to be admired.'

She put her hand over his, her cool blue-grey eyes flashing with something hard and fierce. 'Promise me you're not misusing your medication.'

'I'm a man who likes to be in control, and the medication takes that away. I only use it under my doctor's guidance, and only as a last resort; however, if you want me to stop, I will.'

'I don't want you to fall into the trap I did.'

'Nothing will happen to me because I have people around me to protect me. Who talked to you and told you there were other ways? That the choices being made for you by your doctor were wrong?'

She took her lower lip between her teeth. 'Let's just say, I hid it well.'

'You shouldn't have had to hide. You should have been protected, *cara*. Cherished and cared for by those who were supposed to love you, not left to be numbed because there was no one there when you needed them.'

'We all make our choices, Sandro. You once said to me that everyone has their cross to bear. It's no use comparing the wood and the nails.'

She remembered. There was so much of that night he could never forget. The freedom of it, the sense of possibility that sustained him over the months since. The hope it gave him. He had that sense of hope again. Fragile, flickering, but it was there none the less. The hope that in a selfish world he could find someone else who could be selfless. Who offered him comfort, her body. Who he wanted to offer the same in return.

'I should have a shower, then we can talk some more.'

Victoria stood. Sandro almost mourned the loss of her gentle ministrations; however, he needed to feel more like a king than this half-version of himself. He sat up, the world still a bit fuzzy but not as bad as usual. They'd caught the headache early enough this time.

'You okay?'

He nodded. In the dim light from the en-suite bathroom she looked down at him, her expression unreadable because she was good at hiding, as she'd admitted. He recognised it now because he hid so much himself. Yet he didn't miss the way her gaze tracked over his naked torso, and lower, to his legs.

He couldn't miss her appreciation. It almost burned him

alive, the power of it, and then she'd see how she affected him. He stood and he thought he heard a sharp inhale. Part of him that had no shame and plenty of ego relished the sound and her admiration of his body. He made his way to the shower, passing the mirror as he did so. He looked like hell. A growing shadow on his jaw. Dark rings under his eyes. Skin pale. The fallen King he'd never wanted anyone to see, especially not Victoria. This was not a man who could rule a country. Who would trust and put faith in him like this?

Yet Victoria deserved to know everything, including brutal truths about the accident that left him still infirm. Especially considering what they now suspected about how much danger she and Nic might truly be in.

CHAPTER EIGHT

SANDRO TURNED ON the shower to hot. Let the water rush over him till he was clean. Once done, he lashed a towel round his waist. Brushed his teeth. Righted himself.

He walked into his bedroom and the curtains had been pulled back, the French doors to the terrace opened, letting the cool evening breeze drift over him. Everything about him was still too on edge and sensitive. He dressed in old clothes, ones he'd kept when he wasn't a king but simply a man in exile. It was a reminder of how easy it was to fall from his lofty perch.

He opened his door to the lounge area of his suite to the scent of coffee and almost groaned. Victoria handed him a small cup.

'I asked the kitchens to bring up a light meal.'

He sat on the plush couch. Took a sip from his espresso. The caffeine did its work, his stomach sensing the pang of hunger. He took some of the bread, meats and cheeses the kitchen had delivered. Ate his fill. Finished his drink. Victoria sat next to him, leg tucked under her. He shut his eyes and dropped his head back as he did so because she watched his every move, and, despite both of their admissions and what they'd shared, her unrelenting gaze was like a needle of censure pricking his skin.

Hiding his headaches had a cost. At least he didn't have

to worry any more about Victoria finding out. One less stress to trouble him in a litany that plagued him each day.

'The doctor said you had an accident,' she said.

Sandro blew out a long breath. He felt better, improved by the food and coffee, sure. Maybe improved by Victoria's presence as well. Yet he had more admissions he didn't want to make. He'd tried not to scare her, but it was imperative she know all the fears that still plagued him. He opened his eyes, leaned forward, his forearms on his knees. Hands clasped.

'It wasn't an accident. We believe it was an assassination attempt.'

Vic gasped as the blood drained from her face. 'What?'

'A truck hit my vehicle. It happened on a mountain road. The driver said his brakes had failed. Had the car gone off the edge, as we now believe had been planned, and not into the mountainside, I wouldn't have survived.'

'How can you be sure it was an attempted assassination?'

'We weren't. Then we found out about Nic. The accident happened six months after he was born. The truck was destroyed soon after the accident. Crushed without insurance checking it, so the brakes were never assessed. The man driving the truck disappeared, but we discovered he'd once been employed by Gregorio as a driver.'

'You really think that's what's going on?'

'You called the palace and were intercepted. My cousin knew about my child before me and intervened. I don't believe in chance, not where my life is concerned. Neither does my security team, especially since you confirmed Gregorio couldn't have children. We believe it was planned. With Gregorio in control of my son on the throne, he could have done anything. My people are tired of war—they want peace. What better way to take the throne back than with the real child of the true heir? With me out of the way, Nic would have been the last link to the royal family.'

Victoria's face paled. She wrapped her arms round her waist.

'It's like he's everywhere. This man, he'll never stop, will he? We'll never be safe.'

If Gregorio couldn't have what he wanted—Nic—then Sandro wasn't sure what desperation might make him do. Victoria was right: his cousin would likely never rest. They'd all been fooled into complacency, so desperate for peace they hadn't recognised the covert war still being waged.

No more.

'I've promised to keep you safe, and I will. I'll *never* let anyone harm you.'

'I'm scared, Sandro.'

He wanted to grab her, draw her into his arms, absorb her energy and vibrancy into himself, but he knew the steps he should take here were tentative. Victoria was unlike anyone else around him. No matter how trapped she might be, she always gave off a sense of freedom. He envied it, wanted to soak some in for himself. He'd never been free; he knew that now. Any thought he might be had all been a carefully cultivated illusion.

Instead of hauling her into him as he craved to do, he held out his hand, palm up. Inviting her. A strange concept when he'd come to expect people around him would simply do what he wanted. But not Victoria, never her. She was everything complicated about his existence, when all he'd sought in the past was order.

That might have been enough to make him pause. He'd spent a life determined to need no one. Not physically or emotionally. Yet he allowed himself to crave her.

Victoria slipped her hand into his and it jolted like a

shock, stunning him. That small touch wiping his brain clean. He brought her hand to his mouth and kissed it. The mere brush of his lips and she gave a pleasured exhale. Her pupils dark in the blue-grey stone of her eyes. Her mouth partly open, as if she'd been shocked too. Sandro couldn't explain it, this connection. He knew Victoria's body now, what she liked. What made her gasp and cry out in pleasure. Both of their nights together had been a journey of discovery, making love till dawn, learning each other's desires. Yet each time they touched it was like the first time. That same sense of wonder and excitement. Would it ever feel familiar?

Sandro threaded his fingers through hers and drew her into him.

'I vow to protect you, with all that I have. And I promise, you don't need to fear *for* me. The only thing I risk becoming addicted to, Victoria, is you.'

'Sandro.'

Her voice was a whisper as he slid his free hand behind her head, leaned in and kissed her, her lips soft, tasting like berries. Her mouth opened under his and he couldn't help seeking more of a taste. She reminded him of the sweetest lazy summers, in those few moments as a teenager he'd had a crush on some girl and he'd dreamed of possibility. Now, with her, he felt as if there were more than possibilities open to him. He drew the thread of them together, once again spinning a future. She'd rejected him once, but he knew he'd been wrong in his approach. This, their connection, they could build on *that*. He wouldn't give up on it. In truth, he couldn't.

Victoria's fingers tightened in his as her free hand slipped behind his head into his hair. Their kiss deepened, slow, luxurious, as if they had all the time in the world. The blood roared in his ears, the need to take her, make love to her, make her *his*, driving him on. He was hard, aching for her when she let go of his hand, stood and straddled him. Sandro groaned as she rocked on his body. He wrapped his hands round her, drew her into him. With each flex of her hips the pleasure spiked like lightning through him. He cupped her breast and stroked it through the fabric of her top, the nipple beading under his fingers as she moaned, her movements harder, more insistent.

'You want something from me?' he murmured against her mouth.

'I want *all* of you.'

He wanted to tell her she had it, but he couldn't because he feared she meant far more than he could ever allow. Something of him would always be held apart. He'd never given himself totally over to anyone. Only in his fantasies. In reality, he belonged to his country. He could never truly belong to a person.

Sandro stood, supporting her in his arms as she squealed. She wrapped her legs tight round his waist. 'You're going to let me fall.'

'Never.'

The word was out of him before he could take it back. He shouldn't have said it but in this moment, it was the truth, and what was sex if not the ultimate fantasy? He would protect her with his life, but he feared what failing to give all of himself to her might do. Then her lips were on his again and he didn't care. He walked into his bedroom, with her clinging to him, mouth hungry on his own.

The falling sun painted the room gold. She unhooked her legs as they reached the end of the bed, slid down his body. He released his grip, allowed her. When her feet were on the floor, he slid his hands under her top, her skin roughening with goose-pimples.

'You should always be naked, then I wouldn't have to waste time removing your clothes.'

Victoria gave a throaty laugh as he lifted her T-shirt, dropping it to the floor. Undid her bra, so it went the same way.

'We have plenty of time tonight.'

She wiggled out of her jeans and underwear till she stood before him, naked like a nymph in the glowing evening light. He tugged at the hairband holding her hair in a rough ponytail. It came loose, spilling about her shoulders. Sandro wanted to touch her all over, absorb her, she was so beautiful. He took her into his arms, kissed her hard and fervently, her skin warm and soft under his hands. She ground into him, making desperate noises till she pulled her mouth away.

He smiled as her trembling hands tugged at his shirt. He loved that she was as affected as him. That their need for each other was acute. Urgent. Sandro tore off his own T-shirt as she worked at his jeans, boxers, till they were both naked, the breeze blowing through the open French doors, cool on his overheated skin.

They tumbled to the bed, all searching hands and questing lips, everything slick and needy. He *ached* for her. Feared he'd go too fast when he wanted tonight to be so much more. Victoria's body was on top of his, her hair a curtain about them. She writhed, moving as if she were desperate almost to crawl inside of him. He could have flipped her over but he wanted to take his time, feeling the slip of her smooth skin under his hands, the glory of her warm body sinuous against his own. Then she sat up, her lips the colour of plums, face flushed, eyes over-bright. Her hair tumbling about her shoulders, skimming her breasts. Looking like a goddess.

His goddess, though he wasn't sure why that thought assailed him now.

'Condom,' he groaned. What he wouldn't give to slide inside her, unprotected. Yet he'd promised to protect her and he would, in *all* ways.

'Where?'

'Second drawer.'

She crawled over the bed and he watched her, her moves seductive and enticing. She came back to him with a sultry smile and a foil packet, which she tore open and handed to him with trembling fingers. He loved the way she seemed as overcome as he was.

'Put it on me,' he said. 'I need to feel your touch on my body.'

'I—I've never done this before, but okay.'

She'd been married, yet in so many ways her innocence astonished him. Even more, her trust, her willingness to be free with him.

'Let me show you how.'

He guided her hand, cool against his overheated flesh. She began to roll the condom down and he gritted his teeth because the pleasure of this almost overcame him. When she was done, she sat back a little and cocked her head to the side. He let out a pained laugh.

'Admiring your handiwork?'

She looked at him, her pupils dark, a shy smile on her lips. 'Admiring you.'

The admiration went both ways, yet for him it was far more than physical. She'd overcome so much, and still retained such openness with him in the bedroom, when she had every reason to close herself off for ever.

'There are other ways you can show your admiration.'

He sat up and reached out, placing his hands gently on her hips, guiding her as she straddled his body once more. What he wouldn't give to thrust up into her now, but he needed to check, to ensure her pleasure. Ensure she was ready for him. He released her hips, slipping the fingers of his right hand between her legs. So slick and hot, he groaned. Victoria flexed her hips back and forth, riding his hand as he stroked her till her movements became desperate, out of control. He knew she was close.

'I need to be inside you,' he murmured, moving his hand and notching himself against her welcoming body.

'Yes. Now.' She began to sink onto him, throwing her head back, her mouth open in ecstasy.

The way she took him, the blush that spread from her throat to her chest and breasts, the beautiful pink tinting her skin, her nipples tightening as she sank lower, till there was no space between them... For a moment she didn't move and neither did he. The elemental shock of the pleasure with her wiped him clean. Then she rose, and that pleasure heightened as she rode him, her thighs flexing, her movements liquid, demanding, as the prickle taunted at the base of his spine, a heaviness that told him he wouldn't last long. He watched where they joined, how erotic it was. The ecstasy of the rise and fall of her, seeing himself slip from her body, slide back in. He flexed his hips, pushing up as she sank down, her pants music in the quiet air of the room. Her eyes glassy and unfocused. The pleasure an endless feedback loop of touch, sight, sound.

He smoothed his hands over her thighs, the skin soft under his palms. 'Touch your breasts. Your nipples.'

She did as he demanded, plucking at them between her thumbs and forefingers. He had a better use for his hands right now. Sandro was about to fall over a precipice, and he wanted her to fall right with him. Her head dropped back, the hair spilling over her shoulders. He was there, almost there. So close the blood roared in his ears. He licked his thumb to wet it. Slipped it between her legs to her clitoris and circled it in the way he knew drove her wild. The moan that came from her lips was deep and low. Then her movements became choppy, uncoordinated. Her breath held and the first few flutters of her orgasm began as he lost control, the pleasure roaring through his body as she clenched and released around him.

She collapsed onto his chest as he wrapped her in his arms. They were still joined. Replete. No matter how many times they did this, it was like the first time. The way she unmade then remade him with her body. And he wondered how he'd ever lived without it.

CHAPTER NINE

VIC DIDN'T WANT to move. She lay on Sandro's warm, strong chest, wrapped in his arms. Safe.

Except that had to be a delusion. He wasn't safe. He was anything but. From the first moment she'd met him, he was all risk. An attraction that sizzled through her veins and burned everything clean. All her worries, fears. They disappeared till she was left blank as freshly fallen snow. He was like the drugs she'd once been addicted to. Her eyelids drooped as their breathing came down to a normal level from the desperate gasping of their lovemaking. She softened. It would be so easy to go to sleep, to stay here and not leave. But that wasn't their reality. She shifted a little.

'I should deal…' Sandro moved away from her, left the bed. She watched him walk into the en-suite bathroom, naked, the strong play of the muscles in his back, the firm backside that she'd gripped as he loomed over her. His confident stride. She should get dressed, leave, but her bones were as if they'd been made of noodles. It was okay to lie here a little longer, to enjoy the sensation of being truly satisfied, the scent of him in the bed, the spice of him mixed with the heady musk of sex. Already her body began priming for him again. Those pinpoints of desire that told her once was not enough.

It never was when they were together.

He returned to the bed and his smile when he saw her still lying there was soft and slow. Sandro was still half hard and the sight of him drove another spike of desire right through her. He crawled over to her and drew her into his arms again, stroking his fingertips over her back in a move that might have been meant to soothe, but only inflamed.

She allowed herself to melt into him, to pretend. The problem was, she wanted him. Wanted this to be real when all they could ever be was some fantasy.

'Your husband. He hurt you?'

She stiffened. Of all the things they might talk about in this bed, that man was the last she wanted to invade here. She tried to squirm away. The memories were things she didn't want to revisit.

'Don't run from this,' Sandro said. His hand still stroked her, and she stilled. She didn't run from anything, not any more. Running was what had got her into all the trouble in the first place.

'Why do you want to talk about it?'

'To learn about you. You know my worst.'

And he wanted to know hers. All those wasted years. The indifference, the self-recrimination because she thought if she could give her husband what he wanted, things would work out. But the goalposts constantly shifted. Not even Lance knew the full truth of what had gone on. He'd guessed some, but she'd held it in for so long and it was hard to say the words because they were trapped by a tangle of shame that snared and silenced her even now the man was dead.

That shame remained a prison she needed to break free from. She didn't want to be caged.

'The answer's yes.'

'Physically?'

'Not in the beginning. And then not all that often. He

didn't want any evidence of what was going on behind closed doors. He liked being more subtle than that.'

Pushes, shoves, shaking. His greatest weapon, though, was psychological. Eating away at her confidence.

'Why did you stay?'

She stiffened. 'Are you blaming me?'

'*Never.* I want to understand, so I never trigger the fear that trapped you with a man who didn't deserve you.'

She took a deep breath and realised she'd never really been afraid of Sandro. And in that way, he was nothing like her husband had been.

'It's insidious. The chipping away of self. Isolating me from Lance, my friends, so that he became my world and the only truth was what he told me. Then with my foster animals, the sly threats of what would happen if I wasn't there. I knew he'd do terrible things. He was always hard on animals. It's how he died in the end, in a fall while pushing a horse too much, too fast. But I knew if I left, the animals I cared for would suffer, and I did everything I could to prevent that from happening.'

Sandro gave a pained exhale she felt more than heard. His arms wrapped tighter round her. 'If he wasn't dead, I would have killed him.'

'If he wasn't dead, we wouldn't have met.'

Sandro dropped his lips to her forehead, the kiss affectionate, tender. 'And that would have been the truest tragedy.'

Her heart leaped at his words, the apparent sincerity of them. 'Would it?'

Yet in a terrifying way she knew it was the truth. Despite what had happened, she was glad to have met Sandro, to have him in Nic's life.

'We wouldn't have our son.'

He was right, of course, but part of her wanted to believe the truest tragedy of their not meeting had something to do with her, not the child they'd made together. She hated herself for those thoughts. But it was what it was. Without Nic, she wouldn't be here. She wasn't enough on her own to hold this man.

A man who could have anyone.

'No, we wouldn't. I treasure him every day.'

'Who treasured you?'

Wasn't that the question? She couldn't answer, because that answer was no one. Not in the truest sense of the word. Sure, there'd been Lance. He loved her, but he was a sibling. In an ideal world she should have been treasured by her parents. But the world wasn't ideal. The rose-coloured glasses of her youth had been torn off and stamped on in the rage and recrimination of her marriage. She didn't have those futile, teenage dreams of a handsome prince riding in to save her.

'Nic does.'

'Of course. You're a wonderful mother. No one could have hoped for better.'

'You didn't always believe that.'

His hand stroked over her hair, his fingers twisting into it.

'You asked me whether my parents would be proud of me, or ashamed.'

She lifted from the comfort of his embrace to prop herself on her elbow staring deep into the troubled blue of his eyes. 'I'm sorry. That was a terrible question.'

'You were right to ask it. The answer is yes, and no.'

'Sandro—'

'They would be proud of the way I returned to be King. That in the end I didn't give up the hope, or my drive to take the throne. However, they wouldn't be proud of the way I treated the mother of their grandchild.'

What could she say? She'd never expected an admission of guilt from this man and what he said was so close to it she didn't know where to begin.

'Fear is a good motivator, and a terrible one. You can't imagine the fear I suffered when I discovered I had a child. When I believed you and my cousin had hidden him from me. I was furious, terrified. It made me rash.'

He stroked his hand up and down her arm and goose-pimples bloomed over her skin. 'Believe me when I say this: if I could take it back, I would. My desire to protect was in-grained from birth. My whole life has been about returning to the throne, protecting my people. No matter whether or not I believed you were in league with my cousin, the fact you didn't accept the danger you were in drove me to act. I should have talked to you, told you.'

'But you didn't trust me.'

Though, she supposed, how could he? People had tried to assassinate him as a child, as an adult. How could he trust *anyone* when his life had been one lived with the certainty that there was someone out there who wanted to end you? How could she understand a life where someone wanted to snuff out your existence for simply having the temerity to have been born?

She couldn't.

She might have judged him harshly, but that judgement came from a place where she hadn't understood him. Not at all.

'I was trained to think the worst,' he said.

'That's no way to live.'

'It kept me alive.'

He cupped her cheek, the look on his face as tender as

she could imagine him ever giving her. She shouldn't trust it, rolled up in the post-coital haze, her body still humming. Yet she couldn't stop the overwhelming feeling of wanting to give him…everything.

'You need to realise,' he went on, 'that the protection I'll give to Nic as my son is yours as well. It's what you deserve. It's what you should always have had in your life, someone to care for you and your generous heart.'

She tried to stop the tears pricking at the backs of her eyes because no one had ever truly offered her something so encompassing. His touch was tender, his words carried weight. She wanted to believe them, to believe someone. Victoria also knew what he'd ask of her, the question from earlier that day hovering between them.

He stroked moisture that dripped to her cheeks. Tears that she shouldn't allow to fall. How did this man have the ability to shred her the way he did?

'With you as my queen, there will be a whole country behind you. The protection of Santa Fiorina. Nic will have the future he was born to.'

What about love? she wanted to ask. Whilst she'd never wanted to tie herself to a man ever again, she'd still held on to some dreams that love might find its way to her.

'I've been in one marriage of convenience.'

'You know what our marriage will be like. There are no illusions. I can tell you what I can promise: that you'll have my unending respect as my queen. You'll carry the care and hope of a country for a bountiful future. I can look after you both as you should be looked after. As Nic's parents, we'll be together, for him.'

Common sense told her that he was right. But nothing about their situation made sense.

'You might find someone one day you want to be with.'

Someone he loved. Where would that leave her and Nic? Although if she didn't marry him, they'd be faced with that as a certainty, not a possibility. The whole of her rebelled at that idea. She wanted to claw the sheets to ribbons at the thought of him marrying anyone other than her.

His fingers gently traced down the side of her body and she shivered with the pleasure of it. This man had woken her body from some kind of dormancy with a touch.

He leaned over her, kissed the side of her neck. Her shoulder, her collarbone. 'I can't get enough of you. What we have is something rare and special. An attraction I want to explore.'

Her body went up in flames. A marriage based on sex was a terrible idea but this, between them, obliterated all common sense. And in truth she had to think of more than herself. Of Nic. Of the life and stability that marriage could give him.

She now understood so much more about Sandro than she had this morning. What drove him, the kind of man he was. A good man. In the end, her needs were entirely unimportant. Was it enough? The promises that he made? They had to be. Nic's safety and happiness were more important than her own. Yet she had some demands she wouldn't allow to go unvoiced.

'I don't think I'd do well, sharing you with anyone.'

His eyes darkened, his gaze narrow, yet blazing with heat. 'If we married, there'd be no one else. For either of us. It would be a true marriage in every way.'

Except, there wouldn't be any love. This would have to be enough.

'I have one condition.' Sandro's face smoothed out, as if waiting. 'I need to tell my brother first, before any press announcements.'

'Of course. Family should always be told first.'

She didn't know why she found that inexpressibly sad, that Sandro had no family to tell, when a marriage should be a wonderful, joyous thing. *Should* being the operative word. Once again, she was entering into an agreement that was really about a few names on a piece of paper and nothing deeper.

He took her hand, threaded his fingers through hers. 'Marry me, Victoria, and bring joy and hope to my whole country.'

She squeezed his fingers with her own. 'Okay.'

Not the most romantic response but there was nothing romantic about this situation, not really. Sandro closed his eyes, took in a deep breath, released it. 'Tomorrow I'll set the formalities in train, after you've spoken to your brother. Tonight is for us.'

He kissed her, his lips lush and warm on her own as he eased his hand between her legs. Stroking, caressing, inflaming her. He was right. Of all the wrong between them, this was something they couldn't deny.

She only hoped it was enough.

Sandro strode towards Victoria's suite, a leather box in the inner pocket of his suit jacket, carrying a surprising weight for something so small. Except the weight wasn't a physical one, but emotional. What the symbol he carried represented—the chance of a family. Victoria, Nicolai. Him.

A beginning.

Arriving at the suite's door, he took a moment, realising how important these next minutes were. A restart, if he was being honest with himself. Sandro knocked and a muffled voice sounded through the burnished wood.

'Come in.'

Victoria sat on the sofa, a laptop he'd asked his secretary to provide for her personal use open on the coffee table before her, mobile phone to the side. She smiled at him, but the smile didn't really reach her eyes. Something was wrong, he knew it deep in the heart of him. How had he become so attuned to her moods?

'Where's Nic?' he asked.

'Isadora took him to the garden, to feed the kittens. I needed to call Lance to tell him…'

Ah.

She bit her lip. Her shoulders rose and fell as if she took a deep breath.

'I'm guessing it didn't go well.'

'You could say that.' Victoria stood, began to pace. 'He said I must have Stockholm Syndrome.'

A chill settled in Sandro's gut. 'Is that what you think this is?'

Her responding laugh was short and sharp. 'No. Don't worry. I looked it up. It's not a real thing. Anyway, I know what this is.'

She did? That was a surprise, since he still had no idea.

'I've told you you're not a prisoner. I should have told your brother as well.'

He hadn't handled this properly. Perhaps he should have asked Lance for his sister's hand in marriage? Except Victoria was a person in her own right. A strong woman who could make her own decisions and who didn't need someone to give her away or give any permission. Sandro walked towards her, still moving as if filled with nervous energy. He stroked his hand down her arm and she stopped.

'He's just trying to protect me.' Her face began to crumple. 'I was hard on him when I was unwell and he didn't deserve any of it. Now this.'

All Sandro wanted to do was to comfort. He slid his arms round her waist, cradled her gently against his chest. She melted into him and sighed. Something about this felt so *right*. A marrow-deep realisation that in his arms was where Victoria was meant to be.

'He loves you, and he wants to know this marriage is based on your free will. So do I.'

Her arms tightened around him. She nodded into his chest. 'It is. I've accepted that this is the best thing for Nic.'

Sandro wanted to ask, *What about you?* Although he knew the answer to that question. Everything that had been done, had been because of their son. Being a parent was about sacrifice. However, he needed her to know that this was about her too. Hence the box in his pocket.

'I wanted to be sure.'

Victoria pulled away and shrugged. 'I'm as sure as I can be.'

'I want us to build a home here, where family is always welcome. I want to ensure you and Nic are cared for the way you both deserve. These are things I promise.'

She smiled then, but it was a little uncertain. Tremulous even. He hoped that he could turn her smile into something real. Genuinely happy. He reached into his pocket.

'I have something for you.'

Her eyes widened slightly, seeing the box in his hand. His staff had scoured what was left in the treasury but he hadn't been able to find a ring that suited her. Something she wouldn't fear wearing every day, that was as beautiful as she was. That showed some thought in its choice, some meaning. Not selected because of ostentation. He hoped what he'd found with the help of the Crown Jeweller was perfect.

He opened the box. Victoria's hand fluttered to her chest. Her mouth forming a perfect O.

'What's this?'

He removed the glittering ring from its bed of blue velvet and placed the box in his trouser pocket. Then Sandro took Victoria's left hand in his own.

'Since our engagement is being formalised once all the necessary arrangements are in place, you need an engagement ring.' He gazed deep into her grey-blue eyes, hoping she could see how humbled he was reflected in his own. 'I understand that this isn't the way you might have wanted to get engaged. That you didn't want to marry again. I can't tell you how much your acceptance of my proposal, practical as it was, means to me.'

He slipped the ring on her finger. It was the perfect fit. *Finally,* it seemed as if something was going right.

'Sandro, this is exquisite.'

The ring flashed on her finger as she held out her hand to the light, turning it this way and that. Two gems of the same size. A flawless round diamond and an exquisite round yellow sapphire the colour of Santa Fiorina's summers, set in a crossover style of white gold, flanked by baguette diamonds in the band. The gems nestled together, symbolising their union as a couple.

'It's called a *toi et moi* style. You and me. That's how I want our relationship to be. A true and equal partnership.'

She flung herself into his arms and he caught her, both of them laughing. The sound was glorious, one of true happiness. He lifted her off the ground and swung her around. Sandro couldn't recall ever feeling like this, so *full.* As if life was somehow falling into place.

'It's perfect.'

She kissed him. This wasn't tentative, it wasn't troubled. It was free and alive and heated. He returned the kiss, glorying in it. As if joy had overcome them and was spilling over into the moment. A moment poetry could be written about but not something tragic, something brimming with life. *Love.*

Though he wasn't sure why that last word entered his consciousness. It was their connection and mutual love of Nic, that was all.

Any thoughts were soon obliterated by the deepening of their passion. The need that grabbed a hold. He pulled away briefly, both of them panting. Victoria's lips a beautiful, dusky rose. He craved to kiss them again and never stop.

'When will Isadora be back?'

Victoria's pupils darkened. 'About twenty minutes.'

All of him grew heavy with anticipation and desire, temptation overcoming him. 'If we're quick... I want you.'

She backed away, smiling. 'Then you'd better hurry.'

Victoria turned and raced to the bedroom, giggling. Sandro followed, laughing himself. Knowing that, whilst this might be a sprint, he'd make sure there were two satisfied winners before Isadora and Nicolai returned.

CHAPTER TEN

SANDRO LAY WITH Victoria sleeping in his arms, feeling the gentle rise and fall of her breath, her body soft and pliant against him. He was overcome by the peace these moments brought him. The rightness, certainty, even though he knew he needed to wake her soon. He'd tried to move Nic into his own room so she could stay with Sandro each night, but she didn't want him disrupted again, when he'd only just settled in. Her argument was fair, yet for the most part she insisted that she return to their son.

The one precious time she'd stayed had given him the first peace he'd experienced since returning to Santa Fiorina. A blessing, and a curse, because he wanted her with him constantly. Around Victoria, his stress seemed to have eased. She was in tune with him, able to tell even before he could that he needed a break to avoid another headache. He began to see a future with more clarity than ever before...

Tonight, he simply held her. In a few days, an announcement would be made to his people. Firstly, a carefully crafted revelation about his son, secondly, the news that he would marry Nicolai's mother. He'd introduce them both to the world.

Something about that caused a pang deep inside. The knowledge that he didn't want to share Victoria and Nicci with anyone. Nothing about his life had ever been his own.

It had all been lived for his country, for others. These rare, quiet times were precious, and he'd protect them. Once their engagement was formalised, he'd lose something of this. Victoria and Nic would become the property of Santa Fiorina too.

For the moment, he didn't want to share. He wanted to wrap them up, keep them safe. He'd sworn he'd do that, and he would.

Yet there was no way to keep this hidden any longer. Staff in the palace had all been chosen carefully. Trusted explicitly. But it was time, as much as a voice inside him howled that there would never be a good time for this. This introspection caused the doubts to creep in that plagued him. He'd been born to the role, accepted it. Nic hadn't. His child's life had been a simple one. He was a happy, secure little boy all because of the woman he held, a gift who should be cherished. A mother who had given their boy unconditional love.

She stretched and began to stir. He stroked his fingers up and down the smooth skin of her spine and she snuggled back into him. Another five minutes and he'd wake her. Let her return to her suite and wait to see what the morning would bring.

There was a commotion outside his bedroom. What the hell? The door was flung open. Victoria flinched in his arms.

'What is it?' Her voice was confused, soft with sleep.

'Your Majesty.' The light flicked on. He squinted against the harsh brightness after the peaceful dark. His personal-protection officer stood just inside the bedroom, directing the rest of a team of bodyguards who moved through, securing the space. Some of their weapons were drawn. Sandro pulled the sheets over Victoria's body, his heart pounding as she huddled into him.

'Our apologies, Sir.' His head of security walked in, all business and readiness, armed as well. 'There are intruders in the palace—'

'Oh, my God.' Victoria sat up, clutching the sheet to her even as she started to get out of the bed. 'Where's Nic?'

'Lady Astill, please stay where you are.' The head of security's voice was firm, inviting no argument.

Sandro felt impotent in this bed, naked. He needed to leave, to be the *King*, and yet he couldn't. The security team continued doing their job. Moving onto the terrace and securing the perimeter of the space. It was a drill he knew well, as it was a practised one. He wrapped Victoria in his arms.

'*Cara*, we need to listen.'

'Sandro, I need Nic.' Victoria's voice trembled and cracked. 'To make sure he's okay.'

She clung to him. Hair mussed. Grazes on the side of her neck where his stubble had scraped across her skin.

'Trust my team. Isadora will protect him. She's trained for this.'

Tears welled in Victoria's eyes. He knew his security would have done everything to ensure Nic's safety. He was the country's heir. Obviously, Victoria didn't have that same level of assurance because she hadn't lived with the constant threat. The need to trust that there were people who would give their lives to save yours. He couldn't bear her fear. Every shuddering breath stabbed at him. A deep, unrelenting pain Sandro wanted to *fix*. But there was no way to fix this, not now.

'We need to get dressed,' he said. Victoria looked as if she would climb out of her skin, and he needed to *move*. There were a few nods, murmurs of assent. Some people melted from the room. Others turned their backs. Victoria leapt up and began to scramble for her clothes.

'It'll be okay,' he said as she dressed. The words carried no emotion behind them. Meaningless platitudes. He was helpless in this situation, the way he had been years before, exiled in a foreign country. His parents dead…

He couldn't think of that right now. Sandro grabbed some clothes as well, suit trousers, shirt, the costume of a king.

'I—I was here when I should have been with him. Nicci must be terrified.'

The fury that welled inside Sandro threatened to spill over. Having an intruder in the palace was bad enough. Any risk to Victoria or Nic caused red to colour the edges of his vision. A rage he hadn't felt since he first flew back into Santa Fiorina after his exile. Saw what had been done to *his* country, *his* people.

There was nothing he could do here. No way he could rid himself of the fear that roared through him at the thought of any harm coming to his son and Victoria at the hands of his cousin. Once more, he was a straw man waiting on others to secure his safety. Like his exile. He'd been kept safe in a foreign land, not shedding blood with the people of Santa Fiorina, fighting only with words and diplomacy. Being returned supposedly victorious when he'd won *nothing*. Others sacrificing themselves for his family's name.

'What's taking so long? Nic's only down the hall.'

Victoria's voice may have been the barest of whispers, but he heard it like a shout of accusation. Her face pale and waxy. Looking as if she wanted to fall. He strode to her and wrapped her in his arms. Held her tight as her body shuddered with tears and terror. All the while he knew he'd done this to her. He'd failed to protect them as he'd promised to do. Allowing someone to get into the palace. No matter what anyone said, he accepted this as a personal responsibility.

'I'll find out. My security will know.'

Victoria moved out of his arms and wiped at her tear-streaked face, her eyes red. She sat on the end of the bed as if her legs wouldn't carry her any longer.

'Please tell me he's okay.'

He stalked from the bedroom to the lounge, his head of security barking orders into a mouthpiece. The man didn't stop or acknowledge his king. Sandro knew better than to interfere. These people's role was to protect the royal family. Anything else, including deference to his position, was incidental. It was humbling.

The man finished what he was doing, turned.

'Tell me what's happening,' Sandro commanded, the only control he had over this whole blighted situation.

'Intruders breached the walled garden, breaking in through the northern door. It appears the lock was faulty although it may have been interfered with.'

'How many?'

His head of security said *intruders*, which meant more than one person. Not some opportunistic act, but planned. A chill flashed through him, sharp and cold as an ice storm.

'Two small teams. Both armed. We intercepted one in the grounds. Another managed to enter the palace. Both had mud maps. Your suite. Nicolai's. Both marked.'

Sandro ran his hand over his face. The buzz of white noise filled his ears. This was what he'd feared, what he'd tried to prevent, and yet here in the palace, which should have protected his son, protected Victoria, he'd left them at risk.

'Then why isn't Nicolai here now?'

'One armed intruder remains on the loose. He was last seen near your son's—'

'*No!*'

Sandro spun round to the sound of Victoria's wail. She gripped on to the back of an armchair, knuckles white. Face contorted, eyes red-rimmed. Her breaths sharp and fast. He strode to her and took her in his arms again as she clung to him, murmuring over and over into his chest a jumble of words pleading for the safety of their son. Dark memories overwhelmed him then, of another murderous night when he had lost everything. The wash of hopelessness, helplessness, making him feel like that nine-year-old boy again, and not the King he must be.

His head of security retreated, giving Sandro time with Victoria. How could he have forced her into this position, placing her in danger? He didn't know how to fix it. So he simply held her, unable to do anything more, as the interminable minutes ticked by for some word of Nicolai's safety. And he could do nothing, nothing at all.

'Your Majesty.' His head of security had joined them once more. How much time had passed? It was as if the world had sped up and slowed down, all at the same time. 'We're confident all the intruders have now been captured.'

Victoria's head lifted from his chest and she pulled from his arms. A sharp knock sounded at the door of the suite. It opened and Isadora entered, holding Nic. His face a little tear-stained, his eyes wide at all the bright light, the people. Victoria moaned and ran to them, taking Nic and clutching him to her chest as he snuggled into her neck. Sandro went to them both. Enfolded them in his arms, accepting the fiction that there they were safe. Being a king could wait. For now he allowed himself a moment of profound relief as a man.

Whoever did this would pay. He took a long, slow breath. As much as he wanted to stay, he had a job to do. The tension inside him wound tighter and higher. He clenched his teeth, so hard he feared they'd crack.

He looked over at his head of security. 'Take me to them.'

Victoria stiffened in his arms.

'Sir, that's unwise.'

'What's "unwise" is what they did tonight. I want each one to know what they've unleashed, coming near my fiancée, my son.'

He pulled back, cupped Victoria's cheek. 'I have to leave for a little while. What do you need?'

'You,' she whispered, and the words almost cleaved him in two.

He hadn't protected her and he certainly didn't deserve her. Yet she still wanted him.

'Soon. Anything else?'

She nodded. 'Some milk for Nic.'

Isadora moved into view. 'I'll arrange it.'

'Thank you for looking after him,' Victoria said.

'Lady Astill, it's my privilege.'

With reluctance he turned and strode from the room surrounded by his personal protection. As they made their way through the palace, thoughts whirred in his head. What if his security hadn't stopped them? Would Nic have been kidnapped, or worse? What of Victoria? They wouldn't have needed the mother, she'd be dispensable. Everything inside him rebelled at the thought of *any* harm coming to her. Sandro blew out a long, slow breath. He couldn't think like this. He needed to focus on what he could control, not on the horror of what might have been.

'Are they in the cells?' he asked his head of security as they journeyed to the bowels of the palace.

'Yes.' The man nodded.

Good. They'd know the brutal history of those rooms from the last twenty-five years of his uncle's and cousin's reigns. Let them fear what might befall them.

'I want to speak to one. Your choice. I want the others to hear as well.'

'We can open the intercoms between the rooms if that's what you wish.'

He did. He'd send a message that would never be forgotten.

His head of security stood faced with a number of doors as if in contemplation, then chose one and opened it. More security officers were inside. The room sparse and grey. Dimly lit with a single, naked bulb. A scarred and stained table at its centre, and the temperature set too cold. A man sat in a chair, handcuffed. Dressed in black. The bile rose in Sandro's throat. He clenched his fists as he tried to keep the reignited rage from overflowing.

Who had this man been coming for? Him? Victoria? Nicolai?

Yet no matter how furious he was, he was the King. He would live up to the expectations set by his parents, of those who'd kept him alive as a figurehead for the moment he could walk back into his country as its leader. Because he had a message to pass on, and he would make sure each person here heard it.

He stood, glaring at the prisoner. The prisoner glared back, bruises blooming on his face. Sandro didn't waver. He hoped this would-be assassin could see the loathing and contempt on his face. Then the man looked away and Sandro took it as capitulation.

'You think you can win, but you won't,' he said, so quietly the man almost leaned forward to hear, before checking himself. 'Your employer's come for me before and failed. Yet I treated him with more grace than he deserved so long as he disappeared into history. No more. You made a fatal error, coming after my *son*. For that, there'll be no forgiveness. No mercy unless you tell us where Gregorio is. I want him now, like never before.'

He'd thought he could keep Victoria and Nic safe, and all he'd done was place them in greater danger. He'd essentially forced her into another arranged marriage, after the disaster of her first. A woman who deserved the love he couldn't give to her. The safety he'd failed to provide. She was owed more than *him*. It was a modern world. He didn't have to be married to the mother of his son. She didn't need to be queen. He could find another, even though the thought of it stabbed a pain through his heart. His obligation now was to keep her safe, Nic safe. He had no higher calling than that.

He placed his hands on the battered tabletop, cold under his fingers. Leaned forward, and the man's eyes widened as he pressed into his seat.

'Fail to give the Pretender to me and I promise I'll rain hell down on all of you and I will not stop until you're crushed like dirt under my shoe.'

Sandro had lied. The truth rang in his mind loud and clear. In truth, he would never stop. Not until he was assured Victoria and Nicolai were safe.

Victoria sat on the sofa, fidgeting. She tried to look at her computer again. Attempting to answer emails with an international humane society working in Santa Fiorina to talk about funding for local organisations, but even that had trouble holding her interest. It had been a little over three weeks since the terrifying night when intruders had entered the palace. A shudder ran down her spine. She'd been told little about what had happened, which she supposed was meant not to scare her but the lack of information made her imagine all kinds of horrors. Her security had been increased and their world had become small, consisting of their suite, the kitchens, and the garden because she'd insisted that the mother cat and kittens had become reliant on the food she gave them. They were getting tame now and it gave her and Nic something to do other than stare at their suite's walls and worry. Because she had barely seen Sandro.

Sure, he'd come in the evening to say goodnight to Nic but he wouldn't stay, saying he had work to do. Sometimes, late at night, she'd wake as he slipped into bed beside her, not moving because it was clear he only did so because he thought she was asleep.

He'd be gone before morning.

She knew a few things from Security, or what they had deigned to tell her. The announcement of their engagement had been postponed, until the situation was more stable. There was a prisoner who might have been providing them with information. They might have been close to finding Sandro's cousin, which was why Sandro was so busy. All ifs, buts and maybes.

But there was none of the passionate lovemaking her body now craved. No conversations over a coffee when Sandro asked about her day, Nic's, when they talked like a normal couple. Nothing. And she missed him in a way that she should have had trouble understanding after all that had come before. Except she'd begun to realise that what he'd done all along was try to protect them, no matter how poorly he'd gone about it. Because he had trouble trusting anyone after what he'd gone through.

A lot like her.

She shut down her computer, not knowing what to do

with herself. It was later than normal, Nic already in bed. When that happened, Sandro usually just stood in the room, watching over their sleeping child. She wanted him here now. The world had fallen dark outside and her heart beat a little faster, the fears creeping in. She shouldn't be afraid. Her suite was surrounded by security, the grounds milling with guards. Sandro had introduced her to his head of personal protection, who'd reassured her that she and Nic were safe, and still the constant concern wore her down.

The door of the suite opened and her heart rate spiked, wild and thready, as Sandro entered. He was such a formidable figure and even more so over the past three weeks, when all she saw was the King. Still wearing his suit, likely just having come from work, he took her breath away—she couldn't imagine a time when he wouldn't. Even with the appearance of being tamed, there was nothing tame about him. She knew the wildness underneath, the passion of him that he tried to hold in, that she coveted all for herself.

'Busy day?'

He nodded, sharp and formal. 'Always.'

Yet she could hear the weariness in his voice. The heaviness of it. She walked towards him, wanting to wrap him in her arms and tell him that everything would be okay. That *they'd* be okay. But why that was so important, she didn't know. When *had* she begun to see them as a team? She wasn't sure. All she knew was that deep inside they were, in a way she'd never had before. That knowledge gave her comfort now.

Yet Sandro stepped away from her, kept his distance. That sliced like a paper cut, but she ignored it. She couldn't imagine what he'd been going through, though he hadn't allowed her in enough for her to even ask.

'Nic's asleep. I think he missed you tonight.'

'I've been busy. The life of a king.'

He ran his hand over his face, the skin under his eyes dark and bruised, the lines etched deeper in his face. Looking so weary that he might fall on his knees.

'Have you eaten? I can order something from the kitchens?'

Sandro shook his head, almost a dismissive move. 'No. We need to have a discussion.'

He wouldn't look her in the eye and it confused her. Even when he'd been working so long and hard over the past three weeks, there'd been some communication.

'Okay.' Something about this was off. A sick sensation rose in her throat. Distance had never been their problem and yet Sandro seemed to be keeping it from her. 'About what?'

'My cousin.' He spat out the words as if they were tainted food in his mouth. 'He's been arrested. He'll be charged locally with many crimes, and likely prosecuted internationally for war crimes against Santa Fiorina.'

'Oh, thank goodness.'

Relief flooded through her, filling her with elation and draining her all the same. The sting of tears burned at her eyes. Nic would be safe. They'd all be safe. His parents could be avenged, everything he held so tight to himself Sandro could release. She walked to him, wanting to hold him, comfort him, thank him. Except he manoeuvred away from her. The sensation of that perceived rejection sliced like a paper cut.

'Yes. Some of the palace invaders were most informative. He won't escape this time.' Sandro began to pace. In a man who always seemed so still and sure, the movement across the carpet seemed discordant. Jarring.

'This means it's time to consider the future.'

They *had* considered it. The future where they were married, she'd be queen. She almost laughed at that. When she'd made love to this beautiful, complex man what seemed like so long ago now, she'd never contemplated *that* for her future. All she'd wanted was one night of freedom, to be herself, much as he had. The thought of what lay in store for them all terrified yet excited her. There was so much good she could do for so many as queen. And she and Sandro would guide Nic to be the best man he could be, when he one day took the throne.

But more important than anything, they would be a family. She'd sensed that was what they'd become in their time together here, but she hadn't realised how much she'd craved it when on her own. Sure, Lance was family too. But he had Sara now and one day soon, no doubt, they'd have children of their own. She'd always wanted that for herself, she realised. A marriage. Children. A home full of laughter and love…

Although love wasn't really on the agenda here. Sandro had made that clear. Yet something warm and expansive that spoke of every possibility imaginable bloomed in her chest. Nic loved his father, loved her, and maybe that love would spill out over them as a couple too. And after thinking for so long that she didn't want it, that love was an illusion, that she and Nic were enough, she realised that love with the right person was no trap. It was the ultimate freedom. She craved that for herself and she wanted it for Sandro too. *He* deserved more. Whatever the future held, it felt big and bright and bold in this moment.

She gave a smile. Sandro didn't return it. He looked cool, dispassionate. Every inch the King he'd been raised to be. The King she'd met for the first time at the private airport before being bundled onto a plane. Right now she needed the man who'd made love to her, the man who loved Nic. Protected them both.

'The future is something I'm looking forward to.'

There was a flicker over his face, almost like a wince.

'Given that my cousin's now in prison and his cronies in disarray or fleeing the country, the dangers to you and Nicolai present when I brought you to Santa Fiorina are minimal. There's no need for you to stay.'

It was as if the floor had opened and she'd been consumed whole. The bottom fell out of her world. 'What?'

'There was danger to you both which required immediate action. That situation no longer exists.'

That couldn't be right. After he'd fought to bring her here. The lengths he'd gone to. The exquisite lovemaking they'd shared. The home he'd promised them both. The engagement to be announced. The magnificent ring he'd given her. Promises that she and Nic would be with him for ever.

'Sandro—'

He waved his hand as if in a dismissal.

'We're unmarried and there's now no requirement for any formal engagement. It's not been announced. There's no risk.'

She shook her head. 'I don't understand.'

'It's quite clear. You don't have to stay in the palace. Should you wish to remain in Santa Fiorina then you're welcome to. Should you wish to leave and return to the UK, flights will be arranged.'

'But Nic's...your heir. How would that work?'

'You said once that you wanted a normal life for Nicolai. He can have it. I remember you told me your greatest fear was my coming to claim him. I can give his life back.'

Her heart pounded, the blood roaring in her ears. 'What are you saying?'

'As you'll recall, there's been no formal announcement that I've acknowledged him as my heir.'

He wasn't just casting her aside, he was casting Nic aside too.

'But the DNA…the rules of succession here.…' There didn't seem to be enough air in the room…she could hardly breathe.

'Things are more grey than black and white.'

No, not in her mind. 'You lied to me?'

'No lies were told. You believed what you chose to.'

That simple sentence hit her like a slap. How had it come to *this*? She saw it now. She'd become so needy in wanting a future that she'd believed anything Sandro told her. Kidding herself, when she should have known better. Her only experience with men was that they lied, they gaslit. Her brother might be a good man, but her former husband had been her greatest teacher and she should have listened to the lessons she'd learned from him.

'No. You turned our lives upside down. Put us at risk, saved us, made promises, and now you're doing *this*? Why?'

'I'm a king. I find there's a great deal I can do within my remit.'

Sandro may not love her, but he loved Nic. Of that she was sure. The night of the intruders. His rage. His distress. Once she'd been afraid Nic would be taken away from her. Then she'd come to believe Sandro was a good man whom his son deserved. And she'd been sure of something else, too. Perhaps there wasn't enough glue for them to stick together, but deep in the core of her being she knew Sandro loved their little boy. He might reject her, but he'd never reject Nicci.

'You might be the King, but Nic's your *son*.'

Sandro turned from her, strode to the windows, where he looked out into the darkness. 'You'll both be looked after.'

The horror of this moment…it began ripping her to pieces. Each word like another assault. In that moment of near-terminal pain, she began to fear what she felt for Sandro was not merely respect and admiration, but something that had latched on to her soul and wouldn't let go. The feeling of soft warmth, vibrant elation, jagged misery. She might never have been in love before, but she feared that was what this was now. How could it be anything else? She'd probably been a bit obsessed by thoughts of him in the weeks after their one night. That had faded to shock, joy and disappointment, but deep in the most secret parts of her she knew. She'd wanted him from that night to now. Nothing had really changed.

But that was an adult problem. They had a child who didn't understand the machinations of his parents.

'I don't need to be looked after. I can look after myself. I can look after Nic. I did well before, I can do it again. That's not what I'm worried about. I'm worried about a little boy who loves his father. Nicci loves *you*. Doesn't that mean anything?'

'Nicolai is young…he'll adjust. Memories dim over time.'

Sandro may be able to reject her. She understood; she'd suffered enough rejection in her life. From her parents, who'd never really wanted her and would likely have preferred another boy. From her husband, who'd seen her as a means to an end until she'd ceased to be useful. But Nicci didn't deserve this.

'Did you adjust to the loss of your parents? Are you trying to tell me that your memory of them dimmed? Because I seem to remember you have a photo of them on your phone. And not just any photo, is it?'

Sandro blanched. 'Enough!'

'No, enough from you! Your memory hasn't dimmed. You're consumed by it. You claim no lies were told but you're lying right now. To yourself. You're hiding who you really are.'

'It's who I've always been, *cara*.' He slapped his hand to his broad chest, which had been her resting place over so many evenings together. 'I've never changed. You simply didn't see me for the man I was. Now that you do, what do you think of him? Has he met your fanciful expectations? I'm a king. My responsibility is to my people. Nothing and no one else is important. Given this, am I the person you want around *your* precious son?'

So Nic had ceased to be his as well? That stabbed like a knife to her chest. All those times he'd insisted Nic was theirs and now, when they'd lost their usefulness, he meant nothing?

'I can forgive most things. There's little you can do to hurt me.' She shook her head, tired, ashamed that she'd fallen for a handsome face and pretty words that promised what her heart secretly desired, even though she'd denied it to herself. 'But the moment I held Nic in my arms I knew I'd protect him with my life. You told me you were the same, and yet you do this? I can't ever forgive you for choosing to hurt him.'

The strangest look passed across his face. The crumple of what looked like devastation before it morphed into something cold, resolute. Resigned.

'There's no more to say. I'll ask my private secretary to be in touch. Should you choose to stay in Santa Fiorina there's a cottage in the grounds which was a retreat. It has a garden which is perfect for a little boy.'

She shook her head. He wanted to start thinking about

Nic now? Enough of this charade. She'd lived through fakery. People smiling whilst stabbing you in the back. Laughing over your misfortune because thank goodness it wasn't their own. She'd believed she'd found something here. Some kind of truth, stability. A man who knew what he wanted and put those desires into action. Now she'd begun to see that he was as fake as any of them.

She looked him straight in the eye. That blue which would always haunt her memories, like golden summer days of a long-gone childhood.

'There's really nothing I need from you. I never have.' She dropped into the lowest, most perfect curtsey she'd ever delivered. It wasn't meant to honour. It was meant to mock because not once in that movement did she dip her gaze in reverence or supplication.

'Thank you for your benevolence, *Your Majesty*.'

CHAPTER ELEVEN

VICTORIA WATCHED NIC as he sat on the floor of her palace suite. Tempting as it was, she'd refused to be moved to a cottage in the grounds. In truth, she didn't know what she wanted, but it wasn't to be discarded. Had she been on her own she'd have left Santa Fiorina immediately, but she had a child, and any decisions she made involved him too.

Nic squealed as he waved a feather-topped stick about, a creamy bundle of a kitten leaping after it. She'd managed to tame the whole litter in the walled garden. The rest she'd rehomed with the help of staff, but Luna had been the favourite. She'd adopted her soon after Sandro had cast her out of his life. Shy at first, slowly coming out of her shell. Growing into herself. Snuggling on Vic's lap in the sunshine, fearless around Nic.

She was always saving something, she realised. Looking after broken creatures when she hadn't been able to look after herself. Yet despite those skills, she couldn't save Sandro. She was tired of it, tired of being unwanted. Yet, having replayed their final conversation so many times in the dark and dismal silence of lonely nights, something niggled in the back of her brain that she couldn't put her finger on. Till it hit her with a slow, creeping realisation.

She'd come to love Sandro, deeply.

She'd fought it, and outright rejected it in the beginning

as delusional, not recognising how far and how completely she'd fallen for him, hidden as it had been by the intensity of their passion for each other. But the indescribable peace when she'd been in his arms, the joy around him, the tearing pain when he turned away from her… There was nothing else it could be to make her feel this way, and she didn't know what to do about it.

She'd never truly loved before, not like this. Certainly not her husband. She'd tried to fall in love like any young woman might when getting married. The big wedding, a beautiful dress, sparkling jewels, made her believe there could be a happy ending even if the marriage had been arranged for her. What she'd had with him was insecure, fuelled by his gaslighting. There had been nothing like the level of emotion she experienced with Sandro. Had felt it the moment he'd sat next to her in a club and told her she looked as if she was running dry.

She was running dry now, on empty. Everything about this too much, too difficult. She was in a foreign place and, although she had Dora, there was no real support here. She was as isolated as she'd ever been.

A sharp knock at the door jolted her from her introspection. She leaped up. Sandro? She hated the pounding of her heart that sense of hope elicited. How she still wanted him after everything he'd done. She ran to the door and flung it open. When she saw who it was, the last vestiges of her strength crumbled.

'Lance.'

She burst into tears. Everything she'd held in, trying to be strong, she let fall.

Lance walked in and shut the door behind him. Gave her a hug like the big brother he'd always be, but it wasn't the same. He was strong and safe and familiar. But he wasn't who she wanted, and she felt terrible about that when he'd clearly come to help her, as he'd always done.

'I came as soon as I got the call.'

She pulled away, scrubbed at her eyes. 'What call?'

'I received a call from the palace saying my visa had been approved and to come immediately.' Lance clasped the tops of her arms gently, scanned her face, a frown of concern on his own. 'What has he done to you? Is Nic okay?'

'Nic's fine.' Her, not so much. She sniffed, rubbed at her face again. 'He's in the lounge. Come and say hi. He'll love to see you.'

They walked through to where Nic held on to the lounge suite, practising his walking. He gave a big, beaming smile to his uncle. Tried to wave his hands with glee and promptly fell onto his bottom.

'Come here, little man.' Lance swept a giggling Nic into his arms. 'Do you want to come home? Aunty Sara misses you.'

Her heart missed a beat. She could hardly breathe. 'What do you mean, come home?'

Lance popped the squirming Nic onto the ground, where he crawled towards some toys. Her brother looked well. Less sharp, somehow softer. Marriage and love suited him. She'd hoped but never really believed that he'd find it for himself. It was a relief to know he was finally happy.

'Back to the UK, though it was one hell of a negotiation with Baldoni to get there.'

'Sandro wants me to leave the country so badly?'

Her legs wouldn't work and she dropped to the couch. Lance raised an eyebrow. 'You don't want to go.'

It wasn't a question.

'I…' She knew in that moment that she didn't. She wanted to be here, with Sandro. To make it work because it *did*.

When they were together, they were stronger. This being apart…she felt as if a vital piece of herself was missing. But how could she stay when the man she loved didn't want her? It would be constant punishment each day, eventually seeing him marry someone else.

Never. Every part of her rebelled at the thought.

'Vic.' Lance sat next to her, his voice tender and full of care. 'He forced you to leave the UK without a word to anyone other than lies to me. That's not right.'

'What if you had a child with Sara? What if that child and Sara were in immediate danger and didn't want to do what would keep them safe? What would you do?'

'I'd talk it through—'

'What if that wouldn't work?'

Lance's mouth tightened. He took a sudden interest in his wedding ring, twisting it on his finger. 'I'd do whatever it took to keep them safe, even if they hated me for ever.'

'See?'

'Look at you. He's made you cry. You've had enough tears in your life.' He shook his head. 'Sara and I love each other and would never be in this situation. That's the difference.'

She frowned. 'I'm not sure it is.'

Just that moment little Luna zoomed through the room.

'A kitten?' Lance asked. 'You're clearly…settled here.'

'I found a litter in the gardens, rehomed them except for her. She was the smallest.'

Lance's gaze softened. 'Still saving lost creatures. Protecting them. You always had the softest of hearts, even when you tried to be hard.'

She stilled for a moment. She'd believed that she and Sandro were building something, until that terrible night when intruders broke into the castle. Then, everything stopped. He became colder, harder. Like the man on the tarmac at the airport and not the one she'd first met at the club, the one he'd grown into again over her time here. Except, had he really grown into that man, or was that truly who Sandro always was, when he loved...?

No, she couldn't think like that. But he'd been the protector to her. Saved her and Nic even though he denied it. Deep down, what if he'd been trying to be hard because that was all he'd been taught? Hardness, a fear of being soft because of what he'd lost as a child. She understood the fear of relationships borne of bitter experience, yet Sandro had awakened something in her which made her want to fight those dark shadows and believe that she was entitled to love. That it was there for her with the right man. She'd seen it before with Lance, and knew how love had transformed her brother.

Love could transform Sandro too.

But did he love her back?

That day she'd confronted his doctor. Opened Sandro's bedside drawer and found a piece of paper with her lipstick kiss and the words *Thank you* she'd written, because he'd set her free and she knew she'd never forget him. What if he couldn't forget her either? A hard man wouldn't keep that scrap of paper. That was the act of sentiment. Something...romantic.

What if he loved her too, and thought by sending her away, he was saving her? Protecting her in a way that was misplaced?

There were so many questions in her head to which she had no answers. She'd never know if she didn't take the chance of breaking her heart all over again. Vic wouldn't give him up, not without a fight. She just had to convince him that letting her go was not the right thing to do for any of them.

'What did you and Sandro talk about, in that call?'

Lance shrugged. 'A lot. In the end I thought I was going to have to sell my soul to get you home, but it was worth it.'

Vic looked at her brother, narrowed her eyes.

'I know that look,' he said. 'You're determined.'

'I'm sick of people making decisions about what they think's best for me, when all they need to do is ask what I want. So, I need you to tell me *exactly* what Sandro said in that phone call.'

Because she was sure there were answers, and she was going to get them all before she fought for what she and Nic deserved.

Sandro walked into the small walled garden where he'd found Victoria and Nic that day which seemed so long ago. A bucolic scene. Mother and child, with kittens. It had given him such peace, watching their happiness. Knowing for sure in that moment that Nic would always be loved. That no matter what happened, Victoria would protect him. Now everything was gone. There was nothing left.

He sat on a garden bench where Victoria and Nic had spent so much of their time here. Even when he'd broken their informal engagement she'd come here with their son. He'd watched from an upper window of the palace, catching his final glimpses of them both. Then they'd stopped. He'd asked his staff why. Why there were no kittens frolicking in the gardens any more. He was told they'd been rehomed.

As Victoria and Nic would be, too soon, and for his sanity, not soon enough.

He'd done the right thing. There was no doubt in his mind. When Victoria had told him about her disastrous first marriage he'd thought this, between them, would be different. He was *not* her former husband. Their world was one of passion, mutual respect. A child they shared. Yet he was the same as her husband, a man whose memory he'd come to despise. Deceiving her, even if it had been to protect her and Nic. Taking her away from a family who loved her. Placing her in danger. Her tears and terror for their child had broken him. It had all been his doing. Like her parents, he'd taken away her choices and she deserved whatever the world had to offer her. Every choice, not the opportunities dictated to her by others, by him.

Victoria deserved to find someone to love her, and not be forced into another arranged marriage because it seemed the sensible thing to do. She should have a grand passion and love. She needed poetry written for her. Nic needed to be a little boy, unlike what he'd been allowed as a child. His life had always been about duty.

This was better for them. He wasn't sure what love was, wasn't sure he was capable of it. He'd never loved romantically before. There'd been no opportunity or expectation for him. Yet this pain…so all-encompassing he wasn't sure he'd survive it. In some ways, it was even worse than the pain of losing his parents. That couldn't be love. He'd always thought of love as a tender, sweet emotion which made your life soft-focus. That had no place in his life, since kings had to rule, be strong. Tenderness and a lack of focus didn't fit the job description.

There was nothing tender and soft-focus about his emotions now. They were sharp and eviscerating. Something like grief.

Didn't he read somewhere that grief was the price you paid for love? He'd loved his parents, that he knew. Even though he'd never really remembered grieving for them. So much of that time had been blocked from memory. His terror, fleeing in the night, being called Your Majesty for the first time at nine and knowing that that was *wrong*. That His Majesty was a king and he couldn't be the King because he had a father. Then being told the terrible news, the reaction that he realised now any child would have. Of fear, disbelief, fury that what was being said *had* to be lies. Then being told that those were not the reactions of a king but a child, and he was a child no longer. He must do his parents proud.

That day, everything for him had stopped. He'd ceased to be a little boy, yet in so many ways it was as if he'd never grown up. Victoria had been right.

It wasn't love; it was abuse.

He took his phone, opened his gallery. Once, it had only contained one dreadful photograph. Now, another photograph joined it. Of Victoria and Nic in this garden, snapped in secret the day he'd first seen them here. Those two photographs represented the worst of his life, and the best. Today was about moving forward. It had to be. Her brother was here and he would take her home. He was sure she'd want to leave. The security assessments after his cousin and his henchmen had been arrested meant any risk was no longer imminent. It was a hypothetical one at best. Interpol had rounded up the dregs who'd fled. Lance had violently assured him Victoria and Nic were safer with him than with anyone. It was the right thing to do.

His life had to be about doing the right thing, for if not that, what?

Two photographs, both parts of his life that were now at an end. He opened the one of his parents that had haunted him since the day he'd been shown what his uncle had done, and told in time he could avenge the crime. That photograph was a reminder of what had been lost, of what he must fight against. It had controlled him for as long as he could remember.

That past had died. He could never bring it back. Revenge would never be enough. His finger hovered over the screen. This should never have been the last memory of his parents. He should have been allowed to recall them smiling, happy, before everything had been stolen from him.

It's abuse, not love.

He pressed delete on the picture, the pain visceral, the relief profound. One photograph left... That photograph was a fresh reminder he'd keep for ever, no matter the pain, because it represented his best and not his worst. One that would serve to remind him of what doing the right thing meant, and what it cost to be that man. What it cost to be the King his parents would have aspired for him to be.

Sandro dropped his phone to the ground, put his head in his hands and wept.

CHAPTER TWELVE

VICTORIA WATCHED SANDRO for a while, sitting on the bench where she'd spent so many days in this small, walled garden, contemplating her past and her future. He'd not moved, head down in the sunshine as if contemplating life himself. Phone on the gravel at his feet. She began to move towards him, to make her greatest pitch for the future she wanted, the future she wasn't afraid of any more. Her shadow fell across him and he stirred, picked up his phone. She wondered whether he was happy for what he'd done. Then he looked up at her. His eyes widened. Haunted, red-rimmed. The lines on his face etched deep.

Looking as if he hadn't slept.

Looking…wretched.

Much like herself. This wasn't a happy man. She had some ideas of what could bring joy back to both of their lives, if he'd only allow it. She had to fight for this, for them. If she didn't win the battle…?

She'd decide what to do then. Allow her heart to break for good. She was strong enough to survive it, even though she wouldn't want to.

'Victoria.'

That voice, so laced with grief and pain it sounded as if it was grinding from him. Forced out of him like cut glass. Then he stood, and something about him changed. His face blanked. He straightened, grew to his full height. In that moment Victoria knew that Sandro the man was gone. She was receiving the full force of King Alessandro Nicolai Baldoni.

It thrilled her.

Still, she curtseyed, playing the game a little longer.

'Hello, Your Majesty.'

If she didn't know him so well, she wouldn't have caught the flinch, that tightening of his eyes. But she *did* know him. She knew all of him. More importantly, she *loved* him.

'Where's Nicolai?' he asked, his mouth a thin, brutal line.

'With Lance. He's happy to see his uncle.'

Sandro's jaw hardened. Clenched. His hands flexed and released. 'I'm sure he is.'

Sandro's whole body screamed loudly what it really wanted. Her. If only she could switch off his brain for a little while to let his heart take control.

'Do you have something to say to me? I have a country to run.'

'Santa Fiorina will endure without you for a few moments.' She took a deep breath, ready to make her speech. 'You know what hurt the most?'

'I don't know what you're talking about.'

He was lying. A muscle at the side of his jaw ticked.

'It's not the rejection of me. I'm a big girl. Been there, done that, got the T-shirt. It was your rejection of Nic.'

He shook his head. 'I never...'

She held up her hand and he had the good grace to be quiet, yet he turned his back on her. That hurt too, except his shoulders slumped. Maybe it was because he was ashamed and didn't want to hear what she was about to say, because she had no doubt he'd remember his words.

'You said there'd been no formal acknowledgement of Nic as the future King. That things were more grey than black and white. There's no grey where Nic's concerned. Not for me. Those words are *etched* in my memory.'

They still ached like a knife being thrust into the heart of her, but she'd come to believe he'd said them to force her away. Because everything changed the night intruders broke into the palace, then after his cousin had been caught. The distance. She had to believe he was a protector at heart. Protecting them. Lance had told her all about their hours of negotiation. Not about Lance coming to the country, but about her and Nic's security. Everything had been thrashed out over long video calls, with Sandro taking the lead in the negotiations. Lance said nothing he'd ever suggested was good enough. That in the end Sandro had demanded, *'Vow to me you'll keep them safer than I ever could.'*

That was the final piece of the puzzle, confirming that he was doing this out of love, as she suspected. And she loved him right back, with her own cracked, broken and imperfect heart. Was prepared to fight for him, for them, for the little family she wanted them to become. Was prepared to fight *dirty*. She smiled.

'I only spoke the truth,' Sandro said.

'I'm not sure you did. I think you're lying, more to yourself than anyone else. But here's the thing you need to remember: I'm fighting for my son. I have right on my side. And now I've spoken to my lawyers.'

He hadn't been able to look at her before because he needed to set her free, not hold her captive. But the shock of her words... He wheeled round. What did she mean? She must want certainty. Clarity now she was taking Nic away. Their original legal agreement regarding custody arrangements had been meaningless, given it was a fraud negotiated by his cousin, that was all.

'Of course,' he said, trying to inject a lack of care into his voice, which wasn't all that difficult, given he was tired, so tired. Yet the look on her face—cool, detached...

'Nic should be the one who decides what he wants for his future. You don't have that right.'

'What are you saying?'

'My solicitors advise that, given you personally requested a DNA test, the situation isn't as grey as you claimed. Like you told me before, it could be considered an acknowledgement that Nic's your heir, should I want to push the point in the courts.'

He'd always claimed she'd be the perfect queen. In this moment she was the one who should carry the crown on her head. She held her head high, more regal than, in truth, he'd ever felt. When he'd first discovered Nic, the advice to him had been clear, as he'd said. The mere fact of DNA evidence could be seen as an acknowledgement. The catch had been that he hadn't requested it. His deposed cousin had. Now, however...

'It's more grey than black and white.'

His words came back to haunt him. He'd been trying to do the right thing, and she had no idea what would happen if she took this path. Whilst he was impressed by her bravado, the heat of his anger spiked.

She'd never be free if she carried on with this course, and neither would Nic. So far, he'd kept Victoria and Nic's existence out of the press. Publicity meant Sandro's hand being forced. His choices would cease to exist. He'd *have* to marry Victoria. Nic would be his formal heir. He wanted to grab her, to shout. She had to know if she followed this course there would be no escape for any of them.

A little like a sunny day on the hot tarmac of a private airport...

A day when he'd given her no choices either. He stared at her, the softest of smiles teasing her perfect lips. Did she see the realisation flooding over him, cold, then hot? His heart thumped, beating against his chest as if trying to escape.

'This is…blackmail.'

'Funny, that. It seems to be how our relationship tracks. So, how does it feel, this position I'm putting you in?'

'You'll leave me with no choice.'

'We always have choices, some more difficult than others. I thought long and hard about the consequences of backing you into a corner. Although as an adult I've always believed you should talk out your issues, rather than just…dictating what's going to happen. Though I suppose you are a king, so being dictatorial is probably in the job description, which I suggest we change. So how about we talk? Tell me what you really want.'

Did she believe he didn't want her? If he could have his own way, he'd keep her for ever. He'd never let her go. 'You wanted your freedom. I couldn't protect you.'

'Oh, Sandro. Don't you realise, you saved me? I'm not interested in what you think I should hear. All I wanted was someone to consider my feelings. To talk through decisions like an equal. I don't need a martyr. What I need is a partner. And the thing is, the partner I want is you.'

Everything in him stilled. It was as if the breeze dropped, the birds were silent. After all that had happened, after all his failings, she wanted him?

'You…can't.' He was unworthy of her in every way.

She cocked her head. 'I can and I do. I love you, Sandro. And I'm hoping…you might love me a little bit too. Because if you didn't, why did you keep this?'

She reached into the pocket of her jeans and drew out a slip of paper, held it between two fingers. A kiss, in pink.

Her beautifully lettered words. The truth stared him in the face, startling as a slap. He'd never been able to forget her. The disappointment when he'd found her gone after the night they'd shared hadn't left him in the months after he'd last seen her. He'd thought about her constantly.

'I'm not sure I know what love is.'

'You love Nic. Remember how you are with him. It's simple.'

Occam's razor.

Could it be as easy as that? Was this what caused so much pain at the thought of losing her? Did he love Victoria?

The simplest answer to a question is often the correct answer.

He loved her.

It sizzled over him like a lightning bolt and he was totally unprepared for it, the shock. His sense of love had been so tangled up with pain and loss he hadn't recognised the truth. This sensation cut through him, brutal in a way he didn't think he'd survive. He wanted to crush her to him and never let her go.

'You wanted to know how I knew about Nic. I told you we were keeping tabs on my cousin. That was a lie.'

Victoria frowned, tucking the precious slip of paper he'd held on to from their first meeting back into her pocket. 'What's the truth?'

She deserved to know how long he'd wanted her, even if it left him exposed.

'I wanted to see you again. When my trip to the UK was arranged, I asked my security team to find you. To what ultimate end I'm still not sure. But what you can be sure of, is that you were *never* incidental. My cousin was. We found out about him, about Nic, because I was searching for *you*.'

'You still thought of me?' Victoria placed her hand to her heart.

He saw it then, her engagement ring still blazing bright on her finger. His own heart pumped hard. *Toi et moi.* You and me. That one piece of jewellery containing all his hope for the future. A future built on truth and love.

'That's why I kept the note. As a reminder of a perfect night when you gifted me a moment of freedom, to be myself. To be Sandro Baldoni the man. Not the King of Santa Fiorina.'

He stepped towards her, wanting to take her into his arms, but there were still things he needed to say.

'You can't fathom what I feel—there aren't enough words. There has been barely a moment since we first met that I haven't thought of you. At first I believed it was an obsession, but your strength, what you achieved…how you cared for our son, cared for me when I didn't deserve you…'

He saw them now, the tears welling in her eyes. They broke him. He didn't want her tears. He wanted her smiles. They lit his way in the darkness.

'I said it's simple and so are the words. Say, *I love you, Victoria.*'

'*Cara.* If only it were as simple as love. What I feel consumes me. From the moment we met, there was only ever you, even though I didn't realise it at the time. It felt too much, held me hostage each day.'

'Then why let us go?'

A tear dripped down her cheek. He couldn't take it any more. He strode to her. He might not deserve her but he would also give her anything she wanted. Anything she asked for, even if it was his broken self. As he approached, she threw herself into him and he wrapped her tight in his arms, a space she was made for. Where she was always meant to be.

'Because I loved you, and loving you meant setting you free.'

Her fingers curled into his shirt. 'That's a stupid saying.'

'You came back.'

She looked up at him. 'Like I was ever going to leave. I'm yours.'

'And I'm yours. You have my heart. I want you as my wife, my queen, my everything. If you're sure.' He'd give her an out, if she wanted to take it. Always.

'I've never been surer of anything in my life.'

He smiled, and dropped his lips to hers. 'Then I relish the rest of my days, beginning and ending with you.'

EPILOGUE

VICTORIA STOOD AT the bow of the royal yacht. A warm evening breeze was blowing through her hair as she looked out at the twinkling lights of Santa Fiorina whilst they sailed to the open sea. The deep-water marina contained the superyachts of royalty and others who'd attended their wedding. It had been a long and glorious day, which had now ended, as they journeyed for a week-long honeymoon exploring the islands around the country and the wider Mediterranean.

She breathed in the salty air, the thrum of the boat's engine rumbling through her. Soon, they'd be able to relax. Enjoy the fruits of a busy year since their official engagement. It had been an exciting time. State dinners where she'd met dignitaries of other countries wanting to forge closer ties with Sandro, much to their chef Michel's utter delight, being able to showcase his country's fine food and his own culinary skills. She'd particularly warmed to the King and Queen of Lauritania, Lance's friends and hopefully soon to become hers and Sandro's too. Queen Annalise promised to keep in touch and give her queenly tips, which were welcome as she really had no idea what the role entailed, but wanting to make it her own. Rafe's irreverence and general disdain as a commoner for most royal protocol, keeping Sandro amused during the time they'd spent together. He'd loosened up, become less hard on himself since. And with that, his headaches had continued to improve till they were now a rare occurrence and easily controlled.

She tilted her head back, the moon high in a clear, inky sky. As Sandro had promised, Santa Fiorina's joy at the prospect of a new Queen and the discovery of Nicolai had been effusive. There'd been fireworks round the country on their official engagement, street parties celebrating Nicci's second birthday. She felt more at home here than she ever had in England. Together, they were beginning restoration of the palace, into a place for family and of welcome. Her life had been the stuff of dreams, better than she could ever have imagined...

The prickle at the back of her neck and a slide of warmth told her Sandro was close. His arms came round her, hands gripping the railing in front, caging her in, his shining golden wedding ring glinting in the bright moonlight. But this man was no trap; he represented her ultimate freedom.

Her everything.

'Enjoying the view?' he asked. Vic leaned back into the warmth of his body. He wrapped his arms around her, holding her close, leaning down to gently kiss her temple.

'I'm enjoying your arrival more.'

Even though theirs had been billed as Santa Fiorina's wedding of the century, something about the day had still felt intensely intimate. She'd had no bridesmaids, and Sandro no best man. The only other member of the wedding party was Nicolai, as ring bearer. Lance had walked Victoria down the aisle, not to give her away, but to involve him in an important part of the day so that he could be assured how happy she was. And Lance had grown to understand, after some intense posturing between him and Sandro when they'd first met in person, which she'd found a little entertaining. Although Vic knew that for both of them, their concern was borne out of their mutual love for her, so she'd let them work it out between themselves.

In the end, she and Sara were friends, and soon Sandro and Lance had reached a détente. She'd caught them talking about arranging a charity polo match together once the honeymoon was over. Then discussing the merits of a certain pony Lance had found, as a gift for Nic.

All was well.

'It was a good day,' Sandro said, rousing her from her musings. 'The best day of my life.'

'I thought the best day of your life was the day you met me?'

He squeezed his arms tighter round her, raked his teeth over her ear. She quaked with pleasure, melted further into his embrace.

'It's hard to choose which day. Since you and Nicolai came into my life, how could one possibly be bad?'

Things had settled into a happy equilibrium in the country. There was a new vibrancy and vigour, as if people felt there was something to look forward to, to build towards. Reconstruction had begun taking place. There had been new investment in infrastructure, the arts. There was so much good she could do as a new queen. She'd aligned with charities, become patron of organisations close to her heart. For victims of domestic abuse, organisations saving animals. Every day seemed full of hope and love.

'Did you manage to get Nicci to sleep?'

He'd been resistant to Dora's attempts to settle him down. In the end Sandro had gone to read him a bedtime story.

'After some effort. He's had an exciting day.'

'So have we.'

Vic moved and he loosened his hold as she turned in his embrace, easing her arms around Sandro's neck, sinking her fingers into his hair. His body pressed against her. All of him hard and uncompromising. Well…a little bit compromising, for her at least.

'What are you thinking?' he murmured into her ear, his breath caressing her skin. Goosepimples cascaded down her throat, her arms.

'I'm thinking…' she flexed her hips into him, and he groaned '…that I'd like to get our wedding night started.'

His chuckle was low and deep, curling her toes.

Sandro's hands slid onto her backside, drawing her against his now insistent arousal. 'Who am I to deny my beloved wife exactly what she desires?'

She laughed. 'Happy wife, happy life?'

Sandro brushed his nose against hers, back and forth, feather-light. 'Whatever it takes.'

'I want to keep you happy too,' she murmured against his lips.

He pressed his mouth to hers in a tender, loving kiss. 'I promise, you do.'

Sandro stepped back from her, held out his hand and she threaded her fingers through his. He raised her hand to his lips, and kissed over her engagement and wedding rings.

'It's simple,' he said. '*Toi et moi*. You and me, *cara*. Together.'

She smiled, as he began leading her to the stateroom. Her heart full and complete.

'For ever.'

* * * * *

COMING SOON!

We really hope you enjoyed reading this book.
If you're looking for more romance
be sure to head to the shops when
new books are available on

Thursday 7th December

To see which titles are coming soon, please visit
millsandboon.co.uk/nextmonth

MILLS & BOON

MILLS & BOON®

Coming next month

AN HEIR MADE IN HAWAII
Emmy Grayson

A dull roaring drowned out the sounds around her. Each beat of her heart felt magnified, thundering inside her body as Anika stared at him.

'What?' she finally managed to gasp.

'You want me. I want you.'

'I never said I wanted you,' she sputtered.

Nicholas watched her, his fingers pressing more firmly against her back, his eyes glowing with that same predatory light she'd glimpsed on the catamaran.

'You also never said you didn't. So tell me now, Anika. Tell me you haven't thought about me kissing you. Tell me,' he continued, his husky voice washing over her and sending sinful shivers racing over her body, 'you didn't think about how we'd be together when you were in my arms on the boat. That you didn't imagine me tracing my fingers, my lips, over every inch of your incredible body.'

Say something!

But she couldn't. Not when her imagination was conjuring up carnal images of her and Nicholas entwined, arms wrapped around each other as he trailed his lips over her neck, her breasts, his hips pressing against hers without any barriers between them.

'Ah.' His smile deepened. 'So you have thought about it.'

Continue reading
AN HEIR MADE IN HAWAII
Emmy Grayson

Available next month
www.millsandboon.co.uk

LET'S TALK
Romance

For exclusive extracts, competitions and special offers, find us online:

f MillsandBoon

🐦 @MillsandBoon

📷 @MillsandBoonUK

♪ @MillsandBoonUK

Get in touch on 01413 063 232